I0761776

ARACHNA

A.K. Rohner

This is a work of fiction. Names, characters, places, and incidents either are the product of the author's imagination or are used fictitiously. Any resemblance to actual persons, living or dead, events, or locales is entirely coincidental.

ISBN: 978-1-7333845-4-4 (Ebook)

ISBN: 978-1-7333845-5-1 (Paperback)

ISBN: 978-1-7333845-6-8 (Hardcover)

First Edition: February 2023

Edited by Red Adept Editing

Cover art by Aprampar

www.akrohner.com

“Well, here’s to crime,”

— AGATHA CHRISTIE, *DEATH ON THE NILE*

ARACHNA

PROLOGUE
'TIL DEATH DO US PART

What does it feel like to die?

The questions repeated in the back of her head. *Will it hurt? What happens after?* Every muscle in her body tensed. *Will we get away in time?*

Her steps creaked the dusty floor. She glanced back every few seconds, anticipating a gunshot with each breath. She counted the numbers on each old wooden door as she traveled the narrow hallway, which only seemed to extend the farther she walked as every groan of the walls, every clap of thunder outside resembled his heavy footsteps behind her.

She'd nearly been caught.

She stopped at a door with the number three on it, and after another quick look around, she knocked.

The device was burning a hole in her pocket, and she stretched the tense muscles in her neck. All throughout her life, her nerves had been made of steel. But tonight… tonight, something was different. A crack of thunder sent a rumble through the building.

As if it isn't already falling apart, she thought, frowning at the rotten walls and torn wallpaper.

A man opened the door, his curly black hair disheveled. His brown eyes softened as they settled on her.

Before he could speak, she dashed into the room and closed the door. Then she locked it and jammed a nearby desk chair under the knob.

She turned, and a smile grew on her face as she embraced the man before her. "Jacob."

The man squeezed her tightly. "Willow," he whispered as if saying her name was confirmation that she was real. That she was alright.

When they parted, she fished the drive from her pocket. "I got it… I almost got caught, but I got it."

Jacob stared at the flash drive and gulped. He plucked it from her fingers as if it was made of glass. "This…" He held it up to her. "This could be our biggest one yet."

Willow wrapped her arms around herself, the cold biting into her bare skin. "I'd have brought a jacket if I'd known it was going to be so cold in here."

She surveyed the room as Jacob shuffled through something hidden behind the desk. The room was barely large enough to walk around in. The dresser in the corner had only two drawers, and the air conditioner in the corner of the room lay broken on the dirty floor. She grimaced when her eyes came to a window with stained white curtains blocking the view.

"I thought we agreed no windows," Willow muttered. "That makes another entrance for them."

Jacob rounded the desk with a bundle in his hand. "And another exit for us." He handed her the black bundle. "A jacket. For milady."

Willow couldn't suppress a grin as she took the jacket and wrapped it around herself, savoring its warmth. "Dork."

"But a chivalrous dork."

"Still a dork."

Jacob laughed at the same time lightning flashed in the window, yet even as a shiver of fear crawled up Willow's spine, his laugh broke through it and brought a smile to her face. Jacob inserted the flash drive into his laptop.

"By some God-given miracle, this place has Wi-Fi." Jacob clacked the loud, bulky keys of the computer. "Still, it'll take a few minutes for the drive to put everything on here. Even longer to send it to my colleague. In this hellhole, it's the best I can do."

Willow leaned against the dresser, and it groaned. "I know it's not great, but this was the safest building I could find."

Jacob gave her a knowing look. "Why is it that all the 'safest' places are drug dens? I think we'd be equally safe at a four-star hotel."

Willow rolled her eyes. "On a reporter's salary?"

"What about a soldier's salary?"

Willow scoffed. "They don't pay as well as you think."

Jacob shook his head as a bar on the screen slowly filled up. He tapped his fingers on the desk, bouncing one leg. "Are we doing the right thing?"

Willow crossed her arms. "One hundred percent."

"I mean… if this turns out to be nothing, we've just endangered your job in vain."

Willow glanced at the window, and another flash of lightning stung her eyes. "Probably endangering more than that… Something's wrong here, Jacob. I'm following my gut on this one."

"Well," Jacob sang, "my gut says that it's hungry, so as soon as this is over, I demand we get hamburgers."

The walls closed around her. "If I'm putting you in danger—"

"You're not."

"He wants all of us to take some mysterious drug that his brother made? The other drugs have enough side effects as it is, but he won't even tell us what this one is."

Jacob stood and crossed the room to take her in his arms. He nuzzled his face into her neck, and his warmth defrosted her bones. "It's gonna be okay."

Willow wrapped her arms around him. She exhaled, her lips quivering. "I just… don't like it. It's not even a vaccine, it's… He won't tell us what it is."

"I know," Jacob said.

The computer beeped, and Jacob whirled. "It's ready." He turned to her with his iconic lopsided grin. "You want to take a peek?"

Willow attempted a smile, but it fell flat. She knelt beside him and stared at the contents on the screen.

"Let's see what we've got here." Jacob cracked his knuckles and typed, making walls of numbers and text she didn't understand pop up one after the other. "Let's start with the emails. Any keywords you want to search?"

Willow racked her brain and listed whatever bubbled to the surface. "*Drug... soldiers... vaccine*, and..." She pursed her lips. "*Willow*."

Jacob's mouth quirked up, and he typed the keywords. Seconds passed as dozens of emails loaded.

He opened the first one. "Ugh!"

Willow gasped as two images of an arm appeared on the screen. The first was normal, but in the second, the veins on the arm bulged and glowed... purple?

Willow stuttered before she could get her question out. "Does it say anything in the email about this?"

Jacob scanned through it then shook his head. "Just asking if it's normal for their veins to be this color." He scrolled and clicked another email. "Dear God..."

Before Willow could read what it said, a knock sounded at the door. Jacob clicked out of the emails and removed the flash drive.

Willow didn't take her eyes off the door. She opened her mouth to speak, but the door flew open, scattering splinters across the floor. The chair under the knob narrowly missed her, crashing through the window.

Two soldiers charged into the room, wearing black gear, submachine guns in their hands.

Willow ripped a drawer from the dresser and slammed it into the nearer soldier's head. The wood shattered, and the soldier crumpled to the ground.

Willow threw herself against the other one just as she fired her weapon. They crashed into the wall, cracking the wood. Bullets sprayed the computer, destroying it in a shower of sparks. Jacob yelled and dove behind the bed. The pungent smell of smoke and plastic filled the room.

Heart racing, Willow ripped the gun from the soldier and bashed it into her head. Her nose crunched, and blood sprayed onto Willow's face.

Willow made to slam the gun again, but the soldier caught her wrist.

The soldier reared her bloodied face back and slammed her forehead against Willow's nose.

Willow swore and backed away. Pain rippled through her nose, and warm blood trickled down her lips. The soldier lunged at her. Willow spat blood into her face as they collapsed on the ground. The air left her lungs on impact.

"Get off me!" Willow yelled, gasping for air. She braced her feet on the soldier's stomach and shoved her away then scrambled for the gun.

The soldier made to lunge again, but an air conditioner flew into her head, pinning her to the ground.

Jacob stood near the bed, his face pale. He pointed at the body pinned by the air conditioner. "I just did that."

Willow laughed, breathless. She wiped the blood from her nose and spat in a vain attempt to rid her mouth of the copper taste. "Yeah, you did." She grabbed both guns from the soldiers, wrapping one around her back and holding the other in her hand. "Let's go."

Jacob followed as they stepped through the broken door. His voice shook. "This wouldn't have happened in a four-star hotel."

"Yeah, ye—"

Two more soldiers rounded the corner. Willow whirled, guiding Jacob back into the room. They dove through the broken window, slamming into the metal grating of the fire escape as bullets flew past them.

"Keep moving!" she yelled.

They scrambled down the steps and landed hard on the cold cement of the alley. The rain battered them, and Willow wiped her red hair from her face.

They rounded a corner and were sprinting down the narrow passageway when a car drove into the alley, blocking their exit.

Willow sprayed the vehicle with bullets, shattering the windshield and killing the two soldiers inside.

They dragged the bodies from the seats, and Jacob wiped his hands on his pants.

They clambered into the car, and Willow backed out of the alley then slammed her foot on the gas and sped down the street.

"We're gonna die. We're gonna die. We're gonna die," Jacob repeated, gripping his seat as rain poured in through the broken windshield, each drop like a spike of ice slashing their faces.

"No, we're not!" Willow yelled, silencing his chanting.

"I can't believe I touched a dead body."

Willow turned every corner, using the city as a maze. The road map in her head guided her, and she planned out which turns to take before making a break out of the city.

"Willow?" Jacob warned, looking behind them.

Willow glanced at the rearview mirror and swore as bullets sparked against the car. Two black vehicles just like theirs were tailing them, matching their pace with ease. She swore again and removed the gun from around her shoulders. "Drive!"

"What?!"

"I SAID DRIVE!" Willow turned, bracing one foot on the pedal as Jacob reached over to steer. The car swerved back and forth, dodging the brunt of the bullet fire.

Willow aimed and fired at the driver of the first car, who fell forward into the steering wheel. The car swerved into a shop, shattering glass and brick. Her hands numb from the cold of the rain, she aimed at the next car, but it swerved in a zigzag motion.

"Come on… Come on…" Willow followed the car with her gun, calculating the trajectory.

When the passenger leaned out of the car to fire a shot, Willow took one of her own. The driver went down just as the passenger fired, spraying a hail of bullets into their tires.

The car spun, and Jacob screamed. Willow's world blurred into one image with occasional flashes of lightning, and she could only hold on to Jacob's hand as the car smashed into something then flipped into the air. Time slowed, then the car slammed against the ground. The roof caved, nearly crushing them.

Willow couldn't breathe until the ringing in her ears settled.

She moved slowly, her body aching. Blood trailed down her arms. She could see nothing but blackness with her right eye.

She turned toward Jacob. Blood trickled down the side of his head. His leg was bloodied and bent in the wrong direction.

Tears welled in Willow's eyes as she forced herself to move, scraping her body against broken glass to reach Jacob. A shard sliced her stomach.

"Baby?" She shook him. "Baby, wake up."

Jacob groaned again, and his eyes opened. He smiled at her, some of his teeth missing, and the ones that remained were painted red. He held his hand up, the flash drive still intact. "Got it." He laughed then coughed, blood splattering from his mouth. His smile dropped. "Your eye."

Willow put a hesitant hand to the eye that had stopped working, and something pricked her finger. Her stomach turned, but she ignored it.

"We have to get out of here before more come," Willow muttered, hissing through the pain as she slid out of the car.

Jacob crawled after her, dragging his dead leg behind him. He shouted in pain as thunder shattered the night.

Willow stood, scanning the street in the pouring rain. She helped Jacob to his feet. He leaned on her, his breathing ragged.

"Okay, I think we can—"

Gunfire broke the night, and Willow dove into the alley with Jacob. He yelled as he hit the ground, and Willow urged him back up.

"We can do this," she said. "Just keep going."

Two more soldiers rounded the corner, and Willow dropped them with a spray of bullets.

They rushed down the alley, and when they turned the corner, a dark figure was standing before them.

Willow made to lunge at him, but he fired three rounds into Jacob's chest before she could process who was standing before her.

The light left Jacob's eyes as he sank to the ground. The rain seemed to disappear, as did the pain, replaced by an all-new pain. A weight fell on her chest, and she choked on her own sobs as she cradled his bloodied face in her hands.

"Please don't do this to me, baby. Please…"

He looked past her, his face and body going slack.

He was gone.

Willow awaited a bullet in her back, but none came. Her gun lay beside her, and she turned and emptied the rest of her bullets into the figure. Flecks of warm liquid splashed her face, and she kept firing until the gun clicked. *Empty.* The figure crumpled to the ground, and Willow grabbed the hard drive in Jacob's hand.

She looked down at him one last time and placed a kiss on his cheek. At any moment, he would surely wake up. He would wake up and tell her he was pretending. But the glaze in his eyes was no illusion.

Willow sobbed into his neck, clutching his shirt and pulling him closer as the warmth in his body faded.

She stood, her heart shattering at the sight of his body.

She had to keep moving.

She turned, and the figure stood in front of her again. She stepped back as he stepped forward, and she tripped on Jacob's body, falling back against the cold, wet ground.

Lightning flashed, and his smiling face appeared, his eyes filled with malicious joy, before disappearing into darkness once again.

"You…"

"Me," he said, his voice as formal as ever.

He stepped forward, and his veins glowed purple, first dimly, then brighter than the moon. His eyes glowed next as he stared down at her. Her breath caught in her throat at the sight, the dark figure covered with bright-purple veins. A flash of lightning revealed crumpled bullets falling from the man's body, trickling onto the ground.

The soldiers she'd shot stood up. Like zombies, they rose, their veins purple as well.

"I… I don't understand," Willow said, crawling backward until she was against the brick wall.

The man spread his arms wide. "Surprise." He laughed. "I thought it was you that broke into my office. That was very rude of you, Willow. You could have been one of my best soldiers once you accepted… this." His veins glowed brighter, and a few drops of purple liquid dripped to the ground as his wounds healed. The alley reeked of a sweet smell, like honey.

Willow sobbed, gripping the flash drive tightly in her hand.

Gunfire rang out, and Willow gasped as pain tore through her body.

She looked down at her right side, riddled with bullet holes. She tried to breathe but couldn't, as if she'd forgotten how. She gasped and gasped again, but the air wouldn't come. Panic set in, but she couldn't move. *Please*, she begged to the sky, to anyone. *Just one more breath. Just one more!*

She couldn't fight him, couldn't even stop him as he plucked the flash drive from her hand and crushed it like a bug.

"You look uncomfortable," he said.

She couldn't speak, couldn't get the air to leave her body. Blood rushed to her mouth, and she spat it out, aiming for his face. She missed. *Please*, she mouthed.

Lightning flashed again, and the man's smile disappeared, replaced with something like sadness.

Or disappointment.

"Despite your treachery, I'm afraid you don't deserve to drown in your own blood." He aimed his pistol at her. "I'll have mercy."

Willow closed her eyes, refusing to allow those purple eyes to be the last thing she saw.

A gunshot rang out, and the darkness consumed her.

CHAPTER 1
WHERE ARE MY PARENTS?

"He bit his ear off!"

The shout silenced the other children in the room, who'd just been echoing, "Fight! Fight! Fight!"

The taste of copper was bitter in his mouth. His ears rang, and the walls closed in. The kid in front of him, cursing and spitting only moments before, was curled into a ball, cradling what was left of his ear.

He spat out the blood pooled in his mouth and wiped his bloodied nose. Fear crawled up his spine as a woman tore through the crowd of kids and knelt beside the injured child. Then she looked at him, fear and anger evident in her eyes. He tried to explain himself, but his tongue was dead in his mouth, for any excuse he had would not change that look on her face. Would she even care?

"I'll call an ambulance," the woman cooed to the injured child. She looked at him again, a thick layer of discipline covering the fear in her eyes. "And you… I'll deal with you later." The tone of her voice was cruel and cold.

He expected the children to taunt him for getting into trouble, but as he surveyed the kids, their faces showed nothing but fear.

He opened his mouth, but his tongue remained lifeless.

"Monster!" one of the kids shouted, pointing a finger at him.

"Monster!" cried another one.

One by one, each child joined in on the chant, shouting "Monster!" at him, over and over. The chorus echoed in the room, and he covered his ears, tears stinging his eyes as they chanted ceaselessly.

He looked at the woman, a silent plea to make them stop. He tried to tell her that he didn't mean it, but his tongue was leaden. Shaking his head, he backed away. The fear that clutched the children only moments before dissipated into nothing, and they took a step forward.

What would happen if he stayed here? What would they do?

There was no other option.

He ran.

His feet pounded against the floor, and he burst through the front door of the orphanage. Cold air pierced his skin and stung his eyes, but he kept running.

He ducked into a narrow alleyway and curled into a ball in a dark corner.

He wiped tears from his cheeks with his sleeves, looking up at the starless night sky. He sobbed and curled up tighter. He couldn't go back—not now, not ever. The closest thing he'd ever had to a home was gone, and he was all alone.

"I'm not a monster," he muttered to himself, rubbing more tears from his cheeks. "I'm not."

Eight years had passed since that night, yet he still woke with a start, the same words spilling from his lips.

"I'm not," he breathed.

He blinked a few times, looking up at the cracked ceiling. Paint was peeling from it and the walls of his bedroom.

His heart pounded in his chest, and he sighed, running a hand through his long black hair.

He stared at his ceiling, the dream running through his head over and over. He cursed at it, as if it could hear him, as if it would even care. Almost every night, the dream haunted him. Always the same dream.

He took one look at the clock on the wall and groaned. *Time to get up.*

Maybe after today, he could relieve himself of these dreams.

Maybe.

"Hi, my name is Lance," he said, forcing a polite smile. He rolled his eyes and sighed. "Stupid." He shivered from the cold bath, his clothes clinging to his skin. The dream burned in his memory like an ugly scar he couldn't hide.

"Hi, I'm Lance," he said into the cracked mirror. "Do you have the information?"

Today was the day. The question that plagued his mind in the middle of the night would finally be answered. Any modicum of closure he could get would be worth it.

I just hope this isn't a waste of money, he thought with a sigh. *Either way, maybe I'll finally be able to sleep after this.* Of course, that would depend on the answer he was given. But if there was the slightest hope that he could find them—maybe he could start over, transport his life somewhere much brighter, rather than rotting in the slums of this festering city. No more barely getting by with this structurally unsound store. No more going without bedsheets or hot water. Lance hummed at the thought. *Hot water... and good food.*

Still, his nerves sent his heart racing, even as he kept his breathing slow. He'd never purchased something like this before, and if he didn't get what he wanted, a refund wasn't likely. It was a stupid decision, for sure, but answers were answers.

A rusted bell rang in the next room, and after one last look at himself in the mirror, he grabbed an old rag next to the sink and dried his hair. He stepped out of the bathroom and wound through the small hallway into his store. He opened the door and was greeted by a slim, dark man scanning the aisle of snacks.

Lance approached the cash register, sighing at how bare it was. If the man robbed him, he would be sorely disappointed. Surely the population of the slums would know that by now.

"Can I help you?" Lance asked the man, rubbing his tired eyes and not bothering to hide the boredom in his voice.

In response, the man held up a bag of chips.

The man strolled to the counter, the light shining off his bald head. Lance's gut twisted. Something wasn't right.

Lance tensed. "That'll be a dollar fifty."

The man looked down at a small piece of paper in his hand. "Are you Lance… okay, no last name provided."

Lance's heart skipped a beat, but he kept his face relaxed. This was it. This had to be the man he'd contacted. Now he understood why a glint of fear had shown in the eyes of the customer that mentioned his services.

"Who's asking?"

"You inquired about our services. Information on some family members, correct?"

"Yes!" Lance blurted then composed himself. He cursed himself internally as the man raised an eyebrow. *Be cool.* "Yes," he repeated and cleared his throat. He instinctively brought his hand toward his mouth to bite his nails, but he interrupted the action by crossing his arms.

The man folded the piece of paper and slid it into his pocket. The slight movement showed off the slim muscles underneath his black shirt. "Do you have the money we agreed upon?"

Lance eased to the doorway behind him.

"Sure… just stay right there," Lance said, keeping his voice as steady as possible. He couldn't look timid in front of a man like this, despite how he towered over him. He puffed his chest out slightly and raised his chin. "I'll go get it."

The man crossed his arms as Lance slinked from the store and into the small hallway, deflating his chest as he walked past the bathroom and into the adjacent room. His room. His bare mattress lay next to a pile of dirty clothes.

Lance walked to one corner of the room and pulled out a loose piece of the drywall, revealing a hole concealing a small case. Steadying his breath, Lance reached his clammy, pale hand inside and grabbed the ragged leather case. *I can do this. This is just a simple transaction.*

Lance readied himself, but when he turned, he flinched, unable to hide the action. The case nearly slipped from his fingers.

The man was standing in his doorway, arms still crossed.

So much for trying not to look timid.

Lance swallowed the curse that nearly slipped out of his mouth.

"This is the amount agreed upon," Lance said, opening the case and showing him the money inside. As the man eyed the money from across the room, Lance scanned his body for any signs of hidden weapons. Then he scanned the room. The case would make a good enough weapon in a pinch. *I really need to get a damn gun.*

The man took a few silent steps forward and eyed the money more closely. Lance tensed as he took a stack out, weighed it in his hand, then placed it back snugly within the case.

The man shrugged. "Looks like everything's here." His voice was deep and rich, powerful and unyielding.

"So you'll give me what I want?" Lance asked, shutting the case a little too hard. His own voice was so light and shaky in comparison. He deepened it just slightly as he continued, keeping his face unbothered and his body casual. *Don't look weak.* "I'm… paying a lot of money here, so I hope you got something good."

The man nodded. "I'm afraid the terms of our agreement have changed."

Lance blinked. "O… okay? In what way, exactly?" He gripped the case so tightly his fingers hurt. If the man made one wrong move, he'd swing it at his head. He hadn't been in a fight since… that night. *Shit, I am so dead.*

The man took a step closer. "My boss specifically told me to bring you to him. He wants to meet you. Don't ask me why." The man reached into his back pocket and removed a black hood. "Put this on. I can't have you knowing where I'm taking you."

Lance scoffed at it. A shiver went down his spine, but he refused to show it and raised his chin. The man on the pay phone had mentioned nothing about this.

And with all the kidnappings in this part of town...

"No thanks," Lance said, his voice shaking again. The urge to bite his nails twitched his fingers. "In fact, I think I'm having second thoughts. Sorry to waste your time." Lance dug his nails into his sides.

The man either didn't notice or didn't care. He sighed and pocketed the hood. "Listen, we can do this the easy way or the hard way." He said it so casually, but it didn't stop a cold drop of sweat from trailing down Lance's forehead. He wiped it away.

The man took out a new piece of cloth. "Which is it going to be?"

The man offered the cloth to Lance, who frowned at it. Whatever it was, a sweet smell emanated from it.

"What is this supposed to be?"

"The hard way," the man said. "Don't worry, I'm not going to hurt you."

"Are you crazy?" Lance gripped the case tighter.

It was a trap. The man closed in on him, and Lance threw the case at him. He shoved the man aside, rushing out of the room and into the bathroom. He locked the door and backed against the wall.

"Shit... Oh, shitshitshit," Lance muttered. He caught a glance of himself in the mirror, of the fear glazing his green eyes over and paling his face. He ripped a shard from the mirror and angled it at the door.

Monster, the word echoed in his head.

Shut up, he thought to himself.

His heart was beating out of his chest, his legs shaking, and his breathing was heavy and uneven. *Stupid. So stupid!* He should've known this whole thing was a scam. He never should've trusted that customer. He was so desperate to get answers, and now he was going to die in this rathole of a store. The shard of glass shook in his hand despite his attempts to steady it. Blood dripped from his hands, but he felt no pain.

The lock wriggled, and after a few hour-long seconds, it clicked. Lance swore as the door opened, and he lunged, swinging the shard of glass wildly. His attack was blocked by the man's arm, and the world spun before he landed hard on the ground.

Head spinning, Lance coughed as the impact knocked the air from his lungs. The man grabbed him.

"Don't *touch* me!" Lance yelled.

But the man shoved the piece of cloth against his face. Lance gasped as his lungs allowed him to breathe. He kicked and writhed for what felt like forever, but his vision darkened, and he relaxed.

The man spoke. "You better hope he doesn't charge you extra for this."

Lance groaned as he blinked himself awake, nothing but darkness all around him, save for the hint of an orange glow peeking through whatever was around his head. The sound of crackling, the smell of burning wood, and the warmth blanketing him revealed it was a fireplace. His chest tightened, and he tried to get up, but his hands were tied to the chair he was in. He struggled more in a vain attempt to break the rope, but it barely gave.

He muttered a curse, panic setting in. He couldn't risk shuffling the chair, not when he could barely see anything around him.

So he wasn't dead, but at this point, whatever the man had planned for him was surely worse. Lance's heart jumped to his throat when muffled voices approached. The voice of the man that had kidnapped him rang out clearly, but there was another one. A woman's voice, soft and sweet, yet laced with the sharpness of a knife.

A knife that would likely find his heart if he didn't get out of there.

He took slow, deep breaths and listened. What they said was indistinguishable, and the crackling fire didn't help.

A door opened, and Lance gritted his teeth as he prepared for a knife to the throat. He would've slapped himself if he could, allowing himself to be put in this situation for the sake of answers. He should've known better after living so long in the slums. *Am I even still* in *the slums?*

The bag flew off his head, and he blinked away the pain in his eyes as they tried to adjust to the bright fire across the room. Between him and the fire sat a ten-foot-long dining table made of dark polished wood.

The man that had kidnapped him walked around his chair and sat on the left side of the table, tucking the black hood into his pocket. "He'll be here shortly."

Lance gulped at the sight of him, his eyes watering. He looked down at his stinging hands, bandages wrapped around his palms where the glass had cut. He furrowed his brow.

Two black curtains hung on the walls to his left and right. Surely a window sat behind those curtains—a chance to escape if he could just get out of these ropes.

A clock hung on the wall, ornately designed with webs and spiders carved all over it, but it was hard to tell what time it showed. Lance squinted at it until he could barely make out that it was somewhere around midnight.

No more than an hour had passed since he was taken.

Lance glanced again to his left at the man that had abducted him. "What do you want with me?" he asked. His voice trembled, and fear laced his words. *So much for not looking weak.* Putting on a tough face worked well enough with the customers in the slums, or so he told himself. But this was different. He couldn't bring himself to harden his features, panic blurring his thoughts. He willed his shaking hands to still.

They didn't listen.

The man met his eyes for a few long seconds before folding his hands together. "Calm down."

Lance tensed. The silence gnawed at him worse than the rope around his wrists.

The woman was nowhere to be seen, and Lance nearly opened his mouth to ask, only to shut it before the words could escape. He wouldn't get an answer anyway.

The clock was silent, only adding to the tightness in Lance's chest and the rate at which he darted his eyes to those windows. The faint clicking of the clock was maddening. The crackling of the fireplace only worsened it.

A few deep, slow breaths later, Lance willed his face to look casual and eyed the room for a door, for any other chance to escape if the windows didn't work. He couldn't call for help. If he was in the slums, any passersby would ignore the noise, and the attempt wouldn't be worth whatever consequences came as a result.

He flinched at the sound of high heels clicking against the polished wooden floor, distant at first but rapidly approaching. A door opened to the right of the fireplace, and in walked a narrow-faced woman, the hem of her red dress sliding against the floor. Her eyes were yellow. The grace with which she padded across the room was nothing short of catlike. A murderous smile played at her blood-red lips. Her frame was small, yet Lance felt a shiver of fear crawl down his spine at the sight of her, more fear than he felt when confronted by the man, even.

With a glass of wine in her hand, the woman sat in the chair across from the man and took a long sip. She didn't acknowledge Lance's presence, sparing him her piercing gaze.

The man's square face focused on the hall, where another sound emerged. This sound held no grace. It was clunky and rushed. Two footsteps then a clack.

A man with a long black coat walked in through the same door, a dark cane at his side, its handle obscured by his long, slender hands. His shoulder-length blond hair clashed with his black fedora. With a carefree smile, he planted himself in the chair right in front of the fireplace.

His body was no more than a silhouette in front of the fire. Lance gulped. The sight almost resembled the devil himself.

So he was the leader, then.

"Well," said the man with the cane, smiling through the thick silence that followed. "Isn't this nice?" He looked at the girl, who stared at her nails on one hand while swirling her wine in its glass with the other.

Then he glanced at the man to Lance's left, who looked back at him with rapt attention. "I'm sure Derek gave you the proper treatment."

Lance's ears thumped with every pump of his racing heart, his stinging fists clenching against the arms of the chair, if only to hide how they shook.

"This is Kaela." The man gestured with his cane at the girl.

She glanced at Lance with a bored expression, yet her yellow eyes were completely aware, sending another set of chills crawling down his spine, as if the spiders carved into the clock had come to life with a thirst for his blood. She raised her glass then took a sip, as if toasting his kidnapping.

Lance struggled subtly against the rope. It was just loose enough not to cut off his circulation. He made to move his feet then stifled a gasp. His legs weren't bound. If he could stand and slam against a wall hard enough, maybe he could break the chair.

"And I," the man with the cane started, dramatically placing a hand on his chest, "am Eric." His hand left his chest and reached across the table at Lance. "Pleasure to meet you."

Lance raised an eyebrow and glanced down at his bound wrists.

Eric withdrew his hand with a dark chuckle and placed it firmly in his lap. "Sorry. I sometimes forget not everybody is a handshake kind of person."

Lance frowned. "So… you're Eric… You're the man I talked to on the phone?" His voice hadn't held such flourish on the phone, but it was certainly him. "Why did you bring me here? Why did you drug me?"

"Yes, I am sorry about the drugging," Eric said, maintaining his smile as he stood from his chair and stepped onto the table. "But in my defense, you are the one who decided to fight back instead of simply allowing Derek to carry out his orders." His grin turned wolfish. "Besides, I can't have you knowing where you are until I know I can trust you. Security reasons, you understand. I have to keep my associates here safe."

"Okay…" Lance said, his voice not as shaky. *What the hell is going on here?* He steadied his breath. "What do you want from me? I gave you the money… You said you'd tell me everything I wanted to know about my parents." He struggled against the rope again.

Eric smiled and eyed his two associates. "Don't worry, you'll get your money's worth soon enough." His cane clacked crisply against the surface of the table, nearly hitting Kaela's glass of wine.

She grabbed it and held it to her chest, glaring at Eric.

"I apologize for the bonds." He laughed. "Wouldn't want you attacking us with another shard of glass, now, would we? Derek took exception to that, you see."

Lance couldn't swallow the lump in his throat as Eric towered over him, and he hoped the dim lighting of the room wasn't bright enough to reveal the horror in his eyes. "I was just defending myself." His voice cracked. A flare of anger sparked in him, followed by a paralyzing fear when the room went silent.

A whine interrupted the quiet. Eric removed the handle of his cane, and a blade slid out of its slender body, shining in the light of the fire. Lance didn't struggle against the ropes or try to scoot the chair away. His arms and legs turned to lead, paralyzed at the sight of the blade and Eric's twisted silhouette of a smile.

Lance couldn't resist a glance at Kaela and Derek. Kaela smiled venomously, and Derek just stared, emotionless. The pleas for his life almost escaped Lance's mouth when Eric angled the blade at him. He prepared for the blade to pierce his throat, closing his eyes and biting back a sob.

The ropes pulled at his wrists, and Lance opened his eyes as the rope around one wrist was sliced. Eric leaned over and sliced the other rope with a quick swipe. The blade tore through it as if it was butter.

"I suppose you're right. Perhaps it was impolite of me to have you kidnapped. I can get a little ahead of myself sometimes," Eric said, letting out a small chuckle.

"*Sometimes,*" Kaela huffed sarcastically into her wine glass and took another sip, ignoring the look Eric shot her.

Lance lost his breath, his head spinning. He rubbed his sore wrists and studied the windows before he could stop himself. He could escape at any time now, yet that blade still gleamed in the firelight. The sight of it kept him firmly planted in his seat.

Besides, he needed to know what had happened to his parents, especially since he didn't know where his case of money was.

"Look, I just want what I paid for," Lance said. *What the hell kind of business is this supposed to be?*

Eric just stared at him with a toothy smile.

Lance sighed. "*Please*." The word tasted like poison in his mouth, and saying it in front of strangers was even worse.

Eric ignored him. "I understand you're very confused, but I had good reason to bring you here." He sheathed his blade, and his tone lost some of its drama. "I'm sure it goes without saying how important information is to me. And as someone who loves information, I need as much of it as I can get. Are you following me?"

Lance narrowed his eyes. "No?"

"I have an offer for you." He winked at Lance. "I want you to join my little dysfunctional family here."

Kaela choked on her sip of wine and fell into a coughing fit. Eric grinned and patted her back.

"Boss, are you sure about this?" Derek asked.

Eric ignored him.

Kaela finally finished her coughing and slammed a hand on the table. "Are you batshit insane?!"

Eric smiled back. "Not clinically."

Lance blinked. "You… had me kidnapped and brought here just so you could offer me a job?"

The floor swayed beneath him. *Is this some sick, elaborate prank?*

"I wanted to meet you in person. You have to admit this is one hell of an interview, eh?" Eric chuckled again, a dark, resonant laugh that chilled Lance to the bone.

Some of Lance's fear melted away. This was all too confusing, too frustrating. He couldn't hold back the bite in his tone as he asked, "Who the hell are you?"

"Come now, uh…" Eric motioned to him.

"Lance."

"Lance, yes. I know you're tired of barely getting by in that old, decrepit store of yours. I can fix that."

Lance shook his head. Staring into those dark eyes sent a spike of adrenaline through his body. He ran a hand through his hair. This had to be a fever dream. *No way is any of this real.* Frustration tightened around his chest, and his voice held a sharp edge when he spoke. "I just want to find my parents. Is that too much to ask?" The quiver in his voice was long gone.

"I'm getting to that," Eric said through his now faltering smile. "I need another character in my play. Kaela and Derek don't have any businesses in the slums, and neither's people like to go there very often. But you have your own store there. The things you see and hear can be vital to me. I know an opportunity when I see one. And I think you could give me some pretty juicy info from the slums, being that you're a resident of said hellhole."

Lance's stomach twisted into a knot. Impatience swelled in his chest, and he found himself biting his tongue.

"I..." Lance paused to compose himself. "I don't plan on staying at that store once I find my parents."

Eric's eyes held no warmth—not brown, but black, as if his soul had been sucked out.

Or given away willingly.

"Tell me..." Lance pushed.

Eric flopped back into his seat. "Your mother and father, names Carrie and Charles, were a couple that lived in the slums of our sister city, Agni. They had a child, you, in 1978. When you were around one year old, they left you at St. Farel's Orphanage, where you stayed until you were fifteen. After a nasty fight with another boy, you bit a chunk of his ear off and ran away. Afterwards, you went off the grid for a few years until you gathered enough money to buy a worn-down store in the middle of the slums here in Arachna. Years later, you contacted the best and only information dealer in the city." He smiled and pointed at himself. "The rest is history."

"Where are they now?" Lance asked, his heart racing as he leaned forward. This was it. Years of wondering, of sleepless nights, of thinking about what could have been.

Eric's smile faded. "Dead. Overdosed in an alley here in Arachna. If my sources are right, it should have been maybe a few months after they dropped you off." He cleared his throat and removed a manila folder from inside his coat, sliding it down to Lance. "Here's a copy of their death certificates, if you don't believe me."

Lance reached a shaky hand to the folder and opened it. He'd never seen a death certificate before, but... there they were. His parents' names stared back at him from the documents. His heart sank, and his mouth became too dry to speak. He looked down at his clenched fists, his knuckles turning white. He fought back the tears pooling in his eyes. He *refused* to let them see him cry. He dug his nails into his fists to stop from slamming them into the table. More than anything, he wanted to throw the certificates into the fire and watch them burn into ash as his hopes for the future did the same.

"As for the *other* request you mentioned," Eric continued, seemingly unaware of Lance's anger, "you apparently get your eyes from your mother." He eyed the fire for a moment then looked back at Lance. "For what it's worth, I am sorry that you don't have a family… So what do you say to joining a new family? One that won't abandon you?"

The rage stirred in Lance's gut as he fumed. Something burned inside him, some little lie he'd told himself, that maybe they would be alive and well, that they would want to take him back and he would have a family again. He had nothing now.

Absolutely nothing.

"Fine," Lance said, the blood draining from his face, his hands suddenly sweaty and shaky. "What have I got to lose?"

Lance looked at Eric, whose silhouette smiled lazily in front of the crackling flames. He couldn't shake the feeling that he'd just made a deal with the devil.

CHAPTER 2
A DEAL WITH THE DEVIL

"Let me get this straight," Lance started, staring at the drink Derek had brought him: a crisp glass of whiskey.

Its woody smell fogged his thoughts. He suppressed the scoff clawing its way up his throat. His hands itched to reach for the glass and drain it in one swift gulp. The revelation of his parents' death didn't make resisting any easier. He focused on his breathing, drowning out the noise in his head.

Then again, why shouldn't he give in to his temptations? So many years had been wasted in hoping for more than just closure—a second chance. A chance to no longer be an orphan. Maybe he deserved it for what he'd done to that kid. Flashes came to him in waves: the fist slamming into his chest, the kick to his ribs, the tears sliding down his cheeks, the blood dripping from his nose, the kids chanting their encouragements.

The snorty laugh from the kid as he ignored Lance's pleas to stop.

Then the tunnel vision.

And the taste of blood.

Monster.

Lance shook his head then crossed his arms and legs, closed off to the three strangers in the room in an attempt to hide his discomfort. He slid the drink away, his hand shaking. Kaela eyed it then stared at her own empty glass with a deep frown.

He continued, “You want me to gather information for you, and… just tell you if I hear anything interesting?”

Eric wore a lopsided smile. “I’ll occasionally ask you to get specific info for certain clients, but yes. Let me know all the gossip in the slums that you can gather. Shootings, gang activity, whatever you can get your greasy little hands on.”

Lance sighed. “I don’t know how I feel about letting a bunch of strangers tamper with my store. I bought that place with my own money.”

“And I respect that.” Eric smiled devilishly, his fingers tapping lightly against his cane. “But with a paint job, some extra security, and my leadership, you’ll be making more money than you ever have before… guess that’s not saying much, though.”

Lance frowned, but Eric’s eyes just flashed with amusement.

Eric looked at Derek. “Did you get the chips I asked for?”

Derek removed a bag of chips from his leather jacket and tossed it to Eric, who caught it, opened it, and popped a chip in his mouth with a satisfied hum.

“You never paid for those,” Lance said.

It was petty, and his voice cracked saying it, but it felt good to finally let a comment slip. Just one snarky remark to ease some of the tension in his chest.

Eric waved his hand. “Pay the nice man, Derek.”

Derek reached under the table and revealed Lance’s case. He laid it gently on the table’s surface and opened it. All the money was still inside.

“I… I don’t understand,” Lance said, staring at the case. “You’re giving me a refund?”

“Nope,” Eric said through a mouthful of chips. “I’m going to use that money to fix up your store. Call it an investment. Besides, you seemed disappointed in the info I gave… and I just hate disappointing my employees.”

Kaela rolled her eyes and grabbed Lance's drink. He let out a breath and almost thanked her.

"So that's all I have to do? Just grab information? There isn't anything… else you want me to do?" He avoided the word *illegal*, not that it was unfamiliar.

Those murky eyes peered into Lance's. "Not necessarily…"

Kaela smiled, and Derek scratched at his scruffy chin.

"For the next few days, I just want you to get to know us. Tomorrow, you'll spend your day with Derek at one of his bars, the next day with Kaela at one of her brothels, and then dear old… me." He extended his arms widely, his cane dangling between his fingers.

Lance grimaced. A bar. Of course it would be a bar. God, what he wouldn't give to bite the hell out of his nails right now.

"Any questions, my new employee?"

Derek checked his watch and stood, padding to Eric. He bowed to Eric's ear and whispered something.

Lance let his eyes wander the room until they landed on Kaela, who stared back. Not glancing at him or smirking as she had been doing all night, she *stared* right at him, like he was some puzzle she was trying to piece together. Lance stared back, despite the pit in his stomach. Something about her was more terrifying than he felt comfortable admitting to himself.

She opened her mouth, then closed it, then looked back at Eric. Lance shook his head to regain his focus. Those yellow eyes couldn't be real.

Eric tapped his cane on the floor. "Meeting adjourned. Kaela, Derek, you may leave. Lance, I'm not done with you yet."

"Woohoo," Kaela said unenthusiastically, downing the last of Lance's drink.

Derek and Kaela stood and made their way to Lance's right. They opened a door and stepped out, the night air rushing into the room. Lance gawked at the sight. His escape had been right next to him the whole time. Eric beckoned him over.

Swallowing the lump in his throat, Lance strolled over to him. As if they'd been lifelong friends, Eric put an arm around him, his smile friendly. Lance flinched at the sudden touch, and his skin crawled. His face turned warm, and he shoved his hands in his pockets to stop himself from brushing the arm off.

"This family of mine," Eric started, "you're a part of it now."

"Is that so?" Lance responded absentmindedly, clenching his teeth and waiting for Eric to remove that damned hand from around his neck. His skin burned.

"Of course, Lancelot." His smile curled even farther upward. He led Lance closer to the door Kaela and Derek had left through. "I know this is all very sudden, but think of me as a spider, crafting a web slowly and precisely all around this city. Webs take time, and they take patience. You, Lancelot, will enable me to complete my web. With you, I can wind each strand through the streets of the slums and gain easy access to all its secrets. Does that make sense?"

He opened the door and waved Lance out, but Lance looked back at Eric. His eyes were even darker than before, like a starless night sky. The only contrast to that darkness was the small chip bag he cradled in his hand, labeled: Chipsy Crisps.

"What if the police find out about your operations?" Lance asked.

Eric leaned on the door and stared at Lance with a sick interest, his gangly body still somehow intimidating. Or maybe it was the blade hiding somewhere in that cane. Despite his slender fingers blocking most of his view, Lance made out two black orbs staring at him from the head of the cane. It looked almost like… a wolf?

"Are you planning on sweeping my web away, Lance?"

Dread gripped Lance's stomach. He sighed. "No. I'm just not keen on getting arrested. I'd rather just wither away at my store than be trapped in a jail cell."

Eric looked at him for a second too long, a knowing smile inching along his face. "I assure you that won't be a problem." He popped another chip into his mouth. "As you can see, this is a show of trust. I'm letting you leave without a bag or a drug. You know where my hideout is now. Question is… what are you going to do with that bit of information?"

With a laugh, Eric closed the door, leaving Lance to look around the peculiar alleyway. A lamp hung on each side of the door, the square brick space leading into a narrow passageway.

Lance fumbled for his wallet. All his money was still there—what little that was, anyway. But something had been tucked among the money; a card with three addresses on it. One had "Eric" written above it, the other two labeled "Kaela" and "Derek". Eric couldn't have slipped that card into his wallet when he was leading him out of the room. *Could he?*

A twinge of anger flickered in Lance's chest. He shook his head. The information on his parents was free. And the money was going to be used on his store instead. Lance rubbed his tired eyes. It was all for Eric's benefit, but still—all that just to get information in the slums?

"What have I gotten myself into?" he asked quietly as he wound his way around the mazelike alleyway hiding the headquarters of the spider and his web.

Before he stepped onto the street, Lance leaned against the wall, the cold brick provoking a hiss from him. He slid to the ground and buried his face in his hands.

Tears formed in his eyes, and as hard as he tried to hold them back, a few managed to escape.

He should've known he wouldn't get a happy ending. It was too much to ask for his parents back, for a chance at something better than what he had now. It was stupid, but it was all he had to cling to, the only kernel of warmth he could nestle against his chest in the cold nights on a bare mattress, imagining a life with a family. A *real* family.

Is that why he called them his family? Lance thought, setting his jaw as he looked back down at the card. *To manipulate me? To make me think I would be a part of something? Bastard.*

Frustrated, he wiped the tears from his cheeks and rested his chin on his arms.

He almost laughed. The universe had played a trick on him. He'd asked for a family, and he got one—just not the one he wanted. A 'family' with a handful of strangers that were likely just using him for profit.

He could leave—escape the city and start over. *But where? And with what money?* He'd started over once before. Finding a semblance of life in the slums had taken years of scrambling.

Nowhere else would be any better. Not for him, anyway.

Lance cursed at the ground then picked himself up and stepped onto the street. He wasn't in the slums, that was for sure. The buildings around him were cleaner, sturdier. He passed by offices, boutiques, restaurants, and laundromats. The streets lacked trash and dirt. Bodies weren't lifeless or sleeping on the side of the road. Barrels of fire weren't the only source of heat. He avoided crowds, most of them congregated outside bars, and slinked through the alleyways instead. Somehow, even they were cleaner than the slums.

He looked to the night sky, at the stars all staring down at him, and he hoped they were guiding him on the right path.

After what felt like an hour of walking, Lance finally reached his store. It was rusted and old. Paint was chipping off the walls, and graffiti covered the rest. It was a broken mess, but it was his. It was home.

Lance entered his store. The doors were locked, the lights turned off, and the keys left in Lance's pocket. Derek was thorough, he had to give the man that—thorough enough to kill Lance without anyone catching on. Not that evidence was ever useful in the slums. What was his story? What were any of their stories?

Lance locked the door behind him, shuffled to his room, and fell onto his mattress. The weight on his shoulders was gone, but without its presence, all that remained was an emptiness. He rolled over and closed his eyes.

He was trapped in Eric's web, and Eric had all but confirmed the police would do nothing about it. But it was the closest thing he had to a fresh start.

I suppose I should get used to it.

The smell of stale cigarette smoke, alcohol, and greasy food filled the air. One of which surfaced too many memories… and temptations.

The nightmare had granted Lance a reprieve last night. Maybe the knowledge of his parents' fate played a factor. Or maybe he was exhausted from being kidnapped and offered a job. Either way, Lance refused to question it. He welcomed the first good night's sleep he'd had in years.

He needed it for today.

The flashing neon sign of beer pouring into a glass flashed across the room. Lance looked out at the tables and booths across the room, seating patrons with burgers and steaks and drinks.

And alcohol.

Lance gulped.

Derek—his stone-cold disposition from the previous night replaced with a bright smile and a glint of light in his brown eyes—served every customer as readily as the next, whether they were new customers searching for a buzz or regulars entering together and speaking with Derek like they'd been friends for years.

If only the customers he smiled and laughed with knew he could make them disappear without a trace, Lance thought.

Lance kept conversation to a minimum, excluding an occasional introduction when a regular questioned Derek as to who 'the new guy' was. He kept himself scarce, surrounded by too many people to feel comfortable with anything but watching and listening. He kept his face bored and his movements casual, but his heart raced, and he wiped his sweaty hands on his pants more and more. Too many people were around to calm down—too many faces and sounds and smells.

Lance cleaned out the handful of shot glasses before him, resisting the urge to lick them clean instead, while Derek listened intently to a drunken man's rant about catching his wife cheating on him with another woman.

Derek leaned forward and looked around like he was about to tell the man a secret. "I'll tell you what, pal. Go by The Red Rose and tell them Derek sent you. You'll get a good discount."

Lance stopped his jaw from dropping as the man thanked Derek and left to claim the discount. Derek lazily scratched his chin then leaned toward Lance.

"See?" Derek whispered. "I got what info I could out of him then sent him over to Kaela's business for the rest."

"I don't see the point," Lance said as he slid a shot of whiskey down the bar toward a man waiting on his phone, muscle memory coming into play. More than anything, he wanted to bring the shot glass to his lips instead. Just to taste it. To remember what it was like. "What's the point of knowing if some guy's wife cheated on him?"

"Who do you think he paid to find out?" Derek asked with a knowing grin.

The doors to the kitchen opened, and a server emerged carrying a platter of burgers and fries. The smell yielded a growl from Lance's stomach.

The server set the platter at a table where two men sat then turned and sent a subtle head shake in Derek's direction.

"No good info," Derek said. "That's what he means."

"Why are you telling me this, again?" Lance asked, grateful that the ambient noise of the bar masked his growling stomach.

"Eric told Kaela and I this morning to give you a rundown on how we do things in our businesses. And to teach you what we can about getting info."

"Yeah, well, that explains the thirty-minute lecture on body language." Despite the grumble in his voice, it had been a fascinating half hour. Lance eyed the men eating their meal then surveyed the handful of tables lined against the wall with other patrons eating their own burgers or steaks. The meat looked so tender and juicy, the fries crisp and golden. His mouth watered.

"Feeling alright?" Derek asked.

Lance meant to remain silent, yet he found himself talking before he could stop it. "It's just… weird. This part of Arachna is so different from the slums. It's brighter, cleaner, and people laugh and eat good-looking meals like that." Lance gestured toward the platter of burgers and fries at the table deemed lacking in useful information. "People can lock their doors and feel safe instead of it just being a minor annoyance to anyone trying to break in."

"Yeah, the cops almost never go to the slums," Derek mused. "Makes me wonder how a guy like you managed to survive that long." He chuckled as he turned toward a man taking a seat at the bar.

Lance sighed. *You're not the only one.* He continued cleaning out glasses as he glanced at Derek, who approached the newest patron like a fox stalking a rabbit.

"Shot of vodka," said the man, taking his seat at the stool. He hunched over, leaning his head against his hand. Guilt shadowed his face. "You know what?" He slapped some money on the table, and only then did Derek pour. "Make it two."

"I take it you went to The Red Rose?" Derek said wryly.

"How'd you know?" asked the man, as if he'd been caught in the act of murder.

Lance scanned his face. His eyes were dark and heavy with bags.

"Lucky guess." Derek shrugged, placing the two drinks down and leaning over to better inspect the man. "Feelin' alright?"

"Yeah, sure," the man choked out after downing the first shot. "I just think I'll forget everything that happened this morning. God, I did some things I should never have done."

"It is a bit early for that, but hey, we've all been there," Derek assured. "Happens to the best of us, man."

"I guess." He downed the second shot with a sour look on his face then looked at his watch. "I need to get going."

"What's the rush?"

"I have a meeting to get to, and I don't think my superiors would be very happy about me being late." He gave a fake laugh and slid from the barstool.

"What kind of meeting?" Derek asked as he grabbed the two shot glasses and slid them over to Lance, appearing only casually interested in what the man had to say. Lance perked his ears as he cleaned the glasses, peering at the man from under his hair.

"Just some project," the man said, straightening his tie, his stature turning confident. The stature of a man entrusted with a great secret but proud enough to let the world know he couldn't speak of it.

"Ooh," Derek said, his eyes widening along with his smile. "What kind of project? Some sort of new marketing? Call me old-fashioned, but word of mouth is still the best way to promote any product. How do you think I'm able to keep this bar open?"

"Sorry," he said. "It's a secret." After slapping down a generous tip, the man disappeared, walking with more confidence than he'd entered with.

Derek hummed a tune to himself as he rubbed the back of his neck.

"Anything interesting?" Lance prodded. How much would Derek tell him?

"You weren't listening?" Derek asked.

Lance shrugged. "I didn't think I had to since you were already doing it."

An abysmal lie, but Derek didn't appear to notice.

"Apparently, his company is working on a secret project. And anything involving the word *secret* is interesting, especially when they work for a company that hasn't been around for very long."

"What do you mean?"

"You know about Landreau Corp? How their newest building is in our humble little city?"

Lance nodded. It'd been difficult *not* to notice a skyscraper suddenly appearing in the city last year. Even from the slums, the top of it was visible.

"Well," Derek continued, "one thing that's not hard to spot about them is they all have a tie with that symbol on it. Those hands holding a ball of flame."

"I didn't see anything like that."

Derek smirked. "I thought you weren't paying attention."

Lance's heart skipped a beat. "I still saw the man walk in. Doesn't mean I was listening." He didn't meet Derek's eyes, looking out at the patrons instead.

"I almost didn't catch it either, until he straightened his tie. So now we know that this Landreau Corp is working on a secret project."

"They're a pharmaceutical company, right?" Lance said. "They're probably working on some miracle pill. A lot of companies probably have secret projects that don't mean anything."

Derek rubbed the bridge of his nose. “Do you remember what Eric said yesterday?”

Lance crossed his arms. “Hard to forget.”

“Information is currency. And he’s right. Whatever it is they’re working on, Eric needs to know about it so he can make a profit. If he learns that Landreau Corp is working on a miracle pill, maybe he can let it slip to a few other companies and get paid. That’s how things work around here.”

“Right, well, I wouldn’t know anything about that.” Lance glanced at the clock on the wall. “I think I’m gonna head out.”

Lance rounded the corner of the bar, but a strong hand gripped his arm. He glared at Derek, a snarl on his lips. His heart pounded in his chest, and his skin burned. He followed Derek’s stare to a group of three men laughing as they entered the bar. They stumbled over each other, visibly drunk.

Lance ignored the feeling in the pit of his stomach and glared at Derek again. “Something wrong?” His voice cracked, but he didn’t care. He tried to wrench his arm free from Derek’s iron grip, tempted to kick him.

“Yeah,” Derek said, finally letting Lance go. The maelstrom in Lance’s mind eased, but his arm burned where Derek had touched him. “I know these guys. Kaela told me about them. They’ve been going around different establishments, piss drunk, smashing things and starting fights.”

“What do you expect me to do about that?”

“Stay here and take this.” Derek handed a beer bottle to Lance. “Use it if one gets too close.” Derek rounded the bar, the three drunken men oblivious to what stalked them.

Lance’s gut twisted at the sight of them. He looked around the bar, and none of the customers noticed the tension in the room, brewing like a storm cloud.

Derek was a predator tailing his prey as he weaved through the chairs and tables, the patrons not acknowledging his movements. A ghost amongst the living.

A ghost that was about to haunt three very intoxicated men. One of them, a man with spiked hair dyed blood red and shades on his forehead, stomped to a nearby table and pulled a man's chair from under him with a messy laugh. The man's beer spilled everywhere, and he was on his feet seconds later, shouting at the spiky-haired man, spit and residual alcohol flying from his lips as he listed off every curse in the book.

The spiky-haired man's laugh stopped short, and as he raised his fist to throw a punch, Derek grabbed his wrist.

"Problem, gentlemen?" Derek asked, his friendly attitude slipping back into who he'd been the night before.

"Yeah, this guy's shouting at me for no reason!" yelled the spiky-haired man with slurred words. "My friends and I are here to get a drink and leave, nothing more. I was just taking care of him for you, *sir*." The man tried to free his arm, then braced his leg on Derek to pull harder, but Derek's grip held strong. "Why don't you hop back behind that bar and serve me a drink?" He poked Derek's chest as if expecting him to move back a little. Instead, he winced in pain as his finger jammed against Derek's unmoving form.

Lance parked himself in a corner and kept still, his knuckles white as he gripped the cold bottle. The less attention he could draw to himself, the better. The patrons in the bar turned their heads toward the commotion, and murmurs turned into dead silence.

"I'm gonna have to escort you out of my bar," Derek said, his voice calmer.

When he put a strong hand on the young man's shoulder, the poor sap threw a punch. Derek dodged it and threw one of his own. The man fell back onto a table, his eyes wide and his nose dribbling red. His two friends shouted in a drunken rage and jumped onto Derek's back.

Derek shoved his back against the wall, crushing the two men under his muscled weight. They crumpled to the ground.

The red-haired man wiped his nose and charged Derek. The blood barely noticeable on his dark knuckles, Derek sent a punch into the man's stomach then threw another to the back of his head. He dropped to the ground with a grunt.

Only one of the two lackeys stood back up, a lanky man with skin even darker than Derek's. He pulled a switchblade from his pocket, a lopsided grin marking his face.

The lackey lunged. Derek avoided swipe after swipe of the blade until he grabbed the man's wrist with one hand, his other wrapped around his neck.

"I know you didn't just try to stab me in my own bar," he hissed.

The knife slipped from the lackey's fingers. Derek stretched the man's arm out and sank his knee into his elbow. The only sound louder than the crunch of splintering bone was the piercing shriek of pain.

The third lackey, a fleshy man, groaned on the floor as he reached for the fallen blade.

Derek slid the knife away and kicked the man's face. Blood splattered on the wooden floor. He released the second man's neck and pushed him toward the door. He and his two friends stumbled out of the bar, sobs carrying over from the one cradling his broken arm.

The man that had been pulled from his chair cheered drunkenly while the rest of the bar stared silently. Derek grabbed the switchblade off the floor and approached Lance.

Lance gripped the bottle harder. Derek managed to rip the bottle away and placed the switchblade in Lance's hand. "There," he said with a small smile. "Consider it a welcoming present." Derek cleared his throat and went to the back to wash his hands, ordering a nearby server to clean the mess.

The silence in the bar faded as the patrons hesitantly returned to their meals and conversations. The air was stiff with tension and fear. It was as if none of them had ever seen a fight break out before. *They probably haven't.*

Lance opened his mouth, but no words came to mind. Not even a goodbye. He stared down at the switchblade in his hand, closing it and slipping it into his pocket. He turned to leave, but Derek stopped him.

A worker exited the kitchen with a to-go box and passed it to Derek.

"Don't forget your lunch," Derek said, offering it to Lance.

Lance looked down at the box then searched Derek's face for any sign of malice. But he saw no knowing glare in his eyes, no nervous shifts of movement.

"Why?" Lance asked. He didn't bother hiding his doubtful expression.

"Because you've been here for hours and haven't eaten," Derek said, resting his hands on his hips.

Lance leaned against the bar and pursed his lips. "I know I'm supposedly a part of this group now, but you kidnapped me. And now, today, you've been constantly talking. What's the deal? Is this some way of getting information out of me like everyone else?"

Derek didn't react, only set the box down and crossed his arms. "I was just doing my job yesterday. I'll be honest with you, I thought it was weird that Eric wanted to see you, as he's never brought a client to the hideout before. I thought it was even weirder when he offered to make you a part of the family, or web, or business, whatever you want to call it… but I figure I should do my best to treat you as such."

Lance scanned for any signs that he was lying. No tics. No avoiding eye contact. No exaggerated movements.

"Look, if you don't believe me, at least think of it as an apology for knocking you out in your own store, hmm? I'm trying to make a show of good faith here." He sighed. "If Eric trusts you, then I will too, because I trust him. Is that so hard to believe?"

Lance lowered his voice. "Who are you, exactly? You're more than just a bartender and info gatherer. You didn't leave a trace that you were at my store. You even cleaned up the damn mirror and blood in my bathroom. God knows how you had time to do that." He narrowed his eyes. "And you just took down three guys by yourself. What the hell do you do for Eric, exactly?"

Derek leaned on his hands on the bar, biting his lip and staring at the polished wood in thought. "I… have a sordid past. I learned how to do a lot of shady shit. Eric scooped me out of that life and brought me on with him. He saved my ass. As for those punks, well… I've been in a fair share of fights before." He shrugged.

Lance sighed then hesitantly grabbed the box of food. Derek hadn't attempted to hide his body language at all. He just laid it all bare in front of Lance. Maybe he was telling the truth, but Lance wondered what he'd done in his past to pick up those skills.

Maybe I don't want to know. "Well… apology accepted."

"I should warn you, Kaela's not going to be as willing to give you a chance as I was today. She's a tough nut to crack, and she was pissed that Eric brought in a stranger out of nowhere."

"Yeah, I gathered that." Lance walked to the door. "Thanks."

"Oh," Derek said suddenly, snapping his fingers. "I have a cellar in the kitchen. Would you like me to have a barrel of wine delivered to your store? It's the best in town."

Lance blinked. His heart skipped a beat. He could do it. He had no parents, no second chance. *Well, I suppose I have this one, but... God, an entire* barrel *of the stuff.* He choked on his words a few times, trying to force them out. "No thanks," he said, his voice cracking. "I'm good."

"Suit yourself."

Lance sighed as he stepped out the door and into the bright, cloudy outside. He paused, still shocked at the cleanliness of this part of the city compared to the slums. Fresh coats of paint, flashy signs, and smiling faces; pastry shops, hardware stores, apartment buildings, all as clean as the rest. He felt as if he'd stepped out of a noir film and into… well, the present.

Derek had been kinder than last night, but if Eric ordered him and Kaela to tell Lance how they ran their businesses, he could have easily ordered them to gather info from him as well.

But that doesn't make sense, he thought with a curse. Eric already knew everything about him, right down to his fight at the orphanage. So then, what was Derek's ulterior motive for the act of kindness?

The smell of the food in the box trailed to his nose as he walked the street. He couldn't remember the last time he'd eaten a decent meal. Looking around, Lance cracked the lid and peeked in. The burger and fries stared back at him. He gripped the box tighter when strangers passed, waiting for them to take it for themselves. None of them even tried.

As the minutes passed, Lance sneaked a few fries, then a few bites of the burger, and by the time he returned to the slums, the food was gone, and his stomach was full.

When Lance reached his store, he dropped the empty box on the ground and gasped. At least ten men were ambling around his store.

One of the men turned to Lance with a smile on his face.

Lance closed his open jaw. With steps lighter than even Derek's, the muscular man padded to Lance, his pale hand outstretched.

Lance didn't extend his own hand, but then the man reached down and grabbed the box. "Don't want to litter, now. I know this is the slums, but we don't want anything distracting from your new store."

Lance stared at his store, almost failing to hide his excitement. It had yet to be finished, but a new coat of paint already graced the sides of the building as several men worked on the front. The door was gone, and the inside was filled with more men painting and working. The old, rusted shelves rested on a nearby truck as new shelves were being carried inside. It already looked twice as good as it had before, and it wasn't even finished yet. The money Lance had given to Eric wouldn't cover all this. Why was Eric so invested in him?

The man extended his hand once more. "*Now* I'd like a handshake." His smile was genuine and reached his warm brown eyes. "Name's Rob, sir. Glad to see we've added another underboss to the… what does Eric call it? Web?"

"Uh… nice to meet you, Rob." Lance grimaced at his hand. "I'm not really much of a handshake kind of guy."

Rob furrowed his brow, but his smile didn't disappear. He ran a hand through his fiery red hair. "Ah, I understand. I have a cousin who's a bit of a germaphobe."

Lance opened his mouth to argue but let it go instead.

"These burgers are good, lemme tell you. Least they were back when *I* worked at Derek's bar."

"So… how long is it going to take before my store is done?"

"Probably another day or so. This place was more of a mess than we thought, no offense. We only needed to make some cosmetic fixes. I'm pretty shocked the old girl is as sturdy as she is." His smile didn't falter in the slightest. It appeared even more genuine than Derek's. His face was bright and cheerful. Did he even realize who he worked for? "You picked a good building."

Lance ran a hand through his own hair and allowed himself to nibble at one of his nails. “Did you just call me an underboss?”

Now the smile faltered. “Yes, sir. That’s what Eric told us, at least, that you were a new underboss.”

“Yeah, well, it sounds like Eric dramatized that story a little bit. I’m not the boss of anyone. I’m just apparently a part of the ‘family’ now.” His stomach twisted as the word left his lips.

“I understand, sir.”

That word grated Lance’s ears.

“Please stop calling me that. Just call me Lance.”

Rob raised an eyebrow. “Huh… Not a fan of being in charge?”

Lance paused, considering the question. He shook his head.

Rob’s smile relaxed. “Thank God. I thought I was going to break my jaw smiling that wide.” His demeanor changed entirely, becoming more relaxed, more casual.

Lance failed to hide his surprise. He’d seemed so genuine. *Was Derek faking as well*?

“Well, as I said, we only have a few more cosmetic changes to make, but I wouldn’t recommend you sleep here tonight while we finish up. Eric told us to tell you that you have a room at a hotel over on Widow Street, near The Red Rose.”

“Why were you trying to kiss my ass so bad?” Lance asked.

“Eric made it, um… very clear that we were to be nice to you.”

Lance eyed the men fixing his store, a familiar weight settling on his chest. Eric really had that much power, to make so many men treat a stranger like he was the most respected person in the world.

“Well, it was nice meeting you, Rob. I’ll be going.”

“Yes, s—” He caught himself. “Yes, Lance. We’ll be done with her by tomorrow afternoon.” Rob bit his lip as if trying to cut off more words from escaping his mouth.

Lance turned to walk away, stealing one last fleeting look at his store. It would be the last time he’d see it run down.

It was almost sad to think about.

“Lance,” Rob called.

Lance turned. Worry was written on Rob’s face. Was that fake too?

"You're going to be meeting Kaela tomorrow, right? Derek told me, and… just be careful. She's not very fond of people. Especially strangers."

Lance nodded and turned, beads of sweat forming on his brow. For Derek and his own men to be wary of Kaela, and with those yellow eyes staring him down… Fear settled into Lance's heart, a heavier weight than even Eric gave him at their first meeting.

Well... maybe it won't be so bad.

CHAPTER 3
OH GOD, SHE'S WORSE THAN I THOUGHT

Lance awoke on the cool sheets of the hotel bed, his eyes absent of their usual heaviness.

The room around him was a soft brown. Light from the overcast sky filled the room through a crack in the almost-closed curtains.

Groaning, he clumsily rolled out of the bed, wishing more than anything he could stay under the covers forever. He stretched and finally stood up straight. He rubbed his tired eyes as he padded to the window then ripped open the curtains. The light stung his eyes at first, but he adjusted quickly.

The sky looked only moments away from releasing a torrent of rain.

He looked out at the city. The slums always felt dead and devoid of any happiness, yet in this part of the city, citizens ambled along side-walks and drove down streets in clean, polished cars. A fountain stood nearly out of view. Its statue featured a black widow with its fangs bared, water spilling from them and pooling below. A child stood nearby, tugging at his mother's sleeve. Moments later, he threw something into the water.

The mother grasped her child's hand as he returned from the statue's looming presence. Lance grimaced as they walked away. Where would he be now if his parents hadn't died? On a bus, maybe, or a train. He would walk into a house that smelled of fresh pastries. His mother would round the corner with tears in her eyes and embrace him so hard that he couldn't breathe. His father would hug him as well. They would eat and laugh and tell stories. They would let him stay as long as he wanted. He would be a part of a family.

That dream would never come true.

Tears rolled down Lance's cheeks before he could stop them. He wiped them away, sniffling and swearing at his parents for abandoning him.

His watery eyes glazed over as he stared out at the rest of the city. He focused on the skyscraper in the center, taller than every other building, towering like a king over peasants—Landreau Corp, the company supposedly working on a secret project only a year after moving to Arachna.

Lance leaned forward and rested his head against the cool glass of the window, goosebumps rising along his arms as the cold seeped through and into his bare chest.

Soon, he would have to leave this room and join Kaela for whatever excursion she had planned for him. If she was as bad as he thought, he'd certainly needed that good night's rest.

Again, no nightmare. That was a relief, at least.

A knock sounded.

"One second!" Lance called. He ripped himself away from the window and dressed in the clothes set out for him—under Eric's orders, he guessed.

A pair of black elastic pants cleverly disguised as jeans, and a black shirt. The clothes smelled of pine and lavender, which would've been a lovely sensation had it not smelled exactly like the matron at the orphanage. A copper taste formed in his mouth, and he suddenly had the urge to spit.

Now clothed, Lance crept to the door, taking his time to look around, savoring every moment he could be in this room, safe and comfortable. No risk of being attacked or shot. No more moldy walls, chipped paints, or rancid smell. He stowed a few things from the bathroom in his pockets.

He wondered if he would be able to afford rooms like this once Eric started paying him.

Lance opened the door. Kaela stepped in without a word, wearing a royal-blue dress that covered one shoulder and left the other bare. Glitter shone like diamonds on the skirt as it floated just above the carpeted floors. A sneer played on her lips as she looked around the room, as if she was in a garbage can rather than a four-star hotel room.

"Ready?" she asked, her voice drawling on the word as if she was bored to tears.

Lance had wondered all night how this interaction would go. Already not a good start.

"Yeah," Lance said hesitantly. "I can… barely keep my excitement in."

"Most men can't when they come to The Red Rose."

Lance blinked at how fast her response was.

Kaela sneered down at the floor again, as if expecting the carpet to move out of her way.

What a snob, Lance thought as he stared at her eyes. Those yellow eyes were still a mystery to him, and probably not a mystery he wanted to crack, as the sight of them still sent a cold chill down his back. Those eyes looked at him now.

"Can we leave?" she asked.

Lance put a hand on his pocket, the switchblade resting comfortably within. He checked his other pocket, where two travel-sized bottles of shampoo rested. If he only owned a suitcase, he could've taken some towels as well. "Yeah, we can leave." He nearly added a sarcastic 'Your Highness', but a lump formed in his throat when he considered it.

"Thank God," she said, placing her hands firmly on her hips as she looked around the room once more. "Let's get this day over with."

Lance crossed his arms. "Is there a problem?"

Kaela hummed and glided to the window. "You can almost see it from here."

"See what?"

"The slums," Kaela breathed, a smirk on her lips. "Don't get used to this. You'll be back there before you know it."

Lance balled his hands into fists but relaxed them when she turned around. "Are we leaving or not?"

Kaela didn't answer—just walked out of the room and motioned for him to follow. "Did you learn anything at Derek's bar?" she asked after a few steps down the hall.

Lance wondered what he should tell her and settled for a simple, "Mhm." After a moment of silence, he spoke again. "Is there anything I'm supposed to learn from you today?"

"How to seduce men and women," Kaela said without hesitation.

Lance stopped in his tracks, unable to hide his wide eyes in time as she peeked over her shoulder with a wicked smile.

"Ah, and the mask breaks already." She chuckled. "I thought it would have taken longer than that."

Lance's cheeks flushed, and he waited for the back of her head to catch fire from the glare he shot at her. He racked his brain for a comeback, but anger clouded his thinking. "I'm not sure what you mean, but I'm just here to learn how you run things around here."

"Well, allow me to be frank," Kaela said as she summoned the elevator. "I don't trust you whatsoever, and the idea of bringing you to the business I built from the ground up and telling you how it works makes me want to slap Eric across his grinning face."

"Be a shame if someone were to tell Eric that," Lance said, frustration honing an edge to his words. The way she spoke and carried herself, like she was better than him, made it harder and harder for him to bite his tongue.

"He wouldn't care," Kaela said casually. As they walked through the lobby, she lazily waved to the man at the desk. "See you next week, Johnny."

He waved back with a smile.

When Lance followed Kaela outside, an older man summoned them to a limousine parked just out front.

"Why am I not surprised?" Lance muttered to himself as Kaela got into the car, and he slipped into the seat beside her.

"What can I say? I'm a fan of the finer things in life," Kaela said as she reached for a glass and took a bottle of wine out of the mini fridge.

"So, since I'm obligated to tell you about how I run things, let's go ahead and rip this bandage off. My business is called The Red Rose. There are four spread out across a few corners of the city, with another one dead center, which is where we're going. Derek has about four bars, all of which take up the space that the Roses can't." She took a large mouthful of wine and savored it for a few seconds before swallowing. "I still have no idea why Eric brought you in on this operation. I never know what's going on in that man's head, but he usually has a reason for everything he does. This? You? I haven't the slightest clue as to what he was thinking."

"Maybe you just weren't listening," Lance said. "He said none of you had businesses in the slums. That even your people don't like going there."

She stared at him for a moment. "The pup bites back. Go figure. I would never have guessed you had teeth, with the way you were trembling last night." She took another gulp of wine. "You know, in movies, people like you always end up dead."

"I don't watch movies." *As much as I'd love to.*

Kaela smiled. He kept his eyes forward, watching her out of his peripherals. Her face remained composed and casual. She was impossible to read.

She released a deep sigh and took another gulp. "Whatever. I'm sick of arguing with you. Eric might just be using you for bait anyway, so let's just get this day over with."

Lance spoke before he could catch himself. "Bait?"

Kaela set the glass down gently into a cup holder, crossed her legs, smoothed some of the creases in her dress, then placed her hands in her lap. She stared at him with an innocent expression.

Lance gritted his teeth. She was toying with him, wasting as much time as possible so he would beg for her to explain. Suddenly, he was back at the orphanage with the constant torment and poking and prodding of the other kids. She was just like them. He balled his fists.

"You serve no purpose to this business," Kaela finally said. "Eric most likely has some plan in mind, and he'll use you to lure out some old enemy, effectively killing you and getting whatever it is he's looking for." She cleared her throat. "If our people were that scared to go into the slums, Eric wouldn't have taken so long to hire somebody. Which leads me to believe that you… are bait."

Lance clenched his jaw and couldn't stop himself from gulping. She still looked at him with that smile. She was enjoying his 'mask' breaking.

"So you're saying that he wants something important," he said, "and the only way he can think to get it is to gain an inordinate amount of information on me, a random guy who lives day by day in a shitty gas station, so I can be bait? Not to mention he's having my store fixed. Seems like a lot of trouble for little reward."

"Fattening you up before he shoves you into the oven." Kaela blinked slowly then picked her glass back up, refilling it with wine. "Oh, I hope I can get drunk enough to get through today."

Lance clenched his fists and gritted his teeth as Kaela sipped her wine, completely unbothered.

Derek had tried to warn him, but she was as intense as he said. Maybe even more. He crossed his arms and stewed in his anger the rest of the way, that word searing into his brain.

Bait.

The limo stopped at a four-story building. The walls were dark red with pink-outlined figures dancing and holding each other in tight embraces. A red neon sign lined the front of the store, *The Red Rose* written in glowing cursive letters.

Brothels had been legalized years ago in Arachna, and they still drew in more business than any other nightlife establishments.

"Here we are," Kaela said, sounding more pleasant than she had minutes before.

The alcohol must have taken effect, Lance thought with a smirk that he hid by wiping his mouth.

He stepped out of the car, following Kaela inside. The moment the doors opened, the smell of perfume escaped from inside. The birch hallway was lit with soft ambient lighting and decorated with paintings and pictures of nude men and women.

Kaela looked back at him with a pleasant smile, the first one he'd seen on her, and said, "Welcome to The Red Rose." She turned and walked gracefully down the perfumed hall.

Lance closed in on himself, unable to shake the feeling that he didn't belong here. The sound of pleased customers from the floor above didn't help. He focused his eyes on the floor, clean and polished.

They passed a hall to the right, which led to an exit door, and only a few steps later, another hall to the left that led to a handful of closed doors, the only distinction of what was behind them in the form of a numbered golden plaque resting right beside each.

Escorts walked by, some scantily clad, others in the finest of dresses. He gulped and kept his focus on Kaela's back.

"Feeling alright?" Kaela asked, smiling widely.

Much as he tried to hide it, nothing could disguise the redness in his cheeks. That smile on Kaela's face told him she could see his embarrassment, and that she was enjoying it.

"Of course I am," he said back, keeping his voice light and casual, despite wishing he could escape into his shirt.

Kaela let out a small chuckle. "We're headed to my office."

Lance relaxed, and when Kaela turned to look at him, she seemed to notice.

"What, you didn't think I was going to force you on anyone, did you?" She laughed. "Maybe I will, yet."

Lance balled his fists. Every chance she could get, she toyed with him. *Moves like a cat,* he thought. *Apparently acts like one too.*

They walked past a lounge area where men and women alike sat and drank. Some had women in their laps, others were sharing drinks with them.

"Since I'm obligated to tell you about my business…" Kaela said as she took a sharp right up a set of stairs then paused, her face twisting as if she was nauseous. "This, as you can see, is an all-female Rose. A couple of others are all-male, and one offers both. Maybe you'd like to drink a little and unwind with one of my girls while I get some work done?" She grinned.

"I think I'll pass."

Kaela's smile grew as she looked back at him. "Surely you're not afraid I'll poison your drink, are you? Or perhaps this isn't your preference. I can always have my driver out there take you to one of my all-male Roses."

"I said I'll pass."

Kaela hummed then continued up the stairs. "Fine. Do you have any questions?"

"It's not about your business, but… how does Eric avoid the police? And…" Something inside him halted the question from leaving his lips. Yet, as he opened his mouth to say something else, they came out anyway. "Are those your real eyes?" His voice faltered, and he cursed himself.

They ascended to the top floor, and farther down the hall they reached a dark wooden door. Kaela's name was written across it.

"I should probably let Eric answer the police question himself, but…" She chuckled then turned around with a smug smile. "Since he trusts you *so* much, surely he'd be willing to tell you, right?" She laughed, but her eyes glinted with something like annoyance, and her posture stiffened. "Eric and the chief of police, Ms. Rotoya, have an understanding. A mutual understanding that Eric provides whatever she needs, including some extra funds for her men, and Eric gets more breathing room to do what he wants. As for my eyes, well… they're real. The real question you have, I imagine, is why they are the way they are."

Lance shrugged. "You took the words right out of my mouth."

"Well, if I told you, I'd have to kill you." A playful smile followed. "Maybe I will tell you when Eric uses you as bait. As a parting gift, you know?"

They entered Kaela's office. The walls were a deep-auburn wood with a web pattern carved into them. A mini bar was nestled in a corner of the room. Lance avoided its gaze.

Kaela slinked to the chair behind her desk and sat upon it like it was made of glass.

Lance sat in the chair across from the desk, halfway expecting a needle to prick him.

"So what's on the agenda for today?" Lance asked. "I don't think I can assist with your business—that much is obvious." He took a deep breath. He *hoped* it was obvious, at least.

His nerves were getting the better of him, and the urge to bounce his leg became relentless. He stretched them instead and leaned on them, then crossed his arms to avoid biting his nails.

"True." Kaela hummed as she left her seat and poured two glasses of whiskey from the mini bar. She placed one in front of Lance then returned to her seat. "You really should have a drink. It'll calm you down."

"What do you mean?"

"Oh, please. When you saw all those pretty employees of mine, your face went redder than the neon sign outside."

Lance raised an eyebrow, looking anywhere but at the glass of whiskey. "Did you ever consider that was just the ambient pink lighting?"

Kaela smirked. "Then why is your face still red?"

Lance scoffed.

"Back to the conversation at hand," Kaela said, making herself comfortable in her chair. "I think I do have a job you might like. And don't worry, it won't compromise your precious morals." The snicker she tried to suppress as she took a sip from her own glass made Lance sick to his stomach.

"And what would that be?"

Kaela took another sip. "What did you think of those three stooges that caused trouble in Derek's bar yesterday?"

When did she find out about that? "I think they're a group of punks that like to start fights. Why?"

"Well, they've been coming around The Red Rose as well and harassing my workers."

"What do you want me to do about it?"

"Yesterday, they robbed one of my girls, stole some jewelry off her. It wouldn't be such a big deal if she hadn't been wearing a special necklace her grandmother gave to her before she died. I'm going to be busy here for a little while—I have some stuff to take care of. However, since you're so eager to help, I need you to go to the abandoned building they're staying at. I know you're just going to be *shocked* to hear this, but it's in the slums. I had one of Derek's agents watch the place, and he told me they usually leave to cause trouble at around three. So, you still have time to get there and take the necklace back."

"They could have sold it already," Lance said, taking a deep breath as Kaela drew a long sip of her whiskey. "What if I can't get it back?"

"Then you can't get it back." She rubbed her temples and took another sip. Then she downed the drink and shuffled some papers before pausing and looking up at him. "What are you waiting for? Go. You'll have a friend of mine going with you. Her name's Amari. Be nice to her, or I'll make your life hell."

Lance nearly scoffed as he stood from the chair. "I hope you're not just trying to get me killed."

Kaela looked up from her papers and grinned. "I mean, if it's not too much trouble."

Lance wanted to dive over the desk, but instead, he walked to the door. "Don't you have any other jobs I could do instead? I wouldn't want to get in Amari's way."

Kaela opened her mouth to speak, her eyes dancing with a deadly fire, but the door to her office opened, and a girl peeked in.

"Kaela," said the girl, "Margaret's here looking for Roderick."

"The old lady? Tell her Roderick's out sick," Kaela said. Then she paused. "And he doesn't even work at this Rose. He would've been at the one on Hourglass Street."

"I told her that, but she refuses to leave."

Kaela sighed, but then a smile inched onto her face as she looked at Lance. "Lance, dear, if you're not interested in pursuing that lead of mine, perhaps you could pursue Ms. Marga—"

"I'll go check out the building," Lance blurted, his face hot and his hands sweaty. He wanted to slap himself for breaking his composure again.

Kaela smiled sweetly and told the girl, "Tell Ms. Margaret the only man we have free at the moment is Bradley, and if she's not interested in him, then she'll just have to wait until Roderick isn't sick. And kindly tell her she's at the wrong Rose unless she's looking to diversify her tastes."

The girl smiled, nodded, and left the room.

It was impulsive, but he'd already broken his composure in front of her, so he said, "I hate you."

"What is it they put on fishhooks, again?" Kaela asked. She made a motion like she was reeling in a fish, then chuckled as she stood to pour herself another drink.

When she turned around, Lance made a choking motion at her then left the room.

The sky threatened to rain down over the city, but it didn't. Even as the clouds hovered above, dark and haunting, the streets remained dry.

Lance walked down the sidewalk with Amari, his hands in his pockets. He held the switchblade in one hand, comforted by its presence. He'd never kept a weapon with him in the slums. Never had the chance. Now he understood the appeal.

Amari was silent, her black coat swishing with every step. Lance glanced at her every few seconds. Her posture was straight, her walk confident and unwavering but just as graceful as Kaela's. She seemed to have no reservations about walking through the slums.

"Kaela tells me you're good at what you do," Lance started. "What is that, exactly?"

Her long black braid swayed as she eyed him. Her eyes were a friendly brown, a complete contrast to the harsh stare of Kaela's. "I'm surprised she didn't tell you." She held a playful smile like Kaela's, yet it felt more genuine.

"No, she's not exactly my biggest fan."

"I'm what you would call a cat burglar. I break into rich people's houses and take every shiny thing not nailed down."

Lance repressed his laugh, instead allowing himself a smile. "What is it like, being a thief?"

He wasn't unfamiliar with the feeling, but when he'd stolen, it'd been food or clothes. Those first few years after escaping the orphanage had been hard.

"Like being able to take whatever I want, whenever I want," she said with a toothy smile that would rival Derek's. "Saves me money at Christmas too. I stole this chemistry set once; I love that thing. Haven't used it in a few years, though."

"Are you from around here?"

"If you mean Arachna, no. If you mean America, yes. My parents immigrated here from Japan."

"Where are they now?"

"In a small town, thinking I'm studying to be a scientist."

"Hence the chemistry set?"

She laughed. "No, no, I've loved chemistry forever. I only know the basics, though."

Lance gave her a smile until she faced forward again, and it slowly faded. She was so friendly. Maybe too friendly. Was she faking like Rob?

"So this is the slums," Amari said once the buildings became shabby and run-down. "I've only been here a couple of times, but I swear it gets worse every time I come around." She looked over her shoulder. "Have you really lived here your whole life?"

"Yep," Lance said. "Since I was a kid."

"Damn," Amari said. "No wonder you look so weathered. No offense. Here we are." She stopped in front of an abandoned building, windows broken, walls cracked. Nothing unusual for a building in the slums. "Why can't guys like this ever stay somewhere nicer? It's always an easy-to-break-into apartment. Just boring and drab."

"Boring and drab," Lance repeated. "Well, let's go before they get back."

"Agreed."

Amari slipped into the alley with Lance, scanning the building. She pointed at a trash can. "I can use that to climb up to the window. Can you grab it for me?"

Lance darted his eyes from one end of the alley to the other, expecting a mugger to show up and gun them down. Gunshots often rang out in this part of the city, and their echo resonated in the back of his head as he moved the bin, waiting for a bullet to catch his back.

Amari balanced on the top of the can with ease then leapt up to the nearest window, peeking inside before sliding her body in with one swift motion. She poked her head out. "Coast is clear. You can come up if you want."

Lance haphazardly balanced on the can. He took a deep breath and leapt. His fingers grazed against the windowsill, but he wasn't high enough. He gasped as gravity tugged at his heels.

Amari grabbed his hand just in time.

Lance's feet dangled in the air, and he lost his breath. "Holy shit."

"Wow, you're so light," Amari said with a small, breathy laugh. Lance braced his feet on the wall as she pulled him up and through the window. "You really need to eat more."

"Thanks," Lance said, out of breath, trying to keep his composure as he balled his hand into a fist, his skin burning where she'd touched him. He wiped it on the back of his pants.

"No problem," Amari said. "Search in the next room." She pointed to the room on the left of the hallway they were in, her voice barely a whisper. "We're looking for a silver necklace with an amethyst gem."

"A what?"

Amari's eyes widened. "You don't…? Just—just look for purple and silver. And make sure to leave everything just as it was." She turned to sneak into a room then paused. "But if you find any other jewelry, take that too. Better with us than with them."

"Sure," Lance choked out, his voice nearly cracking.

Amari didn't seem to notice as she slipped into the room to his right, quiet as a ghost.

The floor was filthy, and trash was scattered across the entire hallway.

Lance slipped into the room as quietly as his feet would allow him. The air smelled moldy and humid, and clothes and empty cartons of food were scattered across the floor, alcohol bottles just as prominent. The bed was nothing but a stained mattress. He searched through the drawers in the room, some of them already ripped out of their place in the dresser. Lance thought his own store had issues, but this…

Lance searched up and down and found nothing useful, so he stepped out of the room and wandered around a few others, not finding anything in those either. Amari made no noise in the rooms she searched. She was so quiet, in fact, that Lance found himself wondering if she'd abandoned him, only for her to slip out of another room. Despite his attempts, Lance's own footsteps creaked on the floor.

In the bathroom, the tiles were ripped out, the sink filled with dirty socks, the bathtub filled with old clothes, and the toilet shattered. Lance gagged at the smell.

He almost yelled to Amari to ask if she'd found anything, but he stopped himself.

The front door of the apartment building scraped open. Lance stepped out of the bathroom and spotted Amari, her eyes like those of a deer caught in headlights, and he waited for any orders from her. She regained her composure and gave Lance a thumbs-up before continuing her search. He narrowed his eyes at her back. If they were caught, Lance couldn't fight them. He felt his pocket, where the switchblade rested. *Better than nothing.*

His vision flashed. An ear lay on the floor. Children screamed. His ribs cracked under the weight of repeated kicks. Kids chanted, "Fight! Fight! Fight!"

Lance blinked, out of breath as he surveyed the room. There was no ear on the floor, no kids chanting. It wasn't real. He gulped down air, composing himself as the vision left him.

The sounds of men talking and laughing among themselves remained downstairs. Amari didn't seem bothered, but Lance could hear his own heart pounding over the men's voices.

Amari sneaked out of the nearest room, shaking her head. She pointed at the other side of the hall, toward another set of doors. She held a finger to her ear then pointed at Lance.

"You want me to eavesdrop?" Lance whispered.

Amari held a finger to her mouth, her eyes burning with annoyance.

Lance inched closer to the stairwell, watching Amari pad to the next set of doors while he listened in on the slurred words of the conversation downstairs.

"I told you to stay back, Steven! Those jackasses might've given us their money if they hadn't seen you. That broken arm makes you look weak."

"Shut it, Grant," another responded, his voice heavy and worn out. "At least my nose doesn't look like roadkill."

"I'll show you roadkill!"

There were sounds of a struggle, then a third person tried calming the other two down.

So Grant was the one with the broken nose, and Steven was the one with the broken arm. Who was the last one, then?

That was the one who'd had the knife.

Lance took that knife out of his pocket, wondering if a name was etched on the blade somewhere. To his dismay, the small weapon had nothing of the sort on it; nothing but rust.

"I can't believe I have to babysit you two all the time," the third guy said, his voice light and growly. "I wouldn't have lost my knife if you two *idiots* would just learn to fight like men."

"Cram it, Andy," Grant said.

"No, *you* cram it, bitch! Cram another tissue up your nose so you stop snorting blood."

One of them chuckled, but it sounded closer.

They were coming this way.

Lance nearly tripped over himself trying to get to Amari. "We gotta go. They're coming."

Amari swore, the steps creaking as the men ascended, one of them laughing. "I didn't find the necklace."

Lance shook his head. "Don't worry about it. Let's just get going. Now."

Amari dashed to the window and leapt out. Lance didn't think, despite his body hesitating. He didn't have time to change his mind. The voices were too close.

He jumped out behind her.

Amari landed on her feet with a graceful thud.

Lance wriggled his arms, trying to maneuver himself so his feet would face the ground, but he was too late and landed hard on his side. Pain rippled through his shoulder and back. He groaned and cursed. Amari covered her mouth.

"Are you okay?" she asked through stifled laughter.

Lance stood up slowly. "I'm fine… except when I breathe."

She looked up at the window. "Come on, let's get out of here."

Lance caught his breath as they dashed from the alley, his ribs aching with each pant. The faint voices of the three thugs barely reached him from the street. He could only make out laughing and cursing, nothing of interest.

"Do me a favor and don't tell Kaela about my landing."

"Your secret's safe with me."

"You found these but not the necklace?" Kaela asked, her voice as flat as her hands on the desk, pressed down as if suppressing a monster from escaping. She scanned the jewelry on her desk: a few rings, a brooch, and a bracelet. "You're sure this is all they had?"

Amari propped her legs on the desk, picking at the holes in her jeans. It took everything in Lance not to gawk at the sight, especially with how Kaela didn't seem to care.

"Pretty sure," she answered. "They came back early before I could search the rest of the place. Sorry, girl."

Kaela gently shoved Amari's legs off her desk. "Don't worry about it. Maybe we can try again another day." Kaela poured a glass of wine and handed it to Amari. "But we have their names. That could be useful, maybe."

"Cheers," Amari said, tapping her glass against Kaela's and downing the wine in one go. "Anyway, I'll be headed home now."

"Alright. See you tomorrow, Amari," Kaela said. They hugged before Amari strutted out of the room. "Love you, girl."

"Right back at you," Amari said as she left.

"Didn't know you were so close with your employees," Lance mused, his arms and legs crossed. Amari hadn't said a word about his fall.

Kaela rolled her eyes. "We've known each other since we were kids, of course we're friends."

A moment of silence passed between them.

Lance sighed. "Sorry about the necklace."

Kaela leaned back in her chair, adjusting her hair. "I can't lie, I'm just the slightest bit impressed that you didn't get caught and beat up by those fools. Or disappointed. I'm not sure yet."

Lance narrowed his eyes. "Thanks?"

"Who knows? Having their names could be useful to Eric."

"Look, why…?" He considered shutting up, but when Kaela cocked her head to the side, he had to commit. "I just… Why hasn't Eric sent Derek to kidnap them? I mean, he does that, doesn't he?"

"No, you were a special case. There are a few things he could do with them. But who knows? He might give them a job like he did you." Sarcasm laced her voice.

"I'm beginning to think you don't like me very much," Lance said, too exhausted to hide his own sarcasm. He wondered if he would have to commit to this back-and-forth game with her forever.

"I don't," Kaela said. "But I guess I must learn to… Really, it all depends on how tomorrow with Eric goes."

She grinned at him, and he already knew the word that was stirring in her brain but didn't reach her lips.

Lance clenched his fists, which he hoped was unnoticeable in their crossed state. With a twinge of fear nipping the back of his neck, he stared into Kaela's eyes. Tomorrow he would have to see Eric's, which were like two black voids.

"I think I should get back to my store and see how much progress Derek's men made."

"You want a drink before you go?" Kaela asked.

Lance was already at the door, and he turned to her. "No. Thanks, though."

That devilish smile appeared on her face again. "I aim to please. Speaking of which, I called a taxi to drive you back. See? I can be nice."

"Maybe you're just drunk." Lance left the room as Kaela's playful voice rang out once more before the door clicked shut.

"Good luck with Eric tomorrow."

Lance pretended not to hear, but the lump in his throat was much harder to ignore.

Lance stepped out of The Red Rose. Amari was leaning against the wall beside the entrance, a cigarette between her fingers.

She spoke through a cloud of smoke. "You did good today."

"Thanks," Lance responded, watching the smoke cloud rise into the afternoon sky.

The clouds were starting to dissipate. Still no rain.

Amari's eyes darted to the entrance, her voice dropping. "She's not all bad, you know." She tossed the cigarette down and stomped it out. "She's cold to a lot of people until she gets to know them."

Lance rubbed the back of his neck. "Why?"

"I don't know." Amari sighed with a shrug of her shoulders. "Just give her time. Prove that you belong with her and the guys. She'll warm up to you."

"Just like a cat."

Amari raised an eyebrow. "That's one way of looking at it."

With a shake of his head, Lance wished her a good night and started walking down the street.

"Hey," Amari said.

Lance turned around.

Amari pointed to her left at a taxi, the driver waiting patiently. "I think that's for you."

"Oh." Lance thanked Amari and hopped into the taxi, giving the driver the address of his store.

The car lurched forward, and soon, The Red Rose was out of sight. He sighed, leaning back into the seat, watching as the sun peeked out from behind the clouds, shining down on him and warming his skin. It was peaceful—hopeful, almost. Everyone seemed to have treated him fairly enough, save for Kaela, though he was unsure of their intentions.

And now he was returning to his store, a completely refreshed version of it, at that. The idea was too much for Lance to resist the smile he aimed toward the sky.

Whatever was awaiting him at his store would be better than what it used to be. Ideas swirled around in his head: a new paint job, perhaps a new register, and maybe even a new bed to sleep in—no more stiff neck and sore back.

Lance was pulled from his trance when the car slowed down and parked on the side of the road. "Uh, sorry pal, but this isn't the place."

The driver turned, taking his hat off, revealing greasy blond hair and two dark eyes peering at him over a pair of shades.

Eric waved, and Lance just looked at him, mouth agape.

Eric mimicked the face, bursting into laughter afterward.

"How the…? What are you *doing* here?" Lance asked.

"Well, hello to you, too, Lancelot," Eric responded, his cane lying comfortably in his lap. "How have your days been so far?"

Lance stuttered and looked around, almost expecting Kaela and Derek to appear out of nowhere as well. "Good… I guess."

"I'm glad to hear that," Eric said, pulling the shades back up over his eyes, smiling proudly. "I know our allotted day isn't until tomorrow, and I'm sure you would love to return to your simple little store and sell your simple little things for a simple brand of people. But wouldn't you rather have some fun? Maybe live a little? I have a very important business deal in a couple of hours, and I figured you should tag along with me. You might learn a thing or two, more than you have in these last two days combined." Eric's smile widened, his teeth creaking against each other.

And despite the shades, Lance could feel those eyes on him.

"Am I correct in saying that?" Eric asked, his head cocked to the side.

Is this… some kind of messed-up test? "Actually," Lance said, that lump in his throat returning, "there is something I've learned in my two days here." He leaned back and crossed his legs.

"Oh?" Eric lowered his shades again, his fingers tapping his cane like they always did. He leaned in a little, making Lance worry that he might find a knife in his gut before he could say anything else.

"There's this trio of guys, names are Andy, Steven, and Grant. They tried to cause trouble at Derek's bar, then they robbed one of Kaela's employees of her grandmother's necklace."

Eric's playful smile disappeared, and he stared intently at his cane. "Fascinating," he said. "I don't believe I know any gentlemen by those names. But I am getting sick of this trio of suicidal maniacs trying to disrupt an honest business with their foolishness." He sounded serious, but his voice was dramatized, like he was trying to sound sarcastic. "So, only their names, huh?"

Lance nodded.

"And those little pranksters took a necklace, hmm? Well, I suppose we'll just have to get it back, then, won't we?" Eric buckled his seat belt. "What do you say about paying them a visit and having a friendly discussion about their antics? I have some time to kill before my meeting."

"Uh, I don't know about—"

"Perfect!" Eric floored the gas pedal, and Lance was thrown back against his seat.

Friendly discussion. The tone in which Eric had said that sent a chill down Lance's spine. He rested his hand on the switchblade in his pocket, Kaela's words forcing their way to the front of his thoughts.

Eric looked pleased with himself as he said, "Lance, if you would be so kind as to direct me to their lovely abode?"

Lance tried to buckle his seat belt as he gave the address, his voice shaking despite his attempts to stop it. He hoped Eric would assume it was from the vibration of the car.

Eric sighed. "Get ready, Lance. The rest of this day is going to be most memorable." He patted his cane absentmindedly. "Most memorable, indeed."

Eric pursed his lips as he parked the taxi across the street from the tattered building. Lance sank into his seat, but when Eric looked back, he straightened himself.

"Well?" Eric said. "You think they're still home?"

"Uh," Lance stuttered, "they should be. I was just here about an hour or so ago."

"How did you sneak in?"

Lance pointed at the alleyway. "Climbed in through a window."

Eric hummed. "Then it's a plan. You'll sneak back in through the window, and I'll distract them at the entrance."

Lance looked at the wolf on Eric's cane, staring him down. What would happen if he said no? What would it matter to Eric if they got back a necklace or not? Was this it? The moment Eric used him as bait?

"Wait a few minutes for me to check the upper floor so I can make sure nobody's up there," Lance said as he got out of the taxi.

Eric followed him. "Sure thing, Lancelot!"

They parted ways when they crossed the street, and Lance slipped into the alleyway, taking a glance back at Eric before disappearing around the corner. Eric had that grin on his face, standing in front of the entrance like it would open for him.

Lance gulped then looked down the alley. He could make a run for it —disappear into the alleyways and never be seen again. He'd done it before. But those first years outside of the orphanage, scrounging and struggling to survive, stealing enough food to eat or selling enough drugs to buy his store—he couldn't do that again.

He balanced himself on the trash can and leapt to the window, his fingers barely finding their grip on the edge. He muttered a curse to himself and braced his feet against the brick. He almost slipped but managed to pull himself through the window.

Breathless, he looked around the messy hallway, somehow littered with even more trash since the last time. No sign of the men. No shouting or talking. He smiled and looked back at the window. *If Amari could see me now.*

He checked each room for signs of the three men as he sneaked down the hall, avoiding crumpled cans and food wrappers. When he reached the stairwell, he glanced down from the railing at the main level. The floor was rotted, and the windows were broken and boarded up. A chair was tucked under the doorknob.

The men were sleeping in old sleeping bags, huddled close to each other.

Wait, Lance thought, scanning the floor. *Where's the third one? Where's Steven?*

Lance sighed at the handful of doors at the end of the hall as a knock sounded on the front door.

Lance froze, his heart skipping a beat. "Crap," he whispered. "Dammit, Eric."

"Hey!" Steven's voice rang out from one of the rooms at the end of the hall. "Who's at the door?" Footsteps approached, stomping the floor.

He was coming.

Lance whirled and made a run for the bathroom door. The boards creaked and moaned under his rushed footsteps. He reached out for the knob when his foot landed on an old can. He gasped as the can slipped out from under his foot.

His body crashed onto the moldy floor, his teeth piercing his tongue.

"What the hell was that?" Steven asked.

Lance hissed, his ankle aching and a copper taste filling his mouth. He spat, and a few droplets of blood dripped onto the floor. He looked down at the blood, the world freezing around him.

Whispers filled the hall, muffled and indiscernible, as if they were coming from inside the walls. Lance forgot to breathe, spitting out more drops of blood. The pain withered away, and the shouts of someone behind him faded in the cacophony of chants growing louder in the walls and under the floorboards.

"Monster!" they cried. "Monster!"

Lance was only brought back from his trance when cold steel pressed into the back of his neck.

"Hands up, shitheel!"

Lance instinctively put his hands up. He allowed himself to crane his neck enough to spot Steven, one hand cradled in a tied-up T-shirt, the other gripping a revolver.

"Hey, guys!" Steven called out. "We got a visitor!"

The gun nudged Lance's head. With the windows being broken, he hoped Eric would hear their shouts from outside the entrance. Eric would save him, right? Kaela couldn't be right. He couldn't be bait.

"Down the stairs," Steven said.

Lance followed the order without question, the switchblade burning a hole in his pocket.

His ankle pained him with every step down the staircase, and his mouth filled with that revolting copper taste, but he kept walking. His heart raced as the whispers licked his ears, indiscernible.

He glanced at the front door on the way down, then at the two men shuffling lazily out of their sleeping bags and rubbing their eyes.

Maybe if he was fast enough, he could knock the gun out of Steven's hand. But could he move faster than Steven's finger could pull the trigger?

Then again, he thought, *he only has one arm. Surely he can't hold a revolver* that *well.*

The thought was stupid. But it would be more stupid to let these men do whatever they wanted to him once he reached the bottom of the stairwell.

Andy and Grant were both looking at him now, sick smiles on their faces. Somehow, even in this situation, they still weren't as scary as Eric's.

He paused for only a second, considering whether it was worth the risk, and Steven shoved him. He caught himself with his aching foot, and pain shot through his ankle. Lance nearly collapsed, catching himself against the wall.

This is it. All or nothing.

"Oh my God," Lance said, looking at the entrance, allowing the fear in his chest to rattle his voice.

Steven turned his attention to the door, as did Andy and Grant.

Lance pulled his switchblade out of his pocket and whirled, slapping the gun out of Steven's hand. The blade flicked out from the handle, and Lance plunged the knife into his broken arm.

Steven shouted in pain. Lance made to push past him, but Steven was quick. A strong arm found Lance's body, and Lance spat the built-up blood in his face, his skin burning at the touch.

Steven yelled and sent a punch into Lance's chest.

Lance flew down the rest of the stairs, landing hard on the ground. The air left his lungs, and he clawed at his chest, begging them to work again. He gasped for air as kicks found his arms and stomach. He curled into a ball and waited for it to stop.

The whispers became louder, turning to shouts.

To chanting.

"Fight! Fight! Fight!"

Lance's vision darkened around the corners.

Finally, the air returned to his lungs, and he gulped it down. The kicking stopped, and someone pulled him to his feet. He was face to face with Andy.

"You," Andy hissed. "I remember you from the bar. Your friend beat the hell out of me and my guys here. Hurt our feelings pretty bad." He released a breathy laugh and sank his fist into Lance's gut.

Where the hell is Eric?

"Is that who was at the door, huh? Your bar friend coming back for round two?"

"I don't know him," Lance wheezed. "I was just working there for the day to make some extra cash."

"Oh yeah?" Andy threw him to Grant, who threw a punch to Lance's face. Pain seared through his jaw. Stars dotted his vision.

His vision cleared enough to see Andy marching over to Steven and pulling the knife out of his arm. Steven screamed in pain, but Andy didn't seem to care. He marched back to Lance, holding the bloody knife for him to see. "Then why the shit do you have my damned knife?!"

Lance didn't get to respond before another kick plunged into his stomach.

"Fine," Andy said, wiping the blade on his pants and pocketing it. "Since you're such a fan of my knife…" He grabbed Lance by his shirt and held him close to his face. His breath reeked of alcohol and fast food. His teeth were rotting. "I'll just have to use the rusted one to gut you."

Something pressed against Lance's stomach, and he looked down to see a rusty knife angled at his belly.

Lance almost called out for Eric, to beg him to do something. Pain tore through his body, and a knife was about to do the same.

A car engine ignited across the street.

Lance looked toward the entrance, fear and anger and disappointment flooding him.

So he *was* the bait—nothing more, nothing less.

No, Kaela was wrong. He was worse.

He was a loose end.

Now it made sense why Eric wanted to renovate Lance's store; and, even more, why he wanted to do it with Lance's own money. He wanted the slums and its information, but he didn't want Lance as an employee. He would likely put one of his own people in there. All that information Derek and Kaela had given him was for nothing because he would end up dead anyway.

Eric had fed him to the wolves, and now he would die alone in the slums.

It was bound to happen sooner or later, he supposed.

He almost laughed at the irony. Some small part of him thought that maybe he would see his parents again, but the cruel realization immediately hit him that they'd never wanted him anyway.

But the sound of the engine didn't fade away.

Andy glanced at the entrance. "That your friend?" He smiled. "Well, we'll just take care of him too. Pay him back for what he did to us." He flipped the knife in his hand, angling it at Lance's neck. "Starting with you." He raised the knife above his head to plunge it into Lance's neck.

A crash like an explosion or a clap of thunder shook the building. Wood splintered, and a cloud of dust filled the room. The force sent them all to the ground.

Lance blinked away the dust in his eyes and crawled to a corner of the room, pain searing his body. Tears welled in his eyes. He leaned against the wall, almost smiling when he saw the taxi sticking into the building.

Eric hadn't abandoned him after all.

Gunshots rang out, followed by the quiet clicking of an empty cylinder.

A gangly figure stepped out from the smoke, his hat and shades gone, replaced by greasy blond hair and onyx eyes.

Eric waved a hand in the air, dispelling some of the residual dust floating in the room. His smiled faltered when his eyes landed on Lance. Something flashed in his eyes, a deadly look that sent a cold chill down his spine. His smile returned when he looked at the three shaken men scrambling to their feet.

Steven pointed a revolver at him, pulling the trigger over and over as the gun clicked.

"Evening, gentlemen," Eric said as if greeting old friends. "What's with the revolver?" His eyes widened like he was excited. "Ooh, are we playing Russian Roulette? I love that game!" He laughed, and a gunshot went off.

For a moment, Lance thought Eric had been shot.

But Eric stood with his own revolver in hand.

The revolver dropped from Steven's hand, and a red stain grew on his shirt before he collapsed. Blood pooled around his lifeless body.

"I win," Eric said, lazily pointing the gun at Grant and Andy. "Do either of you want to play?"

They looked at each other, fear evident in their eyes, and stood still, as if scared that they too would be shot if they so much as flinched.

"I guess not." Eric put his revolver back into his trench coat and leaned on his cane. "What a disgusting place. You guys really should clean up around here. I mean, seriously…" Eric walked to Steven's body and tapped it with his cane. "Corpses on the floor, ripped wallpaper, and for the love of God, what is that stench?" Eric sighed and reached into his coat again.

Grant hid behind Andy. Lance almost laughed when Eric pulled a handkerchief out and pressed it against his nose.

"Anyway," Eric continued, facing the two men again. "It has come to my attention that you three… well, two now, I suppose, have been terrorizing my establishments. Is that correct?"

Andy just shook his head, the rusted knife gripped firmly in his hand as if he'd completely forgotten he was armed. Grant was still hidden behind him.

"Y-yeah. Yeah, we have, but we didn't mean anything by it," Grant said, glancing down at Steven's body. His voice shook worse than his hands. "Look, man, you can see where we live. We're just trying to get by."

"By robbing and beating the hell out of my employees." Eric took one step closer, his hand placed firmly on the handle of his cane. "Well, let me tell you both something." The blade unclicked from its holster, but Eric didn't unsheathe it fully yet. "None of you are leaving this room alive. Not you, not your friend, and certainly not that dead body." Finally, the blade was out in the open, a few inches longer than Eric's forearm. "Question is… who wants to go first?"

Andy's breathing became labored, and his grip on the rusty knife tightened. He roared and charged at Eric.

Eric smiled at the challenge and tossed his handkerchief. It landed on Andy's face, blinding him. Eric sidestepped the charge, swiping his blade along the back of Andy's arm.

Andy shouted in pain and turned around to face Eric once again, switching his knife over to his good arm, teeth bared like an animal. Instead of charging, Andy lunged for Eric, swiping wildly at him.

Eric stepped back, avoiding each attack as nimbly as Derek had. Grant pulled out a knife of his own. Lance opened his mouth to warn Eric of the attack, but he'd already sidestepped again, and Grant and Andy clashed their knives against each other's. Eric twirled like a ballerina on stage and sliced his blade through the air.

The room was silent for a breath. Then a thud followed as Grant's hand landed on the floor. Grant screamed and fell back, blood spurting from his arm. Andy watched in horror, his skin paling.

Eric whirled again and plunged the blade into Andy's chest. Blood splattered on the floor, the blade jutting out the man's back. He gasped and gurgled, trying to speak.

Eric leaned in close and whispered something in Andy's ear. Andy's eyes widened.

The slick sound as Eric pulled his weapon out of Andy's chest cavity sent a wave of nausea through Lance.

Andy fell back, dead the instant he hit the ground, and Eric took the gun back out of his coat and fired two bullets straight into Grant's head, silencing his groans of pain.

Eric said nothing. His gun was already back in his coat. He picked the handkerchief off the floor and wiped the blood off his blade.

Eric knelt next to Steven and searched through his pockets. "Ah," he said, fishing out a silver necklace with an amethyst. "Is this the one?"

Lance nodded.

Eric's blade slipped back into his cane with a click. "Family is very important, Lance. I'm sure Kaela's employee will be very happy to have this back."

Lance sniffed and swallowed the blood that traveled to the back of his throat. The taste gagged him. The blood on the floor—there it was again, the ringing of the word in his ear.

Monster.

"Your nose is bleeding," Eric said, picking a new handkerchief out of his coat and tossing it to Lance. "Here. You need to look clean for the meeting."

Lance took the cloth and held it to his nose. He tried with all his might not to glance at the severed hand on the floor, yet the way it twitched still caught his attention.

"Won't the cops come when they hear the gunshots?" Lance asked, running a hand through his hair to get a better view of Eric's face. He rolled his eyes. "Forget I said that."

"We're gonna be late," Eric responded with a serious glance at the bodies scattered across the floor. A flicker of his smile returned when he looked at Lance. He walked outside the building, and Lance stepped carefully around the bodies to follow, keeping the handkerchief to his nose.

They got into the taxi, and Eric had the simplest smile on his face as he backed out of the building, as if he hadn't just murdered three men. Wood crumpled and fell from the ceiling. The taxi was bent in the front, and the windshield was cracked.

Lance had seen Eric in action now, graceful but deadly. He fixed his gaze on his own two feet, the sight of those men burned into the back of his eyes.

Lance tried not to scowl as he stared out the window, watching everything pass by in a blur. Whatever this meeting was, he just hoped it ended much better than the events of a few moments ago.

"Well, that could have gone better, eh?" Eric said, as if he'd read Lance's mind. "Are you okay?"

Lance tried not to show his surprise at the question. "Y-yeah… fine. I don't think my nose is broken."

"That's good," Eric said. "Try to clean up as best you can. I don't think our potential business partner will believe that's ketchup on your face." His smile returned to that lazy, wolflike grin.

Lance tried to think of something in response, but all he could do was look at the cane in Eric's lap.

CHAPTER 4
THE SPIDER AND THE ELEPHANT

The adrenaline kept Lance awake enough on the drive to the meeting. But as Eric parked the damaged taxi in front of a coffee shop, smiling and humming to himself, Lance's eyelids became heavy.

Lance blinked and saw the horrified faces of those men again. He'd seen death before. He'd seen men and women alike riddled with bullet holes on the side of the street, only for their bodies to disappear within a day's time.

He'd always kept walking.

Yet the sight of Eric killing those men in cold blood, the way he enjoyed it, made Lance shift uncomfortably in his seat. He touched his swollen nose, taking glances in the rearview mirror at how purple and blue it was.

He'd gotten off lucky.

"Here we are," Eric said.

The Grand Brew, the sign in front of the store said, illuminated by lights above the shop. The idea of a nice large cup of black coffee swirled around in Lance's head as he stared dreamily at the building from the backseat. The last time he'd had coffee was when he was younger and the matron allowed him a small cup every now and then. Those were the only times she'd acknowledged him. *Well, that and...*

"Wait," Lance said, his tongue aching. "You don't own this place, do you?"

Eric laughed. "Oh, Lance, when will you learn?" He faced him. "I *own* this city. Every building, every*thing* is mine."

Lance furrowed his brows. "I don't know how much I believe that."

Eric sighed. "Okay, okay, maybe not *everything*, but can't a guy dream? Besides, I may as well own this place with all the information I get from here. I like to send one of Kaela or Derek's agents here to order a coffee and just listen to all the conversations they can. You'd be surprised how talkative people can be when they think nobody's listening. The secrets they try to whisper to their friends over the background noise, not realizing that more than just their friend is listening in… You should try it one day." He put a hand to his chest. "Eavesdropping is an underappreciated art form."

Lance glanced at the bloody handkerchief to his right, tempted to throw it out the window and be rid of the images it brought to his head.

"So who are you meeting with?" Lance asked, leaning around the seat to look at Eric, hiding his hands behind the seat to pick at his nails.

Eric's eyes flashed with excitement. "*We* are meeting Landreau Corp. More specifically, one of the Landreau brothers himself."

Lance blinked. "How did you even *manage* something like that?"

"I have my ways, Lance. I'm a very persuasive person, in case you haven't noticed."

Lance felt a sentence bubbling up to his mouth. He knew he should keep quiet. He knew he shouldn't say the words. But his chest tightened the longer he waited. "Persuasive like you were with those men back there?"

Eric's smile dropped. He peered at Lance over his shades. "I had every intention of profiting off those fools, you know, but *somebody* got caught sneaking around. It was either lose a chance to make money or lose you. Where's my thank you?"

"Oh, please. Don't act like you weren't going to kill them anyway."

"I wasn't," Eric said with a roll of his eyes. "I *was* trying to distract them so you could steal that necklace back. When I heard the commotion on the other side of the door, I realized they'd spotted you. I wasn't about to let them kill an employee of mine, even if it meant killing them." He sighed. "What did you expect me to do? Blow them a kiss?"

Lance picked harder at his nails. "No, I just…" Some of that copper taste tainted his mouth still, resurfacing the images of that kid in agony, the matron staring at him.

"The world's not black-and-white, Lancelot, and it sure as hell ain't gray. It's *just* black. *Pitch* black. And if you can't dip your toes in the darkness long enough to get the job done, you won't make it out alive. You should know that as well as I do."

Lance dug his nails into his palms as he leaned back against his seat. "Thanks… for saving my life." The words tasted bitter in his mouth.

Eric chuckled, his smile returning. Lance narrowed his eyes. The dark look on his face had disappeared so quickly, almost as if… he was wearing a mask of his own.

Those dark eyes scanned him, but Lance pretended not to notice, instead looking out at the customers drinking their beverages and eating their pastries.

"I would have thought you were used to death," Eric said. "It happens like clockwork in the slums."

Lance kept his eyes pointed at the coffee shop. "What is that supposed to mean?"

Eric huffed. "Those men tried to kill you. They weren't going to stop. It was going to lead to someone's death regardless of my actions, whether that be them or someone innocent." Eric's stare weighed on him again. "So in a way, I did a good thing. Does that readjust your moral compass?"

Lance ignored him and changed the subject. "So why are you meeting one of the Landreau brothers here, anyway?"

"I want to know what sort of secret project they're working on," Eric said, his wicked smile returning to normal.

"And you expect him to just tell you?"

"I expect to find out one way or another. Whether that be convincing him, bribing him, maybe even blackmailing him. But based on my research, this one is more malleable than his brother. The smartest yet the weakest." Eric chuckled. "And wouldn't you believe he's the head researcher on whatever this new drug is?" He hummed. "And there he is, Malcolm Landreau himself, looking like he had quite a hearty breakfast this morning." Eric's stare was directed at a corpulent man stepping out of the backseat of a black car, suitcase in hand. His eyes wandered around as he stepped into the coffee shop and sat down at a nearby table.

Eric turned toward Lance. "Showtime."

He stepped out of the car, and Lance followed, pretending not to notice Malcolm staring at both of them. The setting sun had disappeared behind the clouds once more, and the chilly air sent goosebumps along his skin. It would be dark in a few minutes. Still no rain.

There was a skip in Eric's step as he pranced into the shop, Lance trailing behind him. They took a seat in front of Malcolm. Lance leaned against the chilled window to keep his eyes from closing.

Malcolm wore a friendly grin, but it was blatantly forced. Either that, or Lance was getting better at this info-gathering business. He wondered, as Malcolm cleared his throat, if that was how easily Eric could see through him.

"Eric, I presume?" Malcolm said, holding his hand out to shake Eric's.

Eric looked at the hand offered to him, his smile not fading in the slightest.

"Malcolm, I presume?" Eric copied, shaking the man's hand, his smile finally settling into something more casual and less threatening. Even Malcolm seemed to relax, and he nodded in greeting at Lance.

Lance nodded back with a fake smile of his own then sank into his seat just slightly, wishing he could disappear.

The smell of freshly brewed coffee and muffins trailed to him, and his stomach growled. He hadn't eaten all day.

"You said you wanted to discuss business. I believe your exact words were, 'I can offer you something no one else can.' If you're offering funding, I'm afraid we've got that covered already."

"Mr. Landreau, I'm an information dealer. I can give you a significant advantage in the marketing of your new drug."

Malcolm paused. "How did you—"

Eric nodded. "Information dealing. It's my job, like I said."

Malcolm folded his hands together on the table. "Okay… you've interested me. What kind of information are you offering, exactly?"

"I'm offering information on the goings-on of other pharmaceutical companies. With a heads-up, you can make their drug first, beat them to it with your expanded resources, and make a much larger profit."

Malcolm didn't seem to react to what Eric said, but he brushed his chin with his fingers, obviously hanging on every word.

As if sensing hesitation, Eric continued. "I could also have men of my own sell your medicines for a cheaper price down in the slums. I'd make a little money out of it, and you'd increase your sales exponentially. Inhabitants of the slums can't afford any medicine otherwise, so pricing it cheaper brings in a whole new demographic."

A wave of heat surged through Lance. Surely Eric wasn't going to make him sell this medicine at his store. Lance couldn't stop his head from whirling toward him. Eric didn't acknowledge it, but Malcolm raised an eyebrow.

Lance almost opened his mouth to say something, but Malcolm checked his watch then stared Eric directly in the eyes. "So you're offering to illegally sell any drugs we create and expose the private information of other companies to us. And you expect us to do business with you? How do we know you won't just give away information about our own company to others? This was a waste of time."

Malcolm made to stand, but Eric held his hand up, and Malcolm paused.

"Mr. Landreau, drugs are sold on the street all the time, especially in the slums, where nobody can afford insurance. I'm offering a chance for both of us to make a profit *and* to give you a head start on the production of other medicines." Eric stood and lowered his voice. "And you don't think I can't just reveal information about your company to others, do you? Seems like walking away from a deal this generous would be a foolish mistake. You might just make me angry, and I'll make a deal with another company. One that may be able to appreciate what I'm offering."

Eric took a glance around the coffee shop, where no one seemed to notice the brewing tension, just like in Derek's bar. Lance crossed his arms, unable to shake the feeling that the ripple of emotion that crossed Eric's face was desperation.

"You must think I'm an absolute idiot to agree to a deal like that. Landreau Corp doesn't need money, and we certainly don't need a street hustler's help. We make our medicines to help people, not to make a quick buck."

Malcolm made to stand again, but Eric blocked his path.

Lance sank deeper into his chair, just waiting for a repeat of the abandoned building to play out. If something broke out, he would be out of here. No way was he going to allow Eric to leave him here to take responsibility for whatever went down.

Lance winced as something pricked his knee, for only a split second. A mosquito flew out from under the table, and he swatted it down with a grimace. He scratched the now-itchy spot on his knee.

"Help people?" Eric said. "Then why does your company sell cheap drugs for exorbitant prices? Why is your company paying off doctors to push your drugs in any way they possibly can for kickbacks? Why do you falsely advertise almost every single drug you make? I'll admit it's impressive how you manage to hide it. You've kept it a secret from everyone… except me." Eric stepped closer, hand firmly on the handle of his cane. His voice grew even quieter, somehow more threatening than if he'd yelled. "So don't sit here and pretend like you care at all about ethics. Or the law. I want information, and I want money. Your company has both of those in spades. What I'm offering in return is lucrative for your business."

"I've already made up my mind. I'm not doing business with you."

Malcolm started to walk away, but Eric blocked him again in one graceful movement. His smile turned threatening, and his eyes grew wild.

"Are you sure you wouldn't like to continue discussing business, Mr. Landreau? Would you prefer a *sharp* ultimatum?"

Eric's dagger released slightly from his cane, and Malcolm flinched at the sound of metal against metal. Lance sat up straighter in his chair. The tension grew heavy around them, but as far as anyone in the shop was concerned, they were two buddies having a discussion. Eric was positioned so that his blade was just out of sight from everybody but them.

“I don’t know what you’re talking about. Our company is dedicated to the safety and health care of the public.”

“Is that why a journalist and a Landreau Corp employee on the verge of finding out what you’re doing behind closed doors ended up dead in a ditch without an ounce of news coverage?” Eric chuckled. “You’re a conspiracy theory come to life, aren’t you, Mr. Landreau?”

Malcolm swallowed as Eric’s blade slid even farther out of his cane. He was so close to Malcolm that he could whisper and be heard loud and clear. Malcolm shook, and his hands trembled.

Lance eyed the entrance, tempted to leave and be rid of all this.

“Truly, I have no idea what you’re talking about, and if you try anything, I will have you arrested.” Malcolm’s voice shook.

Eric smiled. “I would *love* if you did that. I happen to have a personal… investment in the police in Arachna. If I lead them toward a huge pharmaceutical scandal that could make them look good? Well, maybe you’re right. Maybe I don’t need to deal with you.” Eric’s blade slipped back into its cane. “You’re no less of a criminal than I am, Landreau. I’m a spider, and you’re an elephant.”

Lance dropped his head into his hands. *He couldn’t resist making a joke, could he?*

“Both very intelligent animals. Imagine if we worked together. Maximize profit, maybe even become great friends that sit on the porch in the old folks’ home and reminisce about this very day when you decided to make the right decision and join my web rather than be trapped within it.”

Malcolm looked as if he wanted to spit in Eric’s face as he walked right past him, bumping Eric’s shoulder.

Eric looked murderous, but only for a few seconds before regaining his composure.

“Let’s go, Lance. It appears this deal didn’t go very well. I suppose we’ll just have to do better next time. Have you eaten yet?”

“No,” Lance said absentmindedly, standing as Eric went to the register and spoke to the cashier. “We?”

Eric returned moments later with a box in hand. He offered it to Lance. “A roast beef sandwich. You look like you’re about to pass out.”

Lance took the box and returned to the car with Eric. Just as he’d thought, the sun had set, and darkness overtook Arachna.

Eric’s calm demeanor was unsettling, and they were both silent as Lance ate. The sandwich was warm and tender and juicy. It was gone in minutes.

Eric tapped his fingers lightly on the steering wheel, his eyes planted on the road.

“Okay… I’ll admit,” Eric said suddenly, his voice more serious but his smile still wide. “That didn’t go as planned.”

Lance almost laughed, grateful that the darkness hid his expressions from Eric’s borderline omniscient gaze. “Resorting to threats probably wasn’t the best idea.”

“It’s worked before.” Eric shrugged. “Guess I’ll have to find a new way to get to Landreau Corp.”

Something about that sentence twisted Lance’s stomach into a knot. The taxi drove under a streetlamp, the orange light revealing a deep frown on Eric’s face.

Lance held the empty box in his lap. “Is it true that a journalist and an employee died?”

Eric was silent for a long moment. “They were found in an alleyway. Shot dead. Their bodies disappeared from the morgue a few days later. Rotoya, the police chief, said she didn’t know how they disappeared.”

“You believed her?”

“She wasn’t lying.”

“How’d you know they were on the verge of finding something out?”

“Because I hired them.”

Lance’s stomach twisted into a knot. “Why were you so hell-bent on making a deal with a company like that?”

Eric blinked slowly. “A few reasons.”

Lance raised an eyebrow. “So give me one.”

“Money.”

Lance leaned his head against the window, looking up at the dark sky. “Don’t you have enough money already?”

"I do, yes."

Lance was about to ask what he meant when the taxi turned a corner and his store came into view. The walls were covered in a fresh coat of beige and blue paint, almost shining under the light of the streetlamps. Graffiti of a black widow was painted on the wall and over the sliding doors.

Eric had a big grin on his face as he pulled the taxi up to one of the gas pumps and turned to Lance. "What do you think? Spider graffiti isn't too much, is it?"

Lance stepped out of the taxi and looked it up and down, trying to contain his excitement. He smiled, if only because he couldn't hide it. "It's… actually pretty nice."

Eric got out of the car as well. "You can thank little old me for that one… and Derek's men, but you know, my money, my orders, my credit to take."

Lance walked to the doors of the building, which opened by themselves, air blasting down from above. He suppressed a laugh as he stepped through and into the store itself. New bright lights had been put in, replacing the white glow with a yellow one. All the shelves were restocked, the coolers filled, the walls painted beige with a black web pattern across them.

"Here," Eric said, handing Lance some money. "Taxi needs gas."

Lance took the money, placed it in his new register, and set the amount of gas Eric could pump with his new machine.

The buttons don't even stick*!*

"Where do you get most of your gas business anyway?" Eric mused.

Lance raised an eyebrow, his smile harder to fight with every second. "Almost nobody in the slums. A lot of people come here because it's cheaper."

Eric shrugged and stepped out to the taxi.

Lance whirled around and rushed into the back room, finding the design of the web on the walls of the hallway as well. The bathroom held an entirely new mirror, better lighting, and an actual *shower*.

In the bedroom, Lance nearly fell over at the sight of a brand-new bed, twice as large as his last one, now with an actual bed frame and sheets. Across from it, a dresser sat against the walls, which were painted beige with a blue trim at the top and bottom.

"No way." Lance turned toward what he'd glimpsed from the corner of his eye. His mouth agape, he stared at the TV sitting across from his bed, a remote placed right in front of it. "Wow," Lance whispered, looking around at his new room, his smile almost painful. *I haven't watched TV since the orphanage.* He sat on the bed, soft as a cloud.

"Someone's adjusting pretty well," someone said.

Eric clacked into the room and rested his cane in front of him. "Well… you like?"

"I like," Lance said, unable to wipe his smile away. "It's better than I thought it would be after only two days of renovation."

Eric shook his head. "Well, you've had it rough these past few years, so I figured you deserved a bit of luxury." He glanced at the TV. "But if you really want some luxury, this bad boy actually has cable."

Lance ran a hand through his hair. "Probably the only TV in the slums that has that."

Eric shrugged. "Probably the only TV in the slums at all."

"I…" Images rushed to Lance's head: those men dead on the floor and Eric threatening Malcolm. *But even so, to have all this…* "Thank you… You know, for this." This time, for the first time, those words didn't hurt to say—didn't taste bitter or sour in his mouth.

Eric straightened like a proud bird as he looked around at his accomplishment. "I'll tell Rob and the others that you like it."

Lance went quiet, letting it sink in. A proper store, a proper room—all those years of getting by, of barely surviving. Maybe things were starting to look up.

Just maybe.

If he was still alive to enjoy it.

As Eric made to leave, Lance stopped him. "Why did you do all of this?"

Eric stopped, and for a moment, Lance was sure he would lose his hand, but Eric turned around with a smile on his face. "Kaela has a limo, a closet full of stylish outfits, and a lifetime supply of alcohol, Derek has more weapons than he knows what to do with, yet you wonder why you have a decent bedroom with a TV?"

Lance tried not to frown as he said, "I just… can't figure you out." He wished he could explain, but it escaped him.

Eric hummed as he turned back around. "Just a spider expanding his web." He chuckled as he stepped down the hall. "And a spider that treats his employees right!"

"I really wish you'd stop calling yourself a spider," Lance called out to him.

"Never!" Eric yelled back.

Lance held back a smile. From the moment he awoke in his new bed, to trying his new hot shower, a smile formed on his face and remained until he stepped out of his store. Even as he sat in Eric's hideout, the overcast morning light shining through the windows, he realized just how foreign the feeling was of stifling a smile for so long.

The sight before him was familiar. Kaela absentmindedly played with her nails and sipped her coffee in the chair to his right, and Derek leaned back in his chair to Lance's left, biting his lip and staring at the table with his arms crossed. The ominous atmosphere the room had held his first time here was erased. The stone fireplace was dead, the mahogany walls lighter, the curtains drawn back to reveal the street outside.

When he asked about it, Kaela's eyes flashed like she was about to make a joke. "They can't see in."

The door opened, and Eric walked in, humming happily to himself like a father on a Sunday morning. He was holding his cane in one hand and a newspaper in the other.

He seemed rather pleased with himself as he slammed the paper down and sat in his chair, smiling at the three of them. Lance swallowed hard, reading the headline a second time, then a third.

"What the hell?" Kaela said. "Malcolm Landreau, cofounder and head researcher of Landreau Corp, overdosed in an abandoned building in the slums at six thirty this morning. Police are currently investigating." She scoffed. "Yeah, sure they are."

"Coincidence is a wonderful thing," Eric breathed. "It's quite a shame that Mr. Landreau denied my very generous offer, but it seems that the universe has a way of working things out."

Lance stared at the paper then gawked at Eric, not bothering to hide his shock. His voice was breathy. "You killed him?"

Eric shrugged with an uncaring grin.

Derek crossed his arms and leaned back in the seat with a deep frown on his face. "Eric… are you sure that was a good idea?"

"Yep."

Derek furrowed his brows as he looked at the paper. "An abandoned building… like the one those three punks were staying at? Are you trying to pin the blame on them?"

Eric sighed. "That would have been nice, but I'm afraid something didn't go as planned, and they had to be removed from the equation. My cleaners took care of it… I did leave the bottles and food cartons, however. Who's to say Malcolm wasn't staying there every now and then before his untimely death?"

Kaela scrunched her face. "And how is that supposed to be at all believable?"

Eric's eyes lit up. "It wouldn't have been if not for the drugs 'accidentally' found stashed in the walls."

Lance's stomach twisted into a knot as he read the headline again. If someone as high up as Malcolm could be killed and made to look like an accident victim, how easily could Lance be removed from the situation? And why wasn't he already?

"You're really desperate to get this deal with Landreau Corp, aren't you?" Kaela asked after another sip.

"Not desperate," Eric countered. "Determined."

Eric opened his eyes with a gasp, sweat dripping down his face and his body, his chest rising and falling heavily, his heart beating rapidly. He clicked the blade of his cane out, pointing it at whoever had woken him.

He scanned the darkness of the room, but nobody was there.

Eric sighed and sheathed his blade. He swung his legs over the bed, standing in one swift motion, and looked out the window. He cracked it open and let the cool air flood in. The sky had lightened, and a fog had settled over the city. It would be another overcast day, it seemed.

"Another night," he said to the curtains, "another nightmare." Among the usual flood of faces and voices, four more had been added to the mix. One haunted him more than the others:

Mr. Malcolm Landreau.

He'd been so scared. An otherwise innocent man, who'd presented no immediate threat to him, was dead because of Eric's desperation. Even Lance had been able to sniff it out. He was losing his grip.

So things hadn't gone as planned. It wasn't the first time and wouldn't be the last. Having to rethink his approach to Landreau Corp coaxed a groan of frustration from him, but at least he had dirt on the company and a new plan to get into their good graces. He stared out at the city, *his* city, and scowled at the tallest building, trying to overshadow his business, his operation. Despite Malcolm's judgmental eyes staring at him while he slept, killing the man had eased that feeling that plagued his mind: the feeling of a loss of control. It nagged him much worse than any nightmare ever could. It would all be worth it in the end. He just needed more time.

Willow's and Jacob's deaths couldn't be in vain.

Eric ran a hand through his blond hair, greasy from rarely being washed.

He would have to dye it again soon.

His heart tired from its beating tirade and slowed, and his breathing steadied. The thrill of the nightmare faded away, and with it, Eric's alertness. His eyelids became heavy, but a quick look at the clock in his room made him refuse another few hours of sleep. He would have to wake up soon anyway.

Eric reached over to his bedside table, grabbed his flask, and took a long sip from it. The liquid burned as it travelled down his throat, the sensation waking him up. He set the flask back in its place, grabbed a slim metal cylinder, and slipped it into his coat. *Never can be too safe.*

With another sigh, he gave Landreau Corp one last glance before turning away to get dressed, picking up clothes off the floor and smelling for which ones were the cleanest. His plan brewed and formed in his head, like clouds in the sky. He had to get to Landreau Corp, but he needed one more thing—an extra push, perhaps.

That was all poor Malcolm needed.

And Lance… poor kid was practically thrilled just at the sight of a TV. If he could get another chance with Landreau Corp, the side business of selling their drugs for cheap would make his profits soar. Those lost souls in the slums would do anything for a chance to get proper medicine. Though, he hadn't expected Lance's reaction to selling them to be so strong. The glare he sent him back at the coffee shop had burned, especially with those piercing eyes. It had slipped his mind that Lance had sold drugs before, or so his information claimed. It had also slipped his mind that he'd told Lance his parents overdosed in an alley.

Then there was convincing him to abandon his store when the time came. Eric huffed. That would be an adventure.

Dressed in his usual attire, Eric grabbed his revolver from under his pillow and glanced over his cane. He ran his thumb over its body, tracing the silver web laced around the black metal. It was cold, weighty, and powerful. Not a scratch ticked the metal, thankfully.

Eric kicked aside more dirty clothes and empty bottles and left his room, locking it behind him. He clicked his way down the mahogany stairway until he reached the hallway leading to the main room. The sense of power that emanated from the cane intoxicated him. A crooked smile grew on his lips, no doubt mirroring the snarling silver wolf handle with its cold black eyes to match.

He stepped into the main room and lit the fireplace with a match from a box resting atop the mantel, enjoying the warmth in contrast to the cold he'd embraced earlier. He sat down in his chair and stared across the empty table. It wouldn't be much longer before Derek arrived, as timely as ever. Kaela would slink in late but still ready for business.

Then there was Lance. He would walk in with that casual expression but likely deep in thought about something else. Nervous and unsure.

Eric leaned back, listening to the crackling fire behind him as it calmly waited with him. Before he knew it, the sun had risen, and Derek walked into the room, wearing blue jeans and a gray hoodie.

“Good morning,” Derek said, his voice dripping with respect. “Sleep well?”

“No rest for the wicked,” Eric groaned back.

He stared at the dark wood of the table. Something felt off about today, like the world was holding its breath in anticipation of a disaster. Whatever it was, it put a cold sweat on Eric’s forehead that he casually wiped away. He would handle it. He always did.

He shook the feeling away for now and asked Derek to give him the highlights from the latest information he’d gathered. Derek nodded and reported nothing out of the ordinary.

Kaela walked in holding a coffee cup. She wore a simple white dress with a thin coat over it, her hair curled down to her shoulders. She sat in her chair like it was fragile and crossed her legs with a sip of her coffee.

“White is the color of purity,” Eric said, a playful smile reaching his lips. “How ironic.”

Kaela gave an annoyed grin back. “What’s ironic is that you smile at your own jokes even though they’re not funny.”

“Someone has to smile around here.” Eric grinned back. “Any good info for me?”

Kaela pursed her lips and sipped her coffee again, obviously trying to test his patience. But Eric simply crossed his own legs and set his cane on the table.

“Well,” Kaela started, “as far as we know, Landreau Corp still doesn’t know Malcolm was murdered, so that’s a plus. As far as anyone’s concerned, the poor man just couldn’t take the stress of his job, got a little too high, and killed himself.”

Derek had his arms firmly crossed. He didn’t approve—that much was obvious—yet he said nothing.

“That’s good,” Eric muttered. “Anything else?”

“Not really,” Kaela said. “Everything yesterday was mostly about Malcolm’s death. It was honestly starting to get on my workers’ nerves.”

She took a sip of her coffee. "Pillow talk doesn't usually involve murder."

"But that's the best kind."

"And that's why you don't have a girlfriend."

"Rob wanted to know what Lance thought of the improvements to the store," Derek interjected.

Eric chuckled. "He loved it. I don't think I've ever seen someone so excited to see a television in my life."

As hard as Lance had tried to hide it, he'd practically trembled with excitement.

Derek smiled. "I'll be sure to tell Rob."

The door opened, and Lance walked in. There he was, Eric mused, with that distracted look, like always. Lance pointed his thumb at the door, his face twisted in confusion.

"Everything alright?" Derek asked.

Lance just looked straight at Eric and said, "I think there are people watching the building."

Kaela went rigid. "Did you *lead* them here?!"

Derek pulled a pistol out of nowhere. "How many?"

"I don't know. They were standing on the rooftops. I didn't know if they were Derek's agents or not."

Eric's heart skipped a beat, but he remained calm and still as he considered the feeling he'd had earlier. His instincts screamed to get everyone out, but despite the panic in his chest, he kept his face calm and uncaring.

"Well, Kaela," Eric said as thunder rumbled, "it appears your information was incorrect."

Kaela's face paled, and her eyes widened, one of the few times he'd ever seen her shaken up. Lance closed the door, locked it, and stepped away.

The room filled with tension. Derek pointed his pistol at the door. "Eric… what are we gonna do?"

Eric opened his mouth to speak, swallowing his panic. "Lance, you need to—"

The door blew open.

CHAPTER 5
SURVIVE

The force of the explosion sent Derek and Lance to the ground. Splinters shot through the room, and heat ran along Lance's arms.

Armed men in dark, armored outfits stormed the room and pinned Derek down. Kaela stood with her hands up as two men pointed their guns at her. Lance was thrown down onto the table and pinned. His face stung where it hit the wood, and his ribs screamed. His arms burned where their hands touched.

More men charged at Eric, guns pointed. Eric was still sitting patiently in his chair, his smile gone but his demeanor calm and unbothered. He didn't even raise his hands. When the flood of men stopped, another man walked in, wearing a matching outfit. He sipped from a flask and slipped it into his shirt as he marched toward Eric. Confidence carried his steps.

"You," said the armored man.

Eric smiled pleasantly at him.

"I'm afraid you can only see me by appointment." Eric looked around. "This isn't usually how you book one."

Lance rolled his eyes and winced with every breath of air. Of course Eric would be this calm.

"Bastard!" The man yelled and smacked Eric across the face with the back of his hand.

Eric's face barely even moved, his expression unreadable. "If it's information you want, I'll have to raise the price to pay for a new door."

"You killed my brother, you son of a bitch!"

"Ah, I see." Eric smiled up at him devilishly. "I thought you looked familiar. You must be dear Malcolm's brother. Daniel, right? I've seen you in the papers… Funnily enough, your brother also made the papers, didn't he?"

Daniel seemed taken aback, but then he raised his hand, and one of his men smacked Eric with the butt of his gun. This time, Eric almost fell out of the chair.

Lance blinked, and Daniel was suddenly wrapped in Eric's arm with a cane blade against his throat.

"If I hear so much as one gunshot, his head comes off!" Eric yelled.

Lance flinched at the force of his voice. He never thought he'd be grateful to see this side of Eric again.

"Now," Eric continued, his eyes so wild he looked almost feral. "What you all are going to do is let these three go. They're just clients; they have nothing to do with me. After that, I'll let your boss go, and you can do whatever you want with me."

Lance's heart dropped to his stomach.

"Mr. Samuel, was it?" Eric asked, glancing at Derek. "You should probably go *home*."

"Do it," Daniel said with a growl. "It's him I want."

Kaela bared her teeth at the two men aiming their weapons at her. They backed away, guns still trained on her. Derek was forced to his feet, and Lance was pulled away from the table. His ribs were sore, but at least breathing was easier. Kaela carefully backed toward the entrance, followed by Derek and Lance.

Lance held his breath. At any moment, a bullet could find his heart. His eyes darted to each gun in the room. Just one pull of a trigger, and that would be the end. As soon as they were out the door, they ran. Lance paused as they rounded the corner, stealing one fleeting look at the building snugly fit into the alley. One of the soldiers stood at the door, staring him down. Rain was falling in a sprinkle.

"Lance!" Kaela shouted, knocking him out of his trance.

Still out of breath, he ran, ignoring the looks he and the others were getting.

Eric smiled as the trio left. Every gun turned toward him, a dozen men staring at him down their barrels. He slipped the cylinder out of his coat, pushed Daniel toward his men, and held it up for them to see.

"You little—" Daniel started to shout, turning toward Eric until he saw what was in his hand. "What is…?"

"A detonator," Eric said, laughing at Daniel's shock. "You know what a detonator is, right, Daniel? It's a device that makes things blow up? Like you did with my door. Oh, and by the way, you can shoot me now. Because as soon as I let go of this button, you'll get a free preview of Hell."

Daniel's men shared looks, their guns lowering.

Eric took the opportunity and sneaked a few steps to the right.

If he could just make it a few more…

But Daniel narrowed his eyes. "You're bluffing," he said. "Fire!"

Lance didn't know how long they'd been running before the explosion went off. His bones shook from the distant force as he covered his ears. Smoke billowed from where the hideout was.

People screamed and ran from the sound, scurrying like rats.

"Well," Kaela said, her voice shaking. She looked down at her outfit and brushed it off. "We'd better get going."

Lance stared at the smoke for an extra few seconds before following the duo. Derek's eyes filled with rage. He was dead silent as they continued down the sidewalk.

The rain became a downpour. Kaela cursed and held her thin coat above her head.

"What just happened back there?" Lance asked over a rumble of thunder.

"Eric made a mistake," Kaela responded grimly. "Now he's paying for it."

"But did he actually just—"

"Save the questions for when we get to the hideout, Lance," Derek interjected. His voice was a low growl.

After a few minutes of jogging through the slicing cold rain, Kaela suddenly made a turn into an alley. She looked at Derek, who pushed a large trash bin out of the way. Kaela kicked at the brick wall behind the bin with her heel until a patch of it loosened. She kicked again, harder, and the patch fell away, revealing a space underneath the building. Lance shouldn't have been surprised, but his jaw dropped anyway.

Kaela scoffed at her soaked dress and slid into the room, waving for Lance and Derek to follow. Once Derek slid in, Lance moved to do the same, but someone grabbed him from behind. He gasped and choked at the smell of cooked meat. He struggled against whoever had him, hearing a crackling sound like baked bread behind him. He gagged.

He got a glimpse of a black uniform and the scorched face of one of the soldiers that had broken into Eric's place. His eyes were red and bloodshot, his face burned. It was the same one who'd been watching them from the door.

"Got ya!" he said, his voice gravelly, his eyes unsteady, his grip strong.

Derek was already climbing back out of the hideout, but something snapped; something that whispered in Lance's head; something that writhed within the pit of his stomach. Time slowed, and Lance's fear disappeared. The panic settled into a steady flow of adrenaline.

There it was again.

The whisper.

Survive.

Strength surged through Lance's body. The cold of the rain no longer stung his skin. His heart beat slower and stronger in his chest, so strong it pounded in his ears. His vision cleared, as if a blurry lens had been removed from the world.

Lance's elbow flew back hard into the man's stomach. The tightened grip loosened around his neck, and the man backed away, coughing and gurgling.

Lance could've made a run for the underground room, but his body whirled around and grabbed the burned man's arm. He flipped the man onto the ground, splashing water everywhere. The man's skin flaked where Lance's hands gripped him. He screamed and shouted, and Lance raised his foot. The man gasped his last breath as Lance slammed his foot onto his skull. Bone crunched under his shoe.

Time sped back up, and Lance gasped as though he'd been holding his breath the entire time. His strength faded, and his heart sped up. The rain froze his skin, and his stomach turned at the sight of the man before him. He stepped back, tripping and falling on the slippery concrete. *Oh, God,* he thought. *What did I just do?* His wet hair covered his eyes, and he brushed it away, revealing the charred body of the man that had just attacked him.

Derek's mouth was agape, and his eyes almost looked fearful. "How did you do that?"

Lance didn't respond—*couldn't* respond.

Derek dragged the man's body into the trash bin and shut the lid. He ushered Lance into the hideout and slid in behind him.

"I don't know," Lance said as he ran a hand through his wet hair, distracted by not only the smell of the man's burnt body seeping into the room, but the realization of what he'd just done. To be able to throw a man like that… Since when was he so strong? "Did I kill him?"

"No," Derek said. "His burns did. What you did was give him mercy." He grabbed the cluster of bricks and shoved them back into place, as if the wall hadn't been tampered with in the slightest. "But seriously… what the hell, Lance? I didn't think you could hurt a fly, much less do that." He wiped his hands on his wet pants. "I guess now I know how you managed to survive the slums all those years."

"That man," Lance said, swallowing the bile rising in his throat, "was burned to a crisp. He wasn't strong enough to do anything anyway."

A lie. Lance's grip had been much stronger than it should have been. Even his arms were fragile and small. No way should he have been able to throw a man like that. Lance looked around the concrete room, the only light coming from the flickering flame of a lamp Kaela sat near, a box of matches in her hand. The room wasn't much bigger than Lance's back at the store, but with that awful cooked smell, it felt smaller.

"Why didn't you tell us you could fight?" Derek pushed.

Lance balled his fists. "I didn't know! I haven't been in a fight in my life! Except… you back at my store and… that kid at the orphana— Look, I've barely been in two fights!" His heart wouldn't slow down. He sat against the wall, and Derek sat across from him.

"Guess I was wrong," Kaela interjected, looking at the ground, her hands held up to the flame. "Seems like Eric *does* give a shit about you. Go figure." She looked down at her clothes, her jacket discarded on the ground. "I'm freezing." She scowled. "And my clothes are ruined."

Derek sighed and removed a flask from his back pocket, taking a sip before offering it to Lance. Lance took it and stared at it. It called to him, whispering sweet promises that he knew it wouldn't keep. His clothes were soaked, he was freezing, and his hands trembled. He breathed in that smell… Maybe just one sip wouldn't hurt.

He hesitated at first then put the flask to his lips. Before he could get so much as a taste, Kaela snatched the flask from him and drained it in seconds. She wiped her mouth and tossed the flask back at Derek. Lance let out a sigh, almost grateful.

"He'll be here soon," Derek said. "I know it."

"Who?" Lance asked.

Derek tried to knock even a few drops from the flask into his mouth. "Who do you think?"

Kaela leaned her head against the wall, her makeup running down her face.

"I don't think he made it out of there, Derek," Lance said, his voice quiet.

As if she could read Lance's mind, Kaela opened her eyes and said, "I'm sorry, but can we talk about the fact that our hideout has been *rigged to blow* this whole time?!"

“Did you know about the explosives?” Lance asked Derek.

Derek shook his head.

Lance expected the conversation to continue, but Kaela went silent, and Derek sat against the wall, looking up at the ceiling.

The minutes went by like hours. Kaela fell in and out of naps, Derek resorted to pacing, and Lance just sat there, letting his own thoughts consume him. Thankfully, the smell of the dead man dissipated, replaced by the pungent zing of rain and alcohol. He looked down at his hands and balled them into fists, testing their strength. How he’d done that, he had no idea. Memories resurfaced, and the face of that boy appeared as he blinked—the taste of copper in his mouth, the screams. He gulped as a bead of sweat formed on his brow.

A monster and now a murderer.

“Derek,” Lance said after a while, “he’s not coming back.”

“Oh, shut up before I throw you out in the rain,” Kaela said, her words slurring. She pointed at her shadow covering the adjacent wall. “That means you too, buddy.”

“Well, I wouldn’t worry about that,” someone said in a strained, muffled voice. The patch of fake brick wall flew across the room, nearly striking Lance in the head, and Eric slipped in, as slick as a snake. His coat and pants were charred and torn but soaked and dripping as well. His face was covered in ash, and his hand gripped his shoulder as well as his cane.

Lance gaped. “Holy shit, you *are* alive.”

“What did I say?” Derek said, a proud smile on his face. “Glad to have you back, boss.”

“Devil probably kicked him out of hell,” Kaela muttered, pinching the bridge of her nose. “Can’t blame him, either.”

Eric grunted. “I’m happy to hear such an accommodating formality, but I was never gone to begin with.”

“How did you even survive?” Lance asked. The smell of smoke and rain swept through the room.

“Skill, speed, and a hell of a lot of luck.” Eric leaned against the wall, catching his breath. “I jumped out of a window and got blown out into the street. I caught fire, but the rain took care of that. I crawled into a nice little alley to pass out in, woke up, and here I am!" He spread one of his arms out, the other sagging at his side.

"What's wrong with your arm?" Derek asked.

"Dislocated, I think," Eric said. "Did I forget to mention the blast threw me into some poor slob's car?" He laughed. "You should've seen his face." He tried to move his shoulder and grimaced. "Derek, will you do the honors?"

Derek reached out and felt along Eric's arm for a moment before shoving it back into place with a pop.

Eric grunted then tested his shoulder out with a smile. "Ooh, that felt good."

Kaela stood, almost losing her balance. "You could have told us you had the place armed with explosives, you jackass." She made to slap him and missed. She rubbed at her head. "I swear I didn't have a headache until you came back."

"Calm down. They weren't going to blow up until I detonated them."

"And that's supposed to make me feel better?"

"Yes, actually. Now that you all have the comfort of knowing I'm not dead, I need to get going."

"Whoa, whoa, hold on." Lance grabbed Eric's arm before he could slip back out of the hole, then released it when his fingers burned. "What do you mean you need to get going? You just got here. Besides, we need to regroup and figure out what we're doing next. We don't know that there aren't more men coming after us."

"I doubt that," Eric mused, his smile wild and impressed. "But good on you, Lancelot, finally taking the initiative."

"No, that's not what I—"

"What happened to Daniel?" Kaela asked, rubbing her temples.

"While his smell currently permeates the air, I must inform you Mr. Landreau was horribly burned to death with his soldiers in an unfortunate gas explosion," Eric said almost gleefully.

"I'm pretty sure that's the guy in the trash you're smelling."

"Lovely," Eric remarked with no shortage of sarcasm. "I'm off. And Lance? Keep these two in line, will you?"

"You never said where you were going." Kaela stood from her spot. "Or are you keeping that a secret too?"

"It's no secret, Kaela." Eric smiled. "I'm going to Landreau Corp's corporate building in our lovely sister city. With the death of the two Landreau brothers, the company's bound to hold a meeting to determine what their next move is. I intend to use this to my advantage."

Kaela shook her head. "If Daniel knew you were the killer, don't you think everyone else would as well?"

"Not likely. They would have kept it a secret to avoid panic. The only ones that could have known are the Landreau brothers themselves and Daniel's merry little gang of men… and I don't think they'll be speaking to anybody anytime soon." Eric removed a folded slip of paper, charred at the edges. "Here you go, Lancelot."

Lance took the paper and opened it. A key was tucked inside. "An address?"

Eric nodded. "To a special hideout in case of situations like this. You'll want to stay there for the rest of the day. Maybe even a few days, just to be safe."

"Why are you giving me this?"

"You're in charge while I'm gone. Think of yourself as my… understudy. Yeah, I like that."

Kaela's jaw dropped. "Are you kidding me?!" She stomped over to Eric, pointing her finger in his face. "Are you trying to get us killed? He knows almost nothing about how we work. Did you forget that?"

Eric moved her finger aside. "I never forget. And I beg to differ. He has a decent idea as to how our operations work now, having spent a day with each of us. And besides, with him as the leader, you and Derek can focus more on your businesses. Lance only has one business, so he can afford the sacrifice."

Derek was dead silent.

"Adios." Eric started to slide away then paused. His voice turned serious. "And you, Kaela. Think of this as a big game of follow the leader. That's exactly what I expect you to do while I'm gone. I better not hear about you giving Lance any trouble. This is my decision, and you'd better respect it."

"Respect this," Kaela said, showing him her middle finger.

Eric narrowed his eyes then looked at Derek. "I have no doubts you'll follow my orders, Derek, but do me a favor and make sure to remind our fiery Kaela of what I said when the alcohol wears off."

"We're all going to die," Kaela said, placing her hand on her forehead.

Eric smiled and walked away.

Lance pocketed the key. Kaela's frown was so deep it looked painful. Lance scanned the piece of paper, marking a mental path.

"Well," Lance sighed, "I guess it's time we got out of here."

"What do we do about him?" Derek waved his hand toward the entrance, where the burnt smell was permeating the room once more.

Lance racked his brain, ignoring the look Kaela shot him. "Why not just leave him in there?"

She gave a small giggle, and Lance glared at her as she covered her mouth.

"Sorry," Kaela said. "I was just remembering something funny."

"And what would that be?" Lance mumbled.

"Eric making you leader." She burst out in a hearty laugh, nearly falling over. Her cheeks were red.

"What was in that flask, Derek? All she's had besides that was a cup of coffee."

Kaela laughed even harder, shaking her head. "It wasn't coffee." She wiped a tear from her eye. "Well, maybe like ten percent coffee."

Lance balled his fists as she finally calmed her laughing fit. "Fine, since you think me being in charge is such a terrible idea, then what do you propose? Eric told you to help me, after all. It's part of your job, *underboss*." Lance blinked. The words had just… slipped out so easily.

Derek raised an eyebrow at his change in tone.

Kaela's smile dropped, and she glared at him. "Fine." She put her hand to her chin in thought. "How about you… hide him up your ass?"

Lance gritted his teeth. "This is going to be the whole time Eric's gone, isn't it?"

"Pretty much, yeah."

"I expected more from you."

“I believe that’s the first time a man has ever told me that.”

Derek rubbed his temples. “Look, the best thing we can do with what little time we have is drag the body out of the trash can and leave it there.”

Lance crossed his arms. “Is that… going to work?”

Derek shrugged. “If his body is found in the trash can, they’ll know somebody hid him. If he’s lying on the ground, it just looks like he was caught in the explosion, tried to find help, and collapsed here.”

“Oh,” Lance said. “Okay.”

“We need to be quick about this. Lance, can you make sure nobody’s walking around?”

Lance stuck his head out from the entrance. The streets were empty. The rain had stopped, and dark clouds blocked out the sun, casting the city in gray. “Nobody right now, and it’s cloudy.”

“Then let’s be quick.”

Derek and Lance climbed out of the hideout. Lance kept watch as Derek heaved the man’s body out of the trash and positioned him on the ground. Kaela climbed out last, tearing her dress on a loose piece of brick. She swore as Derek slid the cluster of fake bricks back into the hole and moved the trash can in front of them.

Lance gulped with every glance he stole at the body. He looked as if he’d simply collapsed from his wounds, just as Derek said. A flash of blood and tears and the matron’s stare flooded his mind. He turned away from the corpse, rubbing his hands together for warmth, his wet clothes sticking to his body.

“Let’s go.” Lance handed the paper to Derek. “I’m not familiar enough with this part of the city. Do you know where this is?”

Derek stared at the paper for a moment then nodded. “I can figure it out.” He tore the paper to pieces and shoved them into his pocket.

They walked in silence, crossing streets and slipping through alleyways. Nobody seemed to give them any looks other than pity for their soaked clothes. The new hideout should’ve been no more than a few blocks away.

“Derek,” Lance said. “I… What does it feel like? You know, to be you?” He gulped as Derek gave him a confused look.

"What do you mean, boss?" he asked, his voice not faltering in the slightest.

"Dear God, please don't start doing that." Lance rolled his eyes. "I can't think of anything I would like to be called *less* than 'boss'."

Derek chuckled. "Habit, I guess."

"Did Eric make you call him that?"

Derek shook his head. "I guess I just like to be professional. Eric doesn't care much about what we call him as long as we get our jobs done."

"Hmm. You're really loyal to him."

"I already told you—the man gave me a new life. I owe that life to him."

A flicker of annoyance sparked in Lance's chest. If Eric hadn't murdered Malcolm Landreau, none of this would have happened in the first place. That didn't seem worthy of loyalty, to him.

"So, your question?"

"Yeah… I was wondering how it feels when you… kill?"

Darkness crossed Derek's face. "Why do you ask?"

"It's just… You said you had a bad past. I assumed that maybe you'd killed before. You seem like the kind of guy that has."

Derek let out a defeated sigh. "The first time… it depends. My first time was awful. It just hovered over me, like I had a second shadow. But over time, it faded… They all did. Every kill after the first gets easier until it's just… part of life." Derek paused as if in a trance, his eyes holding a faraway look. "I still see the faces sometimes, but… for the most part, you get over it a lot quicker than you think."

Lance grimaced.

They took a shortcut through another alley and back onto the sidewalk. They had to be getting close.

Derek shook his head. "You didn't kill that man, Lance. He was as good as dead already. Though I never expected you to be able to flip him like that. Maybe Eric was right, after all. Maybe there is something special about you."

Kaela huffed behind them, but he ignored it.

Derek stopped. "We're here."

Before them stood an old, abandoned auto repair shop. The two garage doors were rusted and chained shut, and the glass door on the left side of the storefront was cracked.

Lance looked around at the other buildings, most of them in good shape. “I never thought I would see a decrepit building in this part of the city.”

Derek shrugged. “We may not be the slums, but every city’s got abandoned buildings.”

“Eric sure knows how to pick ’em,” Kaela said. “About as well as he does his leaders.”

“You really should stop,” Lance remarked before he could stop himself. “It wasn’t funny the first time.” He blinked again at his own words. A snarky comment was one thing, but since when was he so confrontational? *Probably just the adrenaline.*

“Maybe not to you, but it’s been funnier for me every time.”

Lance ignored her and used the key on the door. The lock clicked open, and he stepped over the threshold. The stench of motor oil made his nose crinkle. The place was empty, save for a handful of toolboxes against the walls. A metal door stood at the back of the room, a broken ‘Exit’ sign atop it. A wooden door stood at the far-right end of the garage, its blurry glass panel revealing nothing but darkness on the other side.

I really wish I was back at my store, Lance thought as he stirred up dust, walking across the concrete floor. He looked over his shoulder at Derek and Kaela. She locked the door behind them and wrapped her arms around herself.

“I really need to change,” Kaela mumbled. “You don’t think Eric would have left a spare set of clothes in this place, do you?”

“Don’t know,” Derek responded.

“There’s no way in hell this is the hideout.”

Derek put his hands on his hips and looked around. “I’m inclined to agree with Kaela. This place is too exposed to be a hideout.” He pointed at the door they’d walked through. “That door’s made of glass, and people can still look through it even if it’s cracked. Not to mention there aren’t any beds, food, anything.” He popped his knuckles. “Kaela, can you check that room over there?” He pointed at the wooden door.

"Whatever," Kaela mumbled as she trudged to the door.

"Lance, was there anything else on the paper besides the address?"

"No, but the key worked, so this has to be the place," Lance said, looking around. Derek had a point, though. It did seem too exposed, especially after the last hideout was underneath the building. "Wait… maybe there's a secret entrance like the one we were just at."

"And our glorious leader has figured out the puzzle." Kaela opened the wooden door and looked in. "It's some kind of office." She looked beside the door and flipped a light switch. Lights flickered on in the office. "Huh… this place still has power."

"Does anything look out of place?" Lance asked.

"Yeah, this place has power," Kaela snapped, glaring at him. She stepped into the office and disappeared behind another door.

Derek furrowed his brows. "Well… that ice cream cooler over there seems pretty out of place."

Lance looked over at the waist-high ice cream cooler attached to a nearby wall. Faded pictures of frozen treats adorned its side.

Derek padded to the cooler and looked inside. He slid the glass door open and felt along its walls and the floor.

Lance did the same.

Nothing—just the smooth bottom of a cooler, though it could have benefitted from a dusting.

Lance sighed, then stood and sent a frustrated kick into the side of the cooler. It made a hollow sound.

Kaela groaned as she stepped out of the office, wiping her arms and shoulders with one hand and holding a roll of toilet paper in the other.

"Kaela… is that…?" Lance began.

"Don't. Say it," she growled. "I just want to be dry."

"Wait…" Derek stared at the wall absentmindedly for a moment before shoving his arms back into the cooler. He knocked on the floor of the cooler, first on the left side. He moved his fist to the right as he knocked. The sound changed from a stable clack to another hollow sound.

Derek scratched his chin. "Huh… I wonder." He braced his palms against the floor and pulled. *Click.* The bottom slid back, revealing a hole in the ground and a ladder that led down into the darkness.

Derek's excited, breathy laugh echoed through the room. Lance reached inside the hole, feeling along the concrete walls.

"Hey, Kaela," Derek said from inside the cooler. "Get over here."

Kaela continued drying herself. "Derek, I'm sorry to have to break it to you, but climbing into the cooler isn't gonna make me any warm—" She froze as she approached the ladder. "Well…" Kaela started as Lance looked down, just as surprised as she was. "Not bad."

"Do we have a light?" Lance asked.

"What's this?" Derek felt around the underside of the panel. With another click, a long string of lights wrapped around the sides of the ladder lit up, spiraling down to the concrete floor. It reached about a dozen feet down.

"Wow. That's flashy, even for Eric."

"He blew up his own building. Nothing can beat that," Kaela said. "I'm going first. There'd better be towels down here." She climbed into the cooler and descended the ladder. "Maybe even some tequila. These freezing clothes are killing my buzz."

Lance went next, then Derek, who slid the panel back into place with a click.

As they reached the bottom of the ladder, a new, more piercing cold bit into Lance's skin. His teeth chattered as he looked around. A narrow concrete tunnel lined with string lights led to a steel door.

Lance went first, the lights guiding him. His breathing became ragged. The already narrow walls closed in on him.

"I gotta ask—" Lance said, his voice trembling.

"Sounds about right," Kaela interrupted.

"How does Eric come up with this stuff? Does he hire psychopathic construction workers or do it himself?"

"We don't know," Derek said. "Eric doesn't tell us everything. He just kind of…"

"Plays games with us," Kaela finished for him. Her words weren't as slurred. "Can't stand it, either. But I gotta admit, the man is an evil genius… in a way." She paused. "Sometimes I feel like we're just pawns in his elaborate chess game. We just do what we're told, go where we're ordered to, and see what happens."

Lance reached the door, but when he tried the freezing-cold knob, it wouldn't budge. The key burned a hole in his pocket. He took it out and slid it into the lock. With one twist, the lock clicked. He pushed the door open and stepped in.

There was nothing but darkness inside, save for the last bit of string lights wrapped around a light switch. Derek walked in and flipped it, and a new row of lights on the concrete ceiling blinded Lance.

The room was all concrete—not just the ceiling, but the walls and the floor. Lance shivered. A new, more piercing cold dug into his skin through his soaked clothes. Kaela swore.

A computer with a desk and a chair sat on the right side of the room, a large metal cabinet to the left, and a row of beds across from the entrance.

"Oh my God, blankets," Kaela said suddenly, rushing to a pile of folded blankets on one of the beds and grabbing one. She held the blanket in her hands, caressing the material. Then she set the blanket back down and began to peel her dress off.

"Whoa whoa whoa, what the hell are you doing?" Lance asked, turning his head and blocking his view with his arm.

Derek turned around casually, his hands behind his back and his eyes pointed at his shoes. He cleared his throat nervously.

"What does it look like? I'm getting these soaking clothes off."

"Well, do you *have* to do it in here?"

"Oh, I'm sorry, princess, have you never seen a tit before?"

"It's freezing in here!"

"Yeah, and I'd rather be cold and dry than cold and wet. You and Derek should get yours off too. Here."

A blanket hit the back of Lance's head, and he scrambled to grab it before it landed on the floor. Kaela was already wrapped tightly in one of her own, her soaked clothes piled next to her.

"She's right," Derek said, easily catching the blanket she tossed at him. "It'll be harder to get warm with these clothes on." He met Lance's eyes then Kaela's. "I… think I'll just go change upstairs."

Kaela sauntered to the computer and took a seat in the office chair.

Lance shivered, the cold gnawing and digging into his skin. Maybe getting these clothes off wouldn't be such a bad idea, but being naked didn't seem much better.

"Yes," Kaela whispered excitedly to herself.

Lance squinted. "Is that…?"

"Internet." Kaela crossed her arms, looking rather proud of herself. She picked up one of the many wires that dug their way into the wall. "Not sure where the router is, but it's somewhere upstairs, I guess." She glanced at him. "You seriously need to get those clothes off. You're shivering. Unless you want hypothermia, in which case, be my guest."

Lance balled his hands into fists. She was right. He'd get sick if he didn't at least get out of these clothes. He groaned. "Fine, just… don't look, okay?"

Kaela scoffed. "I'll try to restrain myself."

Lance looked up the ladder for any sign of Derek, then at Kaela as she typed at the computer. He tugged at his wet clothes, the fabric clinging to his skin and refusing to come off easily. The cold sliced into his bare skin. When the last of his clothes were off, he wrapped the blanket around his waist then grabbed another and draped it over his shoulders. He curled into a ball on one of the beds, still shivering.

"How is this supposed to make me feel better?" Lance asked.

"Give it a minute," Kaela responded calmly. She stopped what she was doing on the computer and spun back and forth slowly in the chair. "What's in that cabinet, anyway?"

Lance padded to the cabinet, the cold of the cement seeping harshly into his feet. He opened the doors and raised an eyebrow.

Inside were a few bottles of water, plastic utensils, cans of vegetables, and light-brown packets.

Lance grabbed one of the light-brown packets and read the front. "MRE." He set the packet back in the cabinet and shut it.

Derek walked in, a blanket wrapped around his waist. "Hey, there's a hand dryer in the bathroom. I'm going to see if I can dry our clothes."

"I didn't see a hand dryer in there," Kaela said.

"Probably too drunk," Lance said before he could stop himself. His eyes widened, and Kaela glared at him. He couldn't stop himself from saying the words. Whatever filter he'd had on his tongue before was no longer there.

"You're such an ass."

Lance almost rolled his eyes. "Like you aren't?"

"And I don't even mean the ass kind of ass. You're just a complete donkey is what you are."

Derek picked up Kaela's pile of clothes then Lance's, sighing in frustration. "You two can fight later. For now, come upstairs with me until we're all dry."

Lance and Kaela shared glances then followed Derek up the ladder. Lance could hardly touch the rungs of the ladder, his fingers already aching from the cold. When he climbed out of the cooler, thunder rumbled distantly outside.

People walked past the door. If it wasn't for the cracked glass, they'd be easily visible. If nobody peeked in, they'd be fine.

Lance and Kaela followed Derek to the office, and Lance curled up in the office chair. Derek closed himself in the bathroom. The hand dryer whirred from behind the door.

"And then there were two," Kaela said, perching herself on the desk and rubbing her hands together for warmth. "You want to keep fighting? Because frankly, I think I'm already getting a hangover, and this headache does not help my mood." Her stare lingered on him. "Wow, your face is pale."

Lance sighed. "You know, you started this crap to begin with."

Kaela stared at him blankly, but then her eyes fell to her shoes. "Well, I guess I should get this over with." A moment of silence passed between them. "I'm sorry." She said it with an eyeroll, and her head lurched forward like she was about to gag. "Call me petty, but the truth of the matter is I've been in this family much longer than you have, and for you to just come in here and sweep Eric off his feet—" She crossed her arms. "I wouldn't even have been mad if he'd chosen Derek. I just really thought you were going to be—"

"Bait. Yeah." Lance looked at her. "I didn't ask to be put in this position."

She sighed. "I've decided I don't like the constant arguing… Granted, I do like making crude remarks, and I refuse to stop doing that. This arguing, though…" She winced. "It's really not fun anymore."

"What are you planning on doing about that?"

"I can try to make it up to you, I guess," Kaela said breathily, checking her nails. "From what I can tell, you haven't seen Arachna's good side."

"I thought this *was* the good side." Lance gestured around the room.

Kaela grimaced like she'd just tasted something sour. "I suppose it's all a matter of perspective. Regardless, Arachna has its good spots. You just have to know where and when to look."

"When?"

"Lance, the nightlife in Arachna is somewhat of a hidden gem. People like you only crawl out from under their boulders during the day and slither back in when it gets dark out. You should be doing the opposite."

"Call it what you want, but in the slums, we call that survival."

Kaela stood and peeked out the glass of the office door. "I plan on getting some sleep tonight. We'll meet up tomorrow night, and I'll show you what Arachna has to offer."

"Isn't that dangerous?"

She tapped her fingers against the wooden desk. "I doubt it. Like Eric said, Daniel probably wanted to keep his little operation a secret. And if anyone *is* still alive, they'll be after Eric, not us."

Lance bit his lip.

"We can't stay in here forever, Lance," Kaela added.

"Hard to believe I managed to squeeze an apology out of you," Lance said, changing the subject to hide the nerves coiling around his chest.

"First and the last time," she said back.

The hand dryer stopped, and Derek stepped out, redressed in his clothes. "Okay, I think everything's dry." He handed Kaela her clothes, then Lance his.

"I wouldn't want to offend you two gentlemen again, so I'll change in the bathroom this time. I'll dry my hair, too, while I'm at it."

Derek ran a hand across his bald head. “At least I don’t have to worry about that.”

Lance stood there with his clothes, silently waiting for a chance to change with no one looking.

“Oh.” Derek seemed to realize Lance’s intent and left the room.

When Lance had his clothes on, and Kaela was done in the bathroom, he closed himself in next. He leaned his head against the wall and let the loud hand dryer drown out the noise in his brain. Warmth filled the room, and he was tempted to stay like that the rest of the night.

He blinked, and the smell of burnt skin filled the room. Crackling sounded in his ears. He looked down at his hands and could almost feel the flaking skin. He squirmed, and his stomach twisted.

He sat up, bumping his head against the dryer.

The air was different. Everything sounded and smelled and looked the same—but different. Could killing a person really make everything shift like this?

He was a monster. The nightmares had tried to tell him for years.

They were right.

CHAPTER 6
A NIGHT TO REMEMBER

Sleep eluded Lance. He lay on the mattress, the smallest of pops or sounds of movement startling him.

He had nobody to blame for this but himself. He never should've joined this group to begin with.

A pile of blankets sat atop him, and a beefsteak MRE warmed his stomach, but he shivered like he was having withdrawals. He gritted his teeth at the memories that surfaced. A small part of him wished for it, for the sweet relief those substances brought; something that could calm him down and get him to sleep. He rubbed at his arm, tracing the faint marks left behind from years ago.

Lance didn't know how long it took for him to fall asleep. All he remembered was the darkness surrounding him, lingering over him like a predator.

Someone shook him awake.

"You going to sleep all day, oh leader, sir?" Kaela asked. The contempt in her voice was gone.

Lance waved her away as he rubbed his eyes and said with a yawn, "Only if I can get away with it." He sat up and looked around the room, ignoring the tightness in his chest. "Where's Derek?"

"He went out the back door a few minutes ago," Kaela said. "The building next to us has a fire escape, so he's going to get on the roof and see if he can spot anything out of the ordinary."

"What time is it?"

Kaela glanced at the computer. "About six."

"In the afternoon?"

"Nope."

"Then what was that about me sleeping all day?"

Kaela shrugged. "I was bored, wanted someone to talk to."

Lance rubbed his face as he imagined his real bed and his TV awaiting him at his store. The two best luxuries he could have ever asked for, and he'd only had one night with them. But he would give them up in a heartbeat if it meant he could get out of this miserable underground nightmare. "What have you been doing?"

Kaela sat in the computer chair. "I've been doing some research on Landreau Corp."

"And?"

Kaela gave a thumbs down and blew a raspberry. "Nothing important. These people are pretty good at making themselves scarce." She clicked her tongue. "Waste. Of. Time."

Lance rolled out of bed, stretching his stiff back. The cold floor sent a shock through his feet and up his spine. That Kaela could even act rested this early baffled him. "Any news on Eric?"

Kaela shook her head. "Derek hasn't heard from any of his agents, and I haven't heard from any of my escorts… I sent out an email to Amari, but I don't know when I'll hear back." She leaned her head on her hand and stared at the screen. "I hope they're okay."

"I'm sure they are."

Kaela hummed. "Well, I'll check on them once Derek gives the okay for us to leave. Then I can go get changed." She sighed. "A nice hot shower wouldn't be too bad, either."

The ladder creaked, and Derek walked in a moment later.

"How is it out there?" Lance asked.

"Pretty good. Everything looks normal. Once nightfall hits, we should be able to leave." Derek's eyes lit up, and he took a pack of cards out of his pocket. "But until then, I figured we could waste some time with a few games of poker?"

"Wait… wait, what do you mean nightfall?" Kaela asked. "I need to change, pick up a dress, check on my businesses. I'm not waiting until *night* to leave this dump. You said yourself everything looks normal."

"Night gives us better cover. And it's Saturday night, so we can blend in with the street traffic."

Kaela groaned and rubbed her face. "Fine… fine, I'll wait until tonight." She marched to the cabinet and flung the doors open, rummaging through the packs of MREs. "But I am *not* playing some stupid card game with you!"

"Royal flush, bitches!" Kaela yelled as she laid her cards flat on the mattress with one hand, a cracker smeared with cheese dip in her other. "I win again!"

Derek made a motion like he was about to throw his cards and covered his face, swearing into his hands. "There's no way you haven't played this game before."

Kaela set her cracker down on a napkin and shuffled the cards, a sweet smile on her face. "Sorry, Derek. You're either going to have to admit my infallible skills or your lack thereof."

"Or you can admit you hustled us."

"Can't hustle you if we didn't bet anything," Kaela retorted.

Lance smiled, the blanket around his shoulders warming him. The salty bean-and-rice-burrito MRE was settling easier on his stomach than the beefsteak. "I don't know, I feel pretty hustled right now. I played a lot of poker back at the orphanage, and you're still kicking my ass."

Kaela shrugged. "Then I guess we'll all just have to agree that I'm the queen of poker." She stretched with a yawn and squinted at the computer. "Well, it's eight o'clock. Can we go now, please?" She finished her cracker and stood.

Derek nodded. "Yeah, we can go. While you two are gone, I'm going to meet with Rob and see if I can gain any intel." His expression grew serious. "But once we're done, we meet back here. If Rob confirms everything to be normal, we can all go back to our homes."

Kaela smiled. "Then it's settled." She walked to the ladder. "Let's go, Lance."

They climbed up the ladder and left through the back door. The night air was cold but still warmer than the bunker. Derek disappeared down one end of the alleyway, and Kaela led Lance down the other.

Lance eyed the rooftops, scanning for any movement or silhouettes watching them. His heart skipped a beat, and his feet turned to lead.

Kaela walked onto the street, looking back at him. Lance hesitated, let out a long breath, then dragged himself out of the alley.

Derek hadn't been lying about the street traffic.

A steady line of cars drove the streets, and an unsteady jumble of people cluttered the sidewalks—laughing, cursing, drunken stumbling, all melding together.

Lance gulped, following Kaela closely.

Too many people.

Way too many.

The humming engines of the cars and the conversations of the people deafened him. Perfumes and colognes assaulted his nose. The streetlights were blinding.

Lance put a finger to his neck, his pulse pounding against his trembling finger.

"Calm down," Kaela said. "The more suspicious you look, the more likely we are to get caught. Just pretend like you own these streets… I guess you do, actually. Temporarily, anyway."

"Yeah, that's real comforting," Lance said, his voice shakier than his fingers. "I'm the new leader, which paints quite the target on my back."

"I never thought of it like that," Kaela said with a pouted lip. She laughed. "I guess I'm glad Eric didn't pick me after all."

"Har har," Lance said. He breathed deeply and kept his eyes forward. "So where are we going?" He didn't care. He just needed to get his mind off the crowd. He almost missed the slums.

Kaela smiled wickedly. "That's a surprise. But just trust me, it'll be fun." She sighed with her eyes closed. "And have lots and lots of alcohol."

"Have you always been such a heavy drinker?" Lance squirmed when a man walked too close.

"Yes, I've been downing bottles of champagne from the moment I was ejected out of the womb. In fact, my first words were 'Chardonnay, please'."

"Funny." Lance wrapped his arms around himself.

"I'm aware of that. That's why I said it with such a confident smile."

Kaela turned onto a new street, where there was a lull in the traffic. Only a handful of people dotted the sidewalk now. Lance breathed for what felt like the first time.

Kaela gasped.

"What?"

"It's my dress. Every time I look at it, it gets worse. And people are starting to stare at me—not in the good way, either. Good thing we're heading for a Rose first." Kaela grabbed Lance's arm and dragged him behind her with more strength than her arms showed. His skin burned, and he dug his nails into his palms to keep from struggling against her grip. She mumbled for the whole handful of blocks they took to get to the nearest Red Rose. "Can't believe I have to walk the streets looking like this." Her hand was still wrapped firmly around Lance's wrist. He was almost grateful. When they came across another big crowd, Lance shut his eyes and let Kaela guide him, drowning out everything but his burning wrists. Somehow, it helped.

When they turned a corner during another lull in the traffic, Lance opened his eyes to a blue neon sign: *The Blue Rose.* The building was nearly identical to the other Rose, except the walls were blue instead of red.

"What is a blue rose, exactly?" Lance asked, an eyebrow raised.

A fire lit in Kaela's eyes. "This is my all-male Rose. So don't expect to see a lot of cute girl employees here."

"I don't understand."

"All of the escorts at this Rose are men," Kaela said. "Can't *just* have all-women Roses, you know?"

"So… there aren't any girls here?"

Kaela hummed. "Well, our clientele is mostly women, but there are men that like to come here too."

"I remember this place now," Lance said, his eyes stinging from the bright neon sign. "A woman named Margaret was looking for it, right? She was looking for a Roderick, I think."

Kaela side-eyed him. "Not a bad memory. Ah, Ms. Margaret. Bless her heart, that woman has a fire in her loins. Let's go inside before someone confuses us for homeless people."

Kaela swung the glass doors open and stepped into the Rose.

The interior was even more like the last Rose; birch walls adorned with paintings and pictures, primarily of nude or barely dressed men. The ambient lighting was cool as opposed to the warm lighting of the Red Rose. Several male workers were dressed in either suits or casual attire. Music played subtly in the background. A well-groomed man in a dark-blue suit stepped out of a room. His eyes lit up when he saw Kaela.

"Kaela?" the man said.

The sound of her name alone stirred a chain reaction of men appearing as if from nowhere to see their boss. In the sea of voices, Lance only picked up a couple of things.

"Heard about the explosion."

"Are you okay?"

"Your dress is ruined!"

"Guys, guys," Kaela said, quieting the small crowd, "I'm fine… My dress isn't." She turned to Lance. "Stay here for now. I'm going to change." She parted the sea of her employees and walked past. "Can anybody tell me where Taylor is?"

A dark-skinned man with a purple suit and a single earring appeared at the top of the stairs at the end of the hall. "Kaela," he said, a hand on his chest, "you look awful."

"I know, Tay." Kaela pouted. "Think you can give me a helping hand?"

Taylor rubbed at his chin. "I think I have just the thing. Come with me, baby, I'll get you straightened out."

"You're the best." She stopped midstep then smirked at Lance.

"Boys, find Lance here something nice to wear. Casual, if you can find it. He's not much of a suit person."

Lance looked down at his dirty clothes, suddenly realizing that they were as bad as Kaela's. Most of the men disappeared down halls and through doors—business as usual. Some carried platters. They all had smiles on their faces. Kaela certainly knew how to get respect from her employees.

One man with bright eyes and blond hair returned with a set of clothes in hand and said with an even brighter smile, "Here you are, sir."

"Thanks," Lance said.

"I'm willing to dress you, if you'd prefer."

Heat rose to Lance's cheeks, and he shook his head. "Uh… no. No, I can handle it."

The man kept his smile and nodded. "Let me know if you change your mind. Bathroom's over there."

A lump formed in Lance's throat. "Sure… Thanks."

The man walked away. Lance cleared his throat, trying to keep his view on the floor and not the suggestive posters on the wall as he walked to the bathroom. He had to give Kaela credit; her workers knew what they were doing.

He slipped into the bathroom and leaned against the cream-colored wall. He savored the peace and quiet as he changed into the clothes: a black dress shirt, jeans, and new shoes. He lingered in the bathroom before splashing cold water on his face and returning to the lobby.

Almost a half hour passed with Lance sitting on a soft couch in the waiting room. Men passed by with women or other men in tow. They disappeared into the numbered rooms.

Lance wrung his hands, flashes of the burned man's face striking him every time his mind wandered. He blinked, his breath hitching. The smell of burnt skin stained the inside of his nose. Even the perfumed scent of the Rose failed to replace it.

Finally, Taylor descended the stairs with a proud smile on his face. "Ta-da!"

Kaela appeared. She wore a sleek black dress with a slit exposing her leg. A trail of silver traced down the side of the dress and formed a peacock on her hip. Her hair was up in a bun, and her face was decorated with black eyeshadow and bold red lipstick.

Lance held his breath as she sauntered down the stairs.

Kaela held her arms out. "*That* feels so much better." She turned to Taylor and embraced him. "Thanks, Tay." She rejoined Lance's side. "Hey, you don't look half bad. Ready?"

Lance couldn't think of the words to say as she approached him in that dress. "Y-yeah."

Kaela held her chin high as she walked past him.

"So… where we're going next… What I'm wearing is decent enough, right?" Lance asked.

Kaela rubbed a single finger across his shoulder, inspected it, and said, "It'll do. Black was a nice choice." She kept her graceful walk all the way to the entrance. "Same goes for me. Last time I ever wear anything white."

Lance chuckled. The safety of the Rose escaped him as the bitter cold of night surrounded him once more.

Kaela stopped, her eyes focused on the road. She turned around and opened the door again. "Taylor!" she called.

Taylor perked his ears.

"I'm not walking in these heels. Get my keys."

She wiggled her fingers in the air, and Taylor gave a knowing smile and left. Moments later, he returned and tossed a set of keys across the room. Kaela caught them and rounded the building. Lance kept glancing at the rooftops as he followed her.

Kaela unlocked a small gate leading to an alley. She locked it behind them and led Lance to a small parking lot. Lamps on the damp brick walls illuminated the darkness, revealing the cars filling the space.

"Why is this so separated from the street?" Lance asked.

"I try to keep my employees as safe as possible. Why risk walking a block to your car when it's right outside the back entrance?"

Kaela walked to a car as sleek and black as her dress, opened the door, and slid into the driver's seat. "Come on, slowpoke."

Lance slipped into the passenger seat as Kaela cranked the car. The vents blasted him with a cloud of heat, relieving some of the chilly tension in his bones.

"Listen to that baby purr," Kaela said as she revved the engine. She shifted the car into drive. "Let's get out of here."

Lance warmed his hands at the vent. As the car pulled out into the street, he relaxed—no more crowds and no more danger of someone following them. Still, as he let himself fall into a sense of security, something stirred in his stomach like the growl of a predator somewhere deep within him.

"Here we are," Kaela said, almost singing the last word as the car came to a halt.

Lance followed her gaze to the sign above the entrance.

"Nightlife... Seriously?" Lance said, his tone flat. "You think they could have tried to be a little smarter with the name?"

"They make up for it in service." Kaela stepped out of the car. "But oh, perhaps I've forgotten that our grizzled leader doesn't like fun."

"Are we seriously going to do this now?"

"I don't plan on winning another argument, Lance, but nothing is going to stop me from making jokes."

"Yeah, well, they're not funny," Lance muttered as he stepped out of the car.

Kaela ignored the comment. "Well... ready to experience some fun for once in your life?"

Lance rubbed his clammy hands on his pants as he followed Kaela inside. When he stepped through the doors, he could barely see anything in the dim, colored lighting. The hallway led to a large room with a dance floor in the center. Tables and booths surrounded it.

A bar stood in the far corner, right next to the DJ. Kaela's eyes flashed when she saw it.

"Well?" Kaela said, her arms spread out, gesturing to the room. She had to yell for her voice to reach through the music. "What do you think?"

"I think…" Lance trailed off, heavy bass slamming into in his chest and throat.

Colored lights flashed in rhythm with the music. Dozens of people were dancing on the expansive floor.

He cleared his throat, swallowed, and tried again. "I think that this isn't really my thing."

"Aw, you're breaking my heart over here." Kaela put a hand on her chest and grinned. "Come on, let's get some food."

Lance followed Kaela through the crowd of people, sweat beading on his forehead, his eyes darting at every person that came too close. Every bump burned his skin. *Too many people. Too close. How does Kaela not mind this?*

As the music quieted, Kaela dragged Lance to a booth and slid into a seat. "Finally, food that's not in a bag," she said from across the table.

Lance grabbed a menu and flipped through it, the writing barely legible in the dim light.

A waiter approached. Kaela ordered a cup of coffee and an appetizer of fried pickles.

Lance asked for more time, staring at Kaela with a raised eyebrow.

Kaela laughed. "What?"

"I just…"

She leaned forward. "I'm driving. I love a good drink, but I'm not *that* irresponsible. Feel free to throw a few back for me, will you?"

I wish.

Lance muttered an apology, but she didn't hear it through the music. The waiter returned and set down the plate of fried pickles. Kaela downed one after the other, but Lance only picked at them. The loud music and the smell of sweat and fried pickles didn't stimulate his appetite. He scanned the sea of bodies, writhing and sweating against each other. The place was stifling. He almost preferred the hideout.

"So," Lance started, his leg bouncing and his voice shaking, "I'm grateful for you bringing me here and all." He looked around, the words heavy as he tried to speak. "But I don't know… This really just isn't my kind of thing."

Kaela looked up at him with a mouthful of pickles, seemingly unfazed. “I figured you’d freak out at seeing this place. Eric mentioned how excited you got over a TV.”

Lance was glad the dim lighting hid the redness forming in his cheeks. *Eric* told *them?* He swallowed the frustration. “Guilty as charged.”

Kaela popped another fried pickle into her mouth. “Well, the night isn’t over yet. Let’s get some real food in our stomachs, and then I’ll bring you somewhere a little more your speed.”

Lance nodded. As if on cue, the waiter returned, and they placed their orders.

Lance forced down bites of his wrap, and Kaela scarfed her burger with the might of ten men.

“I can’t lie, the food was pretty good,” Lance said as he climbed into the car with Kaela. The city air smelled so much sweeter than the body odor infesting that place.

Kaela groaned as she slid into the seat, her hand placed firmly on her stomach. “I think I overindulged.”

Lance chuckled.

“Alright, so this place wasn’t your speed.”

“Not really.”

“Mm-hmm.” Kaela smiled. “But our next destination has something a bit different.”

Kaela drove down the road. Lance leaned back in his seat as he allowed his food to settle. He stared out the window as they passed under streetlight after streetlight. The car hummed as it glided down the road.

The streetlights stopped, and Lance realized he’d closed his eyes. A wave of sleepiness washed over him. He lifted his head from the cold window.

“If you drooled on my window,” Kaela said. “I will personally wipe it up with your face.”

Lance rolled his eyes then carefully checked the window through his peripherals. He almost breathed a sigh of relief when he spotted no drool on the glass.

“Are we… leaving the city?” Lance asked as the sight of buildings turned into trees.

Kaela kept her eyes forward. "Yes and no. You'll see. Don't get impatient on me just yet."

A moment of silence passed, then a snicker.

"What?" Lance asked as Kaela's snickers turned to chuckles. "What's so funny?"

"It's just weird," Kaela said. "Doing something like this with somebody I hated yesterday."

"So you're saying you like me now?" Lance poked.

Kaela shrugged. "Let's not reach that far yet. You're an acquired taste that I'm still getting accustomed to."

Lance let the silence hang over them for a moment. "I suppose that's fair."

Kaela drove up a dark hill, the headlights their only source of light. Lance kept his eyes on the forest line, his nerves ruffling. Someone could easily attack them from the trees.

They traveled farther up the hill until it plateaued. There, Kaela stopped. They were in a clearing in the woods with a bench across from them. The night sky was in view, dotted with bright stars.

Kaela's silhouette smiled through the darkness. A sad smile. She opened the door and stepped out, the interior lights of the car igniting in response. Lance followed suit and walked with her to the small clearing, devoid of all trees except one right next to the bench.

Kaela sat and patted the empty spot next to her without looking back. Lance froze and waited for her to say something, but she didn't even turn her head toward him, as if she was entranced.

Please tell me this isn't some awful scheme to get rid of me, Lance prayed silently to whatever would listen as he approached the bench. If this was just some ruse and it took him this long to figure it out, he would roll himself off this hill right here and now.

Lance dropped that line of thinking when he sat on the bench and followed Kaela's stare. The city of Arachna, spread out before his very eyes like a canvas. The dark of night was cast away by the lights of the city. Landreau Corp's building stood tall in the center, a beacon.

The streets and the alleyways formed a shape resembling a web. Lance almost laughed.

“So this is the place, huh?” Lance said. “Now *this* is definitely more my speed.”

“Glad to hear it,” Kaela responded casually. “It’s odd when you think about what’s going on in the city at this very moment, while we sit here in the quiet and watch. People sleeping in their apartments, thugs robbing each other in the slums…”

“I’m starting to see why Eric refers to this city as a web,” Lance mused as he took in the sight. “It really does resemble one.”

Kaela cocked her head to the side. “I guess it kind of does… doesn’t it? When you squint.”

“Is this why this place is so special to you?”

Kaela pursed her lips. “No… it’s the farthest away I allow myself to be from this city. I like my job. I like the nightlife. I even like Derek.” She paused to smile deviously at him. “Besides, it’s peaceful. The tree is shady, the bench is comfortable, though a bit dirty. I’ve come here at least once a month every month since I was a kid.”

“Oh? When was the first time?”

Kaela frowned as if considering the question. But her eyes softened, even as she rolled them, and she said, “Yeah. At first, it was with my mom and dad. Eventually, it was just me and my mom. And now…” She looked down at the grass, smooshing the blades flat. “Well, let’s just say it feels good to be here with someone again.”

“I’m sorry to hear that.”

“Eh, we all have losses.” She smiled again. “Least I got to spend time with my parents.”

Lance scoffed at the remark, but there was no playful spark in Kaela’s eyes. It wasn’t an insult—just an observation.

“Do you mind telling me what happened?” Lance pried.

“I very much do mind telling you”—she crossed her legs—“unless you’re willing to share something in return.”

Lance shrugged. “You already know how my parents died.” The reminder echoed as a pain in his chest. “Can’t believe I wasted all that time searching for a couple of corpses.” It hurt to say, but knowing it was true hurt even worse.

“Didn’t you ever consider that possibility before?”

Lance sighed. "Yeah… but somehow… I still wasn't prepared to hear it. It was all I had to cling to out in the slums. Hope."

"Hope is stupid," Kaela said bluntly. "But I don't blame you."

A heavy silence fell between them. Lance found nothing to say, so he stared out at the city. Hope wasn't stupid—not to him. If he hadn't held on to it, he would've died, just like his parents.

Kaela let out a long sigh. "Cancer got my dad."

Lance looked at her.

She was staring forward, her jaw set. "My mom died because some… *animal* couldn't keep it in his pants and didn't want anyone to find out."

"Oh my God."

Kaela's face twisted with fury, and she wiped her eyes. "Don't worry about it. He didn't last long."

"What does that mean?"

Kaela let out a slow, shaky breath, her hands balled into tight fists. "Eric approached me when I started my first Rose." She took another shaky breath. "He said he'd pay me whatever I want if I joined his 'web'. I said I wanted revenge. He took care of it for me."

"What did he do?"

Kaela shrugged. "All I know is that the bastard didn't go easy. Or quickly. That's all I care about."

Kaela's face twisted again, and she turned away.

"Kaela, I…" He stopped, not knowing what he could possibly say. He reached a hand out but paused before it reached her shoulder.

She wiped her eyes again and sniffled. "I shouldn't have told you that." She cleared her throat and adjusted her position on the bench. "Shit, that was stupid."

"It's okay," Lance said. "As far as I'm concerned, you didn't tell me a thing."

"Good."

A chilly wind whistled through the limbs of the trees, brushing Lance's hair into his face. "Thank you… for bringing me here. It feels good to get away for a while."

Kaela scratched her nose. "Sure." She looked out at the city, and Lance mimicked her. "Consider it an olive branch. I was going to say that I still don't trust you, but I just spilled my guts out to you, so go figure."

Lance allowed himself a small chuckle. "What made you change your mind about me?"

"Hell if I know."

They looked at each other, and after a small pause, both broke into a low chuckle. The tension eased, and Lance breathed easier.

Kaela opened her mouth like she was about to speak, but among the sound of rustling, a twig snapped behind them.

Kaela whirled toward the sound, her body going still and alert. Lance looked back at the car.

Nothing.

Lance hovered a hand over his pocket, the blood draining from his face when he felt no switchblade waiting for him.

"Kaela?" Lance whispered.

"Yeah?"

"You heard that too, right?"

She didn't respond. The world around them went silent—no crickets, no wind rustling the trees.

Lance's heart pounded in his chest as he stood from his spot on the bench, his eyes glued in the direction of the sound.

Kaela was at Lance's side in the blink of an eye.

"I think we've been up here long enough, wouldn't you say, Lance?" Kaela whispered, watching the trees as she stepped carefully across the grassy hill toward the car.

"I'm in full agreement," Lance whispered back. "You have a weapon with you, right?"

"There's one in the car."

Kaela opened the door on the driver's side. She reached underneath the seat, mumbling to herself almost prayerfully for a weapon to be there.

She paused for a second, and Lance held his breath until she withdrew a small pistol. They locked themselves in the car. Kaela swore, then swore again and slammed her fist into the steering wheel.

"What?" Lance asked, scanning the trees and the grassy plain around them.

Kaela's face was pale. "I think I dropped the keys."

"What do we do?" Lance's voice shook, his pulse throbbing in his ears. They should never have left the hideout and come to a hill *alone*. He cursed himself.

"Shoot the first person we see, no questions asked."

"Better than nothing, I guess."

Please let us get out of this. The words repeated over and over in his mind as he turned his head toward each window.

Lance froze. A dark figure stood at his window. He opened his mouth to scream, but his window shattered. Shards of glass sliced his face, and above the stinging pain… time slowed. A voice whispered to him in the back of his mind, like the purr of a predator.

Survive.

Calm washed over him, and he let out a breath. His stomach writhed, as if something was crawling around inside.

Kaela screamed as the window on her side shattered as well. He meant to duck or react, but his body was stiff.

The figure at Lance's window drew a knife.

Kaela screamed again. Gunshots popped, flashes of light filling the car.

Lance's arms moved as if by themselves. He grabbed the man's arm and wrenched it upward. *Snap.* The man cried out in pain. Lance ripped the knife from his grip as he crumpled to the ground.

Kaela had a gash on her leg, trickling blood. The man on her side of the car was also wielding a knife. Kaela pulled the trigger, the now-empty gun clicking over and over. The man twitched. A gurgling sound spilled from his mouth. He collapsed.

Lance leaned out his window. The man with the broken arm was no longer writhing on the ground. He'd disappeared.

Kaela dropped the gun, cursing at her leg. Tears streamed down her face.

Lance's body moved before he could tell it not to. He opened the car door and stepped out. No sight of the man with the broken arm, but… a sound slipped from under the car. A panicked breath. Lance crouched and spotted him. The man scrambled to get away.

Lance felt no fire or anger in his chest. Just cold.

The man crawled out from under the car with his one good arm, the other dragging at his side.

Lance almost stopped in his tracks when a smile crawled across his face. He shook it away as the man tried to run and tripped over his friend's body.

Lance rounded the car, the knife firmly in his grip. His stomach twisted as if a snake writhed inside of him. The man took the knife from his friend's hand and pointed it shakily at Lance, his other arm limp at his side.

Lance felt that smile again, but he suppressed it, then suppressed the fear that came along with it. It was as if he had no control over his movements anymore. He told his body to stop, but it ignored his pleas.

Lance was on the man in an instant, his hand wrapped around his one good arm. The man struggled in vain, the knife slipping from his fingers. Lance slid his hand up to the man's wrist and wrenched it. It broke with a sickening crunch.

The man yelled in pain, and Lance swiped his blade clean across his neck. A small amount of blood shot out at first, but then the man writhed and grabbed at his neck, more and more blood spewing violently out of the artery. He reached out to Lance as if begging for help.

Lance just watched. He dropped the knife. The calm left him in an instant, and he stared at the lifeless eyes of the man before him.

"I'm sorry," the words slipped out. The world sped back up, and a breeze drifted by. Lance slowly turned around.

Kaela's eyes were pointed right at him, wide and shocked.

His body felt warm again as he walked over to the man Kaela shot and picked up the keys lying in the grass, shining just bright enough to spot in the moonlight. Without saying a word, he handed the keys to Kaela and returned to the passenger seat. Kaela started the car and drove back down the hill. He tried with all his might to ignore the bodies lying still in the grass.

Kaela was quiet as they wriggled through the narrow passageway back to the spacious concrete room of their safehouse. Derek wasn't awaiting them like Lance thought he would. He hoped he hadn't also been attacked. Blood stained Lance's clothes as much as his mind. Every time he blinked, that man's fearful eyes stared back at him.

Kaela's wound was wrapped tightly with fabric ripped from her dress. She took a seat in the computer chair and leaned back, her eyes fixed on the ceiling. Lance cleared his throat and paced, biting his nails.

"I hope we weren't followed," Lance said, eyeing Kaela carefully.

She didn't even seem to hear him until she said, "We ditched the car in the middle of nowhere and wound through a bunch of alleyways before we even came here. I'm sure if we were being followed, we lost them."

"Did you also think that when we went to that hill?"

She glared at him. "Are you seriously trying to start an argument with me right now? I thought we would be safe." She jumped from the chair. "And what the hell was that back there with that man?"

Lance choked on his words. His stomach twisted, and nausea curled around his throat. He didn't know what made him sicker—that he had killed again, that he had lost control over himself… or that Derek had been right. This one had been easier. Much easier than the burned man.

"I don't know," he said.

"You murdered him."

Cold rage sent a chill down Lance's spine. "Don't act like your hands are clean, either. You riddled the other guy with holes because he was going to kill us. I did the same thing."

"No, you didn't." Kaela took a hesitant step forward. "That was… different. The look in your eyes… like you enjoyed it."

The words bubbled to Lance's throat before he could stop them. "What was it you said? 'Wasn't quick, and it wasn't easy'? Don't sit on your high horse and judge me when you've spilled your share of blood."

Kaela's face softened, and her eyes glistened; but then her expression hardened, and she slapped him. "Don't—" her voice cracked. "Don't you dare throw that in my face. I knew I shouldn't have told you that."

Lance tensed, his hand against his stinging cheek. The whisper returned to the back of his head, quieter than usual, but still present. Kaela raised an eyebrow. She noticed.

"I'm sorry," Lance said. "I didn't mean to say that, it just… came out."

"Like hell it did," Kaela scoffed. "What are you?"

Lance bit his tongue, his eyes watering. The way she looked at him—so similar to how the matron did that night. "Please don't look at me like that."

"How am I supposed to look at you?"

"It was either him or me."

Kaela looked sick as she said, "You were crying over that guy we left in the alleyway just yesterday, but back there, you… I don't know… *savored* it."

"I don't know," Lance said. "I guess… I was just caught up in the adrenaline or something."

Kaela stared at him for a long moment before turning away and letting her hair down. "Shit… Eric saw it before I did, but he was right. There is something about you… I wouldn't use the word *'special'*, though. *'Dangerous'*, maybe."

"I'm not dangerous."

Kaela sat on her bed, staring at him with that look again. Lance turned away from her. It was enough that the men he'd killed stared at him from behind his eyelids, that the memories of the matron and the kids stared at him, but now Kaela was doing the same.

Kaela sighed. "I hope not."

CHAPTER 7
MURDERER, BUT NOT A DESERTER

Lance couldn't sleep. He lay in bed and stared at the ceiling, flinching at every creak of the bedsprings. He didn't know how he could hear such small noises when his own thoughts screamed at him. The memory of that man's begging face melded with Kaela's shocked, accusing glare. Together, they stared at him from behind his eyelids. His nightmare had come to life.

Monster.

Guilt weighed down more heavily on him than the bitter cold of the room. He closed his eyes, and the man's face was there, eyes widened in shock then empty and glazed over.

He'd wiped the splatter of blood off his face; the shirt had already dried.

Lance rolled out of bed and dragged himself to the computer chair. The only light in the room came from the string lights spilling in from the entrance and circling the light switch. It was comforting, if only in that it prevented him from being trapped in the dark, *underground.*

In the dim lighting, Lance scanned his reflection in the dark glass of the computer. He leaned closer, searching for what Kaela had seen that scared her. Maybe it was the same murderous flicker that sparked behind

Eric's eyes, or the hollow gaze of a common criminal. Lance had seen enough of those in his days in the slums.

But nothing was there. Just his own eyes, given to him by his mother, if Eric's information was correct. Small flashes of memory were all he had left of her. Just the silhouette of a woman cradling him, and even that might've been the fuzzy memory of the matron from the orphanage. He chose to believe it was his mother, if for no other reason than to have something left of her. She owed him that much, especially after leaving him behind to overdose with his father.

Can I really blame them? he thought. He'd almost done the same thing just a few years ago.

The chair groaned as he leaned back and rubbed his eyes.

Those men that had tried to kill them must have been Landreau Corp agents. Maybe Eric was dead already. Worse yet, maybe he'd made a deal with Landreau Corp and left them in the dust. And Derek still hadn't returned. Lance chewed on his nails.

As if on cue, the ladder creaked. Lance froze.

But when Derek reached the bottom of the ladder, he relaxed.

Now it was just a matter of telling him what had happened.

"So you think it's Landreau Corp?" Derek asked once Lance and Kaela recounted the events of last night.

After a moment of hesitation, Lance nodded.

"Well, if they attacked you at the hill, then they're trying to be subtle about it. The Red Rose is always busy, and so is the bar, so our businesses should be fine. I doubt any of Landreau Corp's assassins would try to attack us in broad daylight… Then again, they did burst into Eric's place, so maybe nothing is off limits." Derek sighed and looked up at the sickeningly white lights above him. "Has anyone contacted the cleaners to get rid of the bodies?"

Kaela shrugged. "I don't know how to get a hold of them."

"We figured you would know," Lance said.

Derek shook his head. "Eric usually handled that… Well, you said it was a secluded spot, so maybe they won't be found… hopefully."

"Did you meet with Rob?"

Derek nodded. "We met in an alley not far from what's left of Eric's place, and I laid out new patrol routes for my men. We can't prioritize all the other information in the city with Landreau Corp after us, so I told Rob to shut down my bars for now and only focus on Landreau Corp. He gave me his email, and he'll be sending me updates on anything he and my men find. I… may have made that decision without your approval, Lance. So, are you fine with only getting info on Landreau Corp?"

Lance's mind went blank. He'd forgotten he was still the temporary leader. That Derek would even bother acknowledging it knocked him off balance.

Lance shrugged. "At this point, I don't see how we have much of a choice."

"Anything else?" Kaela asked.

Derek sighed. "I also have some men at the city's entrances to see if they can spot Eric when he comes back."

If he comes back, Lance wanted to say. Somehow, he managed to stop the words.

"That's it?" Kaela scoffed. "We just sit here and wait?"

"What else do you propose we do?"

Kaela bit her lip. "Maybe… maybe we can go to the police chief."

"And risk going out again?" Lance asked.

"If we can tell her what's going on, we could have the whole police force keeping an eye on Landreau Corp. Why not?"

"I've heard worse ideas," Derek said. "But we just have one problem."

"Yeah." Kaela nodded and looked at Lance. "We need to make sure she doesn't find out that Eric's left the city."

Lance looked at the two of them. "I thought Eric and the chief were on good terms."

"They are, mostly," Kaela said. "But if she finds out Eric's not here, she may try something."

Lance gave the ground a lazy kick. “So, we go to the police chief, ask her to keep an eye on Landreau Corp, and… what then?”

Derek shook his head. “Play the waiting game, I guess.”

“And if we get attacked?” Lance offered. The thought of that killing calm returning sent a chill down the back of his neck. He almost put a hand on his stomach, where it twisted every time that calm settled over him, like a parasite writhing within.

Kaela shrugged. “It’ll be the three of us. As long as we can make it to the police station, we should be safe enough. Landreau Corp wouldn’t be stupid enough to invade an entire precinct full of armed men and women.” She laughed a little at the ground. “And if they are that stupid, then all the better for us.”

“As long as we go in the middle of the day, we’ll reduce our chances of getting attacked.” Derek furrowed his brows and focused his gaze across the room.

“We have a few hours until daylight, so I think it’s time to get some sleep before we get out of here.” Kaela turned toward her bed, but Derek stopped her.

He reached into his coat and removed a leather sheath with straps hanging from it. “The strap goes around your thigh.”

Kaela grabbed the sheath from Derek’s waiting palm. She lifted the part of her dress that wasn’t ripped and strapped it around her thigh. “Wow,” she said as she walked in a circle. “Not bad.”

“And now”—Derek removed a long, slender blade—“your weapon.”

Kaela hesitated as she reached out to grab it. The forearm-length blade looked sharp enough to cut anything, and the hilt was a slim silver grip with a cat’s head engraved at the end.

“Thanks,” Kaela said as she took the blade and sheathed it. Her dress covered it perfectly. “It’s like it’s not even there.”

Derek smiled and nodded. “Don’t thank me. Rob said he thought of you when he saw it, so he wanted me to pass it along.”

“Why?”

Derek shrugged then looked at Lance. “As for us…” He pulled a handgun from the back of his jeans and offered it to him. “He said pistols are the best he can give us for now. He'll try to get something more useful later."

Lance stared at the handgun in Derek's palm, but as he reached his hand out to grab it, that man's face flashed in his mind again. "I don't want it."

Derek furrowed his brow. "Well, you're going to need something to defend yourself with."

Lance wished he had his switchblade back. *Then again*... The man's face reappeared, the image of blood spurting from his neck sending bile to his throat. Maybe it was for the best that he didn't have a weapon at all.

"Would you look at me," Kaela said, lifting her skirt to show off the knife. "I look badass." She stood in a fighting stance and took the knife out, swinging it and adjusting to the weight. After a few swipes, she sheathed it again then smiled at Derek.

"Well, I'll keep it with me in case you change your mind," Derek told Lance, returning the gun to his jeans.

When it was out of sight, a pressure left Lance's chest. Instead, a knot formed in his stomach, as if it protested his refusal of the firearm. He shook the feeling away.

"Rob also gave me these." Derek took out two pagers, handing one to Kaela and dropping the other into Lance's hands. "In case we have to separate and need to contact each other."

Kaela leaned against Derek, one arm on his shoulder. She raised a single eyebrow as she asked, "Rob didn't happen to send any alcohol for me, did he?"

Lance stepped forward, his mind free but his body moving without his approval. A man lay in front of him, dressed in all black, one arm limp at his side, the other held out in some measly attempt at defense.

"Please," the man begged, his voice shaking. "I don't want to die." His voice echoed across an empty field. The moon shone down on them like a spotlight on a performance.

Lance stepped forward again, his foot digging harder into the ground when he tried to reverse his direction.

This scene was familiar. Something clicked in his brain as his hand gripped the knife tighter.

No, he thought. *No, not again.*

"Please!" the man shouted, his voice distorted. "Please!"

That face haunted him. Plagued his mind.

"I didn't mean to!"

Lance tried to open his mouth, tried to explain, but his tongue turned to stone.

Step after step, the man's demise drew nearer. Lance tried to drop the knife, to speak, to do anything but hover over the vulnerable man.

His face burned into Lance's memory, forever staining his thoughts with blood.

"Monster!"

In one swift motion, Lance swiped the knife across the man's neck. He sputtered and gagged, blood shooting from an artery.

Lance breathed for what felt like the first time. The knife fell from his hand.

In a flash of light, the man's face appeared in Lance's vision, his expression twisted in blank horror as his eyes stared past him.

Lance opened his mouth to scream, but no sound came out. Nothing.

With a gasp of air, Lance shot up in bed, his hair wet with sweat and clinging to his face. His eyes darted around the brightly lit room.

He exhaled, his heart racing. The remnant of the man's face flashed in his memory, but he shoved it down. His stomach turned.

Lance put his head in his hands. Voices rang out. He looked up.

Kaela was sitting in the desk chair while Derek leaned against the wall beside the entrance. Neither seemed to notice Lance was awake.

"Oh-ho-ho, if the chief really did send those guys after us, then Eric's gonna raise some hell," Kaela said, fire in her voice.

"Right, well, Eric's not here right now, so it's up to us to get to the bottom of this," Derek said, his voice lacking the same fire. "Are you sure you couldn't find anything?"

Kaela shook her head. "Not a thing. You'd think Eric would've left *something* in here for us." She popped her neck. "If we could just get in contact with the cleaners, this would be so much smoother."

Lance groaned and stood from the bed. Kaela and Derek both turned their attention toward him. "Can someone tell me what's going on?"

Kaela turned her chair to face him, revealing a newspaper. "Yep. Derek here was nice enough to bring me this lovely little piece."

Kaela threw the newspaper to him, and Lance barely managed to catch it. A chill crawled down his spine as he read the headline:

Two Police Officers Found Murdered outside of Arachna.

Kaela pursed her lips. "Seems a bit odd that our local newspaper would manage to get information on two bodies in the middle of a low-traffic spot in Arachna in just a few hours." She frowned as she grabbed her knife sitting next to the computer and inspected it. "I have a feeling the chief got paid off by Landreau Corp."

Lance didn't look up from the paper. "Maybe… Maybe they acted on their own."

"I don't know, but something's off about two police officers dressed in black randomly trying to kill us, don't you think?"

Lance laid the paper next to him on the mattress then rubbed the crust out of his eyes. "You don't think Eric…"

Kaela's mouth formed a thin line, and Derek shifted his weight, suddenly very interested in the ground. Lance didn't know whether they were thinking the same thing or refusing to, but all of this had started when Eric left—not being able to contact the cleaners, the police officers attacking them, Eric going off suddenly to make a deal with Landreau Corp. All of it screamed betrayal, regardless of what Kaela and Derek thought.

"Anyway," Lance continued, clearing his throat. "What do we do now? Are we still going to the precinct?"

"Yeah," Derek said suddenly, biting his lip. "Yeah, we definitely are. I might have an idea."

"Then let's hear it," Kaela said. Her tone of voice was as playful as ever, but her eyes were dark and tired. Last night was still affecting her, but she was playing it off like it was nothing.

Lance wished he could do that so skillfully.

"Did they give the names of the officers?" Derek asked.

Lance picked the paper back up and scanned the article until he spotted two names. "Officers Terrance and Harper."

Derek seemed lost in thought for a few seconds then snapped out of it. "Lance, you and Kaela will go into the precinct while I find a way to sneak in. Maybe I can search Terrance and Harper's offices, see if there's any evidence that they were planning this without the chief's knowledge."

"Got it," Lance said.

"Aye aye," Kaela remarked, saluting him.

"Once I have everything, I'll contact you with the pager. You both need to get as much info as you can from the chief. Find out what she knows. If anything goes wrong, I'll get us out of there."

"Sounds good," Lance said. "It also sounds like if this goes wrong, we're all done for."

"Yeah, well, we're all done for if we don't do anything either," Kaela interjected.

"Very true." Dead one way or dead another. If he ever got the chance to see Eric again, he would have much to answer for. A whisper spoke in the back of Lance's head, and his stomach twisted. "So… we're clear on what we need to do?"

Derek and Kaela nodded.

Lance shook his head. Best-case scenario, the chief hadn't stabbed them in the back and could help them spy on Landreau Corp. Better than nothing. "Then let's get going."

Lance had washed his bloodied shirt in the sink then dried it under the hand dryer. He wasn't sure how much he'd actually washed out, but whatever blood remained was hidden in the dark fabric.

Kaela hung from his arm as they walked through the doors of the ACPD precinct. Desks peppered the room, most of them occupied by an officer doing paperwork. A man sat at the large desk across from the entrance.

"Hey, Kaela," the man said, his face lighting up. His smile wavered for a moment as his eyes scanned her. "Your dress has a tear in it."

"Hey, Reggie," Kaela said sweetly, her arm slipping from around Lance's. She glided over to the desk and leaned on one arm. "I have a favor to ask."

"Anything for you," Reggie said. "Just name it."

Kaela let out an amused hum as she turned toward Lance. "This is my newest colleague. Lance, say hi." Before Lance could open his mouth, Kaela continued, "I want to introduce him to the chief."

"Really?" Reggie said, tilting his head to the side like a curious puppy. "Why?"

"It's business. Can we go see the chief?"

"Yeah. Yeah, sure, I'll let her know you're coming."

"Thanks, Reg," Kaela said, her voice smooth as silk. She motioned for Lance to follow her as she wove around the desks. Most of the officers sneaked glances at her as she passed. Either they were admiring her, or they were about to attack.

Lance gulped. He didn't know how to act with so many eyes on him. He glanced at the second level of the building, at the balcony above, wrapping around the room, where many smaller offices were tucked. Some of the rooms had the blinds down and the lights off. One of the doors opened, and Derek appeared for only a second, slipping into the office without a sound.

He's good.

Kaela led Lance to a door at the end of the room and knocked.

"So, do any of the officers here know about Eric?" Lance whispered.

No officers seemed interested in him so far, and most that had their eyes on Kaela had already turned their attention back to their paperwork.

"Some do, but only that he's a business partner to the chief. As far as they're concerned, he's a perfectly legal info dealer. No more than that."

Lance considered how close Eric was to being legal. If he didn't so readily threaten people as much as he killed them, he wouldn't have as many skeletons in his closet. It was reckless, and they were suffering from the consequences of that recklessness. Maybe power had gotten to him.

Lance sneaked glances at the officers. Some looked back at him, while others didn't seem to notice he was there. At any moment, Lance thought, they could all turn their guns on them and fire. Two officers were bad enough, but a whole precinct's worth…

Lance's palms were sweaty, and when Kaela made eye contact with him, she made a face like she understood. He ignored the image of the man's body in his head as he turned and looked once more over the officers in the station. If they knew who'd killed two of their comrades…

The door opened, and a woman peeked out from around it. Her badge glistened in the light.

"Kaela," the chief said, nodding. Her brown eyes darted straight to Lance, and he almost flinched at the unyielding discipline behind them. "Who's this?"

"Chief Rotoya, this is Lance, a new guy that Eric brought into the group. He wanted me to introduce him to you."

Rotoya narrowed her eyes and sized him up. Lance puffed out his chest just slightly and kept what he hoped was a professional look on his face. He towered over her, yet she still intimidated him. He was tempted to bite at his nails, so he crossed his arms instead.

"I don't recall Eric bringing this by me."

"He didn't?" Kaela said, looking convinced that she had no idea.

Lance didn't even attempt to replicate her expression and instead stayed behind her, trying to ignore the unsettling feeling that a bullet could find his back at any moment. He wasn't sure what scared him more—being shot or hearing that whisper again and losing control.

"That's unlike him. But then again, he's never been the most predictable man in the world." Kaela laughed quietly then dropped her smile. "Don't tell him I said that."

"Why does Eric want me to meet, uh… Lance, was it?"

"I'm not sure, I'm just the messenger here."

Rotoya eyed them both, sighed deeply, then waved them in. Lance followed Kaela inside and sat down next to her in one of the two chairs across from the chief's desk. He breathed a quiet sigh of relief. The only eyes on him now were the chief's. She sat across from them and folded her hands together.

"I know you're not here to introduce me to Lance. Eric already told me about him, and I know good and well he would've mentioned this half-baked meeting."

Kaela's smile didn't falter, but she appeared to be frozen in time for just a moment, meeting the chief's eyes with a furious intensity. Lance realized he was bouncing his leg and crossed it over the other. He couldn't bring himself to meet the chief's gaze, so he stared at the map of Arachna on the wall next to her.

"It may not be the best story, but it's a good enough one to tell in front of all the officers that were obviously trying to listen in on what I was saying. Surely you don't want me to waltz in here and announce the more illegal dealings you've ignored for Eric's sake, do you, Chief?" Something like annoyance tinged Kaela's voice, and Lance casually glanced at the chief.

Rotoya relaxed and leaned back in her chair, one side of her lip quirked up in an apparent smile. Her wide frame took up most of the chair. "Fair enough… So what's the real story here?" Even someone as professional as her was used to Kaela's hostile tone.

Lance scratched his lip to hide his own small smile.

"Well, we actually had something we wanted to talk to you about, Chief," Kaela said, adjusting a wrinkle in her dress. "You see, Eric's been—"

"What a coincidence," the chief interjected, placing both hands firmly on the desk and standing. "I find out just this morning that two of my officers were killed last night, and here you come, knocking on my door, which you've never done before."

"What?"

Lance kept his eyes on the chief as she stared at Kaela, watching for any small tidbits of information she revealed in her body language, just as Derek had shown him that day in the bar.

Thankfully, Rotoya seemed too focused on Kaela to even notice Lance.

"Officers Terrance and Harper are dead. Harper was shot twelve times, and Terrance's neck was slit open. I happen to know a man that has killed his fair share of people. That same man hasn't contacted me for days and has now apparently sent his lackeys to come ask me for a favor. Looks pretty suspicious to me." She opened a drawer, and Lance prepared to attack. But instead of a gun, she pulled out a newspaper and slapped it on the desk. "Reminds me of another mysterious death that happened only a few days ago."

Lance tensed at the sight of the headline. The same one that came out the day after Malcolm Landreau died.

Kaela looked down at the paper for a second then back up at the chief, straightening her posture.

"I'm starting to wonder," the chief continued, sitting back down, "if Eric decided to skip town and leave his bumbling idiots behind to clean up his mess."

It took everything in Lance not to look at Kaela. He had to admit those same suspicions swirled around in his head, even now.

Eric might just be using you for bait anyway. Lance had allowed Kaela to convince him of that, not realizing that he might have just been using them all as bait the entire time.

Lance shook his head. He could worry about that later. His heart pounded in his chest, and sweat beaded on his forehead.

"Chief, I think you're getting a little ahead of yourself here," Kaela said. "Eric may have killed Malcolm Landreau, but he would never kill two of your officers. If he had, their bodies would never have been found."

"I may not be the paragon my men think I am, but I made a *promise* that I would keep them safe. That I would make sure they could go home to their families."

"Which Eric has contributed to. He funded better gear and weapons when the city wouldn't. He gives you information you want for investigations for cheap. Why would he kill two of your officers, especially now, especially after all he's done?" Kaela stiffened.

She was getting heated. Lance couldn't tell if it was because of the chief or if she was also realizing she might've been bait this entire time and was funneling that anger into her performance.

Rotoya's stone-faced disposition faltered, but instead of calming down like Lance expected, her eyes filled with rage. "Then why the hell can't I contact Eric?"

Kaela spoke, but Lance didn't listen to what she said. The pager beeped in his pocket, and a wave of relief washed over him. Lance cleared his throat to mask the sound. The chief glanced at him but paid no mind to the beeper, if she even heard it.

Lance bumped Kaela's foot with his own. The signal that Derek was done. He hadn't taken very long… Lance wasn't sure if that was a good thing or a bad thing. At this point, it didn't matter. Rotoya was looking more agitated as the seconds passed.

"Rotoya…" Kaela paused, her mouth still open, as if the words were scared to come out, scared to face the awaiting chief. "If you'll just let me *explain* what is going on here, I think we'll both realize we're still on the same side. There's a much greater threat that we have to deal with right now, and if I had to guess, I wouldn't put it past them to be the ones that killed your officers."

The chief closed her eyes and sighed, settling back down in her chair. "Fine."

Lance let go of a breath he didn't realize he was holding, and as Kaela began to speak, he focused on Rotoya's reaction. This would be it, the moment that revealed if she was working with them…

Or with Landreau Corp.

CHAPTER 8
DO WE HAVE A DEAL?

Eric was light on his feet as he strode down the hallway, his cane clacking against the floor.

When he'd entered the building, he'd stifled a laugh at the security. Only one guard had been sitting in a chair near the entrance, and he'd been more interested in the newspaper he held than his surroundings. Malcolm's name was in the headline.

Few people had been in the lobby. Eric had sauntered up to the receptionist, his cane tapping on the white marble floor, and claimed he was there for a meeting. When the man said the meeting was already taking place, Eric had slipped him a wad of cash along with the promise that he was fashionably late. The man had taken the money and told him where to go.

Eric had passed another guard on his way to the elevators and unclipped the keys from his belt. Eric likely wouldn't need them, but he saw no harm in taking them—not to Eric, at least. He wished he could see the look on the guard's face whenever he found out his keys were missing.

Even now, he chuckled at the thought.

Eric's black trench coat didn't scream *businessman*, but with the cloudy weather outside, he was certain nobody would ask questions.

He'd wormed his way through the building, planting little surprises throughout should anything go wrong with his plan. Rain would come soon, and as if on cue, a low rumble of thunder threatened the city of Agni.

A terrible last resort, but an assemblage of sticks in suits weren't going to say no to him—not if enough money and information was offered. He patted the case attached to the inside of his coat.

Eric gulped, a shock of nerves jolting him. He stopped in his tracks. It had been too long since he felt nervous about anything. The feeling was foreign to him now. His plan had to work. It had to. He could finally make up for what he'd done. He drowned his nerves as he'd learned to do years ago and continued on.

Bleached lights shone on the wooden door at the very end of the hallway. Muffled voices resonated from the other side, and as much as Eric tried to decipher them, he couldn't make out what they were discussing. With the death of the two founders, however, he had a fair guess.

Eric cleared his throat, raised his fist, and tapped on the door. The voices stopped, and a middle-aged man opened the door, glowering at him.

"Can I help you?" the man asked, his voice coated in tired frustration.

"Oh, no," Eric said, his face twisting in a smile as he waved the question away. "However, I do believe *I* can help *you*."

The older man responded by closing the door—or trying to.

Eric stopped the door with his foot. The older man stared down at Eric's boot then met his eyes.

Eric ignored the twinge of irritation that prickled his skin. His hand found a splinter as he shoved the door open, pushing the aging man to the ground with more force than he'd intended.

"Ow," Eric said, plucking the splinter from his palm. When he surveyed the shocked faces of the aging men, he suppressed a laugh and let out a half-hearted apology. "I suppose I don't know my own strength." His laugh spilled out, and he stepped into the room. His skin crawled as he helped the man up and gave him a hard pat on the back. He made sure the older man met his eyes, and when his face turned a shade paler, Eric knew his message had come across.

Every head turned toward him. One man at the end of the oval conference table appeared younger than the rest, though the wrinkles under his eyes and the grays of his hair were distinct, even from where Eric stood. His eyes flashed with anger, but his smile said otherwise, as if he thought this was some elaborate office prank.

"Hello," Eric said. Two men close to him flinched. The sight widened his smile. "Boy, do I have a proposition for you gentlemen." He took the only empty chair.

The older man rubbed his sore back and groaned as he left the room.

Eric propped his feet onto the table and studied them all. Most looked uncomfortable, others scared, but the one at the other end of the table was composed. Eric peered at the middle-aged man from under his dark fedora then donned a face of embarrassment.

"Oh my." Eric put a hand to his mouth. "I suppose it's rude to have hats on indoors, eh?" He didn't wait for a response before removing his hat and placing it gently on the table. It rested next to his feet.

"Okay," the man across the table said, his hands folded in front of him, his face going cold. The face of a true businessman. "You've got my attention. And you've scared these honest men. I hope this 'proposition' is more enticing than your bizarre entrance."

Eric scratched the end of his nose. "What was it you said, my friend? 'Honest'?" He couldn't hide his chuckle. "What exactly do you mean by *'honest'*?" He removed his feet from the table. "Because selling cheap drugs to your clients for outrageous prices doesn't sound like honest work to me. And don't even get me started on the bribery and false advertising. But I suppose we shouldn't dwell on that. Let's discuss this secret project of yours."

Eric gauged the reaction of every man in the room with a glance. All the nervous looks at each other confirmed his suspicions.

A laugh bubbled up to his throat, but he swallowed it. He had to be careful how he approached this. He was allowing himself to get too careless. *Tone it down, asshat. This is a business meeting, not a performance. Remember who you're doing this for.*

A flash of light shone through the blinds covering the windows to his right, then a clap of thunder rumbled the walls.

"I don't see where you could possibly have any proof of that. Our company is clean, through and through," the man said, his hands no longer wrapped around each other but gripping the edge of the table.

"Of course," Eric said, forcing a look of humility. "I apologize. It appears we've gotten off on the wrong foot. A man likes to make an entrance, I'm sure you understand."

"I can see that."

"Let's start over, shall we? What's your name?" Eric asked.

"Caleb."

"I'm Eric." Eric smiled then straightened his posture and cleared his throat. "Now, Caleb, I have no doubt that your dealings are less than legal. Which is fine. I offer no judgement. But why don't we both agree we're playing in the same ballpark here?"

Caleb leaned forward. "What do you want?" His voice remained calm, though an inflection of anger shone through.

"I have an offer for you, one that will surely make you forget all about my crass entrance. Would you like to hear it?"

The fire in Caleb's eyes dimmed, and behind the flames shone a sliver of curiosity. He narrowed his eyes. "Gentlemen, you can leave."

Slowly, the older gentlemen stood, as if afraid moving too quickly would incite a fight.

As they left the room, Caleb called out, "And tell Jeremy to get the chopper ready." He turned his attention back to Eric.

"I'll take that as a yes." Eric gripped his cane just a little tighter, the cool metal grounding him. "So, Caleb… I happen to be an information dealer in your sister city, Arachna. I'm sure you're familiar. It is where your most recent building has been erected."

Caleb didn't respond. Eric gritted his teeth at the silence. At the lack of reaction. His blade called to him, like a siren summoning a ship captain. He ignored it for now.

"Anyway," Eric continued, "I believe my services could be beneficial to you in this crucial time in your company, what with expanding your business, scamming people with your medicines, *and* finishing this secret project. You're going to get caught eventually. I can prevent that."

"We haven't been caught because we're not doing anything wrong."

"It's alright, I won't tell anyone. In fact, I'm offering the opposite."

"Why don't we cut to the chase?" Caleb said as he checked the clock on the wall. "Security is on the way. You have until they get here to make your point."

Eric dropped his smile. *Security, huh*? He nearly snickered as he imagined Caleb pressing a secret button under the table. *Oh well.*

"Fine. Since I'm apparently on a time crunch now, I'll do just that." Eric removed the case from his coat, opened it, and slid it down the table. It stopped right in front of Caleb. "Cash is always nice, hmm? But that's more of an apology for barging in here." He allowed himself a laugh, which Caleb matched with a strained smile.

Caleb looked down at the money then back up at Eric.

"What I'm offering is information. Information on nearly anything you could ever want, primarily the dealings of your competitors. I could also sell some of your drugs to my financially challenged clientele. I could take a small percentage of the profits, all while increasing yours."

"Why?" Caleb leaned on his hand as if he was bored. "Why would you break into my building and offer me this? What do you have to gain?"

"Money, mostly. Information, however, is my lifeblood. In the end, Arachna is my city, and that building of yours, standing proud and tall in the dead center of it, is something of a blight at the moment, no offense."

Eric stood from the chair and walked to the large window, lifting the blinds to look out at the city—a brighter, happier city than Arachna, even with the pouring rain. A streak of lightning danced across the sky.

"Besides, I would love to know the secret project your company is working on."

"You're a brazen one," Caleb said.

Eric didn't even look his way, but he held his thumb over the switch to release his blade.

"I might be willing to consider your deal... You said you were an information dealer?"

Eric turned around to answer then tensed as four guards rushed into the room, pistols pointed at him. Yelling ensued as the men ordered Eric onto the floor.

"I'm about to answer this nice man, fellas," Eric responded calmly.

Two of the men inched closer. A few steps farther, and they would have to meet his blade. He had to be quick. He couldn't afford to ruin this deal after gaining Caleb's interest.

"Yes, I am an information dealer. I can tell you nearly anything and everything that happens in Arachna, past, present, and sometimes future. That being said, I'm sure you can understand that having Landreau Corp in my city and not knowing much about it is frustrating." Eric darted his eyes at a guard that was too close for comfort. His finger twitched. If he took so much as one step closer, Eric would have to do something.

But Caleb held a hand up, halting the guards in their place and granting Eric no small amount of relief. "So you know about the murders in Arachna? Malcolm and Daniel Landreau?"

Murders? How did he know they were murdered? Eric clenched his cane tighter and cleared his throat. He had no other choice than to play along.

"I do, indeed. Our news stations would have us believe they were accidents, but my information says otherwise. I offer my sincerest sympathies."

"They were my brothers," Caleb said, his voice catching.

Eric choked on his sharp intake of air. A flash of lightning masked his shocked expression. He wiped it away before Caleb noticed, his heart skipping a beat. A *third* Landreau brother? Since when? *Why didn't I know about this?*

"Brothers?" Eric asked before he could stop himself. "I thought there were only two Landreau brothers."

"Only one, now," Caleb said. "Malcolm never did drugs, and the police claim his body went missing from the morgue. Daniel left this city without a word to me, only to die in a gas explosion? It's too coincidental. I want the culprit found."

Caleb's appearance shifted. No longer was he unreadable. At this moment, he was just a man with two tragic losses weighing him down. A man burning with rage and sadness. The window of opportunity opened, and Eric dove in without a second thought.

"Easy," Eric said. "I can find the culprit and bring them to you. Or, if you prefer, I can kill the bastard myself—whatever your pick. In exchange for all I offer, I want to be a part of your company. That means a percentage of your profit and access to information. For example, oh, I don't know..." Eric rubbed his chin. "Perhaps a secret drug that's shrouded in mystery. Oh, I'm just dying to know, Caleb."

Eric scratched his nose, and the guard closest to him twitched. If this went south, he would go down first. Eric's finger rested on the release for his blade. Even now, as Caleb seemed to be mulling it over, Eric planned his route to the fire escape should his contingency become necessary.

"What concerns me about this deal is your desire to access classified information. A percentage of profits is negotiable if your services prove useful. But I'll offer you this, Eric. You bring me the person who murdered my brothers, alive, and I'll give you all the information you want about the new drug we're creating... *only* this drug. If the murderer is unharmed and I get my chance at revenge, I may even allow you to see it for yourself. If you continue to prove trustworthy, then I'll allow you more and more information as you gain trust within this company." Caleb spoke with anticipation. He wanted to know who killed his brothers. He wanted to wrap his hand around that person's throat and squeeze until they went still.

Eric's head spun. He was so close he could taste it. "That sounds fair enough."

Caleb's posture relaxed. "Then it seems we're in agreement." Something like realization crossed his face, a look similar to Lance's when he'd agreed to join Eric's organization.

The guards lowered their weapons.

"Tell me, Eric, when can you have the murderer brought here?"

Eric kept his smile and straightened his posture. Every movement was important here. "It takes time to find someone guilty of crimes of this caliber. I have a long list of connections in my city, but you have to understand that I cannot simply produce a murderer as easily as a cup of coffee."

Caleb nodded. "I suppose you're right."

Eric looked out the window to the city of Agni. The rain was picking up, the steady rhythm of the droplets hitting the window like hundreds of small drums. Lightning flashed again, and a clap of thunder followed.

"Well," Caleb said, "I suppose you should be going." He stood and extended his hand. "Thank you for your time." He stood patiently as Eric walked over to him.

"First," Eric said when they came face to face, "do we have a deal?"

Caleb met Eric's eyes. "Deal."

Eric grinned and took his hand. A small rumble of thunder vibrated the windows. Eric opened his mouth to thank him for his time, but Caleb's grip tightened on his hand. Uncomfortable, at first, then painful. Eric ignored it and tried to speak again, but Caleb's other hand wrapped around his throat.

Caleb stood and squeezed Eric's neck then slammed him down on the table. The wood cracked beneath Eric's weight, and pain tore through his back.

Eric's cane slipped out of his hand. He clawed at Caleb's face, his eyes, anything. Fear settled in, then horror. He couldn't escape. His legs kicked and kicked at Caleb's body, but the man didn't flinch. Pressure built in his head, and his thoughts ran wild with nothing but his brain shouting at him to do something before his neck snapped. If he were to let himself be killed now, it would all be for nothing. Caleb shoved him farther into the broken table. Splinters dug into Eric's back.

Eric stopped reaching for Caleb's face and instead reached for his tie. He scrambled for it and pulled. His lungs screamed and moaned for him to fill them with air, and his chest ached and contracted. His body writhed, every bone, muscle, nerve, telling him to just breathe.

Breathe.

Suddenly, Caleb released his grip on Eric's neck. He pinned him down, shoving him farther into the splinters.

Eric gasped for air. His head ached. His back ached. Hell, *everything* ached.

Sweet air, Eric thought. *Sweet, sweet air.*

Caleb leaned down to Eric's ear. "*Murderer!*" Caleb spat. "How dare you come in here and pretend like you didn't kill my brothers!" His voice cracked. "I can't believe you had the gall to come into *my* building, threaten *my* people." His voice cracked again, but it sounded odd, almost… distorted.

Eric continued gasping, filling his body with much-needed air. He tried to speak, but he couldn't. Bile rose in his throat, and his stomach turned. The guards were surely still in the room, watching his life flicker out beneath the hands of their boss. That they could all see him like this sent a wave of rage crashing through him.

"I will ensure that you disappear off the face of the earth, and our company will continue to prosper. And since you mentioned Arachna, I may just do a bit of investigating, and I'll have every single person that aided you murdered in the street. But unlike you, I'll do a better job of covering my tracks."

"Wh-" Eric tried to speak, his voice hoarse. "Who snitched?"

Caleb gave a deep, throaty laugh. "You wouldn't believe me if I told you."

Eric looked Caleb in the eyes. They were dark purple, almost *glowing* purple. The veins in his arms and neck bulged and glowed, matching his eyes in color. Eric looked up at the guards, all just standing there, waiting patiently for Caleb to finish his business.

"You know what?" Caleb said, grabbing Eric's neck once more. "I won't tell you a thing about our project."

Eric felt pressure on his neck once again, slower this time. Caleb was savoring it.

"But I think I'll show you instead. Give you one little glimpse of what you want before I crush you into ash." Caleb's veins and eyes glowed brighter, and he slammed Eric into the table again. More splinters, like needles, pierced his back.

Eric kicked off his boot then his sock.

Caleb didn't seem to notice. Eric used his free hand to lazily push on Caleb, to make it seem like he was giving up, like he wasn't trying to grab his cane between his toes. When he had the cane in the grasp of his other hand, he danced his fingers along the body until he found the small latch. He fumbled with it, then the latch came loose. The cold steel of the blade touched Eric's finger, and he unsheathed it.

Then he plunged it into Caleb's neck.

Caleb's eyes widened, and his mouth opened in shock. Eric gasped for air once more as Caleb's grip loosened. Purple blood sputtered out of his neck and onto Eric. A sweet smell filled the room. Sickeningly sweet, like honey. His stomach turned again.

Caleb's body crumpled to the floor unceremoniously. Shouting ensued, and gunfire filled the room. Eric rolled over the side of the table, grabbing the case lying next to him. Money scattered all over the floor, and bullets whizzed past him.

Eric tore out the bottom of the case and grabbed the small device within, flipping open the plastic cover and pressing the button. An eerie roar rumbled beneath him, much worse than any clap of thunder. An explosion—several explosions.

Eric sighed as the building shook. A sigh of disappointment and relief. He looked from under the table at the guards losing their balance.

"A bit above your pay grade, don't you think, boys?" Eric asked, trying to raise his hoarse voice above the shouting. "That was the sound of three bombs going off. If you don't get out now, you'll die."

The men didn't move, didn't speak. Eric put his sock and boot back on and crawled out from under the table, peeking at them over the splintered wood.

Each of the guards matched Caleb's glowing purple veins and eyes. They looked dead… until they took aim and shot their pistols. Eric ducked as gunfire rang out. Bullets perforated the window closest to him. Then he heard clicking.

They were out of ammo.

Eric laughed and stood.

Almost in sync, they dropped their guns and drew batons. Eric groaned and put a hand to his pounding head. He leaned down and ripped the blade from Caleb's neck, frowning in disgust at the purple blood coating it. At the flip of a small switch in the middle of his cane, a scythe flicked out from the bottom and shone with a murderous gleam.

The guards moved gracefully and swiftly, like animals.

Like predators.

One jumped on the table and leapt at Eric.

Eric shoved both blades into the guard's chest as he landed on him, his already-aching back creaking and screaming. He shoved the corpse off and rolled to his feet, catching his breath and wincing through the pain. One guard was standing in front of him. The other two rounded the table to position themselves behind him.

Eric backed toward the wall, waiting for them to strike. The two flanking him swung their batons. Eric slipped between them and planted his blade into one's neck, leaving it there. He ducked under the swing of the next guard and spun, slicing his scythe across his throat. Blood splattered against the window.

The final guard swatted the scythe out of Eric's hand. Eric blocked the next strike of the man's baton, grabbed his arm, and swung him into the perforated window. It cracked from the weight. Before the guard could regain his composure, Eric's foot connected with his chest and shoved him through the glass. His body shattered the window, and he plummeted to the concrete below.

Out of breath, needles of pain piercing down his spine, Eric picked his scythe off the ground and pulled his dagger out of the neck of the guard. He wiped the blades against the man's clothes until most of the purple was gone.

"What just happened?" Eric asked no one, sheathing his blades and rubbing his sore neck. He coughed. Even swallowing sent a shock of pain down his throat. Rain blew in from the broken window, and the cold air sent a chill down his aching back. It ached even more as he tried to walk. He needed to get out of there before anymore guards came. The bombs would serve as a good distraction at best. That gave him time, but not much if the rest of the guards were glowing like that. Smoke flooded the hallway. Eric shoved his questions to the back of his mind, at least for now. He stepped out of the room and kept low to avoid breathing in the smoke. As he rounded the corner of the hallway, a groan emanated from the meeting room.

Eric turned slowly, his jaw dropping when Caleb appeared in the doorway, his neck wound still open and gushing purple blood.

"ERIC!" he yelled at the top of his lungs, his body covered in purple blood. His veins glowed even brighter.

Fear surged through Eric, and his hand went to his throat, the soreness not yet dissipated.

"I'll kill you for this!"

"Can you do it after I get out of here?" Eric yelled back, trying to keep his voice steady. The door leading to the stairway was to his right.

Caleb chuckled, and three guards appeared in the doorway.

The same three Eric had just killed.

"Oh, you've gotta be kidding me," Eric groaned and ran to the door. He swung it open then froze.

Even more guards, all with glowing purple veins and eyes, were bounding up the stairs with pistols in their hands. He saw no way to run past them. *Unless...* The smoke thickened, and beads of sweat slid down his face.

The only way out was up.

Eric dashed up the stairs just as the guards spotted him. Gunshots rang out, echoing throughout the stairway. Eric's ears rang as he flew up the stairs, unable to stay low as he ran, the smoke filling his lungs and the sweat stinging his eyes. More gunshots sounded. Heat ran along his skin where the bullets narrowly missed.

He came to a closed door. He tried to push it open, but the door refused to budge. Eric ran a hand through his hair, breathless. The guards were closing in.

The keys.

Eric fumbled for the keys he'd stolen from the guard at the front.

He tried the first key.

Nothing.

He swore and tried the second one.

Nothing.

He tried the third one, the sound of footsteps encroaching upon him.

Please be the right one, he thought as the lock turned and the door swung open. Smoke billowed from the stairwell. Eric crawled away from it to breathe in the fresh air, coughing and sputtering as he looked around. Rain poured down on him, and he swiped his wet hair out of his face.

Caleb's voice rang out from the stairs as the sound of footsteps closed in. "Don't let him get to the chopper!"

Eric shut the door, locked it, then threw the keys over the side of the building. With a smile, he showed the door his middle finger then looked at the chopper awaiting him. Horror painted the pilot's face. The rotors were already beginning to whirl.

Eric didn't give the pilot the opportunity to snap out of his paralysis and rushed to the chopper, forcing the door open and pointing his cane blade at his neck. "If you want to live, you get us out of here."

The pilot shook his head as if snapping out of a trance then looked down at the blade as if just now noticing it.

Eric had no time. He'd kill the pilot and try to fly it himself if it meant getting away from whatever freak show he'd just encountered.

When the pilot nodded, Eric removed the blade from its threatening position and sheathed it, taking a seat as the pilot prepared the chopper for takeoff. His fingers were a flurry of button presses and switch flipping.

Eric's heart pounded, and he shivered as his rain-soaked clothes clung to his back. None of this made any sense, but he wouldn't bother trying to figure it out, not yet. Instead, he focused on the door and how it shook as the men tried to force it open. At this point, he nearly expected Caleb to phase through it with some other newfound power. He had no plan for how to kill whoever slithered out of there, but he apparently didn't need one as the helicopter rose. The pilot put on his helmet, and his fearful eyes disappeared behind the visor. His exposed neck showed no purple veins. Still, Eric kept an eye on it. If it so much as flashed purple, the man would die instantly.

Even if they were in the air.

The pilot's hands shook, as if he could feel Eric's stare burning into the back of his head.

He needs to calm down if he's going to get us out of here.

Eric glanced at the pilot's nametag. "So, Jeremy, is it?"

"Uh… yes, sir," Jeremy said, his voice shaking.

The helicopter rose off the ground and began its journey away from Landreau Corp. A flash of purple shone on the other side of the door, visible even where Eric was, and then it flew off its hinges. Seconds later, bullets hit the chopper's hull as Caleb stepped out onto the rooftop.

Eric laughed when Caleb took out a knife.

He stopped laughing when Caleb slit his wrists.

Caleb gathered the blood in his hands, and before Eric could even cock his head to the side, a large purple orb of blood floated above Caleb's palm.

The orb shot from Caleb's hands, headed for the chopper.

Jeremy tried to swerve out of the way, but the orb still crashed into the tail rotor. At first, it seemed to do nothing other than leave a stain.

Then it started to glow.

The chopper shook as an explosion destroyed the rotor.

Jeremy swore and screamed as the chopper spun toward the trees outside of the city. He guarded his head with his arms, for all the good that would do.

Eric gripped his seat and yelled, "It was nice knowing you, Jeremy!" He laughed as the pilot's screams worsened, refusing to allow the fear of death to haunt him. If he was going out, it would be with a smile on his face. The helicopter spun mercilessly as it plummeted to the ground. The city and the trees melded together in a blur of gray and green. And then nothing but green.

This had to be it. All that work for nothing.

He was going to die.

I hope you're going to be okay, Lance.

CHAPTER 9
MORE THAN JUST A MIGRAINE

"We came here to ask if you could keep an eye on Landreau Corp," Kaela said.

The chief's eyes flashed, and she shifted her weight. Kaela didn't seem to notice, but she seemed more focused on keeping her own act up.

Lance recognized that look. The first man that mugged him in his early years in the slums had that same look—one of guilt, then resolve. It disappeared from the chief's face as quickly as it appeared.

Maybe he was just seeing things.

Lance kept his eyes on Rotoya, completely still, afraid that any small movement would draw her attention. Kaela was the chief's primary focus. It was for the best if it stayed that way.

"You're asking me to assist in your information racket?" Rotoya asked, incredulous. "Don't I already do enough?"

"I know it's not the usual deal, but I'm sure Eric would be willing to pull some strings and help you find the culprit of your officers' murders."

"Which you seem to think is Landreau Corp. I still find it odd that Eric would send you and this new guy over here to make me an offer. In my experience, Eric has always handled those things himself." She leaned forward. "If I find out that Eric was responsible for murdering my officers, I will have the entirety of my police force cracking down on you." Her voice rose, and she pointed a finger at Kaela. "So you'd better hope—*argh!*"

The chief grasped her head with one hand, leaning on her desk with the other.

Lance exchanged a look with Kaela, and she stood.

"Rotoya?" Kaela said.

Kaela gasped when the chief looked at them. Her eyes were glowing purple, and so were her veins, throbbing and pulsing beneath her skin.

"Kaela…" Lance said, his stomach twisting and his body yelling at him to run. "Please tell me this is normal for her."

"Don't know how to break it to you, Lance," she responded, backing toward the door. Lance did the same. "This is anything *but* normal."

The chief screamed, her voice suddenly deeper.

"Derek!" Kaela screamed as they ran out of the office, only to stop at the door. Every officer in the precinct stared at them, their eyes and veins glowing purple. "DEREK!"

A fire extinguisher flew from the balcony and landed on an officer's head. He crumpled to the ground. Two shots were fired from the balcony, and the extinguisher exploded in a cloud of thick gas. Gunshots rang out from within it.

Lance grabbed Kaela's hand. "Hold your breath."

They sprinted through the cloud of smoke. Lance flinched with every gunshot. His eyes stung and watered, and he could barely see where he was going. An energy electrified the room, and the hair on the back of his neck stood straight. The silhouette of an officer appeared, his gun raised toward the second floor. Lance shoved him aside, and as he fell, a bullet found the cop's chest.

They reached the edge of the cloud as Derek rained down gunfire from the balcony. He leapt down and landed next to Lance.

"What happened in there?" Derek asked.

"We do *not* have time to answer questions right now, Derek!" Kaela yelled.

They reached the exit. Reggie stood in front of the doors, a pistol in his hand. He raised the gun, but Derek fired first, three shots into the chest.

Lance tackled him through the door.

Over the sound of shattering glass, Kaela yelled, "Sorry, Reggie!"

"They've reached the exit. After them!" an officer yelled.

Derek helped Lance to his feet. Lance hissed at his bloodied hands. Before they could run, an officer rushed out of the building and tackled Lance to the ground. His face scraped against the concrete. That familiar calm settled over him as steel pressed against the back of his head. He twisted just in time, and a bullet hit the ground next to him. His ears rang, and heat ran along his cheek. He freed an elbow and sank it into the officer's face. Blood shot from his nose, and before he could retaliate, a silver knife plunged into the officer's neck. Kaela yelled as she pulled him off Lance, purple blood staining her face as she helped him back up.

An empty pistol lay beside Derek's feet, a loaded one in his hand as he shot toward the door. The smoke was clearing.

"We've got to get out of here," Derek called. "I can't cover us forever!"

"We need to split up!" Lance yelled. "You both know where to regroup."

Kaela and Derek nodded, and they all ran in separate directions. Lance didn't know where he would go, but as long as he was alive when he got there, it didn't matter.

The streets were sparse with people screaming and staring at him. Lance had no crowd to dash through to lose the officers, and as he rounded the corner of an alleyway, a bullet hit the wall where his head had been seconds ago.

The alleyway was dark enough to hide behind a nearby trash bin. Another wave of that calm, that... killing calm, washed over Lance, his stomach twisting and turning. The face of that man resurfaced. His pleading eyes, empty of a soul, now staring eternally at nothing and everything. He couldn't allow himself to kill again, not if it meant seeing their faces for the rest of his life.

Lance peeked around the trash can. Two officers eased down the alley, pistols in hand. He swore at the brick wall. His stomach twisted further, and his body readied itself for the coming fight. The whispering became louder, demanding:

Survive.

He tried to muzzle the feeling, but it overwhelmed him, and as one of the officers came close, he kicked the trash bin, sending it wheeling into one of the officers.

Lance slapped the other one's gun out of his hand and rammed him into the wall, harder than he intended. Lance's shoulder stung where it scraped against the brick. The officer's head hit the wall, and purple blood splashed onto the brick. He dropped like a stone.

Lance turned and grabbed the next officer's wrist as he returned to his feet. The officer fired as they slammed against the wall, the bullet shattering the brick. Heat rose along Lance's neck. They struggled, but Lance held firm.

Lance's body moved with ease, barely registering any input from him at all. He struggled and fought for control over it, but it moved without him.

Lance slammed the officer's wrist against the brick, over and over, gunshots popping off, until finally something cracked, and the gun clattered to the ground. The officer yelled in pain, and Lance slammed the man's head against the trash bin. Purple blood splattered against it, and a fleck landed on Lance's cheek. He wiped it off, wondering for a moment if it would infect him.

Lance backed away as the two officers lay groaning on the concrete. Whispers hissed in the back of his mind, and his stomach stirred, as if something were alive within it. It almost seemed angry—angry that he didn't let it kill. Maybe he did have some control over it, after all.

Lance's body moved without his input, leaping behind the bin as a gunshot popped off and a bullet grazed his side. He peeked over to see three more officers with guns pointed, marching down the alleyway.

Lance hissed, pressing his hand against the bleeding wound in his side. It stung and burned where the bullet had grazed. *Too close.*

Shaking himself out of his trance, Lance looked around until he spotted a pistol on the ground. It called to him from only an arm's reach away. *But if I shoot them...* He couldn't afford seeing more faces in his sleep. But as his stomach twisted even more, he knew the men were closing in on him. It was either him or them.

Survive.

Lance moved, and this time, he had full control. Faster than he thought he could, Lance grabbed the gun, nearly losing a finger as a bullet chipped the concrete near his hand.

The calm settled within him once again, and he knew what he had to do, but he hesitated. The gun was heavy, and the grip was warm from its short time in the officer's hands. The whispering grew even louder, like a breathy scream.

Fire. Fire!

Steeling himself, Lance stuck his arm out, closed his eyes, and shot. The knot in his stomach untangled with every pull of the trigger. His hand moved slightly after every few shots, as if the whispering thing was guiding his aim. He fired until the gunshots turned into clicks, barely audible over the ringing in his own ears. He retracted his hand and dropped the pistol, out of breath. The alleyway was silent. The knot in his stomach was gone. He peeked around the trash can. The officers lay on the ground, bullet wounds in their stomachs and chests. They were still.

Lance stared at the pistol, at the bloody grip, then at his own bleeding hands. He had to get out of here. Those shots were sure to attract more officers.

A sweet smell filled the alley, eerily similar to honey.

Nauseous, Lance dashed from the alley and into the next, hoping and praying a bullet wouldn't find his back. As the minutes passed, his hands ached and screamed, and blood trickled from his ear and his side. Every step was more painful than the last.

As the adrenaline wore off, he wondered where Kaela and Derek were and if they were okay. Despite everything, he released a quick request to the sky and whoever resided in it.

Please let them be okay.

CHAPTER 10
HELL'S NOT READY FOR YOU YET

Eric stirred, unsure if he'd crossed over to death's domain or if death had been too scared to allow him in. Heat stung his cheeks, and sweat beaded on his brow. The crackling sound of smoldering embers surrounded him. Surely, he was in hell.

But then he opened his eyes.

He was in the remains of the chopper, and unless the chopper had committed sins of its own, he was still alive.

Laughing hurt, but he did it anyway. Moving hurt worse. His head pounded, and as he straightened himself against his seat, his back popped and crackled. The smell of smoke and burnt metal filled his nose and tainted his lungs. The pilot sat in the seat beside him.

Dead.

His shocked expression was visible behind the broken visor, his empty eyes cast at the thick branch piercing his chest. Behind Eric was nothing but broken trees and embers. The other half of the chopper was missing. The rain had stopped, but not before putting out whatever fire had ignited while Eric was unconscious.

"Thank God for rain."

He drew his attention once more to Jeremy.

"Not a bad landing." Eric chuckled, elbowing the corpse. "Well, for me, at least." Everything hurt as he shifted in the seat and kicked the broken door open enough to crawl out. He slid from his seat onto the cold ground. Sparks shot out from inside the chopper.

Eric inspected himself, and despite the soreness of his body, nothing felt broken. He stood and stretched his back, groaning as it cracked again in several places. He took a step away from the chopper.

A snap sounded from his foot, followed by a wave of pain.

Eric dropped to the ground with a groan.

Okay, maybe one thing's broken, he thought to himself. *Good thing I didn't kick the door with* this *foot.*

Eric picked himself up and swore with every step on his bad foot, grateful for his cane to lean on. "Thanks for the ride, Jeremy. Hope you wanted to be cremated, my friend." He sent a wave back at the corpse.

Eric limped away from the chopper, his body screaming at him to stop moving, to lie down somewhere and rest. But he needed to get back to Arachna and set a plan. First, he would figure out what had happened to Caleb. Those glowing purple veins and that sweet smell—he wondered if that was the result of their new drug, some sort of super serum, maybe?

He shuffled painfully through the forest, searching his mind for any clue as to how a drug could turn a man into a beast. Caleb's men had the same glow, the same purple veins. He'd seen his fair share of crazy things in his life, but *that* was at the top of the list.

But Eric couldn't think about that, not now, not when he had to figure out a way to get back to Arachna. Taking a train wouldn't be safe. Caleb's men could be waiting for him.

A disguise? Eric thought. *No, too risky. I could always steal a car. Not very classy or creative, but it should do.* Eric's leg screamed in pain. He would've kissed his cane for its assistance if it weren't covered with purple blood.

He soldiered on until he reached the outskirts of the city, his eyes scanning his surroundings as he found the nearest alley to hide and rest. The warmth of the burning chopper was preferable to the cold dampness of the alley. No screams or panicked sounds polluted the air. In the distance, though, the sirens of fire trucks and police cars sang. He couldn't have been out for very long if they still hadn't arrived at the site. Eric leaned his head against the brick wall. The pain worsened as the adrenaline faded, and he winced and hissed through his teeth at every movement.

I need to bring pain meds with me the next time I pull a stunt like this. Eric breathed through the pain, scanning each end of the alleyway for any sign of Caleb's goons. Now that he considered his circumstances, he realized that getting back to Arachna would take much longer than he'd hoped. At least Lance was in charge. Eric had a feeling about him. A feeling deep down that he knew what he was doing, and that when Eric returned to his kingdom, everything would be under control.

"Everything is *so* out of control!" Lance yelled as Kaela and Derek sat quietly on their beds while he paced the floor of their hideout. "What *was* that? Since when does the police chief have *glowing purple veins*?!" The shout stung his bullet wound, wrapped tightly in gauze from a first-aid kit Derek had stolen from the precinct.

"Calm down," Kaela said, rubbing her temples. "We're safe right now. We just need to figure out what's going on. Burning a line in the floor and screaming isn't going to help us."

"Oh," Derek said, his eyes widening as he lifted the back of his shirt and removed two rolled-up sheets of paper from his pants. "Almost forgot in all the madness." He crouched next to his bed and flattened out the pages.

"What's that?" Lance asked, glaring at the layouts and marks all over the pages. Dots and circles were peppered across the drawn lines.

"Blueprints." Derek smoothed out the creases in the paper and sighed. "Of Landreau Corp. It's definitely a layout of some of its floors." He pointed at the bottom of the page, where it said just that: *Landreau Corp Arachna—Main Floor.*

"Why?" Kaela tilted her head. "I wonder what those marks are."

"Maybe Eric will know when he comes back… I wonder if he's okay.

We haven't heard any word from him, and my scouts at the edge of the city haven't seen any sign of him."

"I guess..." Lance stopped to take a deep breath, suppressing the frustration clutching his chest.

Rotoya was right. Eric had left them all to handle the consequences of his actions while he went to negotiate with Landreau Corp, unless he'd lied about that too and had already fled the country.

But when Lance opened his mouth to remind Derek of that blatant fact, he only said, "I guess we'll just have to wait for him." He would let Derek figure it out for himself, if he hadn't already and was just in denial.

"I can go out and track him down," Derek said, standing. "I know how to get into Agni. I could make it there on foot in a day if I'm quick, and—"

"I don't think that's such a good idea." Lance crossed his arms and glanced at the entrance, halfway expecting the chief to be standing there. That sweet smell still clung to the inside of his nose, and nausea picked at him with every breath. "We need you more than ever right now. You're the reason we managed to escape the precinct." He rubbed his eyes. "Besides, we don't know what it's like out there. Even if you wait until night and try to sneak out, they may have officers patrolling all over the city for us. You'd just be putting yourself in danger for no reason. If Eric's fine, he'll be back. If he's not, then there's no point wasting time to go get him."

Kaela blinked. "He's right. That's probably the most leaderlike thing you've ever said."

Lance eyed her expression for any sign of a wry smile, but none appeared as she grimaced at her broken nails then back down at the papers.

Derek threw his arms up in defeat and returned to his place beside the bed. "Well, if we don't do something, then we're sitting ducks. If the chief has the whole police force looking for us, then it's only a matter of time before we get caught. And waiting for Eric to get back isn't good enough, especially if he's dead." He shook his head. "I think he bit off much more than he can chew this time."

"Well, Eric will just have to deal with it for now. We need to focus on our own survival for the time being," Lance said.

Kaela hummed at the computer. "I suppose I could try emailing Amari to bring us some extra supplies." She stretched. "While I'm at it, I'll email the rest of my Roses and tell them to shut down for now. Except the one on Main Street. I'll leave that open in case we get any good info."

"Wouldn't that be suspicious, one of your friends coming to an abandoned building?"

"Unless she brings a man with her," Derek said. "Like Rob. A man and a woman slinking off to an empty building can be written off easily in this city."

A smile tugged at Lance's lips. "Then it's settled. Kaela, email Amari to meet with Rob. Tell them to come here with the supplies we need. We'll make a list."

"I'll tell you where she can meet him," Derek said, following Kaela to the computer.

Lance's worry eased for now. Even so, as long as they were stuck in this city, they weren't safe. He scratched the back of his neck as he eyed the blueprints and wondered just where Eric was.

Likely sipping wine in some luxury apartment while we suffer in here.

Eric opened his eyes, disoriented. The smell of trash and rat droppings assaulted his senses, and the events of before came flooding back: Caleb, the helicopter crash, the pain. He groaned as he lifted his pants leg, revealing the bruised and swollen ankle. He tried to move it, but it screamed in response.

A glance at the sky told him he hadn't been out for any longer than an hour. The cold of the brick wall pierced into his back, or maybe it was just the splinters. As he tried to stand, his ears perked. He heard voices. Two men.

The first voice spoke. "That crash was pretty bad. This guy can't be so hard to find, can he?"

The second scoffed. “I can’t believe he survived it, honestly. I’ve never seen Caleb so angry. I wonder what this guy said to him.”

Eric peeked around the trash can, the darkness hiding him in its cloak. The men were dressed in black uniforms, both with pistols holstered. Their veins weren’t glowing, and the alley was too dark to tell if they were purple or not. Leaning back against the wall, Eric shut his eyes and cursed. He rubbed at his sore neck and wished for his revolver to appear inside of his coat. He had no more explosives on him.

He forced himself to move from his sitting position, wincing from the pain. He sat on his good leg, readying himself.

The men approached, and Eric slipped his blade from its sheath. Its whine was faint and deadly. Eric held his breath as the two men walked past him. Darkness was kind and hid him well. They spoke of where they were to search next, and Eric made a mental note to avoid that direction.

Eric smiled as he rose, leaning on his cane. Then with the flip of a switch, it became a scythe. He hesitated for a breath then plunged the dagger into the neck of the first man.

The second gasped, but Eric thrust his cane upward, the scythe impaling him through his neck before he could scream.

Eric grabbed the gun from the man’s hand as he fell to the ground and choked on his own blood. He wiped his blades clean and sheathed them, checking his new pistol for ammo. He grabbed the magazine from the other man’s pistol and limped out of the alley, sunlight warming his cold back.

Despite the pain, Eric kept his smile.

Nostalgia crept up on him, surfacing memories of his childhood here in Agni: fleeing and slinking through the streets, stealing food and money any chance he got, the thrill of being chased by a policeman or having to fight a thug he’d been caught pickpocketing. This was his true element—the sneaking, the fighting, the surviving. It felt good. The pain in his leg even reminded him of the many times he’d had to make do and patch himself up. At that time, he knew nothing of black-market doctors. How ignorant he’d been so long ago.

Eric shimmied into a small space between two buildings.

Something was familiar about this spot, and Eric's smile grew as he slid through another narrow space to a small alley.

A large crate sat in the corner.

Eric moved it and scanned for a familiar patch of wall, slightly more discolored than the rest. With a hearty kick of his good leg, the patch of wall fell inward.

For all he knew, the man that had once resided here was no longer around, but either way, having a place to hide from Caleb's men was a godsend.

Eric went prone and crawled through the open space. Then he stood in the dark and moved the patch of wall back into place. He patted the spot and chuckled. "Sorry for stealing your tricks, old man."

Darkness overtook him. The cold bit at his skin and even more so at his ankle.

A distant light broke the darkness enough for Eric to climb down a set of stairs ahead. With an audible groan, Eric stumbled down each step, his cane taking most of the weight for his bad leg. The light emanated from a room at the bottom, brighter the closer he approached.

Eric reached the bottom of the stairs and took a breather before knocking on the rusted metal door. He smiled at the sound of movement on the other side. The smell of peroxide permeated the air, and water dripped onto the concrete in a steady rhythm. The door opened, and a tired old face looked at him. For a moment, no recognition showed in his aging eyes, but then they sparkled.

"Eric?" the man asked, grinning.

"Hey, Doc," Eric said with his own grin. If he'd still had his hat, he would've tipped it. There was no telling where that thing was since the crash. "Got a bit banged up. Think you could help an old friend?"

The doctor laughed. "Of course, Eric. Come on in. Ah, I almost didn't recognize you with that new hair color." He took another glance at it. "Blond just doesn't suit you. You should go back to black."

Eric closed the door behind him. "No chance, George."

"So what are you doing here? I thought you were in Arachna now. Don't tell me you had something to do with that helicopter crash."

George laughed, but when Eric didn't respond, his smile disappeared. "Wait, *did* you have something to do with the crash?"

Eric opened his mouth to ask how he knew when a small television in the corner of the room caught his eye, an image of the broken helicopter placed right next to a reporter.

"Eh, not really. Though I was a passenger on it at the time."

George scanned him up and down, taking in the bruises and cuts, and sat down in his chair for support. "You're telling me you survived a helicopter crash with nothing more than scrapes and bruises?"

"And a broken foot, I think. I just need some pain meds and a place to sleep for the night, and I'll be on my way."

George burst into laughter again. "Now that's the Eric I know. Surviving all of that, I figured it'd catch up to you one day. Alright, you mentioned your leg, so come here and let me look at it."

Eric presented his leg, suppressing a wince as George examined it.

"Can you walk on it?" George asked, his tone suddenly professional.

Eric cleared his throat. "Yeah, but it hurts pretty bad. Made a nice little crunch when I first stepped on it."

"And I said your cane was useless when you first got it."

"You gotta be stylish sometimes, Doc. Never thought my wonderful fashion sense would save my life."

George finished examining the leg before he relinquished it. He stood and turned toward his table.

Eric squinted at the bright light bulb hanging from the ceiling. "You really need better lighting."

George chuckled. "Well, I need better everything, but on my budget, I have to make do."

Eric shook his head and rubbed his sore throat, ignoring the nausea. "So give it to me straight, Doc. How bad is it?"

"Pretty badly sprained, for sure. I'll give you a brace, disinfect those cuts, then I'll look at your bruised neck there."

"Once you're done with that, I think you should check my back too."

"You got it."

"You're the best, Doc," Eric said with a smile.

George chuckled. "Tell me something I don't know."

The silence in the hideout hung over them like a fog. Kaela leaned back in the computer chair, spinning it around as she stared at the ceiling. Derek sat beside the open door of the entrance.

Lance sat on the other side of the door, twiddling his thumbs and listening for any noises. They couldn't wait upstairs in case they were seen, and Kaela had decided against revealing how to get into the hideout in her email. They couldn't risk it. They were foxes in a foxhole, just waiting to be burned out by the hunters.

Lance sighed and fantasized about his store. His bed and his TV awaited him in that back room, and so did his potential business.

"Lance, I mean this respectfully, but can you please stop sighing?" Derek asked.

Lance released another sigh. Derek glared at him.

"Sorry," Lance said. "I can't help it… I just can't stand sitting in one spot for so long. I have to move." He rubbed his hands together and blew on them, the cold of the hideout suddenly worse than usual.

"Before we met, you were working behind the desk of a store all day. What difference does this make?" Kaela asked.

Lance rolled his eyes. "Um, maybe because in my store I wasn't waiting for somebody to come in and kill me." He paused. "Actually… let me rephrase that. I wasn't being *hunted* by anyone."

Derek nodded. "That's fair."

Lance ignored the look on Kaela's face and kept staring at his thumbs. Kaela turned her head toward the computer screen, probably rereading the email Amari had sent back. Lance reviewed the response in his head:

Consider it done. I'll meet up with Rob and bring everything you requested. Muah. ;)

. . .

Just hearing from Amari had put Kaela in a better mood. One less thing to worry about. Now she seemed worried about the one Rose left open.

Lance imagined the chief barging into the Rose. Whether they would arrest everyone or kill them on the spot was the question that worried him. He could only imagine the worry tormenting Kaela.

Lance leaned his head back against the wall, his eyes closed. "So, what did you do before you worked for Eric?"

Derek asked, "Are you directing that question to me or Kaela?"

At the sound of her name, Kaela stared at them both for a moment before returning her gaze to the screen.

"You," Lance said to Derek. "You told me you had a bad past, but I have no idea what you actually did before you met Eric."

Derek shook his head. "We really shouldn't be talking while listening for Rob and Amari."

"Then we'll stop talking the second we hear something," Lance said. "Come on, I'm curious."

Derek shook his head again and rubbed the bridge of his nose then looked up at the concrete ceiling. "I was an assassin."

Lance nodded. "I guess that makes sense." He considered Derek's ability to fight, his quiet footsteps, his proficiency with weapons… the perfect condition he'd left Lance's store in when he kidnapped him. "How… many people have you killed?"

Derek crossed his arms. "Too many."

"Well, what kind of people did you—"

"It doesn't matter. I don't do that kind of work anymore."

A fog of tension clouded the room, dark and gloomy.

"Well… what did you do in your free time, then?" Lance asked in a desperate attempt to change the subject.

"Read books. Went to shooting ranges. Snuck around the city and explored. That was before I met Eric."

"I remember you took me to the shooting range once," Kaela chimed in. "It was fun."

Lance raised an eyebrow. "Were you any good?"

"Not at first, but Derek taught me some tricks."

"She's not a half-bad shot, either," Derek said.

The silence returned, and Lance squirmed under it. "You said that was before you met Eric. What do you do for fun now?"

"About the same. I do practice mixing drinks more. Look for good recipes."

Lance chortled. "I can just imagine you hunched over a computer, looking for good recipes."

Kaela giggled. "That's cute."

Derek crossed his arms, a small smile crawling across his lips. "Yeah, yeah, laugh it up. But Kaela knows better than anybody that I make a mean drink."

Kaela held a finger up. "He tells the truth."

"If I drank, I'd put that to the test," Lance said. When Kaela and Derek went quiet, he realized his mistake. "Shit."

"You don't drink?" Kaela asked. "*How*?"

Derek cocked his head. "Why not? Have you ever tried it?"

Lance grimaced. *No going back now.* "I did try it. I liked it… a little too much. It got to a point where I couldn't stop. I nearly died one night and decided that maybe it was better for me to take a break… That break hasn't ended yet."

It was an understatement. Truthfully, that night still returned to him on occasion in the form of a nightmare. He still remembered the vomit all over the floor. The shaking and sweating. Slipping in and out of consciousness. His fingers turning blue and his heart palpitating. His body jerking and twitching uncontrollably. Not knowing where he was or remembering his own name. He didn't know how he'd survived that night.

Derek opened his mouth again, but before any words came out, a female voice rang out from above.

"Kaela?"

Derek tensed.

Kaela stood from the chair and whispered, "That sounds like Amari, for sure."

Then another voice spoke. "Derek?"

Derek relaxed and climbed up the ladder.

The hatch slid open, then Lance heard hushed voices.

The ladder creaked as Derek climbed down first. Following behind was Rob, wearing a tuxedo and carrying a cello case over his shoulder. Then behind him, Amari, wearing a sleeveless red dress and a coin purse to match.

"Were you followed?" Lance asked, staring at the cello case.

Rob ripped the bowtie from his neck and tossed it down with a scowl. "If I were being followed, I wouldn't have come here. I hate formal clothing." He set the case down. "Nice to see you again, Lance. What'd you think of your new store?" He reached out to shake Lance's hand then frowned. "Sorry, forgot."

Lance smiled. "It was more than I could have asked for."

"Well, I'm glad to hear that. Shame you haven't had much time to spend in it." Rob looked at Derek. "Everything you asked for is in there, plus some extra little gifts."

Derek rifled through the cello case. He took out a slim metal case then a healthy sum of cash, two pistols, and clothes.

"What's this?" Lance asked, holding up a brick-shaped object.

"C-4," Derek said.

Lance dropped the explosive back into the case, a shock of fear crossing his chest.

Derek sighed. "Kaela." He held up a bottle of wine.

Kaela gasped with a smile on her face, as if she had been presented with a puppy. She glided to Derek and snatched the bottle.

Derek sounded exasperated as he held out a wine opener. "You'll need this."

Kaela took it and opened the bottle, giving it a small kiss before taking a long swallow. She handed the bottle to Amari to get a sip of her own. "I didn't even ask for any," Kaela said.

Amari took a long sip. "I know my best friend. I asked Rob to bring one."

Rob scoffed. "By *asked*, she means *threatened*."

Kaela took the bottle back and sipped from it, then hesitated. She looked at Lance. "Is it okay that…" She pointed at the bottle.

Lance hid his frown. Kaela and Derek knowing was one thing, but he couldn't accept Rob and Amari knowing too. "Yeah, it's fine."

"Great." Kaela took a long swig from the bottle.

Lance shook his head as Derek put the money back in the cello case and opened the slim metal one, revealing a disassembled sniper rifle. It took seconds for him to put it together. Lance wondered how many times he'd done that. How many people had died at the other end of Derek's barrel—how many innocent people?

"How are things out there?" Lance asked Rob as Kaela sipped on her wine and Derek looked through the scope of the rifle.

"Weird, to say the least. The chief has already announced you all as public enemy number one. She claims that you tried to assassinate her at the precinct. Cop cars are on every street corner, and police are patrolling the street. The suit ended up being useless. They were searching bags, so I had to take to the rooftops. Amari managed to slip by on the street, and we met up here. I swear it looks like martial law out there." He rubbed the back of his neck. "That's not all, though. The cops look… weird."

"Glowing purple veins?" Derek interjected.

Rob stuttered. "I-I don't know. They were wearing heavy-duty armor. Like this crazy black armor that makes them look like special… forces—I'm sorry, did you say *glowing purple veins*?"

"Any update on Eric?"

"Nothing, but I have reports that there was an explosion at Landreau Corp's corporate building in Agni and a crashed helicopter in the nearby woods. There are a lot of men patrolling Agni, as well. Whether police or Landreau Corp's private military, I don't know. But what I do know is that they're wearing the same armor." He rubbed the back of his neck again, his expression suddenly nervous. "Also… the police are stationed at the edges of the city. I had to ask the men to stand down and go into hiding. In other words… I don't think even Eric will be able to get back into the city unless he has one hell of a disguise."

Derek shook his head. "Well, thanks for trying, Rob. If you somehow manage to find him, give him a pager and tell him to meet us here."

"Yes, sir," Rob said. "I know it's not my place to ask, but… what happened to the police? And… seriously, I can't get over this vein thing."

Derek placed the rifle on his bed. "I don't know. I couldn't find anything regarding this new armor or their veins. But if it is Landreau Corp's men patrolling Agni and they have the same armor as our police…"

Lance waited for Derek to finish the sentence, but he never did.

Rob ruffled his hair, removed his blazer, and partially unbuttoned his shirt. "I'll keep an eye out for Eric, and I'll continue to update you with what's happening outside. Keep the case. I don't need the suspicion drawn to me." He looked at Amari, happily sipping wine with Kaela. "Amari. Mess up your appearance, and I'll take you home."

Amari removed her earrings and put them in her coin purse, messed up her hair, and took her heels off, holding them carefully in her hand.

"Now, let's go," Rob said.

Amari pulled Kaela into a tight embrace then followed Rob back up the ladder. Derek wished them good luck.

"I hope that girl stays safe," Kaela said after a few minutes and a few more gulps of wine. She spun her chair around slowly. "But a skilled thief like her? She'll be fine."

Derek counted the money, his pager beside him, as if he expected Eric to send a message at any moment.

"At least we have fresh clothes now," Lance said.

"You two go ahead and change. I'll go last," Derek said then continued whispering the amount of money to himself as he counted each bill.

Kaela curled into a ball in the chair, bottle of wine still in hand. "I'm pretty content right about now."

"I wonder why."

"Why are you counting it, anyway?" Kaela asked. "You know it's from *my* safe, right? You even saw me type the amount."

"Making sure it's all there." He counted the last bill and placed the stack in the case. "Which it is."

"You think Rob would've stolen from you?" Lance asked.

"Nah, he and Rob are best friends. He probably thinks Amari stole some." Kaela laughed, setting the bottle on the computer desk. "She *could*, mind you, but she and I have this little thing we like to call trust."

"You can never be too careful," Derek responded like it was nothing.

Silence fell upon them. The only sound that broke through was the creaking of the office chair as Kaela spun it back and forth. Lance stared at the rifle on the bed. He saw that man's face behind his eyelids, and he wondered how many faces Derek saw. Dozens? *How does he sleep at night?*

Lance stared down at the palms of his injured hands, then his arms, as if expecting his own veins to be purple. His head spun with questions. What was this calm that came over him when he was in danger? Why could he fight so well when it settled over him? The question most prominent in his mind sent a chill through him.

Has Eric known about this all along? And how? Eric himself said something was special about him, and Kaela and Derek only mimicked the thought after seeing him fight. Lance grimaced. Eric knew so much.

Lance shook himself out of his own head. Kaela was fast asleep, cozied up in the chair like a cat, her already half-drunk bottle of wine on the desk. Derek was also nodding off, leaning against the wall with his arms crossed.

Lance stared at the ladder through the open metal door. With all the supplies in here, he could easily steal some and go off on his own. He'd survived by himself for this long, and in the slums, no less. He could pack up a pistol, some food, and some clothes and get out of this ruined city. It would be hard, but no harder than being a fugitive.

He took a step toward the entrance, but a knot formed in his stomach. Something inside him halted his steps, and he looked back at Kaela and Derek.

Lance flipped the light switch, plunging the room into darkness. It wouldn't matter if he left with all the supplies in the world. He would have to get past the officers if he wanted out of the city. Even with the killing calm, he didn't know how many officers he would have to face.

Besides, could he really leave Kaela and Derek behind to die?

Would they leave me if they had the chance?

Something told him they wouldn't.

Lance sighed at the string lights wrapped around the light switch then climbed up the creaky ladder. He wouldn't leave. As loyal as Derek was, and even Kaela, he wouldn't leave. They hadn't left him yet, after all.

Maybe one day, they could emerge from their hideout, the rats they'd become, and regain whatever semblance of a normal life they had. Lance smiled at the prospect.

He clambered out of the cooler, rubbing his hands together. He wandered the vast garage, his thoughts bouncing off the walls. *Alone, at last.* He'd told them about his… problem. Saying the words out loud had hurt. He hadn't even mentioned the other substances. He wouldn't, either, as long as he could avoid another slip of the tongue.

"Trouble sleeping?"

Lance jumped. "Son of a bitch, Derek!" He put a hand to his chest, his heart racing. "Don't sneak up on me like that."

Derek leaned against the cooler, crossing his arms. He chuckled. "Sorry."

"What are you doing up here?"

"Came to check on you."

Lance avoided his eyes. "I wasn't leaving."

"I didn't think you were."

Lance joined Derek, leaning next to him on the cooler. "Good, 'cause I wasn't."

"What's on your mind, Lance?"

Lance shifted uncomfortably. "I smiled when I killed that man, Derek."

"The one on the hill?"

Lance nodded. "Why?"

"Hard to say… Killing isn't simple. It's messy."

"Can I ask you something?"

"Go ahead."

The words hesitated to escape Lance's mouth. "When did you decide to become a… assassin?"

Derek closed his eyes for a moment. "Well, I didn't *decide* to become one. It just…" He rubbed his face. "Life has a way of throwing opportunities at you when you're at your worst. When… you don't feel like you have any other choice but to take them. Sometimes, those opportunities aren't ideal."

"Hell, you're preaching to the choir," Lance muttered. "What happened?"

Derek sighed. "I was a teenager. My mom was poor and had a lot of debt. I wanted to get some money to help, and the part-time job sure as hell wasn't cutting it. So I started selling drugs. That was good for a while, but I wasn't satisfied. I didn't think the debt was getting paid off fast enough, so I searched for a quicker way to make money. And it was then that I started gambling. I was good at it, too… really good."

"Did you make a lot of money?"

"Oh yeah." Derek grew a smile. "One night, I got on this huge winning streak. You wouldn't believe the amount of money I won that night. I probably could have gone on longer, but the manager started eyeballing me, and I wasn't exactly of age to be there in the first place. I knew he'd kick me out if I got any more. So that was that. I got my money, left the casino with dollar signs in my eyes, and looked up from my bag full of cash straight into the barrel of a revolver."

"Whoa."

"I don't think I'd ever really seen one before. I'd seen shotguns and rifles, but something like that pointed right in my face was the scariest thing I'd ever experienced. I barely even heard him ask for my money. I just… stood there, my grip tight on that money bag. He knew what he wanted. The gun wasn't shaking in the slightest. He'd done it before. I couldn't even look around, but I knew no one could see. I was in a dark area outside the casino, and everyone else was either drunk or unable to see what was going on."

After a moment of silence, Lance asked, "What happened?"

Derek stared at the ground. "I killed him… I don't know how, but… next thing I knew, the gun was in my hand. I watched this man gurgle and spit up blood as he faded away to hell. Everyone screamed when they heard the gunshot."

"You don't remember killing him?"

"Oh, I definitely remember killing him, just not how. I got scared. I went back to my house, sneaked into my room through the window, dropped the money bag, and left. I never saw my mom again."

"Why did you leave?"

"Like I said, I was scared. I was a sixteen-year-old kid, covered in blood, with a revolver in my hand. It took me a few days just to let go of it. I ran away because I was scared she'd get in trouble for what I did. I realize now that it was a stupid thing to think, and I shouldn't have left, but… well, by the time I realized, it was too late to go back."

"Why didn't you go back?"

"I couldn't face her after what I did. She already suspected the money I was getting wasn't legitimate."

"You should go see her one day."

Derek shook his head. "For all I know, she'll spit in my face the moment she sees me, for abandoning her."

"You don't know that, Derek."

"I don't, but I don't want to risk it… Besides, I still keep tabs on her. Word is she got remarried and has another kid. She's doing okay for herself, now. I don't want to ruin that for her."

"What'd you do after you ran away?"

"I fell into a pretty dark moment in my life. I had no money, I was drinking water from puddles in the ground, and I was emaciated. I fell in with a gang… They fed me, paid me. All I had to do was kill rival gang members for them. I got good at it. I left shortly after and went independent, took contracts for whoever needed somebody offed. I did a good job of it, too. From then on, I just… killed. Good or bad, man or woman—didn't matter to me. If it paid well, I did it."

"Then you met Eric."

"Then I met Eric." Derek pursed his lips.

The room returned to its heavy silence, and Lance allowed his mind to absorb the story. "Thank you for telling me."

Derek nodded. "Feels weird, like I just got a weight off my chest… I don't know if I like it or not."

Lance laughed. "Yeah… yeah, I think I know what you mean."

CHAPTER 11
WE'RE BREAKING INTO WHERE?

Eric leaned against the cold metal table, his arms crossed and his head dipping. His eyelids were heavy. George had wrapped his leg and given him a dose of pain meds, the foul perpetrators of his sleepiness.

Eric doubted his decision-making skills at the moment, trusting a doctor he hadn't seen in years, old friend or not. People changed, and for all he knew, George was in Landreau Corp's pocket as well. The thought depressed him, yet he'd still taken the pills without question, and his grip on his cane was loosening. George had been the only figure in his life he could look up to, had repeatedly patched him up when he was younger, no questions asked.

Now, here he sat, having returned to be healed by the closest thing to a father he'd ever had. Years with no explanation of where he'd been or why he'd left all melted away, and George still treated him the same.

"Do you still have that old van from your mobile business days?" Eric asked after jerking his head back out of the waters of drowsiness.

George chuckled in the darkness, where he was rummaging through drawers. "I do. It's at an old car-storage place a friend of mine owns. He keeps it up for me, and in return, I give him a free prescription for his insomnia." He emerged from the darkness and handed a bottle of pain pills to Eric. "Speaking of friends, how many do you have now? Last we met, you mentioned that you were starting to get some contacts together. 'Crawling my way to the top of the food chain' is how you worded it, if I remember correctly."

"Yeah, I managed to build myself up pretty well," Eric said, pocketing the bottle and hoisting himself onto the table. He crossed his legs with a wince. "I have my own little information business going. Two… well, three underbosses that own their own businesses. Two of them have their own employees, as well." A voice spoke in Eric's head. It whispered, *Too much. You're telling him too much.* He shoved the voice down and drowned it.

"So you collect data on people and sell it?" George wore a proud smile. "Must be easier with the internet nowadays."

"I wouldn't know. I don't trust it."

George rolled a desk chair over to himself and sat. "Why is that?"

"Don't like it, don't need it. Too easy and too accessible. Nothing in the world that useful is without a price." He smiled. "Besides, I've already spun my web in the city of Arachna."

"As paranoid as I remember you being," George said, shaking his head. "So you don't use the internet at all? Not even a little?"

"There's a computer at one of my hideouts that I never use. I have some people there. I'm sure they're eating it up right about now."

George rubbed his chin. "What about cell phones?"

Eric ran a hand through his hair. "Even worse. Don't have an ounce of trust for those things. For all I know, they could track me with it."

George shrugged. "I don't know about that, but I feel like a cell phone would be pretty useful to own, especially now."

"Well, I did have a landline a few days ago, but it, um… short-circuited."

Silence stood between them until Eric said, "I need a way out of the city. I have a bad feeling that Caleb is going to take a stroll through Arachna to find my operation and dismantle it. I can't have that happen, Doc." Eric tightened his grip on his cane at the possibility of everything he'd worked so hard to build shattering into pieces under Caleb Landreau's heel. If that man knew the hellish wrath Eric would unleash if that happened, he would slink back to his corporate office with his tail between his legs.

"I understand," George said. "If you give me an hour, I'll have the van over here."

"So we're using the van, are we?"

George peered over his glasses at him. "I know you didn't just ask about the van because you were curious, Eric." And with a chuckle, George stood from his chair and promptly left.

An hour passed. Eric's leg pain eased as the pills took effect, but the bottle in his coat pocket called to him anyway. He ignored its sweet promise. He needed to be alert if he was going to return to Arachna without being riddled with a hail of bullets.

George returned, and they left the secret clinic together. Eric was giddy as he limped out into the alley and spotted the van. Whoever the doctor's friend was had surely taken care of it. Not a scratch was on it.

"Here we go," George said, opening the rear doors and revealing an empty space behind the two front seats. "Watch this." He climbed inside and braced his hands on the bare metal floor. With a pull, a patch of the floor slid back, revealing a human-sized compartment. "I used to keep extra equipment in here. It won't be the most comfortable for your leg, but you should at least be able to fit."

"It'll do," Eric said. "At least until we get out of the city."

Crawling into the compartment took longer than Eric's pride would have preferred, the pain in his leg throbbing with each movement. Once he'd tucked himself uncomfortably into the compartment, his cane hugged against his chest, George slid the floor until it was nearly closed, leaving just enough room for Eric to breathe; it was hard enough already with the intoxicating reek of rubbing alcohol.

The van rumbled to a start as George cranked it, sending a vibration through Eric's body. It eased the pain in his leg.

"Does this Caleb Landreau have his own private military?" George asked after a few turns of the van.

"Don't tell me…"

"Guards in black uniforms and helmets. Armored from head to toe?"

Eric scoffed. "Not fair. Wish I had a private army."

"Eric, my friend," George started as he made a turn, a chuckle escaping him, "I think we can both agree the world would be worse off with you in charge of a military force."

Eric chuckled along with him. "I disagree. I'd make things a lot more fun around here."

"Hmm, nothing looks very fun about these guys."

Eric's attempts to respond were cut short by a curse from George. "Looks like they're stopping cars trying to leave the city."

The van pulled to a stop, and Eric craned to peek out of the narrow opening in the compartment door.

"How many cars are—"

George shushed him and rolled the window down. The shouts of angry drivers and honking horns blended with the rumbling of the engine. The smell of exhaust billowed into the car, and Eric resisted a cough.

He heard footsteps then a voice.

"Where are you going today, sir?" someone asked in a surprisingly friendly voice to be part of a private military.

Eric peeked through the crack in the compartment door. The officer's voice was muffled by a dark helmet, and a visor covered his entire face. His armor was midnight black.

"I'm going to meet my brother in Arachna. His car broke down yesterday, and he needs one to get to work on Monday."

The soldier leaned forward, his arms resting on the windowsill. "And how are you planning on getting back?"

"I'm not, right now. I'm going to stay there with him for a few weeks."

A moment of quiet thickened the air, interrupted by another car horn.

"Can I see your driver's license?"

"Absolutely." George fumbled for his license and handed it to the soldier.

The soldier scanned it for a moment then gave it back. "Go on through," the soldier said, patting his hand against the roof.

George rolled the window up and whispered, "Those uniforms cover everything. Not an inch of skin was visible."

Eric relaxed. "Definitely to hide the bad case of purple vein… That's going to be an interesting topic of research when I get back to Arachna. I need to know what's going on with this company. What are you going to do?"

"Once we get to Arachna? Find some new patients, make some money until things here in Agni settle down. And if business in Arachna is good? Heh heh, well, I may just stay there."

"I could always employ you, Doc. Another source of information. The reasons why they got injured. It could really give me some juicy intel."

George chuckled again. "I believe there are laws against that. I still took an oath, you know."

Eric slid the door all the way open, and George looked at him in the rearview mirror.

"My dearest doctor," Eric started, "I'm sure you could make an exception for an old friend. And if I can't convince you, my money might."

The doctor laughed and returned his eyes to the road. "The young boy that used to come to me all the time, now offering me a job. Funny how the world works, huh?"

"Funny, indeed," Eric said, his hands resting behind his head. "How's the wife?"

"Still in jail."

"She should be getting parole soon if I'm counting the years right."

"Unfortunately." George went quiet after that.

Eric smiled at the memory. That was the first big scam he'd pulled, and definitely the riskiest, but seeing that lying witch thrown in a cell had been worth it.

"You acted so mad at me when you first learned about her arrest, but I knew you were thrilled. I suppose you were just trying to draw a line in the sand on your morality?" Eric asked, closing his eyes. Prodding, just a little, to know what was going through George's mind.

"I *was* thrilled… but I didn't want to be. I wanted revenge on her, to make her hurt like I did."

"They do say cheaters never prosper."

"But a decade in jail for a crime she didn't commit… It was too far, Eric."

Eric sent a crooked smile to the van's pale ceiling. "We both know that's not true, Doc."

The doctor hummed. "Maybe I *was* just trying to draw a line in the sand… but what's your line, Eric?"

"I haven't found it yet."

"I hope you do soon, my boy. You may have control over Arachna, but you need to have control over yourself. Crack open a history book, and you'll see. The most powerful men in the world that lost themselves lost everything else shortly after."

Eric rolled his eyes and pulled the sliding door, nearly closing it. "Whatever you say, Doc." He reached for his hat to pull it over his face, but he found nothing but his greasy hair. He sighed, wiped his hand on his coat, and lay back, waiting for sleep to carry him off and away from any more awkward conversations with the doctor.

He was right. Admitting it hurt nearly as bad as his leg, but George was right. His own pride and desperation had cost him a deal with Landreau Corp. He should've been more careful. *Oh well.* He would find a way past it.

He always did.

Lance groaned as a hand shook him and a distant voice called his name. Disoriented, he stirred on the hard mattress, the bright white light bearing down on him. He sat up, rubbing his eyes. His arm was asleep.

"We have a plan," Derek said, sitting on the edge of the bed.

Lance massaged the blood back into his dead arm, the tingles like a thousand tiny spiders crawling across it. His body sang for him to lie back down. Kaela was sitting across Derek's bed, staring at the papers from the precinct. Her dress was gone, replaced with jeans and a black shirt.

"Okay," Lance said. "What is it?"

Kaela looked up at him. "We're going to break into Landreau Corp."

Lance shot up, his eyelids no longer heavy.

No glint of humor shone in Kaela's eyes.

She was serious.

"Are you crazy? You understand we're public enemy number one right now. Every cop in the city is after us."

Kaela rolled her eyes. "I'm fully aware of that. Which is why I have a *plan*."

Lance shook his arm, the blood returning. "What plan is worth getting ourselves killed?"

"We're waiting for Rob to get here," Kaela muttered. "Derek paged him and told him to scout the building to confirm my suspicions."

Lance stood, the springs of the mattress groaning. "So how exactly do we go about not dying? Or is this supposed to be some sick form of suicide?"

Kaela smirked. "Look at this." She pointed at the dots and crosses peppered across the page. "What if these marks are where guards are stationed or are going to be stationed? Say the dots are where Landreau Corp's guards are going to be, and the crosses are where the officers will be."

Lance scratched the back of his neck then looked at Derek. "I guess that makes sense. So are we to assume that every officer has a page telling them where to go in Landreau Corp?"

"Or *had*," Derek interjected. "They could have destroyed them by now."

Lance rubbed at his tired eyes. They'd narrowly escaped the precinct, and now they wanted to break into Landreau Corp? Maybe he should've left after all. "So… about this plan?"

Kaela cleared her throat. "When Eric first asked us to get information on Malcolm Landreau, we learned that he generally stayed in an office here in Arachna. We're going to find his office and look for clues. Malcolm was the lead chemist, after all. Surely, if they did something to the police force, there will be proof of it there."

Lance sighed. "Do you really think that Landreau Corp managed to drug the entirety of the police force?"

Kaela glared at him. "The glowing purple veins didn't tip you off?"

"It's just… I've never seen a drug that does something like this." He'd put enough of them up his nose and in his own veins over the years. None of them had that kind of effect. Then again, Landreau Corp had been working on a secret project. *And what better way to get back at Eric than to cripple his police protection?* Lance swore.

Kaela glanced at the computer. "There has to be a way to fix this. If Landreau Corp has drugged the police, then surely there's something that can flush their system of it, like a backup plan in case it failed." She sighed. "And if that doesn't work, we can try to get evidence that Landreau Corp is guilty and get the FBI involved."

"What if Landreau Corp has gotten to them too?"

Kaela shrugged. "Then we're as good as dead anyway."

A knock sounded on the door.

Derek tensed and snapped his head toward the entrance. "It's Rob."

Derek opened the door, and Rob slid into the room, his eyes tired but set with determination. He was out of breath.

"Anything of interest at Landreau Corp?" Kaela asked.

"Guards," Rob said, leaning against the wall. "Everywhere. Practically surrounding the building. I can tell some are police because of the police cars in the parking lot. Other than that, they're indistinguishable from Landreau Corp's men. Employees have to go through metal detectors and show ID before they even reach the entrance. After that, it looks like they go through another round of security." He rubbed his face. "Cameras are pretty scarce, and a handful of guards are peppered across the parking lot. To top it all off, a curfew has been put in place. The streets are nearly empty. Getting here was a bitch."

"Did you take any pictures at Landreau Corp?"

Rob reached into his tight-fitting leather jacket and pulled out a handful of photos. "It's not much, but it's at least enough to make some semblance of a plan."

Kaela looked through photo after photo as Lance peeked over her shoulder. The photos were filled with the grim faces of employees showing their IDs, the guards armored from head to toe.

"Can't see their skin," Derek said. "They're hiding their veins."

Kaela braced her hands on the desk, biting her lip and staring off into space. “We could use that,” she said. “If we can get at least one of their uniforms, we’ll have the advantage.”

Derek scratched his bald head. “Maybe. But it’s hard to tell what their behavior is outside of guarding the place. How do these people act when they’re alone? Do they go back to normal, or are they still affected by whatever the drug does to them?”

“I don’t know,” Rob said. “All I could see was them doing their jobs.”

Lance zoned out, the others’ voices phasing into white noise. They would be breaking into Landreau Corp itself. And after the news of what had happened in Agni, the thought of getting caught, of getting his brains blown out by a crazed officer, chilled him to the bone. Whatever fighting instinct stirred inside him didn’t give him any more confidence in this suicide mission.

His palms were sweaty when he returned to the real world, and he wiped them on his pants.

Kaela grabbed the photos and placed them beside the pages. “Since you’ve seen the place up close, any chance that this is how the interior is laid out?”

Rob nodded. “It looks to be. Derek can enter through here, dressed in a uniform. I’ll be on the rooftop with the rifle I gave you if anything goes wrong. There’s a back door leading to another parking lot, where they throw out trash. You need to get to that door once you’re inside and let Kaela and Lance in. Derek’s told me that you’re something of a formidable fighter?” He looked up at Lance.

Lance flinched under the sudden attention. He cleared his throat. “Yeah… yeah, I can fight.”

“You wouldn’t think, huh?” Kaela smiled, but her eyes held the same shadow they had the night he killed that man. “But he can, as crazy as it sounds. Maybe he’s like that dude in the Bible. The one whose hair makes him all strong.”

Derek grinned for the first time in a while. “You mean Samson?”

“Yeah.”

Derek laughed. “You know, it was a pretty lady that cut Samson’s hair and made him weak. Delilah, I think her name was.”

Kaela's smile grew wicked. "Hear that, Lance? Your weakness is me with a pair of scissors."

"Looks like there are a couple of guards at the door," Rob interjected, a small smile tugging at his lips. "Lance, Kaela, you take them out and disguise yourselves. Once you're all in, you need to find Malcolm's office, which should be somewhere on the top floor." He pointed at two small lines at the same point in both papers. "You should come to a hallway when you enter the back door. These marks in the hallway look like a set of stairs and two elevators. It seems that there aren't many guards near them on the main floor. As for the top floor, for all I know, there could be an army up there, so be prepared."

Kaela idly scratched the back of her head as she said, "While we're at it, we need to be asking around. Casual conversation with the guards, if they're even capable of it anymore. We can probably get some good intel just from what they say." When Lance and Derek looked at each other, Kaela sighed. "You know what, how about I just do the talking? I can get some info without attracting too much attention, but you two need to be looking through the offices for something. Just remember that Malcolm's office is the target."

Lance relaxed. Talking with strangers was hard enough, but strangers that would kill him if they knew who he was? He scoffed.

Rob scanned the photos and plans. "Should anything go wrong, I'll take out as many guards as I can. If not, I'll go down personally and help you escape. But once you're inside that building, my hands are tied. If you get caught in there, you'll have to get yourselves out, or it's over."

A spike of fear struck Lance's heart like a syringe penetrating skin. Derek nodded grimly, and Kaela crossed her arms. If she had doubts, she hid them well. *I wish I could share the same confidence.*

"It's already dark outside, so we need to get going now."

Kaela straightened and breathed deeply, closing her eyes for a moment. When she opened them again, they held a new intensity. "Let's go."

CHAPTER 12
ESPIONAGE

It was worse than Lance had thought it would be.

They crawled out of the hideout, sneaked out the back door, and clambered up the fire escape to the roof of the neighboring building. They hopped rooftops until they had to climb back down, make a mad dash across the street, and start all over again. Derek and Rob jumped the gaps with no problem. Kaela and Lance took running starts and a lot of deep breaths to reassure themselves that they wouldn't plummet to the unforgiving concrete below.

No civilians were around, just empty streets, police cars, and an occasional patrolling guard. Rob was right. They'd enacted a curfew.

They stopped on the roof of a pastry shop, where the smell of cakes wafted up to his nose. It was euphoric, after having to deal with the smell of dirt and body odor for so long. Lance stared up at the night sky, at the stars speckling the black canvas, and he breathed in the refreshing, pastry-laced night air.

A moment of calm before the storm.

Landreau Corp towered above the rest of the buildings in the city, its entrance closely guarded. At least five men stood at the glass doors, which were reinforced with iron bars. More men patrolled a closed-off pathway leading to the door. A few employees were leaving the building, all looking normal.

So none of the employees had been affected.

“Look over there,” Rob whispered, pointing at a small parking lot to the side of Landreau Corp.

A short brick wall surrounded it, just high enough that nobody would notice the two guards on each side of the back door.

“They’re completely out of sight, so taking them out shouldn’t be too hard.”

Derek hummed. “So how do we get a uniform so I can get in there?”

“I… procured one for you.” Rob stood and went to the stairwell door. Hidden behind it was a bag. He returned and promptly dropped it in front of Derek.

Derek reached into the bag and took out the helmet. “Lighter than I thought it’d be.”

“I know, right? The body was a lot easier to drag than I figured.”

Kaela crossed her arms. “And… where is this body, exactly?”

Rob smiled sheepishly. “Same place as the uniform.” Before Kaela could respond, he continued, “I wouldn’t go back there if I were you. It’s already starting to smell.”

Kaela groaned in disgust and walked closer to the edge of the building, probably trying to avoid the smell in case it wafted her way.

Derek was already putting the uniform on, cursing and stumbling as he struggled to fit into it.

“Yeah, it might be a bit small on you,” Rob said. “Try not to walk funny.”

Kaela dropped her head into her hands.

“How are Kaela and I going to get to that parking lot unseen?” Lance asked.

Rob followed Lance’s stare to the parking lot, where the two guards at the door stood like statues, watching for any movement. “Don’t worry, I have someone positioned across the street. They’ll make a distraction for you.” He stared down from the roof. “There’s a stairwell over here. Once the distraction happens, you and Kaela make a dash for it.”

"Okay," Derek said, the entire outfit on except for the helmet, which he cradled in his arm. "How do I look?"

"Like a corrupt policeman," Kaela said, "who gained some weight."

Derek grimaced. "Har har." He moved around a bit, then his grimace darkened. "This is squeezing me in all the wrong places."

Kaela covered her mouth, a breathy laugh spilling out. Lance chuckled a bit as well, a welcome relief from the nerves, and seeing a hesitant smile grow on Derek's face eased his nerves more. God, how were they smiling now when they were about to die?

Rob had a cool smile on his face. "Okay, not bad. I was following the guard before I took him out. Just tell the guards at the entrance that you're done with your patrol. Now, get down there and get into the building."

Derek secured the helmet on his head. "Is it that easy?"

"We're about to find out. If anything goes wrong"—he patted the rifle secured to his back—"I'll cover you." He then reached into the bag where the uniform had been and drew a pistol, which he promptly tossed to Derek.

Kaela crossed her arms. "And once Derek gets in, Lance and I make a run for it?"

"Precisely," Rob said, already positioning himself on the edge of the roof, rifle pointed right at the guards at the entrance.

Derek nodded, the action hardly noticeable with the dark helmet seamlessly blending with the outfit. He holstered the pistol. Not an inch of skin could be seen—perfect for hiding purple veins.

Or an intruder in the building.

Derek jumped down to the stairwell and descended to street level. He stepped out into the street and strode across to Landreau Corp.

Lance held his breath as one of the guards held a hand out and stopped Derek. He could barely hear the guard speaking, but he couldn't tell what he was saying.

Derek said something back, and the guard leaned in closer, looking at Derek's chest.

His badge.

The guard silently stared Derek down. Derek's hand slid carefully to the pistol at his hip, and while the guard didn't notice, all he had to do was look down at Derek's hand to be suspicious.

Rob cursed, and his finger slid from the guard to the trigger.

The guard turned toward one of the others, waved his hand, and said something, and Derek relaxed. The rest of the guards nodded in response, and Derek was let by. Rob relaxed, and his finger returned to the guard. Lance allowed himself to breathe as Derek ascended the steps to the door, where two guards nodded to him. Derek nodded back and disappeared into the building.

"Okay," Rob said, not looking at them, but adjusting the rifle toward the parking lot. "Go ahead. I'll signal for the distraction."

Lance gulped, and his heart skipped a beat. Kaela seemed confident, but her posture was rigid. She was nervous too.

Just like Derek, they clambered down the stairwell to street level. They eased to the edge of the alley, where Kaela eyed the guards.

"Wait for it," Kaela said, but it seemed directed more at herself than at Lance. The guard that had questioned Derek turned away and walked to the other end of the building. The guards at the entrance scanned the area, left and right.

Lance surveyed the street for any sign of a distraction. "How are we supposed to know when—"

Before he could finish, an alley at the end of the street fizzled and popped and filled with smoke.

"Firecrackers," Kaela whispered. "They're not looking. Go!"

Lance and Kaela sprinted toward the parking lot. Lance's stomach didn't turn, and the calm didn't settle over him. They were safe for now. When they reached the lot, both of them looked back, catching their breath.

"They shouldn't be able to see us from the entrance now," Kaela said. She turned toward the two guards at the back door. A man and a woman, judging by their frames.

"Copy," one of them said. "A firecracker. Can you believe that shit?"

"Probably kids," the other guard said. "I hate kids."

A pause. "You *have* kids."

"I didn't say I hated *my* kids."

Kaela and Lance shared a look.

Lance whispered, "At least they sound like they're normal."

"That's a good sign, at least. Let me distract them while you sneak around those cars." Kaela pointed at a set of three cars parked beside each other. "When I make a move, you jump in and finish them off. Ready?"

Lance nodded and ignored his dry mouth as he dug within himself, searching for that whisper, that calm that came over him in danger. He'd never tried to control it before. It usually worked the other way around. But as he searched, he found nothing—no twisting stomach, no whispering, nothing.

"Go for it," Lance said as he sneaked around the car and waited.

Kaela stood, painting a worried expression on her face. She approached the guards.

Lance reached out for that feeling, but it wasn't there. His chest tightened. It was as if it disappeared. What if he couldn't fight?

"Hello?" Kaela said to the guards, keeping her voice fragile and worried. "I need help."

Lance peeked around the car. The guards looked at each other before one stepped out to face Kaela, a hand on his pistol. Kaela's body language screamed panic, and her face was ghostly white.

Quite the actress.

"You're not allowed to be here," one guard said. "You need to leave."

"Please," Kaela pleaded, "I need to find my daughter. We were walking home, and she disappeared. Please!" She leaned on the man's chest, desperate sobs spilling from her.

The guard pulled her hands off his chest. "I said you need to l—" He stopped and looked at Kaela's face in the light of the lamppost shining on the lot. "Wait… I know you. You're one of the—" He was cut off as a knife found its way into his knee. He tried to shout, but Kaela ripped his helmet off and covered his mouth, falling to the ground with him.

Lance looked at the second guard, who pointed her gun at Kaela. He sprinted toward the guard, that calm refusing to grace him with its presence. The guard spotted Lance, pointing her gun at him instead. He charged into her, slamming her into the wall. The fact that the gun didn't go off was a miracle.

The guard grunted at the impact. Lance pulled the gun from her grasp and threw it aside. He was already out of breath. The guard cursed and drew a baton.

Finally, time slowed down. The calm washed over him, that stirring within the pit of his stomach. A voice whispered in his head.

Survive.

The smile that tugged at his lips unsettled him as much as it relieved him, and he kicked the baton out of her hand. The weapon flew into the air. She threw a punch at Lance, and he grabbed her arm, whirling her around and throwing her into the brick wall. The baton came down, and Lance caught it. He ripped her helmet off and bashed the baton over her head. She collapsed.

He turned toward Kaela. She made to pull the knife from the man's knee, but he pushed her off. Kaela swiped the helmet from the ground and swung it into his head. Purple blood sprayed from his nose. Again, Kaela swung the helmet, over and over until he went still.

Out of breath, she sat against the wall. "Help me drag them out of sight."

Lance and Kaela dragged their unconscious bodies into a dark spot behind a car and stole their uniforms. They stepped out from behind the car and looked around.

"That went easier than I thought," Kaela said, adjusting a loose strand of hair in her eye. "Now, we wait for Derek to—"

Before she could finish, the door clicked and opened, revealing a uniformed guard. Lance and Kaela froze, but then the guard took his helmet off, revealing Derek underneath.

"Come on," he said, and Lance and Kaela slinked inside the building, donning the helmets.

When Lance stepped in, he gawked at just how much he could see with the helmet. Even with the dark visor, he could scan the entire hallway in front of him without moving his head an inch.

The hallway was lit with bright white lights, similar to the sickening lights at their hideout. The sight of them nauseated him. Two shining silver elevator doors stood to his left, with a stairway at the end of the hall. Beyond that was a wall then a turn to the right, which likely led to the lobby. It was exactly as it was drawn on the paper back at the hideout.

Derek cleared his throat. "We're taking the elevator to the top floor. Kaela, find out what you can from the guards."

Kaela saluted him and, with sarcasm painted on every word, said, "Aye aye, captain." She ended the salute with a wave and sauntered down the hall, taking a right at the end and disappearing around the corner.

"Ready?" Lance asked Derek as he pressed the elevator button.

Derek leaned against the wall. "Hmph. I was about to ask *you* that, actually."

"What do we do if we find something?"

The doors opened, and they stepped inside, pressing the button for the top floor. Even when they were in the elevator, Derek spoke quietly.

"Hope and pray that we can escape."

Lance rolled his eyes. "That's comforting."

It wasn't, but somehow, the helmet was. There was no need to hide his facial expressions. He could roll his eyes, frown, or look anywhere he wanted, and nobody would know. That didn't matter around Derek, but still, this past week would've been so much easier if he'd had a helmet like this one.

Derek broke the silence. "I wonder what we're going to find."

"I can't stop thinking about what we're going to do if we don't find anything."

The cheery elevator music did nothing to prevent Lance's heart sinking into his stomach. They'd just infiltrated the most dangerous building in Arachna, and they were wanted by the police force guarding it. Taking out a guard at the back entrance was one thing, but if a dozen came flooding in after him, he'd be finished.

The remains of that calm stirred within Lance, like a parasite slithering through his body, hissing and snapping at anything that put its host in danger. He knew he shouldn't ask the question floating in his head, that he should keep it to himself and not show that weakness, but as hard as he tried to shove it down, he soon sighed and went for it.

"Do you ever feel like you can't control how you fight back… like you don't have any control over your body? I feel this calm feeling when I'm in danger, and then… next thing I know, I'm alive and there's bodies around me…"

Derek looked at him, though Lance couldn't tell what expression he was holding. "That sounds like adrenaline to me. You'd be surprised the things you can do when your life is in danger. Sometimes, that's just how surviving works. Time slows down, everything goes by in a blur, and you're either dead or alive at the end of it."

"I wish I had more control over it," Lance said, more to himself than to Derek. His stomach turned, but it wasn't the calm.

Derek was quiet for a second. "You will one day."

Lance sighed, focusing on his feet. "I don't know… It just feels weird, being able to do this. It's like watching myself do it. I—"

"Lance…" Derek sounded frustrated. "You need to stop overthinking it. I made that same mistake when I started out as a fighter, and it only made things worse. Just do what you're doing now. It's obviously working for you."

Maybe he was right, though Derek probably didn't hear voices when he fought.

Maybe with all that was happening, he truly was losing his mind. With the drugs and the alcohol and the years in the slums, the possibility that he was just imagining things made sense.

The elevator reached the top floor, and Lance's heart rose back up into his chest. When the doors opened, the duo tensed.

Three guards were facing them. For a moment of tense silence, Lance felt it again, that calm stirring around within him. Except no voice spoke to him this time.

One of the guards in the trio nodded, and Derek returned it. Holding his breath, Lance stepped out, shimmying between two of the guards entering the elevator. He didn't allow himself a breath until the elevator doors closed behind them, and he and Derek were left in the hallway of the top floor.

Alone.

"Okay, you check at the doors on that end." Derek pointed down the hallway to the left of the elevators. Then he pointed to the hallway to the right. "And I'll search here. If you find something, just knock on the door loud enough for me to hear. I don't want anyone to hear us calling each other, especially by name."

Lance nodded. Derek was already looking at the slim golden tags placed at eye level on every door.

Lance turned and started the search on his side of the hallway. He muttered the name on the closest door. "A. James." As he padded down the hallway, he read the tags on each one with a glance. "E. Newman. G. Hasan. M. Singh." Lance searched until he came to the end of the hallway. "Aaand T. Banes." He sighed. "Nothing."

A faint sound perked Lance's ears, a knock on the other end of the floor. He padded back down the hall. Derek was standing next to a door, his helmet raised as he scratched his chin. The tag read: *M. Landreau.*

"I found it," he whispered as Lance approached. "Come on."

Lance couldn't suppress a few nervous glances down the hall. He racked his brain for some excuse he could use if anyone caught them up here. Derek cracked open the door, only worsening Lance's nerves, and peeked in before slipping inside. Lance followed and shut the door behind them with a soft click. He felt along the wall until his fingers found a switch and flipped it.

Light flooded the room. Derek spun on his feet and flipped the switch back, plunging the room into darkness once again.

"We cannot let anyone know we're in here," he hissed. After a glance at the light under the door, he removed his helmet and began searching the room.

Lance removed his own helmet, standing perfectly still. He could hardly see anything in the darkness.

Derek padded easily over to one side of the office and ripped open a set of curtains. The moonlight shone into the office, casting the whole room in a dim white glaze.

"How did you—"

Derek shrugged. "I'm used to having to see in the dark."

A fake plant sat next to the window, its shadow casting the shape of a monster on the floor. Derek looked out the window, down at the streets below, and just stood there for a few seconds before he stepped quietly around the desk and set his helmet down.

Lance set his own helmet beside Derek's.

"Looks like everything is calm down there," Derek said as he opened a drawer and rifled through it. "You hid the bodies behind the building well, right?" He paused. "Did you kill them?"

Lance hesitated then shook his head.

Derek cursed. "Then we have a stricter time limit than I thought."

"Sorry," Lance responded, locking the door to the office and stepping around the desk like Derek had. But while Derek was focused on the contents of the drawers, Lance found himself drawn to the bookshelf standing tall and proud behind it.

He tapped his finger on each of the books, the titles all referring to medicine, biology, or chemistry. *Lots of books on chemistry*, Lance thought as he continued down the shelf. One book in particular looked worn, the spine loose and scratched. He slid it out from between its brothers and let it fall into his hand. He thumbed through the book, finding notes scrawled across each page. A few pages had been torn out. Lance continued flipping through the book, watching as the notes transformed from meticulously written words to nearly incomprehensible scrawls, like a madman had scribbled them.

MUST BE BETTER!

The words were circled and underlined. Lance flipped through more pages and found one that was entirely scrawled out, the words barely visible any longer. At the top of that page, written in a different color ink: *FOOLS!!!!*

Lance stepped closer to the window and squinted at the words at the top of the page, the moonlight providing him some assistance. Unlike the red ink used for past notes, this one was in a purple ink. *Or...*

"Derek," Lance whispered.

The rifling stopped.

"What?" He was already behind Lance, looking over his shoulder at the book. He swore when he saw the scribblings.

"Is that..." Lance couldn't make himself finish the sentence, but an odd smell emanated from the purple ‘ink’. He turned toward Derek, his face twisted in disgust.

“Keep looking,” Derek said.

Lance turned the page again, then again. The scribblings lessened, as if Malcolm had entirely lost interest in making notes in the book. He flipped the pages faster and faster until he reached the very end of the book, where one last sentence was scribbled on the inside of the back cover. It was difficult to read, but he could just make it out:

I was careless… FOOLISH! Just like them! Must go back to the church! Must continue my research!

Derek took the book from Lance and reread the page. Lance leaned against the window and looked down at the streets. From where they were, the guards were like ants, guarding the entrance to the building, completely unaware of the intruders crawling around in their nest. He looked at the rooftop where Rob was positioned, but he was nearly invisible. The darkness hid him well, as if he could manipulate it at will. This was the company Lance kept now, and with his current predicament, that didn’t seem so bad.

God, this view. The whole city was laid bare before him. Even the slums were visible from here. Under any other circumstances, Lance would’ve killed to sit against this window and stare out at the city forever. *Kaela would love it too,* he thought. No wonder she loved that hill so much.

“So now what?” Lance asked through a breath, somewhat comforted by the moonlight shining down on him.

Derek ripped out the page mentioning the church, closed the book, and slipped it back into the shelf. He took the ripped-out piece of paper and tore it to shreds, pocketing the pieces. “I suppose we go to the church… wherever that is.”

“There’s only one church in Arachna that I know of.”

“Maybe he left something there, some clue as to what he was doing.”

"He didn't seem so crazy when Eric and I met with him. Nervous, maybe. But nothing like the way he wrote. And he didn't have any purple veins."

Derek closed the curtains, and the room was dark once again.

"Was he wearing clothes that might have covered him up?"

Lance shook his head. "No, he was perfectly normal... I don't understand."

"Well maybe we can—" He stopped when a shadow slithered across the light on the other side of the door.

Derek grabbed his helmet and plastered himself against the wall next to the door. Lance stood paralyzed, comforted only by the fact that he'd locked it behind him.

But then the shadow returned.

And it stood still right at the door.

The doorknob jiggled and rattled, then someone spoke from the other side.

"Are you sure you saw somebody go in here?"

Someone else responded, "Absolutely. I saw them on the camera myself. Two officers went in there."

Thanks to the light leaking under the door, Lance could see Derek's silhouette move. Then it moved again. After a few times, Lance realized Derek was gesturing to the left of the door, telling him to plaster himself against the wall too. When the doorknob rattled again, Lance grabbed his helmet and did just that.

"It's probably just some young couple from the police precinct tha—"

Lance would've felt relief if the other voice hadn't interrupted and said, "Just check!"

A sigh sounded, then the jangling of keys. Derek's silhouette flattened itself against the wall. Lance did the same and held his breath. The door opened, and his heart fell as a man holding a rifle stepped in. Following him was another guard. Lance's heart was beating so hard, he thought one of them might hear it. Sweat poured down his face, and a knot formed in his stomach.

Worry crept in, but then the calm began to settle. The serpent within his gut slithered and hissed.

No, Lance thought as his body ached to attack them. *Not now.*

"Hello?" the first guard said, pointing the rifle behind the desk. Lance gulped, and the second guard turned toward the noise.

Lance thought his chest would explode as the guard took a step toward him, then another, his black visor staring right at him. Every second he investigated the darkness felt like an hour, and Lance's throat, his chest, his entire body was tensed hard enough to hurt. He was grateful for the dark uniform blending him into the wall.

Survive, the voice whispered.

Not yet! Lance hissed back.

If the guard made so much as one move toward him, he would have to fight. And if they were detected, being on the top floor, they would be done for. No amount of fighting would get them out of the building.

The guard turned back around, but Lance didn't allow himself to relax yet.

The rifleman searched behind the curtains and asked, "Is there a light switch somewhere in here?"

The other guard was leaning against the desk and chuckled. "Right, sorry." He strode toward the light switch, right where Derek was hiding, flattened against the wall.

Lance's eyes burned with sweat, and his chest hurt from the lack of oxygen. He allowed himself small, short breaths through his nose and told himself everything would be okay. When the guard's hand reached for the light switch, Lance expected Derek to reveal himself, to snap his wrist in an instant and send both guards out the window.

But Derek did nothing.

And light flooded the room.

CHAPTER 13

A PIT IN THE STOMACH, AND A BULLET IN THE CHEST

Lance's heart almost stopped as light banished the darkness and the first guard pointed his rifle at him. The other one drew his pistol on Derek.

Lance's breathing became rapid. He waited for the killing calm, but it didn't rear its head. Horror crept up his spine. Now *it chooses to shut up?*

"What are you two doing in here?" asked the guard with the rifle.

"We…" Lance started, but he couldn't think of anything with the gun pointed at him.

The calm stirred somewhat in his chest, but he tried to ignore it. If it had appeared seconds before, he could have taken them, but now the officers had the advantage.

Yet that stirring was persistent. It lingered and spoke to him, whispering for him to attack. If this went on much longer, he wasn't sure he would be able to resist. His body struggled against his mind, tensing and urging him to rush the men.

"I'm sorry," Derek said. "We'll just leave. But can you please put those weapons down? We're on the same side here."

The first guard lowered his pistol, and the other lowered his rifle. Lance tried to keep his sigh of relief quiet.

"Sorry," the rifleman said, turning his attention from Lance. "You just caught us off guard. But you still haven't answered my question. What are you two doing in here?"

Derek looked at Lance. "Do you want to tell them, or should I?"

Panic rose within Lance again, but as he stuttered, trying to come up with something, Derek inched within arm's reach of the pistol. Lance showed it no attention and said whatever came to his mind.

"I… I wanted to get a picture of the view outside the window. Seriously, have you looked out at the city from here? It's beautiful."

The guard with the pistol looked at the rifleman, who said, "You seriously snuck in here just so you could take a picture?"

Derek paused for a moment, a predator preparing to pounce. Then, in the blink of an eye, he ripped the pistol from the officer's grip and bashed his visor in.

Lance charged the guard that was already aiming his rifle at Derek and disarmed him, tackling him into the desk and slamming his head until the visor shattered and violet blood splashed onto the polished wood.

Relief swept through Lance. His body relaxed just slightly, as if releasing that bit of energy had tamed whatever beast lay within his gut.

Derek flipped the light switch, returning the room to darkness. Lance slipped out of the office with him and started to shut the door quietly. He turned to speak, but Derek stopped, turned around, and peeked into the room. He nodded at the two unconscious men on the floor, gesturing with his hand as if he was talking. Then he shut the door and muttered to Lance, "Act calm. If someone else is watching the cameras, they can't suspect anything."

"At this point, I think they already do," Lance said. "I wish we'd noticed the cameras."

"I didn't see any when we first stepped on this floor, and I don't now." Derek shook his head. "We're lucky. If either of them had managed to get so much as one shot off, these halls would be flooding with men right now."

They reached the elevator, and Lance summoned it with the press of a button. He stole a glance at the ceiling and walls. Just as Derek had said, no cameras were visible. Wherever they were, they were hidden well enough that even the professional ex-assassin hadn't noticed. The thought sent a chill down his spine.

"I guess," Lance said. "At least we have a lead now. I'm ready to get out of this place for good."

"Yeah, I wonder how Kaela's doing."

The elevator door slid open, and six men poured out, guns pointed.

"Hands behind your head, now!" shouted a guard.

Derek and Lance backed against the wall, following the order.

Rotoya stepped out of the elevator, wielding a malicious smile.

The whisper in Lance's head strengthened its resolve. It'd had a taste of combat, and it wanted more; a hungry beast awaiting more food, not satisfied by the morsel it'd been given. But they stood no chance against these men. They blocked the hall on both ends, surrounding them.

No way to escape. No way to fight.

They were stuck and at the mercy of the chief.

Lance fought as hard to calm the beast as he did to keep his expression neutral.

"I felt something off about an hour ago. A shift in the wind, you could say. Wouldn't you believe, one of my officers went missing? And then two more at the back entrance?" She laughed. "Don't worry, they're all fine. Even the one your friend on the rooftop thought he killed. That'll be a nasty shock."

Lance glanced at the men around them, waiting for some kind of sign from Derek.

As if she knew he was looking around, the chief set her attention on Lance, her smile disappearing. "You're not going to get away. Not unless I want you to."

"What happens now?" Derek asked, murder in his eyes.

"Now," the chief sang, "I'm going to get you two all settled and comfortable outside, and then I'm going to retrieve your little friend down in the break room. If you try to escape, I'll have you both executed on the spot."

There it is. Lance swallowed as the calm stirred within him again, a snake coiling to strike. The chief stopped and looked at him, as if she, too, could feel the calm within him.

An awkward silence grew, just like the smile on Rotoya's face. "Let's go."

Kaela rounded the corner of the hallway, the sound of elevator doors sliding open behind her. When she stepped into the lobby, she nearly thanked the darkened visor of her helmet.

The room was bright, brighter than the inside of a car dealership at night. Kaela wasn't sure how the receptionist could look her way without squinting.

"Shift change already, Allen? Martinez just came in with the donuts. He's in the break room," the receptionist said, nodding her head toward a door down another, much wider hall. Kaela almost thanked her but instead chose a polite nod.

Kaela took a deep breath as she walked across the lobby, the armor hot and heavy—and worst of all, ugly.

She reached the break room and looked through the small glass window at eye level before stepping inside. Only one other guard was in the room, his helmet off, snacking on a donut, the smile on his face like a kid's. The veins in his neck were purple, nearly protruding from his skin.

"Martinez?" Kaela said, deepening her voice slightly to sound more authoritative.

This 'Allen' woman's voice was deeper than Kaela's, and she hoped her impression was close enough. It was a risk—a monumental risk—but one she had to take if she was going to get any good info.

Martinez turned his head, sprinkles falling from his chin. His veins looked dead, not glowing like the officers' at the station.

"Hey," he said through a mouthful of the treat, setting the remains of the donut next to the box. He sat on the table across from her and smiled. "Well, I got the donuts you asked for. Baker even gave me a discount. I think she was scared of me, though."

He laughed heartily, but Kaela could only look at those veins. Even his eyes had a tint in them—bloodshot, but even those veins were purple.

“Thanks,” she said, her throat protesting at the voice she was putting on. On any other day, in any other building, with anyone else in the room with her, Kaela would have gladly devoured the treats presented to her in the box on the shiny metal table. Even with the helmet on, the smell permeated the room. “I appreciate it, but… I’m feeling sick to my stomach.”

Martinez’s face twisted into concern, but even then, those veins made every movement of his features look cruel and sick.

“You okay?” he asked, licking his fingers.

Kaela nodded and scanned the room until she saw the small bathroom in the corner.

“If you feel like you’re gonna be sick, you can take your helmet off, you know. It’s pretty suffocating in those things sometimes.”

“No,” Kaela said, committing to the role. She hunched forward just slightly and slurred her words, feeling the nausea she didn’t have swelling in her throat. “No, I don’t want to do that.”

“Come on, the chief said it was okay as long as none of the R&D guys saw us, and they’ve all gone home.” The smile he gave her would have been beautiful. His teeth would have gleamed in the light of the room. But even they had the slightest purple tint to them.

Kaela’s fake nausea wasn’t so fake anymore. “Do you think I’m sick from…” She paused as she took a step toward the bathroom. “You know.”

Another risk…

Martinez’s eyes shone like an innocent pup’s, and he said, “You mean that sandwich you ate earlier? I told you that meat smelled funky. That’s why I don’t eat at Jerry’s.”

Kaela continued her slow shuffle toward the bathroom, trying not to overdo it. “No, I mean… the other thing.”

She refused to turn her head toward him as she closed in on the bathroom, instead looking at him through her peripherals. But if she saw it correctly, a spark of realization flickered in those puppy dog eyes, and as he spoke, she stopped.

“Wait,” he said, eyeing the donut he’d left next to his helmet, “are you pregnant again?”

Son of a bitch, Kaela thought. "No, Martinez," she said, frustration flickering in her fake voice. "I'm talking about the drug."

Martinez shrugged. "I guess it could be that. I mean, the shots were a couple of weeks ago, but they did say there might be some side effects, right?"

Kaela tried not to seem too interested as she looked at him. "Do you remember what they were, again?"

He stood and shoved the rest of his donut into his mouth then brushed the crumbs off his hands.

"Well, weird cravings, for one," he said with a chuckle that ejected crumbs onto the table. "Let me think… Mood swings. I got mad at a citizen earlier just for tripping over her own feet. Didn't fall down, just tripped a little." He shook his head. "Made me so mad, but I don't know why. There are probably a lot more, but you'd have to ask the chief, and even then, I'm not sure she even knew."

Kaela closed the door to the bathroom, and through the door, she could hear Martinez's footsteps close in as he kept talking to her.

"Gotta admit, despite the side effects, the stuff we get in return is pretty worth it, right?"

"Yeah," Kaela said, forgetting in that second to lower her voice. Even with the helmet on, she put a hand to her mouth.

Martinez was silent, then he said, "You know, you do sound kind of sick. Do you need me to leave so you can get it all out?"

Kaela took her helmet off, breathing in the cool air of the bathroom, the smell of air freshener keeping her grounded. It was starting to hit her that she was inside a building full of people that wanted her dead. *And if either of the guards we knocked out wake up soon…*

"Allen?" Martinez called.

Kaela returned the helmet to her head and said, "No, no, just stay here. I'll be out in a second." She sat on the toilet and stared down at her feet. "Why did we even bother taking this crap if it's making us sick?"

Martinez chuckled again. "Chief told us to. But come on, who wouldn't want to be a superhuman? And believe me, we'll need the extra strength." After a moment of silence, the door creaked as he leaned on it. "I think you're just feeling sick because you're nervous. Those shots haven't been giving anyone else nausea, especially after several weeks."

"Me? Nervous?" She tried to fake a hearty laugh. "Never."

It must have been convincing enough, because Martinez joined in. "Don't think you can fool me. Look, I honestly don't think we'll have to kill anybody. When they all hear what they're being offered, they'll beg for it. Those fugitives, though… I don't know, I don't think we'll have to kill them either as long as they don't come busting up in here."

Kaela's stomach turned. She was grateful for the bathroom, for the sanctity and safety of the small space. She took her helmet off again and breathed in the air. She even took off one of her gloves and braced her hand against the wall—anything to ground her, to calm her racing thoughts.

Is Landreau Corp planning a hostile takeover of the city?

Her mouth was too dry to speak anymore, and Martinez must've sensed it.

"Uh huh. I knew you were nervous about it," he said. "But just think of the end goal here. It'll be glorious to see the rebirth of Arachna. You just have to remember that what we're doing is right."

Kaela forced the helmet back on her head, every fiber of her mind screaming for her not to. Her stomach did somersaults inside her, and bile rose in her throat. "How do you know?"

Then the helmet came off again, and Kaela flipped the lid of the toilet up. The last thing she'd expected was to become as nauseous as she was pretending to be.

"Because the chief says so," Martinez said. "And she's never led us wrong, so I have no reason to believe she will now. I trust her." When Kaela didn't respond, Martinez continued, "Well, I gotta get back to patrol. You feel better, okay?" His shadow disappeared from under the door.

Kaela leaned against the wall, wishing with all her might that none of this was real, that everything could just go back to the way it was. When she could work at the Rose and laugh with the girls or dance at the club or even sit in meetings and hurl jabs back and forth with Eric—anything but sitting in this dreadful bathroom and thinking about the deaths of the people of Arachna if they didn't accept whatever this 'offer' was. *The drug, maybe?*

Kaela had told herself plenty of times over the years that she didn't care about the people of Arachna—that, for the most part, they could burn, for all she cared. But hearing the words coming out of someone's mouth, hearing that people would die if they didn't obey their corporate masters, sent bile to her throat.

She couldn't live in a city where everyone was forced to comply, to walk around with those purple veins.

Oh, and how ugly they would be.

She couldn't handle the nausea anymore and vomited into the toilet. This whole thing went much deeper than she'd thought. The quiet of the bathroom weighed heavy on her as she steeled herself. She had to get out and learn more about this. Martinez had been enough of a help, but any more questions would make him suspicious.

She stood, her legs wobbly, her chest tight and her stomach turning like waves in an ocean. She leaned against the wall, feeling the cool wood on the back of her head. The armor was more constricting with every passing minute, and after a few shaky breaths, she walked out of the bathroom with her helmet back on, keeping her back straight and her steps rigid.

But when she did, she found four guards outside the door.

All were looking at her.

None of them said a word.

She stared at them all, then at the pistols on their hips, at the soulless visors, imagining the menacing faces behind them.

Her hand twitched to grab her own pistol, but she wouldn't be able to take them all out before they shot her down. She wasn't as proficient with guns as Derek. And even he surely wouldn't have that quick a trigger finger.

She opened her mouth to spit out some excuse, but the leftmost guard stepped around her and into the bathroom, closing the door behind him. She let out a sigh, smelling the remnants of her regurgitated MRE on her breath, coughing at the stench.

"Sorry," she said with a laugh, remembering to keep her voice low. "I'm not feeling well."

"I can tell," said the guard on the right. "Your voice isn't what it usually is, Allen. You sure you shouldn't be on sick leave?"

"No, no, I'm good. I don't know what it could be, though. Martinez said it could be something I ate or even the shot."

The guard in the middle grunted. "I doubt that. There've been some weird side effects, but no one's gotten sick."

"Martinez said the same thing. But even if it was the shot, it's worth being a little sick if it means being stronger, and… you know, the *plan*."

"Yeah, the *plan* is worth any pain, any sickness… any sacrifice."

The uniforms they wore made it harder to read their body language, but Kaela could still feel the tension glowing around them. She swallowed, her mouth suddenly dry again, her nose crinkling at every breath she took.

"Which is funny," the guard continued, stepping over to the box of donuts and looking in. His hand grasped the box much more firmly than he should have. "From what the chief told us, the shots are supposed to give us a resistance to poison… disease… and sickness."

Kaela started to take one slow step back, but she stopped herself when her back pressed against another body. She balled her fists and craned her neck at the guard standing tall behind her, his arms crossed.

The guard had either exited the bathroom quietly, or he hadn't gone in at all.

"I was just feeling nauseous, that's all," Kaela said, her hand and mind fighting over whether to reach for her gun or not. "Not actually a sickness. Martinez said it was just nerves, and I'm starting to think that's what it is. Besides, what about all those headaches we get every now and then? I swear, I had one earlier, and I think this nausea could be left over from that."

The guard's hand relaxed, just a little, on the box. He looked at his friend.

The breathing of the guard behind Kaela was loud and heavy in the tense silence—a big mistake on his part, as Kaela followed the sound and marked the spot where he was. Behind her, more to the left. One quick strike of her elbow in the right place, and he would be down for the count, armor or not.

The guard looking at his friend spoke again. “I’m sick of this game. Take off your helmet, *Allen*.”

Dammit. Her cover was as good as blown. With the armor she wore, a bullet or two wouldn’t do too much damage. And with the uniform being loose on her anyway, maybe… just maybe she could get out of this.

The guard’s hand inched toward his gun.

“Sure,” Kaela said, shrugging. Her hands shook as she reached for her helmet, pacing herself as she grabbed it. The helmet slid off easily, and before the guards could draw their weapons, she threw it at them.

Kaela shot her elbow back against the man’s neck. He choked and gagged as she grabbed him from behind. She ripped his helmet off and drew her gun, pointing it at his head. He raised his arms in surrender, his purple veins glowing and his head turned as far as it would allow for him to glare at her.

He was bigger than her, and with the drug, he could tear her grip from his neck easily. Kaela released him but kept her gun pointed at his head. She grabbed the pistol from his holster and pointed it at the rest of the guards.

She had the advantage, but only for now.

The armor was heavy, and her movements had been slower than she wanted. But now here she was, peeking out from behind a guard’s back at the three others pointing their pistols at her.

“If you call any of your friends in here, this one dies,” Kaela said, grateful that her shakiness had not reared its ugly head in her voice.

But the guard to the right laughed, the first time he’d even made a noise. He said, “What was that you said about sacrifice, Raymond?”

Before the words could settle a chill into Kaela’s bones, gunshots rang out. Blood splattered from the hostage guard’s neck, and he fell backward.

In a blind panic, Kaela squeezed the triggers on both guns. Two more ear-splitting pops echoed in the room, and the guard’s limp body fell back on her. If she hadn't been wearing armor, she would've been crushed. Her head struck the floor as she landed.

She didn't have time to blink the stars away from her vision or wait for the ringing in her ears to stop. She didn't have time to consider that she'd taken another life or care about the pain searing her hands and wrists from the kick of the pistols. Shots were fired again, and Kaela couldn't contain her scream. She fired back and squirmed out from under the guard's body. Purple blood stained her armor and painted her face. She flattened herself against the wall of the bathroom.

"She got Tray and Daymon!" a guard shouted.

Only two left, then.

Kaela flipped the light switch, dimming the bathroom. Light spilled in from the break room. *Still not dark enough.* She took a deep breath and blindly fired at the ceiling. Two of the lights shattered and sparked, and the bathroom finally fell into darkness. Dim light still lit the break room.

More shots rang out, and Kaela pressed harder against the wall, goosebumps rising on her skin. She crouched and turned, spotting the two guards with their guns pointed at the door.

They couldn't see her.

Good.

With two shots to the helmet, another guard crumpled to the floor in a splash of violet blood and broken visor pieces.

One left. Just one.

She held her breath. The sound of heavy footsteps trying to be quiet stomped against the floor, inching closer and closer to the bathroom door.

Just a few more seconds, Kaela thought. *Just a few more...*

The footsteps paused just before the door, and Kaela fired at the floor, flashing the darkness with light for a split second. The guard flinched just long enough for Kaela to grab his gun and throw her weight against him. They fell and clattered to the ground.

Kaela slid her dagger free from its sheath and plunged it into the guard's neck. He choked and gurgled as violet blood filled his mouth.

Kaela ripped the blade out and took a second to breathe, surveying the chaos: purple blood on the walls, dead bodies around her, half the lights off, the others either on or blinking.

"Shit," she said, out of breath. "How the hell do I get out of here now?"

Shouts erupted from behind the door, and seconds later, it blew off the hinges, the wood splintering and crashing against the opposite wall. Kaela fell to the ground, her gun slipping from her hands. She sheathed her knife just in time.

The chief stepped in, her eyes glowing purple and her mouth formed into a snarl.

No. If she was going to die, she was going to take the chief with her. Kaela picked the gun back up and pointed it at Rotoya.

"Wait." Rotoya grinned and unhooked the bulletproof vest from her chest then dropped it to the ground. "Go ahead."

"What the…" Kaela paused then blinked away her hesitation. She fired, riddling Rotoya with bullets. The chief took each bullet with a smile, backing up with each impact until she fell against the wall, splattering it with amethyst blood. She slid down, that haunting smile still on her face. Her empty stare pointed at the ground.

When the gun clicked, Kaela tossed it aside. "Crazy bitch." She leaned against the wall as the pain worsened—her hands, her head, her ears, her back. Her entire body ached. More guards stormed in, and she just glared at them. She should've known this plan would fail. She closed her eyes and prepared for death. She just hoped Lance and Derek would get out okay.

"Hold your fire, boys."

Kaela opened her eyes. She could've sworn that voice was…

Rotoya was still smiling as she lifted her head back up then stood. She looked down at her armor, at the purple blood oozing from the wounds. "Want to see a trick?"

Rotoya raised her arms to her sides, and the bullet wounds glowed. Kaela's jaw dropped as the bullets wriggled out of her body and clinked on the floor. The bullet wounds glowed brighter then closed as if she'd never been shot at all.

The bodies of the men Kaela had shot glowed as well.

Rotoya scanned the room with that smile.

The ground swayed beneath Kaela's feet as each guard she'd shot, one by one, stood. Not even as if they'd woken up, but as if they'd been faking the whole time.

They all stood, surrounding Kaela, each one staring at her. Martinez walked in, matching the chief's smile.

"You can come with us, or we can drag you out," the chief said, her voice distorted, her smile revealing purple-stained teeth. She picked her bulletproof vest up and strapped it back on. "You have three seconds to choose."

Kaela tried to swallow the lump in her throat, but it remained lodged in place. The guards stepped toward her, all of them at the same time.

Am I in hell?

The knowing smile on the chief's face sent a chill up her spine.

Kaela stepped forward, almost losing her balance, and put her hands behind her head. The guards closed in on her, herding her out the door like cattle.

She tried to resist a smile of her own. If only they knew who was waiting outside the building with a rifle pointed and ready. But would Rob be able to shoot them all before one got lucky and popped her? Unlike them, if Kaela was shot, she wouldn't be getting back up.

That thought reawakened the nausea.

The guards circled her, and the chief led the group, walking to the front door.

It was exactly where Kaela wanted them to go, but she couldn't look too ready to get outside.

She stopped dead in her tracks, and as soon as the guard pushed up behind her, she braced for impact. The guard shoved her forward, hard, and she fell to her knees. The chief chuckled, echoed by her men.

"How…" Kaela risked, "How are you just… healing them like that?" She looked around at the men, their wounds glowing purple as they closed. Through one of their broken visors, she spotted bright glowing eyes. "Are you controlling them or something?"

The chief scoffed. "I don't need to control my men. They're loyal. You understand loyalty, don't you? After all, you're one of Eric's little henchmen." Her smile was smug. "I wonder if you'd be willing to die for Eric. Or die *with* him."

The guard pulled Kaela back up, and she wrenched her arm from his grip.

"Why are you working for Landreau Corp? Why did you let them do this to you?"

The cool night air caressed her cheek as the guards shoved her outside. Her eyes relaxed after the brutal light of the lobby. Police cars and armored vehicles littered the street.

The chief kept walking but said, "Simple. I was offered a much better deal." She gestured to the glowing purple veins throbbing in her neck. "And don't worry about anyone seeing this. They'll be too busy watching your friends die."

Kaela looked past her smiling face to the two men on their knees, surrounded by guards. A few civilians were looking out their apartment windows. An audience. No wonder Rotoya had brought them out here. They would be a message, a warning to anyone else that tried to resist.

Derek and Lance had their hands up, rifles pointed at the back of their heads. Kaela wanted to look up at the rooftop, to assure herself that Rob was still there, but if she did, she would risk not just his life, but the others' as well.

So she resisted, hoping he was only stalling because he wanted all three of them together for an easier escape.

"Speaking of you and your friends dying," the chief said, her voice suddenly much smoother, "please take a knee right next to them, or we'll shoot both your legs and force you to."

Kaela wordlessly kneeled next to Lance.

"I'm sorry," Lance said. His voice was filled with a sadness he'd never shown before. "I'm sorry for letting Derek and I get caught."

"I'm sorry too," Kaela said. And though she didn't want to, she risked a short glance at the rooftops, but Rob's figure was nowhere to be seen. She'd sworn long ago not to show weakness, but if she were to let herself slip just a little before she died, well… Maybe it wouldn't be all bad. "You didn't deserve to be dragged into all of this. By any of us."

His breathing was hard, slow. He was trying to calm himself down.

“Is this really where we die?” His voice was shaky, rattled. His eyes were wide and bloodshot. The last time she’d seen him like that was after he killed that man in cold blood. He’d turned around, shock and fear on his face, as if he couldn’t believe what he’d just done. Whoever that monster had been was gone, replaced by who he was now. “I’m scared.”

“It’s okay,” Kaela said. Never had she thought she’d be comforting Lance, of all people. Death did crazy things to people, she supposed. She almost swore as her own voice shook. “We’ll be fine.”

When Lance turned his head, Kaela looked past him at Derek’s emotionless face. He was staring at the ground, but she knew he could feel her eyes on him.

Still, he kept his stare on the cold ground, so Kaela did the same. Lance’s breathing became panicked as the chief turned around. Kaela forced her own breathing to steady, holding it down and pinning it like a wild animal. Her lungs protested, her heart pounding in her chest, but she ignored its complaints. The chief walked to her first and stared her down with that same smile.

A spark of temptation revealed itself to her, the temptation to cry and plead for her life. She ignored it.

Right beside the chief’s head, a slight movement caught Kaela’s eyes. She nearly turned her gaze to it but stopped herself. The movement came from the rooftop where Rob should’ve been. That urge to smile returned, and Kaela’s heart beat in intense anticipation. She watched with the best poker face she could muster as the chief reached for the pistol at her side and aimed at Kaela’s head.

Kaela closed her eyes and waited for the distant sniper fire, for the opportunity to get out and crawl back into hiding like the little rats they’d all become.

Crack!

The shot of a rifle split the night, and a splatter of blood hit Kaela’s cheek. Something whizzed over her head. Damn, if Rob wasn’t an even better shot than Derek. In that moment, she allowed a small smile to slide onto her face.

Then a bullet found her chest.

CHAPTER 14
THE DEVIL IS MY...

Lance watched in horror as Kaela slumped to the ground, her head striking the concrete.

The chief stood in front of her body, her face covered in shock and her hand clenching her pistol. Smoke trailed from the barrel.

Rotoya coughed, and blood spilled onto the ground. Even more poured from her neck. Her pistol fell from her hand, and she crumpled to the concrete.

In the moment of blind panic, Derek took advantage of the distraction and turned on the guard behind him. He wrestled the rifle from him and smashed it through his visor. The officer went down, and Derek sprayed a hail of bullets into the crowd of guards.

Lance waited for the guard behind him to fire, but he didn't. Instead, his attention was directed at the fleeing Derek. Another rifle shot rang out from the rooftop, and the guard dropped like a brick.

"Lance, come on!" Derek yelled.

Lance eyed Kaela as he allowed that twisting feeling in his stomach to churn, that killing calm. Whatever beast writhed inside of him hissed and demanded he attack. Holding it back had taken all the strength he could muster. Now, looking at Kaela's still form, he decided that what happened next didn't matter. He allowed the beast full reign.

Eleven guards surrounded him, but most of their focus was on Derek popping shots at them from the alleyway. Kaela lay on the ground near one of them, surrounded by the bodies Derek had left.

She was still.

Lance closed his eyes and breathed. The scent of honey poisoned the air. He didn't think. He stepped back and let the voice within him take over as it whispered.

Survive.

His body moved without him. He grabbed the pistol on the ground behind him. One of the guards pointed his rifle at Lance. Lance wrenched the rifle aside and fired the pistol into the guard's helmet. He collapsed.

Rifle in hand, Lance fired at the rest of the guards. They scattered and dove behind police cars. The gun jolted Lance's arms with every pull of the trigger, and four of the guards weren't lucky enough to find cover, purple spraying from their bodies as they fell to the ground, limp. The empty casings clinked against the concrete as the remaining guards hid behind their armored vehicles. If only they knew Lance was out of ammo.

Six left.

Lance dove behind the nearest police car and slid across the rough concrete as gunfire rang out. Bullets sprayed against the car. Windows shattered, and sparks flew from the metal doors. Lance curled into a ball and waited for the bullet storm to subside.

"Smoke him!" one officer yelled.

Lance told his body to dash into the alley where Derek was, but when he tried to commit to the action, his body refused. *Refused.*

His own body told him no, so he lay there and waited as smoke grenades flew over the vehicles and landed near him. He stared at Derek, and as the smoke rose, he finally stared back. Lance nodded to him, a silent message that he could go. *Go check on Rob.* Derek nodded and disappeared from view as the smoke thickened and washed away anything that wasn't a few feet in front of him.

I hope you know what you're doing, Lance said to whatever was controlling his movements.

His response was a twisting in his stomach.

Lance stood in the smoke, his footsteps as silent as a jaguar's as he walked. He closed his eyes. Heavy footsteps drew closer, surrounding him. His body ignored the cold metal of the gun in his hand and the stuffy feeling of the smoke as he calmly breathed it in. The men closed in, and he took the magazine out of his gun.

The sound drew their attention, and Lance dropped to the ground and rolled as gunfire rang out. A few bullets grazed much too close for comfort.

He stood again. One guard was much closer than the others.

Three, the bone-dry voice in the back of his mind whispered to him. *Two.* He forced himself to breathe deep. *One.*

Lance dodged under a strike from an officer's gun and threw the magazine into the smoke. Metal clanged against a helmet, then a man hit the ground with a thunk. He threw the rifle through the smoke like a spear, and just like the clip, it found its mark in one of the officers' helmets. The sound of the visor shattering sent satisfaction swimming in his chest.

He hated it.

He dodged another swing of a guard's gun and shattered the man's leg with one swift kick. He ripped the helmet from the guard's head and kicked again, purple blood splashing from his nose.

When silence overtook the street, Lance called out, "Kaela? Kaela, are you—"

His words were cut short as something hit him in the head. A flash of light blinded him, then darkness came. His ears rang, and heat spread through his body. As his vision began to return, a dark figure stood in a background of smoke, and before he could try anything, the figure wrapped its hands around his neck and squeezed.

But then the figure screamed in pain with the voice of a woman and looked down. Lance followed her stare to Kaela, her hand firmly wrapped around a dagger planted in the guard's leg.

Lance used the opportunity to kick the woman away.

The sniper fire had yet to return.

The figure reappeared, and Lance's vision cleared, transforming the shadowy figure into the chief herself, the hole in her chest gone, replaced by the red sinew and muscle of her body. Her skin slowly grew over it.

"You didn't think a little bullet would kill me, did you?" Rotoya smiled. "Get up."

She said it so quietly, but Lance didn't know who she was talking to until, one by one, as the smoke cleared, all the officers rose—broken legs, bullet holes, it didn't matter. They all stood and stared at Lance. The ones who still had guns pointed them at him. Kaela had gone still again, her dagger sticking out of the chief's leg. But the chief wasn't reacting to the weapon at all, as if she no longer felt it.

"You." The chief pointed at Lance. "You're not half bad, fighting off as many of my men as you did. Alone? I underestimated you when we first met. I'm impressed, Lance."

His gut twisted at the sound of his own name in her mouth. Even as she spoke, the skin of her chest was slowly growing back, as if he was watching a time lapse.

"However," she continued, "I am much less impressed with your friend. Bring him in." Again, she spoke as if to no one, but seconds later, the sound of heavy boots on concrete and something dragging behind them grated Lance's ears.

Lance turned and couldn't suppress a gasp. Two officers, covered in purple blood, their armor torn and broken, dragged an unconscious Rob to the chief's side. They dropped him like a sack of fish in front of her, and she pressed her boot to his chest, a smirk on her face.

Two more officers came, leading Derek to Lance. Derek had a black eye and a bleeding lip, but other than that, he seemed fine. A scowl shadowed his face. A prick of fear poked at Lance's chest. He'd never seen such a darkness in Derek. Never.

Derek stood beside Lance, and the guards backed away from him, returning to Rotoya.

Despite Lance's urging, the killing calm didn't return. It had left the moment all the officers revived, as if the instinct itself had deemed the fight hopeless.

Or perhaps it didn't think Lance was in danger.

The chief crouched next to Rob, who stirred finally as she dug her boot deeper into his chest. The moment he groaned and blinked himself awake, she smiled at Lance and Derek and held her hand out expectantly.

"Rob, get up," Derek said, his voice breaking. "Do you hear me? I said *get up*."

In seconds, an officer shoved a pistol into Rotoya's hand, and the chief had no more words, no more remarks or smirks. She simply pointed the gun down at Rob and fired.

And fired.

And fired.

And fired.

Rob flinched at the first three then went limp for the rest. The chief shot until the pistol was empty, and when she was done, it was impossible to tell where the bullets had hit. Blood painted his torso, and a puddle formed beneath him. His shocked face was pointed at the night sky, his eyes blank and glazed over.

"Next time, bring someone a bit more… durable." The words were a mere happy hiss out of the chief's wicked grin.

Derek twitched like he was about to charge her, but even he seemed to realize that whatever he did, it would be for naught. Still, every muscle in his body tensed, and tears rolled down his cheeks.

"But you all fought decently. Even sweet little Kaela got in a nice hit." She ripped the dagger from her leg and tossed it at Derek's feet. "She'll be wanting that back."

"You're letting us go," Lance said flatly. "After everything that just happened, you're letting us leave?"

"I had fun tonight. I like hunting you down. But I'm waiting for Eric to return to start the real fight. Now, that man knows how to play the game. You three take it way too seriously. Once he gets here, I can kill you all… Well, maybe not you." She pointed at Lance. "You could be useful to me." She turned around then looked at Rob's body. "We'll be taking him, by the way. Don't worry, we'll ensure he has a proper burial. I know how to be respectful when I want to be."

Derek cursed her. "You don't really think we're going to let that happen, do you?"

The chief didn't even bother turning around. She just reached a hand out for a nearby officer to hand her another gun and pointed it at Kaela.

The chief smiled and said, "I could always just kill your other friend too." Her smile was gone, and her eyes flickered with irritation. "I'm being nice here. A favor to Eric for the years of partnership, if you want to think of it that way."

Anger twisting his features, Derek took a step forward, but Lance stopped him. Rage was blinding him from seeing the consequences of charging her. They'd already wasted too much time.

Derek settled down, the fury in his eyes dying as Lance planted a hand against his chest. The chief chuckled and walked away, back into Landeau Corp, as if nothing had happened. Two officers picked up Rob's body and carried him inside, blood dripping on the otherwise clean lobby floors.

Lance looked around. The streets were mostly empty, save for the few officers left guarding the entrance. The civilians looking out their windows had all disappeared.

"I'll get Kaela," Derek said, his voice a low growl. Once she was secured in his arms, they slinked away into the shadows. "I don't like that she's letting us go."

Lance eyed the rooftops as they walked, pretending not to notice a shadow disappearing from view. "So you see it too?"

Derek nodded.

"What do you want to do?"

"Keep going. I have an idea."

"What about Kaela?"

Derek sighed. "I don't know. The vest took the hit, but she might still have some broken ribs. And she hit her head pretty hard on the concrete."

"I meant what are we going to do with her?" Lance asked. "If we're being followed, then anywhere we take her puts her at risk."

Derek was silent until the hideout was in view. "It's my fault."

"No, it's—"

"My fault," Derek repeated. "Don't try to tell me otherwise. I'm responsible for what happens to the people that work for me. And Rob's death is because of me."

"I don't mean to make things worse by saying this," Lance started, carefully eyeing Derek's reaction. "But why exactly do you think they decided to keep Rob's body?"

Derek growled. "I'd like to think it was a way of spitting in our face, not letting us bury our own dead." He let a moment of silence pass. "I hope that's what it was."

"What else do you—"

"Shut up."

Lance glared at him. "Look, I know it sucks, but you have to at least consid—" He stopped when he followed Derek's stare.

They'd reached the hideout. The rightmost garage door had lost its chain.

Someone had gotten into the building.

And they had no weapons. *Except...*

Lance reached around Derek's hip and took Kaela's knife out of his pocket. Derek didn't protest as Lance inched closer to the shop, unable to peek through the glass door with the taped blanket covering it. The whispers were silent, and nothing wriggled in his stomach. He slipped through the entrance to the shop, gesturing for Derek to follow.

Lance froze when he stepped in. A white van was parked in front of the garage door that had been opened.

"Shit," Lance muttered. "Please tell me you know someone with a van like this."

"No," Derek said. He laid Kaela down gently against the wall.

Lance waited for the calm to settle over him, but it didn't. Surely it would when he needed it, right?

"Here," Lance said, handing the blade to Derek. "I don't need it."

"I'll search the van," Derek said, taking the knife. "You try to sneak down into the hideout."

"Aren't you the sneakier one?"

"Aren't you the one that took down almost ten guys by yourself?"

Lance opened his mouth to protest, but no arguments came to mind. He padded to the ice cream cooler. The floor panel was still firmly shut.

Carefully, he slid the panel open, flipped on the string lights, and peeked down the ladder to the bottom. No sight of anyone yet. As he took one last look at Derek, who was opening the back doors of the van, Lance slid himself into the opening and climbed down the ladder. Nearly every rung creaked. *I swear it didn't creak this loud before*.

With the killing calm still quiet within Lance, fear took its place. Even his stomach was calm, no twisting or slithering within. Something was wrong. It was as if the killing calm had abandoned him.

Not that he missed that dry voice.

Every step lower into the main room of the hideout was like falling a mile deeper into the ocean. Finally, he reached the bottom step, but before he could turn around, cold steel was pressed against his throat.

A voice even colder than the blade hissed in his ear. "Tell me how you found this place. Did you follow us?"

That voice. "Eric?"

The steel lifted, then a hand grabbed Lance's shoulder and whirled him around. He wrenched himself free of the grip, his shoulder burning at the touch.

"Lance?" Eric stared him up and down. "I thought I recognized that hair, but… why the hell are you wearing a Landreau Corp uniform?" He inspected the outfit. "Wow, looking at these things up close, they really are ugly. You'd think Landreau Corp would have some fashion sense."

A hundred questions flooded Lance's head, but Eric was already walking through the metal door into the hideout.

"Where's Derek and Kaela? You didn't get them killed, did you?" He chuckled and sighed. "Nah, I'm sure you didn't." He slid the blade back into his cane, an infuriating smirk on his face.

After all they'd just been through, Lance was *not* in the mood for Eric's jokes. The calm was still gone. The urge to punch him in the face was all Lance.

"Kaela's hurt," Lance said simply, walking into the hideout.

An older man was sitting at the computer chair. He appeared shy, withdrawn, definitely out of his element.

"Eric, please tell me you didn't kidnap someone from Landreau Corp."

"You said someone was hurt?" The man stood. "I'm a doctor. If you show me where she is, I might be able to help her."

Eric said, "He's a friend. His name's George. Don't worry, we can trust him."

Lance stared into those wild eyes. "Since when do you trust anybody?"

Eric chuckled. "I trusted you to take care of things around here, didn't I?"

"Yeah, we're going to have a conversation about that once Kaela's taken care of." Lance nodded to George, who rushed toward the ladder. "Derek! Someone's coming up. He's a doctor."

"And try not to kill him. He's good people," Eric added. He sat down at the computer chair and rested his cane in his lap. "So, Lancelot, tell me. How have things been on your end of the spectrum?"

Lance balled his hands into fists. He didn't know how Eric could be so casual after disappearing and leaving them to fend for themselves. At least he hadn't abandoned them forever, like Lance had originally thought.

"No. You're answering my questions first," Lance said, more anger in his voice than he intended.

Eric tensed, and his dark eyes went cold, staring right at him. His hand tightened on the cane, and Lance could tell the blade hiding within was already calling to him.

"I want to know *exactly* why you made me leader. Were you hoping I would get us all killed so you could get in bed with Landreau Corp?" His heart hammered in his chest as Eric remained completely still. Maybe he just didn't know how to react to someone speaking to him in such a way.

"I work a very dangerous job, Lance. I need someone to take my place when I'm no longer here. If I die, the web I've weaved in this city will untangle, and all the little bugs I have tied in it will break free and start anew. That's not ideal for me. I need someone who can take over. Derek has Rob, and Kaela has Amari. I have you."

Exhaustion nipped at Lance's heels, and he leaned against the cold wall for support. The adrenaline was wearing off, and new pains emerged all over his body. His eyelids were heavy. "*Why?* Why me? How did I stand out in your messed-up little roster of people you can drag into your damned *web*?!" His chest tightened and twisted at the maddening poker face Eric had glued on.

"I… because…" Eric's tension eased, and his grip on the cane loosened. Those dark eyes emptied of all energy, like he was shutting down. But he picked his head up and spoke, his voice softer, more sincere. He looked Lance in the eye. "Because you're my son."

CHAPTER 15
HE'S ALIVE... RIGHT?

Kaela's head pounded, a terrible pain that came in waves. Then she heard voices. One she recognized, and one she didn't.

Light shone, and the voice she didn't recognize instructed her to open her eyes. She did, slowly. Her body was stiff and groggy. Her chest and ribs ached, but her head was worse, as if a vise was tightened around her skull.

"There you go," the older stranger said, and the light disappeared. The man put the flashlight back into his coat pocket and examined her.

Derek was standing close behind him, and she tried to smile at him, but her head protested.

"You okay?" He wore a smile, but his voice was filled with worry.

How adorable.

"Yeah," she squeaked as her ribs protested. So many questions were swimming around in her throbbing head, but until she could think straight again, the interrogation would have to wait.

"It's hard to tell without an X-ray, but I don't think any ribs are broken. Bruised pretty badly, but not broken. No concussion, either. You're a tough one, young lady. Lucky too. What do you last remember?"

Kaela hissed in pain as another wave hit her head. Even thinking hurt, but she tried to remember what had happened before she went out.

"I remember being on my knees," she started, "in front of the chief. She was about to shoot me. Then I remember seeing Rob on the rooftop. After that, I remember hearing a shot ring out, and that's about it."

The man looked at Derek, who nodded.

"That's good," the man said, standing. "My name's George, by the way. I'm a friend of Eric's."

"Eric's here?"

"That's right. He's down there in the bunker."

Derek sighed and scratched the back of his neck. "Do you think we can get her down there? I don't like being exposed like this. I have a bad feeling about the chief letting us go."

Kaela blinked. The chief had let them go? "Why?" she breathed.

Derek sat next to her with a groan, casting a glance outside. "She said something about it being one last favor to Eric. But I have a feeling she might just want to track us. Which means, if you're able to stand at all, I would really appreciate if we could all go down into the hideout."

Kaela shifted, but her head forced her back down. More than anything, she wished staying in this exact spot was an option, but Derek's paranoia was right. She would rather deal with the pain than be killed by the chief. Rotoya wouldn't aim for the vest next time.

"Okay," Kaela said, and she rose.

The process was slow and frustrating, and her ribs allowed her very little speed as she used the wall for support and slid up to her feet. Derek stood on her other side, keeping her balanced.

"Where's Rob?" she asked. "I need to thank him for what he did."

Derek remained silent, and when Kaela looked at him, his eyes were pointed at the ground. What had happened while she was out? She searched her memory, and in the darkness, a moment of clarity revealed itself. Her hand had wrapped around the cold grip of her knife, plunging it into the leg of some officer. She wasn't sure if that was real or a figment of her imagination. She felt that cold hit her hand again, and when she looked down, Derek was slipping the knife into her palm. She took it and sheathed it against her leg.

Derek wrapped Kaela's arm around his shoulder as she pushed off the wall. Every step she took sent waves of pain to her head and ribs.

George waited patiently at the cooler, and with his and Derek's help, she climbed down the ladder into the bunker. She leaned against the wall until Derek climbed down to help her balance again. George slid through the entrance with some trouble and waited on the other side should she fall. She was embarrassed at needing so much help because of an injury.

Rob... If it wasn't for him, she wouldn't be alive.

Derek's silence had said it all. If he had been simply captured, Derek would have said something. He was supposed to be Derek's replacement. One of the few times Derek's eyes lit up was when he spoke about Rob. If only she knew what had happened, not only when she had been out, but before that. How had Derek and Lance gotten captured in the first place? Tears welled in her eyes from the pain the bright white lights were causing her head. That was what she told herself, anyway.

Lance was sitting in the desk chair, hunched over with his hair hiding his face. Eric was standing on the other side of the room, wearing a careless expression. Tension hung between them.

Neither George nor Derek seemed to notice as they led her to the bed. Kaela's head threatened to split open as she sat and caught her breath, the pain in her ribs more annoying than excruciating.

"I know it hurts, but try to breathe as deeply as you can. It will prevent infection," George said.

Kaela only nodded and risked a glance at Lance. A sadness clouded his green eyes, like he'd just had his world turned upside down.

"Okay," Eric said with a clap of his hands. "Now that the gang's all here, I think it's high time we catch each other up." He cleared his throat. "Obviously, I'll go first."

His son... his son. The words echoed in Lance's head, banging around and trying to burrow deeper into his brain. No way—no way in hell was he that man's son.

He'd had so many questions, so many doubts, but before he could voice any of them, the sound of creaking reverberated from above, and Eric had lunged for him and covered his mouth.

He'd smelled of death, and the darkness in his eyes matched. "You are not to speak a word of this to anyone. If you do, I won't answer a single question you have. If you can be patient, we'll talk about all of this. *Later.*"

Those words still lingered in his head, and the only thing that snapped him out of his thinking was the clap of Eric's hands as he addressed all of them. He didn't wait for anyone to protest and began his story.

Lance listened to it, forcing himself to focus on it, and when he finished, Kaela told hers, then Derek told of what had happened to him and Lance. The two of them caught Eric and George up on everything that happened.

"Lance," Derek called.

Lance looked up, meeting the stares of everyone in the room. He'd zoned out. The bombshell Eric had dropped on him still hadn't stopped blowing shrapnel around. The chaos in his head refused to settle, and the blood drained from his face as he looked at all of them, trying to keep his expression calm. Pretending in front of Kaela and Derek felt foreign now. Eric and George, however, were his biggest motivation to return to the old habit. The way Eric was looking at him told him to steel himself.

"What?"

Kaela sent him a look, but he ignored it. He calmed himself and steadied his breathing, rubbing his clammy hands on the uniform.

"I said that you should probably tell them what happened when we got captured."

Lance opened his mouth to question why, but the sheer sadness behind Derek's eyes answered his question. He wasn't in a talking mood.

Lance swallowed. "Right. Right, of course."

Lance explained everything he could remember, trying not to leave out any details. Everything had gone by in a blur, and clarifying what was stored in his mind was more difficult than it should've been.

"The way she looked at you," Derek said, his arms crossed. "The way she talked to you. The chief obviously sees you as valuable."

"And so does Eric," Kaela said, looking at the very man whose name she uttered. Then she set her sights on Lance. "What is it about you, Lance?"

Lance's heart hammered against his chest, and as tempted as he was to spill what Eric had told him, the threat of not getting any answers kept him silent. But as the thoughts swirled around, he couldn't stop the questions. *Does Rotoya know? Is that why she didn't want to kill me? Does she want to turn me into one of those zombies and kill Eric for her? Is that why I can fight so well? Is it somehow... genetic from Eric? This bloodlust?*

"I don't know," Lance finally said, his voice cracking. "I don't know." He glared at Eric, but his poker face remained unfazed. "But right now, we need to focus on the lead we found."

Kaela didn't appear satisfied with the answer, but she said, "You're right. We need to head to the church and find out exactly what Malcolm was so interested in there."

"Where is this church, exactly?" George asked.

Lance sighed. "It's pretty deep in the slums of the city. Not many people even know about it anymore. It's a ghost town there."

"Only problem is we need to get there. If Rotoya is following us, we need a distraction to give us an opportunity to leave unnoticed."

"So what do we do?"

"This is a terrible idea," Lance said, sitting in the driver's seat of the van. "And it smells like chemicals in this thing."

"I warned you," George said.

"Come on, Lance. Take one for the team," Eric said, his grin as frustrating as his cane clacking against the floor. He tossed it anxiously from hand to hand. He was nervous—the first time Lance had seen him so.

"I hate this," Lance said as George shut the back doors of the van. "I hate this so much. You realize I know sparingly little about driving, right?"

"I've already run you through the basics. All you need to do is cause a distraction long enough for us to get out and sneak to the church. You can meet us there after you use this." Eric handed him the device. The cold metal in his hands should have grounded him, but it only made him more nervous. It was a symbol of commitment. He really was about to do this.

Of all the things Lance had done in the past week, he was about to do the craziest and, frankly, stupidest of them all. But he was the only one that stood a chance of being spared by Rotoya.

"Now what?" Lance asked, his chest twisting in pain. This wasn't like fighting, nothing at all like it.

"Now," Derek said, "you just wait. The police are coming, that's for sure. And the moment you see something suspicious, you ram through the door and hold the chase for as long as you can. We'll be down in the hideout until then, and I'll wipe the computer while we still have time."

Eric's smile widened, and he patted Lance on the shoulder. "Good luck… and be careful." Even with the armor on, Lance gritted his teeth at the touch, like acid on his shoulder. That it was Eric's touch only made the feeling worse. His skin crawled.

Son. Lance shook his head. *It can't be true.*

"Oh, and, uh…" Eric slid his arm over Lance and buckled his seat belt. "Safety first."

Derek ripped the blanket from the glass door before descending into the hideout.

And just like that, Lance was alone as the others climbed down into the hideout. He was stuck in this death trap of a van, looking through the busted glass door for any sign of movement or any red and blue flashes. Thanks to the police force's hesitation to kill him, he was the perfect candidate.

That didn't make it any less nerve wracking. One saving grace was that none of them could see him rubbing his face and whispering curses at the steering wheel.

Minutes passed by, with Lance tiredly rubbing his face and staring out the glass door of the building. His eyelids became heavy, and as time slowly dragged along, he considered, just for a moment, leaving the van.

But then a light shone through the glass door—headlights for sure.

Then more headlights appeared. He woke himself up and straightened in his seat. Cars were slowly closing in on the building.

Derek had been right after all.

The rumbling of other vehicles became louder then halted. Car doors closed, and quiet footsteps scraped the ground and splashed into water puddles.

"Give that to me," someone said, nearly inaudible.

Lance had his hands on the keys when a voice sounded, amplified by a megaphone. "Hellooo? I know you're in there. I gave you enough time to exchange your last words, so I think it's time to come out, or I'm coming in." It was the chief's voice, that unmistakable gruff tone.

The beast shifted in Lance's stomach as if awakening. The calm settled within him.

Lance turned the key, and the engine roared to life. He slammed the pedal down just as the police sirens flashed.

They were too late.

Lance crashed through the garage door, swerving the van and wincing as the tires screeched against the road. The van tilted sideways.

No, nononono…

Lance swore as the van hung in the air then tilted back, slamming down. A shock went up his spine on impact. He stomped his foot down on the gas and sped down the street, burnt rubber tainting his nose.

"After them!" Rotoya yelled, her voice fading in the distance. Two police cars sped after him before he even made it down the street. The few cars sharing the road with him swerved out of his way, narrowly dodging him every time. The two cars behind him blared their sirens, and the flashing red and blue lights kept his foot on the gas pedal.

He swerved down every street that led away from the slums, and a rush went through him with every dodge of a car. Adrenaline coursed through his veins.

No voices spoke in his head, but the calm settled further, and the beast continued to move in his stomach. His driving became smoother, more confident. Swerving was easier, and dodging cars became second nature. Even so, the officers gained on him.

The van wasn't fast enough.

Lance swore, not thinking as he slammed the brakes and turned the car around. The squad cars tried to stop as well but skidded past. One of them stopped too abruptly and swerved. The car flipped over and slammed into a nearby building, shattering glass and brick.

Breathless, Lance sped off once more. The single car left chasing him was farther behind. He smiled at the victory, flipping off the car in the rearview mirror. Then he furrowed his brow, wondering why he'd done that.

His heart pounded, his blood pumped, and his skin tingled. The wind whipped harshly against his face. God, he felt so alive right now.

A flash of light caught his attention. It was too late for him to dodge the armored truck slamming into the side of the van.

It all happened in slow motion. The world spun, and glass flew through the air. Then a terrible screech sounded; he wasn't sure if it was the voice in his head or his own. The van slammed into the ground, and Lance was thrown around, his seat belt keeping him loosely in place.

Everything was blurry until the spinning stopped. Lance caught his breath. His head ached, his leg screamed, and his arm was numb.

He turned his head, fighting through dizziness, and assessed the damage. The van was right side up. Glass was scattered everywhere. The passenger side was bent in, and the back door that wasn't missing was wide open. He slowly turned his head again to himself to search for injuries.

Blood. He had blood on his arms. A drop of blood spilled from his face onto the airbag he hadn't realized had deployed. Finally, his vision returned to normal, and he sat still, awaiting his upcoming fate. Plan A had failed, and Plan B was all that remained. He swallowed, tasting blood, and nearly vomited.

Footsteps pounded toward Lance, but he couldn't move. The beast within him stirred as if reminding him it was still there. No voice whispered to him.

Two officers climbed in through the back of the van, the chief with them.

She looked furious as she ripped the seat belt off his body and pulled him from the van. Pain coursed through his body, and he groaned. The chief dragged him all the way out of the van and dropped him on the ground. Lance spat blood onto the concrete.

"Where are they?" the chief said, so close to Lance's face that he could've spat more blood at her if he wanted.

"Why would I tell you that?" Lance asked, pain blanketing him.

A kick to the ribs, and Lance coughed in response, thankful that no more blood came out.

"Because," the chief muttered in his ear, "if you do, I'll offer you amnesty. I'll forget you even exist. All you have to do is reveal their location, and I'll bring you to a hospital myself. After that, we're done. Good deal?"

Lance's gut stirred. That word floated around in his head, a seductive whisper like it always was.

Survive.

But this time, his body gave no indication of wanting to fight. Instead, it wanted to give up, to accept the deal.

Lance almost smiled. To be forgotten and left alone—it was an offer too good to be true. And if he believed the chief would honor it at all, he probably would've accepted it.

Lance let silence grow tense between them for a few breaths. "Fine. I accept your deal."

"Good. Now tell me where they are."

Lance looked at the van then lowered his voice. "There's a compartment hidden in the floor of the van. That's where Eric is. Kaela's… She's dead. She died before we could help her. Derek ran off. I don't know where he is. He said something about revenge for Rob." To sell his point, Lance embraced the pain torturing his body and released a groan.

"Eric's here? Why should I believe you?"

"Check for yourself."

The chief laughed. "You could have avoided so much trouble if you'd just sold them out earlier. Shame. Officer Terrance."

Lance recognized that name from somewhere, but the officer that approached the chief still had his helmet on.

"Take Lance to the car. When I ensure that he's telling the truth, take him to a hospital. Oh, and ask Caleb for a dose of his *special* medicine. We want to ensure Lance here heals up quick, don't we, Lance?"

"Wait, what do you mean?" Lance asked as Officer Terrance roughly pulled him to his feet. "I'm not taking that shit!"

Rotoya smiled at him then kept walking.

Officer Terrance dragged Lance to the car while the chief stepped inside the van.

Lance smiled and slowly reached into his jacket for the device.

His hand slipped against the cold metal, and he flipped the latch up.

Rotoya eyed the floor then paused. She crouched and felt her hand along where the compartment was. She braced her hands on it and pulled. As soon as the hatch opened, and a look of shock crossed Rotoya's face, Lance pressed the button.

After a heartbeat of silence came a deafening boom. The van exploded in a cloud of fire and smoke. The blast sent Lance and Officer Terrance into the side of the police car.

Lance stood as Officer Terrance gawked at the van, its shrapnel scattered across the street. Car alarms sounded in the distance, and the cloud billowed into the sky. The van was nothing more than a skeleton of what it used to be, and the chief's body was farther down the street, blown back by the blast. Her body was burning to ash right before their eyes.

"What have you done?" Officer Terrance yelled. He turned and faced Lance. "What have you done?!"

"Fuck you, that's what."

Officer Terrance charged him. Lance sidestepped and shoved him into the car. His head crashed into the window, shattering the glass.

While Terrance groaned on the ground, Lance jumped into the police car and drove away, the pain aching his body even with the new shot of adrenaline.

The chief. The explosion. Had it really worked? Her burning corpse was still and lifeless as he drove past, but he'd seen worse happen to her. Lance hissed at a wave of pain in his head then his arm and leg. Every movement of his muscles ached him. His leg screamed the loudest. He needed to find the others, get patched up by George, and get answers from Eric.

You're my son. With no other sounds to distract him, Lance could hear only those words in his head. That was the first time he'd seen Eric sincere. He'd *seen* it right in those black eyes.

Lance found his eyes shifting to the rooftops, the streets, the cars that he passed and that passed him. He relaxed as he drove. The armor he wore served as a police uniform, and any cars or people he passed didn't give him a second glance. However, each first glance was always filled with fear.

The streets had been so active on that night out with Kaela, but now they were nearly barren. How long would this curfew last?

At any moment, he expected the chief to appear out of thin air and fill him with holes, but the farther he drove, the quieter that fear became.

Lance drove around for as long as he could stand the pain before changing direction toward the slums. Every few seconds, his eyes shifted around as he tried to ensure that he wasn't being followed. Sirens had sounded in the distance minutes ago, and Lance envisioned the twisted faces of the men around their fallen chief. Or worse yet, the smiles as she rose from the ashes, more vengeful than ever. He swallowed the lump in his throat and kept driving. He knew he was reaching the edge of Arachna when the buildings transformed from clean to ragged. He drove past broken windows and boarded-up buildings; barrels with fire and people huddled around them; sleeping bodies on the side of the street.

Lance wondered what was held deeper in the slums. He'd always stayed away, in the outer ring. Some of his customers told stories of how bad the inner slums were. Fighting and bodies on the street, gunshots sounding off every other hour, needles scattered in alleys, buildings covered in vines and so worn down that they seemed ready to collapse at a gentle breeze. It didn't sound too different from the outer ring, but apparently, it was much worse.

He hadn't thought much of it at the time, but as he traveled deeper into the slums, his heart sank. He passed a small bakery, halfway caved in and swathed in vines. He also passed three different bodies in only a few minutes, some in puddles of blood, others looking at him with empty, glazed eyes. The smell of fire and blood and sewage mixed in the air. How could they even breathe down here?

The pain in Lance's head came in waves, and every slight movement in the alleyways, every shift in the shadows, had him jumping in his seat. His breathing became labored the longer he drove, the pain worsening as the adrenaline faded. Nausea stirred in his stomach and clawed at his throat.

He focused on his surroundings, diverting his attention to anything else besides his aching body. Movement shifted in almost every dark alley, as if his presence startled whoever hid within the shadows. He almost laughed as he glanced down at his uniform then at the steering wheel of the police car. He was likely the first 'cop' anybody in this part of the slums had ever seen.

He drove until he reached a clearing. A graveyard. Tombstones were scattered across the field, some so old that they looked as if they would crumble at a gentle breeze. So many poor souls had been laid to rest here.

Forgotten.

Lance thought of his name on one of those stones, of the very real possibility of that happening with every plan he enacted with this group. One careless mistake, and Lance would join a field of tombstones. The thought pushed his foot harder on the gas pedal. The shape of the church came into view under the moon's light, standing hauntingly tall next to the graveyard.

The closer he approached, the more details of the church came into view. The memories of the few times he'd visited a church were faded. The matron of the orphanage had always allowed the kids that were interested to attend.

At the time, seeing the families together had made him sick. Even the lure of escaping the orphanage for a few short hours wasn't worth having the unattainable shoved in his face. The church burned down a year later, replaced by a restaurant. Looking back, perhaps he should have gone more often.

This church, however, was abandoned, left to rot by the congregation. Just like all things, it had ended. The small cross at the top of the steeple, outlined by the moonlight, served as another memorial. A much larger tombstone among the many others.

What used to be a parking lot was now an area of broken concrete with grass and roots overtaking it. He pulled into the darkest spot in front of the church and shut the car off. The doors remained locked until the silhouettes of four people standing in front of the church doors came into view. Before he stepped out, Lance glanced at the console.

Something inside of him urged his hand forward to open it.

He flipped open the console, and a handgun slid forward. As one of the silhouettes walked toward the car, he fit it snugly in the holster at his side.

When he stepped out of the car, he could better recognize the man walking his way.

"I heard the boom from here," Eric said. "Nice work." Even in the dark, the taunting smile was audible in his voice.

"I'm glad you enjoyed it," Lance said, lacing his tone with malice. When he took another step, his leg struck him with pain. He nearly fell over but braced himself on the hood of the car.

"Are you okay?" Eric's smile disappeared. He almost looked worried. "You look hurt."

Lance ignored the question. "I know we meant for the explosion to slow the chief down, but the way she looked before I left…"

Eric was quiet as Lance walked around the car, but he held his hand out, his cane dangling lazily from it. "Take it," Eric said, his tone a serious whisper, just as it had been back at the hideout.

You're my son.

Nausea curled in Lance's stomach, and he lowered his own voice. "Why should I accept your help? If this isn't just another one of your *cons*, why would you try to be a father to me now? You weren't for the first twenty-three years of my life. Don't try to help me now."

He tried to sidestep Eric's arm, but Eric mirrored him. "Then don't think of it that way. You're useless with that limp. Just take the cane long enough for George to patch you up."

Lance fumed but took the cane anyway. He wouldn't admit it, but as he stepped forward, putting the brunt of his weight on the cane, the relief nearly coaxed a sigh out of him.

George, Kaela, and Derek were waiting for him when he reached the entrance, and George gave Lance extra support as they entered the building.

The inside of the church smelled of musty wood. The stained glass windows were faded from years of exposure to the sun. The pews were layered in dust. The sliver of moonlight shining in through the windows revealed more dust particles floating in the air.

George sat Lance down on a creaky pew, and memories came flooding back: the bright light of the sun shining in; the laughter of the congregation; the catnaps he took in the middle of the sermon, despite the matron's futile attempts to nudge him awake. Resentment had coated his heart when the people around him greeted each other while he and the other orphans went ignored.

Unwanted.

"Derek, see if you can find some candles. I'm going to need as much light as I can get." George directed his attention to Lance as he opened his doctor's bag. "Now, tell me what's wrong."

Lance did so, wriggling the police uniform off, pain searing through him. With George's assistance, he relaxed on the church pew, the cool air settling in his bones.

Lance checked off the symptoms in his head mindlessly. The smell of the church lingered and fogged his thoughts with distant memories. A stain in his head, forever there, like a scar.

The faint rustling of George's bag rose above the noise in his own head. Sleep nuzzled beside him. A muffled voice told him to stay awake.

He couldn't.

He was too exhausted.

Kaela frowned as Lance fell unconscious, and George swore. Derek brought candles over, one by one. The light of the flame revealed the cuts, the bruises, the dried blood crusting Lance's hair. The cane beside him fell onto the carpet.

Eric walked with a mild limp and leaned against the pew beside Kaela, his arms crossed. The man always had a good poker face, but he bit his lip. It lasted only a second, but she caught it. He seemed worried about Lance. But that couldn't be the case. He never worried about anyone but himself, or at least he never showed it.

"There's something you're not telling us," she whispered.

Derek stepped outside the church while George worked. With Rob gone, she didn't blame him for wanting to be alone.

"What is it?" she asked.

Eric smiled like he always did when he wanted to hide something. "Why, I don't think I know what you mean," he said.

Kaela met his stare and held it. "Something went down while I was out." She finally broke the stare. "Something between you and Lance. And I think it had something to do with why you brought him on the team."

Eric made a grave mistake. He stayed silent. He didn't make a joke or try to cause a scene.

"So that *is* what's eating at you," Kaela said, resisting her own smile. "I've been thinking and thinking about why you chose Lance. I can agree that there's something special about him, but it took me a while to see that. Then it turns out he can fight better than just about anyone here. Even Derek." She paused. "Even you."

"It's really bothering you, isn't it?" Eric asked, smiling. "I could tell the moment I brought him into our organization that you hated him. And when I made him the leader, you were furious."

"Are you saying that's why you did it?"

"No, but that does sound like me," he said with a low chuckle. "Yes, there is a very good reason why I brought Lance onto our team. And it's that very reason why I made him the leader while I was gone. How'd he do, by the way?"

"He had his moments, but I wouldn't say he was much of a leader," Kaela said. "He was as lost as we were, but we also figured it out together. As a team."

Eric hummed. “You were all lost without me, were you?”

“You left us suddenly and gave us a new hideout and a wave goodbye as your parting gift. So yes, we were kind of lost without you.”

“So Lance managed to make you all work together? Doesn’t sound like a half-bad leader to me.”

Kaela rolled her eyes. “Yeah, since you’re so interested. You can’t even give me a hint as to what’s got you so enraptured about him?” She leaned back in the pew with a casual smile. “I think I deserve at least a hint as to what the deal is between you two.”

Eric kept that smile, composed and calm. She’d had him. For just a moment, she’d made him squirm. But he’d recovered, and now *he* had control of the conversation. He would either tell her or not. She was at his mercy, but if he wanted to play this game, she would play it too.

All night if she had to.

“You’re right,” Eric said, and the smile disappeared. The stare he gave her wasn’t a challenge but an invitation to stare back, to see for herself that what he was about to say next was genuine. “Lance is not just an average man.” His tone became sincere and soft. He’d never looked like this before, and despite the spark of skepticism flickering in Kaela’s chest, she let him finish. “In fact, he’s much more than average, but I’m sure you guessed that.”

He chuckled and continued. “Lance…” He paused, as if reconsidering.

Kaela found herself leaning in. She was breathless in anticipation, and she knew Eric was enjoying it.

“He’s CIA,” Eric said, his smile gone. His eyes snuffed out any amusement, and his voice was genuine. “He was given a new identity, to come to this city as a simple storeowner, nothing that anyone would suspect.”

Kaela crinkled her nose. *Smells like bullshit to me.* “And how do you know that?”

“The chief told me before she went crazy. She did some digging and figured it out. She always was a good detective. Knowing what she did is likely why she wanted to spare him. Injecting a CIA agent with that kind of drug could give them access to a lot of information.”

"So you brought him in… why, exactly?"

Eric huffed with a smile. "His timing in Arachna coincides perfectly with Landreau Corp's sudden burst of popularity. I had reason to believe he was spying on them."

Lance stirred then went still again.

"I thought if I scratched his back, then he'd scratch mine."

"So the thing with his parents… it was fake?" she asked.

Eric nodded. "I negotiated a good deal with his superiors. If I did everything in my power to get as much information as I could on Landreau Corp, we'd be gifted a hefty sum of money and the possibility of them using our services later down the line."

Kaela narrowed her eyes. "So why did you leave him here with us to go to Agni?"

"To meet with his superiors stationed in Agni," Eric said. "They wanted to send me in to get information on Caleb Landreau. The rest of the story, I already told you back in the hideout. I just left the part out where I met with the superiors again and updated them on what happened."

Kaela glared at him. His flair for drama burned like flames behind his eyes. A performer on stage, just like the Eric she knew.

"So you're saying Lance can fight because he was trained to?"

Eric nodded, his smile replaced with a serious grimace. "I admit I thought this would be easier than it's turned out to be."

Kaela refused to give Eric a reaction, but her chest tightened at the memory of what Lance had done to those men. But that wasn't professional, not like Derek was or how a trained agent would be.

Not at all.

He'd fought like an animal let out of its cage, wild and free to roam. Even Lance himself seemed frightened of it.

"How sure are you that he won't turn us in when this is all over?" Kaela asked.

"You let me take care of that."

Just like you took care of Malcolm? She felt another twist in her chest. "This story is completely and utterly untrue, isn't it?"

Eric's expression was strained, like he was about to burst out into laughter. "That's for me to know and you to lose sleep thinking about."

She glared at Eric as he limped away and looked up at the stained glass windows.

Kaela scoffed. That entire story was ridiculous, and the smile he sent her only proved her right. She could've bitten steel. She'd let him lead her into that farce too easily. Balling her hands into fists, Kaela sighed with a silent swear to the ceiling then pushed herself from the pew. Derek was just walking back into the church when—

Crash!

The sound of glass shattering rang through the church. Kaela whirled.

"What was that?" Derek said, his voice sharp as a dagger.

"I don't know," Kaela said. "It sounded like it came from… underneath the floor?"

Eric was already walking to the back of the church, peeking through one of the doors.

Kaela slid her hand along her knife as she eased toward Eric. Derek followed her.

"Looks to me," Eric whispered, "like this church has a basement." He pushed the door open wider to reveal a set of concrete stairs.

"I'm not very experienced in church," Derek said, "but I don't know of many that have underground levels like this."

"Hmm," Eric said, stepping down. "Maybe there's a holy artifact I can steal and take over the world with."

"Funny," Kaela said dryly.

Derek huffed. "Thing is, we don't know if he's joking or not."

Eric turned around slowly. "Maybe I'm not." He continued down the stairs then stopped when he reached the bottom.

Kaela crept beside him, Derek on his other side. She froze.

They stood in a crypt. Past its crumbling archway, stone sarcophagi lined the room. Two more sat in the middle.

But the sarcophagi weren't what froze Kaela in her tracks.

A man, his skin gray and lifeless but riddled with bright glowing veins, stood over one sarcophagus at the other end of the arched stone crypt. Torches lined the hall, and the man moved to the far side of the space, revealing lab equipment covering the flat surface.

Derek swore.

"No way," Eric whispered, squinting. "I don't believe it."

Kaela held her knife at the ready.

"I think that's…" Eric stood from his crouched position and stepped forward. "Malcolm Landreau?"

CHAPTER 16
WHAT IN THE HELL HAPPENED TO YOU?

Malcolm Landreau stumbled and fell at the sound of Eric's voice, a beaker crashing to the floor next to him.

Kaela's jaw hung as she stared at him. The way his body moved, it almost appeared... rotten. She would have gasped if her ribs weren't aching. *Is this real? How hard did I hit my head?*

"Can you imbeciles not see that I'm working?" Odd noises came from Malcolm's mouth as he crawled over the remnants of broken glass and swept them away. His mouth hung open, teeth rotted, eyes dark purple and empty of life. But as he looked at Eric, a smile crossed his face. "You."

Kaela expected Eric to smile back, but even he seemed to find the sight too much.

"Malcolm Landreau," he said, calmly looking him up and down. "What in the hell happened to you?"

The man laughed. "I think you know, my dear boy." He laughed again, a giggle almost. "I truly must thank you for what you did to me. Gruesome as it was, you proved my experiment a success. Oh, how I had been dying to see if it worked..." He paused in disposing of the broken glass then looked at Eric. "And I suppose I did."

"You were supposed to be buried," Eric said. His teeth clenched, and his eyes danced with fire.

"Oh, I was," Malcolm said. "I dug my way out. At this very church, in fact. I admit, it was clever of you to have my body brought all the way out here. After I survived, I had my brother Caleb send lab equipment so I could continue my research."

Something flashed in Eric's eyes, and his face fell for a flicker of a second. "So that's how he knew…"

"What experiments?" Derek asked.

Malcolm smiled with those rotten teeth then gestured at himself. "This experiment. The drug that can make a human into a superhuman." A tooth fell from his mouth. He frowned at it for a moment and added, "With some side effects, of course."

Silence hung in the air for longer than it should have, and after a few moments, Malcolm seemed to have lost interest and went back to working on something at his table.

Kaela narrowed her eyes. Why was he so willing to answer their questions?

"I don't understand," Derek said. "How does this drug work? Do you know about what happened to the police chief?"

"So many questions," Malcolm muttered rapidly, sounding like he was talking to himself. "The one in this city? Hmm, this city… 'Full of suckers,' my brother once said. Which one, I wonder? Perhaps both."

"Malcolm," Kaela said. "The question?"

"Ah, yes. Chief of police was unwilling at first. Claimed she knew her men better than anyone. Claimed they needed no drugs to make them better. But my brother convinced her." He giggled again. "*Convinced*, I say. That is the word my brother used. She found that herself and her men were much better off with the new medicine. Very few side effects. I was not so lucky." He was silent for a moment, staring at the ground as if in shock. He composed himself and continued, "Though I suppose that was because mine was a different strain. Regardless, this drug was a genius idea. *My* genius idea. My brothers helped. Caleb knew how to sell, how to *convince*. Daniel is much stronger, much tougher. Head of security, so he needed—"

“What does the drug do?” Eric asked with a frown twisted in an unnatural fashion, nearly resembling a toddler with his toys ripped away.

Perhaps it was the stench permeating the room.

“The drug,” Malcolm repeated, “triggers bursts of adrenaline in controlled waves. Stronger, faster, quicker thinking. However, some have opposite effect. Mental fortitude plays large factor. Different strains may have different effects. Also aids immune system. Resistance to dozens of diseases and sicknesses. Miracle drug.”

“What do you mean?” Kaela said.

He hummed. “This strain of the drug provides me with immortality. Life expectancy increases exponentially.”

More silence, and as if forgetting what he was talking about, he resumed his work.

“Immortal?” Eric said, his eyes bright. “What do you mean, ‘immortal’?”

“Immortal,” Malcolm said. “Virtually speaking. Nearly impervious to damage, but can still technically die. Greatly slows aging process. Double, maybe triple usual life expectancy.” After another chuckle, he continued what he was doing. “Does not slow decomposition process, however. Then again, drug had not activated then. Perhaps it *can* slow decomposition. I must add that to my research!”

“This is exhausting,” Kaela said. “I need a drink.” She had one last question, after seeing what the chief had done. “What’s the connection between the police chief and her men? When they were injured in ways that should have killed them, she… did something. And the men would rise back up and keep fighting.”

“Ah,” Malcolm said. “Yes. Drug has two primary strains. Beta strain and alpha strain.” He writhed his hands together like they were cold. “Chief of police given alpha, her men beta. Marvelous things, she can do. Control the drug in their blood. Turn off pain receptors, heal them, raise them from near death, even. Unexpected results, however. She now holds control over them. Theoretically could control blood outside of bodies as well, almost like telekinesis. Haven’t tested theory.” He laughed then looked scared. “Caleb. Had his men take a similar drug. Gave himself alpha drug, for when he would need to awaken it within them. Only in emergencies, only when he lost his temper. Yes… gave the chief of police a cocktail of both, unfortunately. He can control her as well. Not sure that she knows that."

Malcolm pointed at Eric with a smile. "It is you he does not like. He will only shut alpha drug off once you are dead. Only then will he and his men return to normal. Or so he claims. Fascinating."

Again, as if nothing had happened, he resumed his work.

"An alpha drug," Kaela repeated. "Does that even make sense? I mean, what can something like that be made of to be remotely activated?"

She stared at the rotting man before her. He claimed immortality, yet his body was so distorted. Whatever this drug was, it was not to be played with.

"What is in this drug, Malcolm?" Eric asked.

But Malcolm said nothing.

Eric asked again.

And again.

But Malcolm remained silent, as if he couldn't hear anymore.

"Is there a cure?" Eric pushed.

Only then did Malcolm react. He said, "Of course not. Why ask for a cure to a cure? Putting a bandage on a clean patch of skin. Why do such a thing?" He laughed again, and purple blood splattered to the floor.

"Doesn't look like much of a cure," Kaela said.

"All things require some sacrifice."

Eric took another step forward. "Is there no possible way to shut off that drug?"

Malcolm paused and stared at him longer than he should have. "I suppose there could be… some method of shutting down the medicine. Death is possible, though unlikely. Decapitation, a thorough burning, things that render the body entirely useless. Irreversible damage of the mind may also suffice. A cure, however, as you put it, a version of the drug that can deactivate the other strains… What a challenge. A challenge I would rather enjoy." He smiled, and another tooth fell out. "I shall begin my research immediately!"

Lance stirred as pain crawled all over his body. His head pounded, and a faint clicking disturbed the silence. Also, a quiet voice was speaking to itself. He turned his head, and an orange glow shone through his eyelids. The voice went quiet, and the clicking sound did the same. His eyes were heavy.

Finally, he opened his eyes. At first, he had no idea where he was. But then… George was staring at him. His hand was in his doctor's bag.

"How are you feeling?" George asked.

Lance's throat was dry and scratchy. *Water. If I could just have some water...* "Terrible," he answered, his voice like gravel. "Water."

George sighed. "I don't think we have any water. I'm sorry."

Lance leaned his head on the hard wooden back of the pew and swallowed, the feeling akin to swallowing a razor blade. But then he raised his head and looked around the empty church. Only him and the doctor.

"Where is everyone?" Lance asked.

A door was open at the back of the church.

"They went down to the basement because they heard something." He thought for a moment. "They've been down there for a while, but I keep faintly hearing their voices, so I'm sure they're fine."

Lance tried to stand, but his leg protested.

"You're lucky," George said. "None of your injuries are too serious. You'll be sore for a few days—that's for sure. The worst problem is that leg, so stop trying to stand without that cane." He nodded toward Eric's cane on the floor then bent over to pick it up. George offered the cane to Lance, who grabbed it tightly. "It's broken pretty bad. I did my best to make a splint, but that's about all I can do. From here on out, it's up to you not to walk on it."

Lance looked down at his leg, at two small pieces of wood wrapped tightly to it. He tried to move it, and a spike of pain shot through his leg. He swore through gritted teeth and gripped the cane harder.

Lance felt along the cane until his thumb grazed the smallest of switches. That would unlock the blade, he knew. It would come in handy later, especially if he had the calm settling over him, or the serpent—the beast, whatever it was. *Beast* sounded right, the way it hissed and whispered inside him, the way it fumbled around in his gut.

"I've got to say…" George said. "You're tough for someone who just owns a store here. You seem like the kind of guy that's been in a few scraps." He laughed, the sound hearty and warm.

"Not really…" Lance snorted with another look around the empty church, unwilling to show more weakness to this stranger than he already had, especially when Eric trusted him.

"No military experience at all?"

Lance furrowed his brow. "Why?"

"Just curious."

"Okay," Lance said. "You mind if I ask a few questions?"

George shrugged and motioned for him to continue.

"What's the deal with you and Eric? He's not the most trusting guy, so for him to put as much faith in you as he does is surprising. And for you to so easily come to Arachna and join the group like this is odd. Did he threaten you… bribe you?"

George looked at the open door in the back, and the distant sound of voices spiked, only to quiet down again. "No," he said. "I actually wasn't planning on it at first. I was going to find somewhere to set up shop here until things in Agni calmed down. When I saw what was happening in *this* city, I figured my best option would be to stay with Eric, at least until I find my own way."

"You'd probably be safer leaving."

George smiled at him. "Maybe. But I caught a glimpse or two of what those officers are doing to innocent citizens. At my age, I can't really handle myself in a fight, and I certainly can't take a beating, so the way I see it, it's best to keep the company of people who can fight. Besides, you all would do well to have a doctor around." He made eye contact with Lance. "It was a deal I made with Eric on the way in. And I've known him since he was a teenager. At that time, he was more of a petty thief and a con artist. I always patched him up when he was hurt."

"When did he actually start trusting you?"

"About a year or so after I met him. He never understood why I patched him up for free, and he always thought I would ask for something in return. When a year passed and I did nothing of the sort, he opened up more. Next thing I knew, we were friends."

George didn't speak after that, and Lance didn't either, more because of the pain in his throat than anything else. Lance closed his eyes and breathed as George stood. The pew in front of him creaked.

But with his eyes closed in the silence that followed George's movement, something caught his attention. A sound outside the church. A car door shutting.

Lance ignored it at first. Then a familiar voice whispered in the back of his mind.

Run.

His eyes shot open. It was the only word besides 'survive' the beast had spoken. For it to offer such an alternative…

Lance sat upright, and pain seared through his body. He removed his pistol from its holster on the floor and blew the candles out.

George turned to him. "What are you doing?"

"Go to the basement. Now," Lance whispered, the adrenaline numbing most of his pain. "There are people outside, and unless you're expecting company, we need to hurry." With nothing but the moonlight and memory to guide them, Lance stood with the cane in his hand and his arm around George. The doctor's breath became quick and panicked when silhouettes of men passed by a window, their shadows casting over Lance and George as they rushed to the door in the back and shut it behind them. George fumbled around at the door until it locked with a heavy click.

"How'd they find us?" George asked, his voice breathy.

Lance cursed. "The police car," he answered. "There's a police car right outside. It's my fault. I should've hidden it better."

Stupid, Lance thought. *How'd they even think to come this far into the slums?*

George didn't acknowledge Lance's confession as they stumbled down the stairwell.

Derek, Kaela, and Eric were sitting on the stairs, their haunted faces illuminated by torchlight. Lance didn't understand until he and George reached the bottom of the stairway. He froze. A glowing-purple-veined man was fussing over a flat sarcophagus with an array of chemistry equipment scattered across it.

Before he could ask, Derek stood to face them both. His face was grim. "What's wrong?"

George spoke, his voice panicked. "Someone's here."

Kaela whirled her head toward them, but Eric appeared unfazed.

"What?" Derek glanced at Lance and twisted his face in thought. "Why the hell would they have come all the way out here?"

Eric kept his gaze on the purple-veined man, still huddling over his equipment. He seemed completely unaware of what was going on around him. "Is it the chief?"

"Who else?" Lance asked. "It has to be her."

"No," Eric said. "No, I don't think so. You said she was burned, right? How badly?"

"She took the brunt of the explosion, and her body was on fire. How much more could she have been burned?"

They were going to die. Lance could feel it. The calm refused to grace him this time, but the thing in his stomach writhed as if trying to escape.

Eric's eyes flashed at Lance's tone. But then the purple-veined man turned his attention toward them.

"I may know," said the man, and when he stepped closer, Lance recognized him. He nearly lost his balance, the cane preventing him from falling. But he stepped back and sat on the stairs.

Malcolm Landreau, looking as rotten as his corpse was supposed to be.

"Oh, God." Lance gaped at them all, raising his hands to his head. "Did I *die* or something? What in the hell…" He ran a hand through his hair then checked his forehead for a fever. "Am I in hell? Is this a fever dream?"

Malcolm spoke quickly, as if his brain was too fast for his mouth. "As stated before, decapitation, burns beyond function, destruction of the brain—all render drug useless. If chief of police burned badly enough, it is likely she is very dead. However… strongly depends on the amount of damage done by—" He stopped and looked up at the ceiling. His eyes widened, and he smiled, but then the smile dropped, and fear crossed his rotting features.

"No," Malcolm said, backing away. "He's here." He closed his eyes for a moment then reopened them in shock. "He's angry."

Lance's heart dropped to his stomach, then Eric's eyes widened, and something like fear appeared behind them.

Lance froze—injured, scared, and on the verge of a panic attack. The stirring within him slumbered. The killing calm wasn't there, just panic and adrenaline.

Eric smiled, but the fear in his eyes remained. "It seems Caleb Landreau has found us."

Malcolm glanced around. "Can hide in sarcophagi if you like. Brother will be unhappy if you are here with me."

Eric shared a look with Lance. "I don't think we have a choice."

"They're empty," Malcolm said. He held a finger up with a proud smile. "I checked."

Eric looked around at the sarcophagi. "Kaela, George, hide in that one." He pointed at the one carrying Malcolm's equipment. "Derek, you and I take the one on the right. Lance, the one on the left."

Stone ground against stone as they went to work sliding the lids of the sarcophagi enough to hide in. "Not all the way," Eric said. "If the lids fall off, we'll never get them back on."

"Careful with my equipment," Malcolm said as George and Derek slowly slid the lid open, the liquids in the beakers shaking. He stared at Lance, a grin growing on his face. "I remember you. That day in the cafe. Deal was unsuccessful. You seemed calmer then." He frowned and looked Lance up and down. "Something different about you. How do you feel?"

Lance gulped. "Pretty shitty… but better than you, I guess."

"I feel great."

Kaela finished helping Derek get Lance's sarcophagus open.

A bang sounded on the door, echoing down the stairway.

They all shared a look before scurrying to their hiding spots. Lance grabbed Kaela's arm as she walked past. She glared at him with fire in her eyes, but it didn't match the stinging in his hand. He drew his pistol and placed it in her palm. She stared at it then gripped it tightly and climbed into the sarcophagus with George before closing it partway. It was open just enough to peek out and shoot if a fight broke out. Lance could hardly tell it wasn't closed.

Derek slid into the other sarcophagus. Lance tossed Eric's cane to him, and Eric raised an eyebrow.

"You'll need it if we get into a fight," Lance said.

Lance climbed into his sarcophagus and strained to close the stone lid, leaving it cracked open just enough to see the room.

Thank God for the dim torchlight.

"Don't worry," Malcolm said. "I shall pretend none of you are here. This is exciting!" Something squirmed inside Lance. At first, it seemed the killing calm had returned, or the beast was warning him of some danger. But it was just discomfort at seeing Malcolm so animated. A man that appeared to be a glowing, rotting corpse, moving around and talking, looked so... wrong. The smell was enough to elicit a gag, but Lance resisted as another bang sounded at the door leading to the stairwell.

Bang!

The silence in between each bang was colder than the sarcophagus.

Bang!

Lance took a deep breath and closed his eyes.

Bang!

What would happen if Caleb spotted them? Could they all fight him off?

Bang!

Malcolm giggled then gasped, and Lance nearly vomited.

Bang!

The door broke off its hinges and clattered down the stairs. Rushed footsteps followed, echoing throughout the chamber.

Officers stormed the room, surrounding Malcolm. They swept the area, checking corners and walls. But they didn't take more than a quick glance before bringing their attention back to Malcolm.

The room went quiet, then another set of footsteps came walking calmly down the stairs, getting louder and closer.

An older man appeared. His hands were behind his back, and his face held no expression. His veins and eyes were purple. He approached Malcolm, wafting expensive cologne strong enough that Lance crinkled his nose. It didn't blend well with Malcolm's rotting stench.

"Brother," said the man whom Lance could only assume was Caleb. His voice was steady and powerful. "How have you been?"

Malcolm coughed. "I have been well, brother. I see you have activated the drug."

"Yes, and yours still has not restored you yet," Caleb said, stepping closer to Malcolm. "Your body is just as rotten as the last time I saw you."

Malcolm's breath was uneven. "I understood the consequences when I took this strain, brother. I wanted to live forever, and I have my wish."

Now Caleb looked around the room. "Why did you lock the door?"

"I heard a noise. Someone was in the church, I believe."

Caleb hummed. "Yes, there's a police car outside. We're looking for the man driving it. You didn't see anyone?"

Lance hissed as pain shot through his leg, and he covered his mouth. The beast finally stirred in his stomach, and he could've sworn it growled at him.

Caleb stopped midsentence and smiled. He turned his head slowly toward Lance's sarcophagus.

Lance trembled, but not from the cold. The look in Caleb's eyes sent a chill down his spine. The beast went silent.

Caleb snapped his fingers, and the guards, who'd all been standing motionless moments before, turned on a dime and stormed to the sarcophagus. They ripped it open and pointed their guns at Lance.

Lance raised his hands in surrender, his breathing panicked. Strong arms grabbed him and dragged him out of the sarcophagus. His leg screamed in pain, and Lance screamed along with it as the soldiers dragged and dropped him in front of Malcolm.

"Son of a bitch," Lance muttered at his screaming leg.

Caleb harrumphed. "Are we going to discuss the elephant in the room, Malcolm?"

Malcolm shook, and he didn't speak.

"You're not telling me you did this to him, are you?" Caleb kicked Lance's leg lightly.

Lance swore, hissing and fighting the tears welling in his eyes.

"You couldn't hurt a fly."

"I never," Malcolm spat, as if the idea sickened him. "Was injured when he arrived." He giggled. "Said… said he would hurt me if I didn't hide him."

Lance felt a small kick in his side. Then a harder one.

"Get up," Caleb said.

Lance almost spat on Caleb's perfectly polished brown shoes, just to spite him. Instead, he glared at him.

Caleb stared down at him with a deep frown. "I said get up."

Lance did as he was told, struggling with his leg. He eventually found himself eye-to-eye with the man. He suppressed his cries of pain, refusing to allow this man to see anything of him that he didn't want him to.

Caleb's stature was that of a gentleman, a businessman, yet fear pricked at Lance with every movement he made. "Why would you fear pain, Malcolm? Aren't you immortal?"

Malcolm stuttered. "Immortal, brother… not invincible."

"Malcolm," Caleb sang. "Brother… this man is a fugitive. Don't tell me you're helping him." Anger flickered in his eyes, but he covered it up. "He looks exactly like the man you described that day. The one that was with Eric."

"Yes! With the man that murdered me. Thought you looked familiar, sir," Malcolm told Lance.

"We'll discuss this later, brother," Caleb said. He looked at Lance. "I have a favor to ask you."

"What do you want?" Lance asked. He kept his face neutral, but sweat beaded on his forehead, and his leg ached.

"You killed the chief of police."

The words lifted a weight off Lance's shoulders. So fire *did* work. They could be killed. But how many more had been infected with this drug? How many would have to die in order to stop this madness?

"Burned her alive." He turned his head toward a few of the officers.

"The men and women in this room worked for the chief. I wonder what they would do if I left them here alone with you? If I cleared their minds and told them to have at you, what would you say to that?"

Lance expected to feel a stir in response to the obvious threat, but the killing calm remained silent. "It doesn't matter."

"It doesn't? The only thing keeping you alive right now is me. So I'm going to ask you a question, and I expect you to answer it, or I will walk away."

Lance resisted the urge to glance at Eric and Derek's sarcophagus. If Caleb was as powerful as Eric had said, letting him walk away was the best option. Perhaps the killing calm inside Lance knew that, as if it was some kind of entity, a parasite that resided within him and only showed its head when necessary.

"I'll take your silence as understanding," Caleb said. "Where are your friends at?"

"I don't know. I was supposed to distract the chief while they escaped. They told me to meet them here, but they never showed." When Caleb narrowed his eyes, Lance continued, "Now that I think about it, I'm starting to feel like I was bait—"

"You're lying," Caleb said. The words hit Lance like a spear to the chest. "You know where they are, and you don't want to tell me." He shrugged. "That's fine. Just tell me where Eric is, then. He's my priority, anyway."

Lance gave no response.

"I'll give you one more chance, and then I'm walking away. You understand what that means." He took one step closer to Lance, and his eyes glowed. Power exuded from him, and every second that he stood close nauseated Lance.

"Where. Is. Eric?"

Lance kept his mouth shut.

Caleb snorted and leaned back, staring into Lance's eyes.

"Fine," he said. "You don't have to tell me. From what the chief said, you can fight pretty well. I suppose you think you can take on these officers by yourself, even with your leg injury here." He kicked Lance's leg again.

It took everything in him not to yell out in pain.

"That didn't take you down?" The veins in Caleb's arm glowed bright purple. The muscles throughout his arm rippled and bubbled like boiling water. Within seconds, his arm was as big as his head and glowing a bright violet. He smiled at Lance, who was too caught off guard to dodge the blow to his chest. The impact sent him flying into the sarcophagus, and when he hit the ground, he couldn't breathe. He gurgled and gagged, trying to tell his lungs to breathe, demanding it from them.

While he was trying to get his breath back, Caleb spoke again, but it wasn't addressed at him. "I'm so disappointed you would betray me in this way, Malcolm."

Finally, Lance gasped. Air filled his lungs, and his chest hurt with every breath he gulped down. He coughed, praying that no blood would come out. His eyes filled with tears.

Malcolm spoke next. "I'm sorry, brother."

Caleb leaned in close and whispered something in Malcolm's ear. Whatever it was, it elicited a gasp from Malcolm. The ground swayed under Lance as he tried to stand again, only to fall back onto the floor, his leg screaming in pain. Caleb seemed completely uninterested in what happened to him. The officers surrounding him looked ready, like a pack of wolves waiting for their alpha's permission to fight over a pound of flesh.

"No," Malcolm asserted. He giggled. "I shall ensure he does not escape from your… efforts. You have nothing to fear. My body will simply come back from any death I am given… except decapitation, perhaps—still unsure. I shall simply cover my head." He looked at Lance, frowned, and turned back to his brother. "You may go now, brother."

Lance looked up at them, out of breath. Caleb gave a suspicious look to his brother then looked down at Lance and smiled.

"If that is what you wish, brother," Caleb said. "When you're done climbing out of the rubble, come back to Landreau Corp. We'll talk, eat, laugh. After that, we'll discuss your progress on that new project I asked you about." As he ascended the stairs, he looked back one last time with a menacing grin. "Do as you please."

The officers lowered their guns and holstered them. Their veins stopped glowing. Just like hyenas, they circled Lance like the savages they were.

There it was—the stirring within Lance's stomach. The killing calm sensed the danger, but even moving that leg sent pain shooting through it. He gritted his teeth and closed his eyes. The officers closed in. If he didn't try to fight back, he wouldn't stand a chance once they began.

But the calm settled within him, and he opened his eyes again.

The officers were all standing around him.

One tried to send his foot into Lance's face. Time slowed. Lance grabbed the leg midkick and twisted it. The bone snapped. The officer screamed in pain and crumpled to the ground.

Kaela popped up from her sarcophagus and fired her pistol. She hit two officers in their exposed sides, dropping them. Lance's body moved, launching itself with his good leg at the sarcophagus. He dove inside, nearly landing on George, who was curled in on himself with his hands over his head. Kaela ducked back into her sarcophagus just in time as the rest of the officers drew their weapons and opened fire. Bullets sprayed on the stone and equipment, shattering stone and glass alike. Shards of it scattered everywhere. The air reeked of chemicals.

"My equipment!" Malcolm screamed.

The bullets stopped for a moment.

Suddenly, a sound rose above the silence. A quiet sound that none of the officers seemed to hear.

But Lance did.

He peeked out from the sarcophagus, and purple blood sprayed on him as a blade emerged from an officer's throat. Eric's smile shone through the dim light. Derek shot out from his sarcophagus and sent an officer's rifle into her helmet. The visor shattered, and Derek threw her to Eric, who shoved his dagger into her face. The blade pierced through the back of the helmet. Lance's stomach turned.

The last two officers turned to open fire.

Derek fired first, spraying bullets into their bodies. They dropped like bricks.

The room went quiet again, for good this time.

Lance was breathless when he made to stand. Eric wiped his blade on an officer's leg. The clean sound of metal on metal reverberated on the stone as he sheathed his weapon.

"You're going to want this back for now," Eric said, handing the cane to Lance, who took it gingerly to balance himself as he left the sarcophagus.

Kaela emerged from cover with George. "Everyone okay?"

"Yeah," Derek said. He, too, was out of breath. "That was intense."

"Wait," Lance breathed. "Where's Malcolm?"

After a moment of silence, Lance heard a giggle.

Malcolm poked his head out from beneath the stairs. "I am fine." He emerged with a bit of a smile. "We should leave. Brother is going to blow church sky high, he said."

Lance froze and stared at him. "What?" He took a step toward Malcolm. "Is that what he whispered to you?"

Malcolm nodded. "Told me to come with him. I said no, not leaving my research." He leaned in and put his hand to his mouth as if someone would hear him speaking. "But in truth, I didn't want to leave you all behind. My research is all in here." He tapped his head then looked at the equipment on the table, most of it shattered and broken. "Unfortunate. Let us go."

"Where?" Kaela asked. "There are going to be soldiers out there, setting the explosives up. How are we going to get out without anybody seeing us?"

"No," Malcolm said. "Unlikely. These were the only officers he brought."

"What do you mean?" Lance asked.

"We must leave now." He rushed to the sarcophagus Lance had been in and took out a small bag, not unlike George's doctor bag. He stuffed notes and whatever equipment remained intact inside and closed it. "Let us go. I believe there is a side door."

He'd already climbed the first set of stairs when he looked back and waved his hand for them to follow.

Derek cursed. "What choice do we really have?"

The group followed Malcolm upstairs and back into the church. The door to the stairwell had been busted in and knocked down the first set of stairs. For Caleb to be so strong, and for Lance to have survived that punch—Lance's heart skipped a beat. *He was holding back.*

Malcolm looked around carefully and signaled for them to continue following him. He led them to the other side of the sanctuary and disappeared into a thick patch of darkness, then a door opened. Moonlight spilled in, revealing the smiling Malcolm.

They left the church and wound around to the back. At Malcolm's suggestion, they each hid behind a gravestone, peeking at the church from around the corners.

Lance's chest ached, and his leg groaned in pain as the cold ground bit into it.

At first, Lance stared at Malcolm's grave, where the ground had been clumsily dug up and bits of wood were scattered across the ground. But then he realized Malcolm was trying to draw their attention to the church.

Caleb stood in front of the building, his hands behind his back. His eyes glowed, and his veins glowed even brighter. Like a beacon in the night, he lit up, yet he stood as if nothing was happening.

Lance didn't understand what Caleb was doing until a deep rumble shook the church. The ground trembled, and a loud boom sent a shockwave through the night.

Wood splintered, concrete shattered, and the entire back of the church began crumbling in on itself. As if in slow motion, the walls, the roof, the glass collapsed, all broken.

The church folded in on itself as blue flames erupted from the wreckage then disappeared.

When the dust settled, all that was left of the church was the front half. The back half was rubble.

"What just happened?" Lance risked whispering.

Malcolm shook his head. "Not here."

CHAPTER 17
ARE YOU READY TO TALK ABOUT...

Caleb stood proudly in front of the church with a satisfied smirk that didn't leave his face, even as he slid into his black car and drove away.

When he was gone, Lance climbed into the passenger seat of the police car. Malcolm, George, Derek, and Kaela pressed against each other in the back. Eric drove.

The stench of rotting flesh filled the car, and Eric opened the rest of the windows, which only welcomed the new smell of burning trash.

Kaela requested a pain pill, and Eric took the bottle from his jacket and tossed it to her. She swallowed one then offered one to Lance. "For your leg."

He yearned to grab the bottle, take a handful, and forget about the world for a while. More and more, he missed that sweet relief. Still, he managed to refuse them.

Kaela fell asleep minutes later. Derek nodded off soon after, and Malcolm frowned at the window and muttered to himself. It sounded like some kind of formula.

"Were you really telling the truth?" Lance whispered, glancing back at the group.

Eric was silent for a moment as he aimed a lingering stare into the rearview mirror. “George, do me a favor and cover your ears, will you?”

George raised an eyebrow but followed the request anyway. Malcolm grinned and mimicked the action. “Yes, of course. Blocking out the noise should help me think.”

Eric surveyed them with another glance at the mirror before muttering with a sigh, “Yes, I was telling the truth.”

Lance rolled his eyes. “And is that all you have to say about it?”

“I will give you answers once we are somewhere more private.”

With an annoyed snort, Lance leaned his head out the window, just to breathe in some night air, bitter as it was. The moon cast its soothing light on his face. He gripped the cane loosely and rubbed the smooth metal handle with his thumb. He traced every crevice and indentation in the carving. A wolf’s head. His thumb rubbed over the cold metal eyes, the ears, the snarling mouth.

“Why a wolf?” The question came out before Lance could stop himself.

Eric smiled and glanced down at the cane. Finally, a question he seemed willing to answer.

“The wolf is a symbol of loyalty and perseverance.” His smile widened. “It’s a reminder to have both at all times.”

Lance hummed. “You weren’t loyal to me, though. Dropped me off like I was a broken toy.”

“You’re right,” Eric said. “I wasn’t loyal to you. And that’s why I chose that carving. Every time I hold that cane, I know it’s a wolf’s head I’m holding onto. It’s a reminder of what I did and a warning not to make that mistake again… or try not to, anyway. It’s good to stay with my pack, and I’m working on it.”

There it was, that rare sincerity that hid somewhere within Eric. Underneath the instability of his actions, his mind seemed perfectly fine. All a show, a performance for them, to look unpredictable to friends and enemies. Lance scoffed as he thought about it, then scoffed again as he considered just how fake that sincerity might be.

“Trying to stay with the pack, yet you left us behind to go to Agni and put me in charge?”

Eric smiled again, but it wasn't the taunting grin nor the wicked smile like the snarl Lance ran his thumb over.

"I did say 'working on it'. Besides, leaving was as much for you as it was me." Eric stole another glance in the rearview mirror. "I was curious to see how you would be as a leader. Should anything happen to me, I need someone willing to take my place. I told you this." His voice was barely a whisper, and even Lance had trouble hearing it.

"And what makes you think I would ever want to take over for you? Maybe I want to go back to my store and live some semblance of a normal life."

Eric's smile faltered. "Call it a hunch. I just have this feeling you'll change your mind. And anyway, I think with some practice, you could make a great leader. You have potential."

Lance dug his nail into the cane handle. Anger gripped his heart, and that beast stirred within him, just a little. "Whatever. I'll allow you to keep that fantasy in your head. When this is all over, I'm out, and I expect to keep my store with its renovations in return for all I've done." It wasn't an act this time. He didn't puff his chest out, nor did he hide his expression. The anger and the demand were as genuine as the beast stirring in his stomach.

Eric said nothing after that, and Lance didn't bother looking at him to see what his reaction was. It didn't matter, anyway. He was in pain, being hunted, and could die any day. If there was any time to make such a demand, it was now.

Eric parked the police car on the side of the road once they reached the outer ring of the slums. They woke Derek and Kaela and abandoned the car, treading lightly until they were out of the slums and crossing the street to an empty parking lot. After the dash, they stopped to catch their breath, shrouded in darkness.

"So now what?" Lance asked, sitting against a wall and laying out his sore leg. "Our last hideout's probably guarded by now, and we dealt with the chief, but now we have to deal with something ten times worse."

"I'm more interested in learning how Caleb managed to blow the church up like that," Derek said. "It didn't look like any explosives I've ever seen."

Everyone looked at Malcolm, who perked his head up and shushed them. A second later, a police car drove by. Once it rounded a corner, he settled down.

"Yes, should explain," Malcolm said, his voice shaky as his eyes darted all around the alley. "Blood connection. Drug given to Caleb, chief of police, Daniel. All alpha strain. More special than beta strain given to officers and Daniel's soldiers." He paused. "Appears to be more of a connection than originally hypothesized. I could… sense the blood, the drug within it. Brother ignited it like gasoline within the fallen soldiers and used their bodies as explosives. So powerful, it blew up the back half of the church." His eyes widened. "Truly incredible. Shouldn't even be possible. Not for him, anyway." He grinned. "Very creative brother." His smile became a frown. "And scary."

Derek shook his head. "I don't understand how he can turn blood into an explosive."

"Oh," Malcolm put a hand to his mouth and laughed quietly. "Did I forget to mention the secret ingredient of my magnum opus?" His question was met with silence, but he answered anyway. "Nanobots." He tried to suppress another laugh but failed. His face brightened like a child's.

More silence, until Derek said, "You mean like… the kind of nanobots you see in those sci-fi movies? Those nanobots?"

"Inspired by the same premise, but not quite executed in the same way."

Kaela rubbed her head. "Did I hear that right, or are these painkillers stronger than I thought?" She glared at Malcolm. "So you made a drug to control people and use them as… robots, basically?"

"No," Malcolm said, nearly singing. "Had no such intention. I wanted to rid the world of disease… longer life spans. Nanobots within their bloodstream would attack viruses and diseases more effectively than any other medicine in the world. And I… well, I wanted to live forever… to continue my research unhindered by age. Began working on a strain that would work exclusively to keep me alive for centuries. Much more potent than the strains given to my brothers. I cannot control nanobots, however, only sense them."

Derek crossed his arms. "That doesn't explain how Caleb blew up a church using those… nanobots."

"A fault of my brothers, unfortunately. Daniel wanted his own strain for him and his soldiers. Was how the idea of alpha and beta bots came to me. Daniel could issue orders to his men wordlessly. Combat effectiveness increased by tenfold. Alongside healing them, making them stronger." He went quiet, and the police car rounded the corner again before disappearing. "Harmless, I thought. I developed his strain as a side project while working on my own. Must have done something wrong. Alphas could… manipulate his soldiers' thoughts. Convince them of things they wouldn't believe, like a whisper in their ears. And then Caleb found out… I don't know how he has such control over the bots… He has not had the time to understand them as I do.

"He has always lusted for control. Sees city as one big experiment. With Landreau Corp's men, and control over police department, he can practice control over beta drug. Somehow alpha drug has twisted his mind. Made his obsession for control overwhelming. He intends to take over country, maybe even world, with these nanobots. Holding world leaders under his thumb." He shook his head, and his hands trembled. "I do not wish to know what such a world would look like, especially with the influence of nanobots."

Eric leaned closer. "How could you make a drug like that?"

"I did not intend to create the alpha and beta bots for their current purpose. It was supposed to increase the effectiveness of Daniel's men—that is all… Somehow, the nanobots can… speak to each other, and alphas can manipulate betas in nearly any way fathomable." He sighed. "A modern-day blood magic, if you think about it." He started a laugh then cut it off. "Would be proud if my creation were not being used in vain."

Lance watched carefully as a smile started to crawl onto Eric's face until he wiped his mouth and it disappeared. "So you *willingly* made this drug for your brothers?"

"I did," Malcolm said. "Though at the time, my judgement was clouded. Was busy trying to perfect the nanobots that would be going into my bloodstream. To ensure it was safe. Never knew it would turn into this." He looked out at the street, toward all the chaos created by Landreau Corp and triggered by Eric. "I am no better than my brothers. So caught up in my own selfish desire. Should've seen this coming."

"You can still fix this," Lance said. "If you can make a cure."

"We can talk about this later," Kaela said. "We've wasted enough time as it is. We need to go somewhere."

Eric looked her in the eye. "What about the Rose?"

"I closed all of my Roses except the one on Main Street," Kaela said. "Does Caleb not know about me owning that business?"

Eric shrugged his shoulders. "I'm not sure. It depends if Rotoya mentioned anything about it. There's always the chance she told Caleb, but the closest safe place for us is the Rose, and surely Caleb wouldn't think we'd be dumb enough to go there."

Kaela narrowed her eyes. "But we *are* dumb enough to go there."

Eric sighed. "We don't need to stay there. We just need a place to wash up, get some food, and get out before Caleb even suspects us."

Kaela sighed and rubbed her head. "We have a basement that we could hide Malcolm in…" She cursed then held a finger up. "*One* night. That's it. Then we're leaving and hiding somewhere else."

"So it's settled?" Derek asked.

Lance stood clumsily. "Even if it's close by, how are we all going to get there without being seen?"

"Well…" Derek looked at the three vehicles parked nearby. "I guess we have to take a car."

Before anyone could protest, Derek was already walking to the nearest truck. He peeked into the cargo bed then turned back to wave them over.

"It should be just big enough to fit all of us." Derek turned his head toward George. "Can you drive us?"

The doctor looked like a deer caught in headlights. "The Red Rose… Yes, I saw it on the way to that auto repair shop." He hesitated. "I… I think I remember where it is."

Derek nodded. "Good, because you're the only one of us that Caleb doesn't know about."

They clambered into the cargo bed and closed the tailgate. They were exposed from above, but at least no cars would see them.

Lance couldn't breathe. The stench of Malcolm wasn't any less sickening than it'd been earlier, and being trapped so close to him, even with fresh air, turned his stomach. Every time the truck lurched to a stop, he almost lost whatever was left in his growling stomach.

"Someone distract me before I vomit," Lance finally said.

"Same here," Kaela mirrored.

Eric coughed. "Babies." His voice was strained, and Lance knew he was feeling sicker than any of them.

"Must admit," Malcolm said, "small possibility I can properly research a cure. Large possibility I will never be able to procure it. Not without proper equipment. Important pieces in my bag, but basic equipment will suffice to complete my set."

"Your office didn't have any equipment that I can remember," Derek said, his voice nasally from pinching his nose.

"It doesn't," Malcolm said. "My equipment is in the labs on the third floor."

Lance rolled his eyes. "Well, you can forget about us trying to infiltrate Landreau Corp again."

Kaela also spoke with a nasally voice. "I have a friend that has some equipment, I think. Nothing heavy duty, but maybe it could help you."

Lance glanced at the rooftops, praying with all his might that no officers or agents were watching them. There were no signs of movement like earlier, but it didn't mean nobody was there.

The rest of the way to The Red Rose was silent, only broken on occasion by coughs or swears when the stench worsened. Malcolm seemed completely unfazed by all of it. The truck came to a stop, and they waited until a pat rapped on the side of the truck to move.

When Lance jumped from the cargo bed, he felt like he'd been underwater, and he gasped for the cool, fresh night air. Kaela and Derek did the same, but Eric looked to be mostly fine.

Probably a façade, Lance thought as Eric stumbled on his footing as if slightly drunk.

Derek bent over for a few seconds next to the truck, and Kaela had to pat him on the back before he stood straight again. He looked sicker than the rest of them, but he'd been placed the closest to Malcolm as well.

Poor soul.

George had parked the truck in the alley next to the Rose, and after a nice long breather, Kaela knocked on the side entrance. The door opened slowly, and Amari poked her head out. When she saw Kaela, the door burst open, and she leapt forward, grabbing her in a hug. The door nearly hit Malcolm, who they'd told to wait behind it so that Amari wouldn't be taken aback at the sight of a living, breathing, rotting man.

When Amari and Kaela separated, she said, "The police have been looking everywhere for you guys. I can't believe you're actually here."

"How's business, Amari?" Kaela asked. "Have the police been here at all, asking any questions?"

Amari shook her head. "Nobody."

"Good," Kaela said. "We need you to hide us for the night, and we're keeping a friend here in the basement."

Amari looked at George.

"Not him," Kaela said. "Just… just let us inside. And don't panic."

"Okay," Amari said. "Whatever you say, girl."

She stepped aside, and everyone walked in, including Malcolm.

Amari gasped, but when she made eye contact with Kaela, she swallowed the scream before it could escape. After a quick look around, she closed the door behind them. "What the hell are you?"

"A scientist," Malcolm responded.

Lance remembered the smell of the place, the perfume that permeated the air, the soft lighting, the glowing neon signs, the sound of giggling girls and jazz music, and the nude pictures and paintings everywhere. Something about it was comforting, familiar—better than the last few places they'd been.

Amari darted past Malcolm and went to Kaela's side, holding her nose. Kaela turned to face them all, and Amari did the same.

"Our… unwell friend, Malcolm, is the one that we'll be keeping in the basement. Have some of the girls spray the place with perfume, light some candles and incense, and for the love of *God*, please tell them not to scream or panic when they see him. Warn them that he looks…" She glanced at him. “Well, dead. Tell them he has a skin condition. Not contagious.”

Amari nodded and turned to walk away.

“And another thing,” Kaela added. “Bring your chemistry equipment down to the basement.”

Amari crinkled her nose. “My chemistry set? It’s already in the basement. I haven’t touched it in years.”

“Perfect,” Kaela said then waved Amari away.

With a nod and a lingering stare of confusion at Malcolm, Amari was off again. Kaela rushed them to her office.

Lance looked down at himself as they walked past some of the girls. Eric and Derek stood on each side of Malcolm in a pathetic attempt to hide his condition. They were all smelly and covered in blood, both red and purple. Their armor and clothes were torn and worn out.

Kaela opened the door to her office and urged them all inside while she addressed two more girls.

“I need one of you to bring us six sets of clothes from the store down the street. Two XLs, three mediums, and just grab me something comfortable from my closet, please.” She turned her attention to the other girl. “As for you, I need you to get all the showers ready. Let me know when you’re done.”

Both girls nodded and were gone in a flash.

Lance stared at Kaela. Her usual grace and balance were still present, still as catlike as ever, but she was unflinching, unmoving, and powerful in every word she spoke, like a strict mother instructing her children. The moment she closed the door and stepped to her desk, the strict manner melted away, and she was the casual, lazy feline once again, even as she held her ribs with a wince.

She sat in her chair with a groan and reached into her desk drawer. “It feels good to be home,” she said, pulling out an unopened bottle of wine and a wine opener. She popped the cork and took a hearty gulp from the bottle. She then held the bottle out for anyone that also wanted some.

Malcolm took a step forward to reach for the bottle, but she drew it back with a glare. He retreated into the corner. Derek and Eric both refused the offer, but then Kaela pointed the bottle at Lance. He took it from her hands, hesitantly.

"Kaela…" Derek said, his voice fading as the aroma seduced Lance's senses.

Lance stared at the bottle, one side of him screaming to put it down, to not take the risk. Then again, the other side urged him to drink. After everything he'd been through tonight, and the pain in his leg not getting any better, a small buzz would surely help.

Better than risking the painkillers, right?

"Nope," Kaela said, yanking the bottle from Lance's hand. He blinked, ripped from his trance. Panic seized his chest as he looked around the room. Eric eyed him, as did George.

"He's allergic," Kaela said smoothly. "Feel free to sit on the floor." She smiled. "And Malcolm, sweetie, please don't lose a tooth in my office."

"When can I begin my research?" Malcolm asked, not a demand but a desperate plea.

Kaela smiled kindly at him, a fire in her eyes. She was about to say something terrible, but then she looked at Lance, and the fire dimmed. Her smile darkened, and she returned her attention to Malcolm. "Soon," she said simply, eyeing Lance as she took another sip from her bottle.

"You shouldn't be drinking after taking a pain pill," George warned.

"Don't patronize me, Doc."

"Hey, be nice," Eric warned.

Lance raised an eyebrow. Seeing Eric defend another person like that… *George really must be special to him.*

A knock sounded on the door, and everyone's attention went to one of the girls Kaela had sent off. "The showers are ready, ma'am."

Lance groaned as the hot water rained down on his back, his head, his arms and chest. He closed his eyes and let the relaxing shower ease the tension from his body. Some of his cuts stung in response, but he couldn't care less. He'd been through so much action and blood and killing and running in the past few days, and he could finally just *sit down.*

He looked down at the dirt and blood rinsing down the drain.

In this moment, with nothing but the sound of the running water in his shower stall and the ones adjacent to it, nothing else mattered. Everyone else was getting their own showers, no doubt enjoying them just as much as he was, the stalls next to him blocked off by a white tiled barrier.

He let the water hit his leg especially, as pain continued to course through it. His splint was abandoned with the rest of his clothes outside the stall, and George had already promised to bandage his leg back up. He was sitting on a small wooden chair, and as embarrassing as it had been to watch one of the workers carry it in with an understanding smile on her face, he was grateful to avoid standing for as long as possible.

After a few generous minutes of just sitting in the shower with his thoughts, he bathed himself, taking his time with the process, having to scrub more dirt and blood off than he'd realized was there.

After a while, Lance finished cleaning and stepped out of the shower with a towel wrapped firmly around his waist. He grabbed for the cane and slipped on the wet floor, catching himself just in time. He looked around the bathroom, but he was the only person left.

On the walk to the door, he tested his leg a bit. The shower had eased some of the tension, and the pain had become manageable. But when he put weight on it, it ached in response, a warning to not continue.

But then he tried again on the next step, pushing harder against the ground. Pain sliced into his leg, and he collapsed, the cane clattering across the floor. "Dammit!"

A second later, the door opened, and without thinking, Lance hissed, "Get out." His wet hair hung over his face as he swore into the floor and pain bit into his leg without remorse.

Whoever opened the door paused then walked in, closing it afterward. Footsteps clacked on the tile floor, then a pair of black combat boots walked into Lance's cone of vision.

Lance sighed as he looked up, meeting Kaela's face, smiling down at him with a raised eyebrow. Her hair was in a tight bun.

"Is there a problem here?" she asked.

Lance cursed and crawled toward the canc, muttering to himself as he imagined the look on Kaela's face, watching him crawl to the only thing he could use to walk.

Kaela sighed and kicked his cane to him.

Lance stopped the growl forming in the back of his throat as he grabbed the cane and tried to help himself up. Kaela sighed again and held her hand out.

Lance knew the look he gave her was filled with anger, but her face remained neutral. After a few long seconds, he hesitantly grabbed her hand and let her help him.

"You okay?" she asked.

Lance sat at one of the benches across from the stalls and took a deep breath. "Fantastic."

She shook her head. "You're lucky your towel didn't fall off." She laughed. "Now, wouldn't that have been a sight to see?"

"Not a sight you haven't seen a hundred times before, I'm sure."

Kaela met his eyes, and her playful smile disappeared. "Well, you can't blame a girl for trying." A glimpse of the smile returned then disappeared again. "Sorry. I know this isn't a good time to be making jokes." She folded both sides of her short leather jacket over her chest, covering the simple white shirt beneath. "Also, I might be a little buzzed."

Lance swiped a chunk of wet hair from his face. "It's okay. A little humor might be what I need right now."

Kaela let out a dry laugh in response. "If it makes you feel better, I usually only want to make jokes like that to cheer up my friends… like Amari. But I'll make an exception this time for you." When Lance gave a half smile, she let herself smile back. "See? I can't help it."

"It's fine, really," Lance said. "Just don't worry about it. Can you ask George to come wrap my leg back up?"

Kaela wiped her hands on her dark jeans. "Sure thing."

She started toward the door, but Lance called her name without thinking. Her hand was on the door handle, and she didn't turn to look at him.

"I, um…" He tried to find the words to say. "I like your outfit."

Now she looked at him, and in those catlike eyes was a flicker of something that resembled confusion.

But she smiled. "I do too. That's why I'm wearing it." She left the room, and on the other side of the door, she spoke again, her voice muffled.

Not long afterward, George stepped in, wearing a simple black shirt and jogging pants. He held the materials for a new splint and a fresh set of clothes.

"How long was I in the shower?" Lance asked as the doctor handed him the clothes, then he started dressing.

"About an hour, I think."

Lance stopped with his shirt still over his head. "Are you serious?"

"I wouldn't have said it otherwise. Eric was cracking jokes, and Kaela may or may not have joined in." He laughed with a shake of his head. "You kids are crazy."

With more trouble than he wished for, Lance changed into the new clothes, black jogging pants, just like George's, with a navy-blue shirt and a black jacket. George wiped the remaining water off the chair, and Lance sat, his leg extended for the doctor to work.

"I heard you fell," George said. "Did you hurt anything else?"

Lance shook his head.

"You tried to put more pressure on it than you should have?"

Lance nodded.

"You're sick of walking with the cane?"

"You're just good at guessing, aren't you?"

George chuckled then continued. The splint fit tightly on his leg, and as uncomfortable as it felt, it was better than trying to walk on it otherwise.

"Does Eric have a limp?" Lance asked through gritted teeth.

George eyed the wall for a second as he wrapped Lance's leg, as if considering whether or not to say anything. "Eric sprained his leg pretty badly when he got into that helicopter crash in Agni." He shifted in his position and continued his work. "I've told him not to put much pressure on it, but he's pretty much ignoring me at this point."

Lance looked at the cane lying beside him. "So… he gave me his cane when he needs it himself?"

George seemed to realize what Lance was saying. "Your injury is more severe than Eric's, but yes, he did give it to you despite needing it himself."

"Hmm," Lance said. "Well, I can't wait until I can walk on this leg again so I can give it back."

"I know you're impatient," George said as he helped Lance to his feet. "I also know that you're not exactly in the best of situations to be injured. But don't push yourself too hard yet. All that walking and fighting—there's no reason why you wouldn't be sore." He opened the door for Lance, who tried to hide his grimace as he walked through. "Right now, the best thing you can do is get some rest."

"I think we could all use some rest," Derek said.

"Where's Malcolm?" Lance asked, looking around. The place was closing for the night. Fewer girls walked the halls, and there were no clients to be seen.

No walking corpses, either.

"He's already in the basement, brainstorming this cure business," Kaela said. "And we are staying here for the night, by the way. We have plenty of rooms. Top floor, scattered so that we're harder to find." She adjusted her jacket again. "So for now, we're safe. Best thing we can do is get a good night's sleep."

Eric turned to walk up the stairs. "Amen to that."

Lance fell back on the soft bed, the blood-red comforter warm and cozy. The pillows were as soft as clouds. He closed his eyes and breathed in the perfumed smell of the room, and when he opened them, he looked at the ceiling. Just like the comforter, it was blood red—the walls too.

The curtains to his left were a soft pink and already partially opened, revealing a sliver of Arachna. Somewhere beyond that sliver, Caleb was either working on his plan for world domination or searching for Eric.

Lance sighed and turned away from the sight, from the realization that he wouldn't be able to safely walk around the city again for a long time. He was clean, in a soft bed, and if Kaela was right, food was on the way. *What I would do for a sandwich right now.*

A knock sounded at the door, and Lance smiled as he slid out of the bed and rushed to answer it. The cane was quiet against the soft carpet of the room. Being rid of that annoying clacking for a while was more satisfying than it should have been. He expected a worker on the other side of the door, bringing him a platter of food. Instead, when he opened it, Eric's devilish smile peered at him from under his blond hair.

"May I come in?" he asked, his eyes sparkling.

Lance leaned out and looked left then right. No worker was behind him—nobody bringing food.

"Fine," Lance groaned and stepped aside.

Eric walked in as if he owned the room, tossing his coat on the floor and falling onto the bed. Just like Lance, he wore jogging pants, but his shirt was a short-sleeve white T-shirt just like Kaela's. He'd kept his trench coat, dirty as it was, and had blatantly refused any of the workers' attempts to clean it for him.

Kaela would kill him if she knew he'd thrown the dirty thing on the floor.

"Nobody touches it but me," he'd said. Lance would've crossed his arms if he didn't have a cane in one of them, so instead, he leaned against the wall, distributing his weight to his good leg.

"Are you ready to talk about..." Lance couldn't bring himself to finish the sentence. Those words still haunted him every time he thought about it.

Eric wasn't smiling anymore. He sat up with that genuine glaze over his eyes, the same one he'd worn when he first broke the news to Lance. The more he saw it, the more it appeared to be an act.

"I think so," he said, looking out the window then promptly leaving the bed to close the curtains further. "But I need you to talk quietly. If anyone hears what I'm telling you, I'll have to kill them."

Lance didn't know why he was shocked to hear those words, but then Eric chuckled, a wheezy laugh following as he tried to silence himself.

"Kidding. I would only bribe or threaten them."

"Are you going to get to the point, or should I skip to the part where I ask you to leave?"

Eric shrugged. "I guess you'll just have to ask me to leave."

Lance swore smoke would blow from his nose as Eric's smile only grew with each passing moment of silence.

"You see? You won't. Because you rely on knowing this information. You need to learn what to say and when to say it if you want to get information out of people. You'll need to know this when—" He stopped at Lance's glare then rolled his eyes. "*If* you end up taking over."

"Thanks for the advice. Now, tell me why you said I was—" Eric put a single finger to his mouth, and now it was Lance's turn to roll his eyes before lowering his voice. "That I'm your… son."

Eric sat on the bed and gestured for Lance to sit next to him. Lance didn't acknowledge the action at first, but putting so much weight on his good leg was tiring. He gave in and limped to the bed then sat next to Eric. His body protested being so close to him, and his hand slid casually to the handle of the cane, where his finger kept a thumb's distance from the switch. He had no reason to be ready for an attack from Eric, yet his body told him to do so anyway.

If Eric noticed the action, he either didn't care, or he pretended not to.

"How long have you known I was your son?" Lance asked as he stared forward.

"Since the day you were born." Lance thought it was a cheap joke, but Eric's face was serious. "I never lost track of you, not really. I knew you were being raised at that orphanage. I was the one that left you there."

"Wait," Lance said. "When did you have me?" His heart sank. "And who with?" He could never remember her face, only fuzzy images of someone with dark hair holding him.

"I was fifteen when I found out she was pregnant." Eric played with his fingers, his hair hiding his face. "I stayed with her for a few months, but she wanted to live a better life for your sake. No more scamming. No more stealing."

Lance swallowed the lump in his throat.

"I was too selfish," Eric continued. "I only cared about myself, so I told her no. That I would keep making money the way I was, and that I would eventually make something of myself with it. I said if she could wait a few years, I would manage something more stable." He tucked his hair behind his ears, and something like sadness showed in his eyes. "I left her not long after that. Gave her a few grand I had saved up over the years, and I just left. I kept an eye on her until she left the city. We were hiding in Agni at the time, living on the streets.

"She went to Arachna, so I left with her. Or… followed her. I was her shadow everywhere she went, and I decided to build myself up in Arachna. She got a job at a burger joint for a while. When she couldn't go out and work, I can only assume she used the money I left for her." He cleared his throat, but his voice cracked anyway when he spoke again. "Months passed, and she went into labor. She took a taxi to a hospital, and… in that moment, I decided I was tired of following her. I wanted to be there… to be a father." His voice cracked again, and his eyes glistened in the lamplight. "I jumped in the taxi with her. She cried the whole way there. She let me hold her and talk to her. All I could say was, 'I'm sorry'.

"Over and over, that was all I said until we reached the hospital. It took hours… The doctors told me that you were a healthy baby boy." He stopped and gripped his knee tightly, then cleared his throat again. "But she, um… She didn't make it."

Lance couldn't look at him, could barely stand to hear him constantly clearing his throat and sniffling. Not a tear rolled down his cheek, but his eyes were like two dams, raring to burst.

"I couldn't handle being a father alone. I couldn't take having a constant reminder that she wasn't here anymore, so I brought you to that orphanage and kept an eye on you until you were old enough. I thought if you were raised by some half-decent people, that you wouldn't grow up in the streets like I did, fighting every day to survive." He stood and walked to the window. "That didn't turn out the way I wanted."

Lance didn't want to believe anything he was hearing, but Eric had no reason to lie now. He thought he'd hated Eric before, but now… He wanted to lunge at him and punch him until he cried blood *and* tears. Instead, he just balled his fists and scowled.

"What did she look like?" Lance asked, and his own voice shook. He hated that too. He hated the cane in his hand, hated the room sat in, and hated his mother for leaving him just as he'd entered the world, for being selfish enough to die on him. He hated *everything*. But he had to know. He *needed* to remember what she looked like.

"Piercing green eyes and long red hair." Eric peeked out at the city and laughed. "She was so short. And she had freckles everywhere." More laughter—quiet, sad laughter. "Her smile made every dark night in those alleys bright."

Lance's heart broke more with every detail. His memory wasn't of his mother. In the brief moment she was alive after he was born, he hadn't seen her. He'd seen…

Lance looked up at Eric and eyed his blond hair. Dyed, as he'd suspected from the beginning, and always greasy, as if it was never washed. "You cut and dyed your hair, didn't you?"

Eric nodded, his cheeks stained with tears. "Right after I gave you to the orphanage." He rubbed his nose. "Her name was Carrie. She always told me I needed to cut my hair, so I did. And I dyed it because I thought it would… I don't know." His eyes dried, and he steeled himself, wiping his face.

If only it'd been Eric instead of his mother. The thought lingered in the front of his mind, even as he said, "How'd you keep track of me once I ran from the orphanage?"

Eric peeked out at the city through a gap in the curtains as if trying to stall. Then he sighed. "The chief."

Lance scoffed. "Of course it was."

"Calm down, it's not the way you think. Back when she was just an officer, she told me about a bad fight at the orphanage. I found out it was you and had my people follow you for a while, but you disappeared. Years later, I found you again, and I bribed the man who owned that old building to sell it to you for cheap."

"And he didn't say anything?"

"Bribed *and* threatened, Lance," Eric said, and that devilish smile half-heartedly returned. A spark where a flame should have been. "He gave you the store, and for the next few years, I kept expanding my business, crafting my web all over Arachna with Kaela and Derek. Once I had everything stabilized, I decided I was sick of watching you work at that same store every single day, miserable." He let the curtain close again. "I made sure you knew there was an information dealer in town. Had some of Derek's men go there every now and then and give little hints. I figured I could bring you in, let you join our group, give you a good life, teach you everything I know, and let you take over when I was gone." He chuckled. "Look how that worked out."

Lance's chest tightened, and his stomach twisted into a knot. His heart beat like a drum, and his knuckles whitened from gripping the cane too hard. That beast awoke within him. Drowsily, it moved, urging him, whispering for him to unlatch the blade from the cane. He thought the beast only came out when he was threatened, but now it stirred in response to Lance's rage. He shoved it down, ignoring the whispers. He was furious, not stupid.

"So every part of my life," Lance started slowly, "you messed with?" Had his nasty, bloodstained fingerprints all over it. Tears welled in Lance's eyes.

"In a manner of speaking, yes…" Eric crossed his arms, and the tension in the room thickened. "I know you got dealt a bad hand in life, Lance. I wanted to relieve that as much as possible."

"Screw you," Lance said, a white-hot wave of rage crashing into him. "If you were going to help me, you shouldn't have abandoned me. You should have stepped up as a father in the first place. Got a normal job, like my mother did." He balled his fists so tight his nails dug into his palms. Tears threatened to spill from his face, but he locked them away, refusing to let Eric see him cry.

"Everything I've done since the day you were born has been for you," Eric protested.

"Don't give me that bullshit," Lance spat. "Was forcing me to distract Rotoya in a high-speed chase for me?"

"You're the only one she would have spared."

"What about pissing off Landreau Corp? Was that for me? Murdering Malcolm Landreau?"

Eric braced his hands against the windowsill, a deep frown etched on his face. "I needed the money."

Lance shook his head. The tears fought harder and harder to escape their prison. "For what?"

"For you," Eric said, turning around. A fresh tear ran down his cheek, and he roughly wiped it away. His voice quivered. "This was supposed to be *the* deal, the one that would have given you the easy life. It… I was desperate, okay? When Malcolm said no, I panicked and killed him. I couldn't let the deal go south. Just… wasn't anticipating that secret project to be nanobots that raised people from the damned dead."

"Oh my God," Lance muttered. "You did kill Malcolm Landreau for me."

Eric didn't respond, just turned back around. "I just want to make up for what I did to you, for abandoning you and your mother. I didn't want you to know I was your father. I wanted to make this last deal, skyrocket our profits, and give you the easy life. You would've had everything you wanted."

Lance scoffed. "You mean what *you* want?"

"What?"

Lance rubbed his tired eyes, tears leaking from them now. He muttered a curse. His leg ached terribly, and the tears flowed harder. "I'm not like you, you bastard! I don't give a shit about information or money. I just want a normal life, and… a family. I want a *family*, and I want to be happy for once in my miserable life. Christ, Eric." Lance sat down on the bed, hanging his head in his hands. He choked down a sob as the pain tightened its jaws around his leg. "Why do you think I spent months saving up the money to pay for info on my parents? Because I wanted to be with them. To start over. I've lived my whole life without info or money or status, and I don't *want* it." A small sob escaped him, and he cursed again. "I am *nothing* like you. Just because you want those things doesn't mean I do."

What he wouldn't give to begin again, to leave the city and start a new life.

"Lance…" Eric started. He took a step closer. "I'm so sorry."

"I don't want your stupid apology," Lance said, wiping tears from his face. How could Eric have the gall to think he would want all these things? "It should've been you… not my mom."

Hurt crossed Eric's face. *Good.*

"Just get out."

Eric remained in his spot, standing stiff. "Lance—"

"I said get the hell out," Lance hissed. "Before I throw you out."

Eric closed his eyes tight then opened his mouth like he was going to say something else.

Lance stood, bracing himself on the cane. The beast stirred again, ready to lunge. Eric flinched then held a hand up.

The beast whispered for Lance to throw a punch, and he almost did, but a knock sounded at the door.

"Room service."

CHAPTER 18
ROB

Lance's thoughts jumbled into a maelstrom. He'd eaten the steak and potatoes and left only a bite of bread on his plate. Eric had slithered out once the worker left. Lance stared down at his nearly empty plate, his stomach aching from forcing the food down.

It was as good a distraction as any.

A man like Eric was his father, begging for his son to take over the business, pretending that everything he did was actually for him.

Lance grimaced.

The man was delusional. He was backed into a corner like a wild animal, and now he was desperate.

There was another knock on the door, and Lance's heart skipped. He tossed the plate onto the tray next to the nightstand, where it clattered against the silverware.

Lance opened the door, his thumb over the switch of the cane.

He relaxed. Derek was standing at the door, a toothpick popped in his mouth.

"Enjoy your meal?" Lance asked as he stepped aside.

Derek stepped in with a "hmph" and said, "As long as it's been since I had a good meal, I almost did a backflip." He sat on the bed.

Lance crossed his arms, the words spoken between him and Eric still resonating in his head. If only Derek knew his leader had been reduced to a teary-eyed wreck and that he was looking at that same leader's son.

"Lance?" Derek called out to him.

Lance blinked, and he was staring at the floor.

"Everything okay?"

Lance stuttered to find the right words, tried to wring the conversation out of his mind. "Yeah, just… stomach troubles."

Derek hummed. "You've really taken an initiative here," he said. "Chief's dead because of you, you came face-to-face with Caleb and took a punch from him, and you had to lead for a few days… All that, and now you have a broken leg."

"What's your point?"

"You've been through a lot, Lance. I wanted to come check on you. See how you were doing."

Lance couldn't keep eye contact. If Derek only knew the real reason for his discomfort.

"I'm doing alright," Lance said. The words came out faster than they should have.

"Try again."

Lance sighed. "I'm not the best… I'm sick of having to use this stupid thing." He gestured at the cane holding him up. "And I never knew when I agreed to be a part of this that it would turn into being a fugitive." He scratched the back of his neck.

"We'll get through it," Derek said. "Somehow." He stiffened. Something was eating at him.

"What about you? Are you okay?" Lance asked.

Derek stared down at his feet for a long moment before he said, "Yeah, just… can't stop thinking about Rob."

The image still hadn't left Lance's mind—the flash of Rotoya's smile and the bang of a gun. He couldn't imagine what it was like for Derek.

"Do you want to talk about it?"

"No, no," Derek said. "I came here to check on you, not the other way around."

"Trust me, I've had enough of talking about my issues for one night… I'd like to get my mind off of it for a while."

Derek sighed and rubbed his hands together.

Wow, he really is nervous.

"I miss him, Lance."

"I didn't know him that well," Lance said, sitting beside Derek. "Why don't you tell me about him? How you guys met? How he came to work for you?"

Derek huffed. "He was homeless. Living out of his car. He came by my bar every now and then to get some food. Then he'd get drunk. He never bothered anybody, so I left him alone. Sometimes, I gave him a free drink. After a while, he opened up and told me his aunt and uncle kicked him out because they found out he was engaged to some guy."

"What happened to his parents?"

"Car accident."

"Oh, man."

"He lived with his fiancé for a while. Turned out he was an abusive prick, so Rob left. His aunt and uncle wouldn't let him back, so he ended up in his car."

"How old was he?"

"About nineteen. He's twenty-five now… He was." Derek gulped. "I talked to Eric about it and offered him a job. Showed him the ropes, how to fight, how to get info. Next thing I knew, he was one of my top guys. Then one of my best friends. He always had my back." He shook his head. "I guess I didn't have his back, though. He was a fine man… and he'd be alive right now if I'd just been more careful."

"Have you lost people before?"

"A few," he said quickly. "More than I should have… It's why I try not to make friends with my agents…" He hesitated, bit his lip, then looked Lance in the eye. "If you hadn't killed Rotoya, I truly think she would've given him that same drug. To make him fight for her."

Lance eyed the nightstand, where the bottle of champagne sat comfortably in a bucket of now-melted ice. He grabbed the bottle and handed it to Derek, who popped the top and drank.

Lance eyed the bottle himself. Its call was softer tonight. Easier to ignore.

"It's not exactly the kind of alcohol you use in these situations," Lance said with a nervous laugh, "but it's something."

Wearing a sad smile, Derek said, "May he be in heaven half an hour before the devil knows he's dead."

"May the devil never find out to begin with."

Derek chuckled and took another long swig from the bottle. "Thanks, Lance."

"Don't mention it." He refused the bottle when Derek offered it.

"Crap," Derek said. "Sorry, I forgot about—"

"Don't worry about it. Kaela forgot too."

Lance took a deep breath. The citrus smell wafted to him, fogging his brain.

They sat in silence. Silence for Rob, who at the very least died fighting and wasn't drugged by the chief.

Derek stood with a groan. "Thanks, Lance… You're a good friend." He made to walk out of the room.

"You see me as a friend?"

Derek turned back around, his hand on the knob. "With all we've been through together, hell, I almost see you as a brother."

Lance wasn't sure why, but a warmth filled his chest. "Thanks… I see you as a friend too."

Derek nodded. "I'll just take this with me." He held up the champagne bottle.

"By all means."

When the door clicked shut, Lance lay back in the bed and stared at the ceiling, shaking the thoughts of Eric as they crept up on him. The room was quiet, dim, and safe. Caleb was somewhere in the city, surely convinced that Lance was dead.

He frowned then sat up. Caleb thought he was dead. If he just left now, he could start over. Leave the city and wait a few weeks. Then he could return to his store and live the rest of his life in a mild comfort.

He looked at the window, and just like the alcohol, it called to him. The starry night sky stared down on him, and he nearly left the bed.

Lance gulped and lay back down, the thought floating around in his head. As with the alcohol, he resisted. If it were just Eric, he'd leave in a heartbeat. Derek and Kaela… He couldn't leave them. They were both his friends. Even Kaela.

He touched the wolf's head on the cane.

"Loyalty and perseverance."

Lance's store still smelled new. Even now, he had trouble imagining it as the same store he'd lived in for years. Snacks lined the shelves, and drinks filled the coolers. Kaela sauntered down the beer aisle.

It wasn't like their previous hideout, but they had no better place to hide now than a business in the slums. The TV and bed in his room were a plus.

They'd all agreed—after a long talk in Kaela's office—that Lance's store was their best option. Staying at the Rose would put Kaela's employees at too high a risk. So they piled into the truck, and George drove them into the slums. Malcolm remained at the Rose, in the basement with Amari. He'd complained that the equipment was enough but not ideal, to which Kaela promptly told him to deal with it.

They'd left at the brink of dawn, hidden in the cargo bed while George drove, relieved by the lack of a horrid smell. The rooftops had been easier to watch for shadows as the sun peeked out from the horizon.

Now here they were, in Lance's store, the only light inside coming from the rising sun.

"Well," George said when the silence grew stale, "I think I'll be heading back to the Rose now. Maybe I can do something to help with this cure. Wouldn't be good for a truck to stay parked outside the store, anyway."

"Be careful," Eric said.

George nodded and left, the back door closing behind him without so much as a squeak. Lance locked the door behind him, letting the silence settle once again.

Kaela sat on the floor and leaned against the cooler door, sipping a beer she'd snatched. She frowned at it as if it had insulted her, but she took another sip anyway. Derek stared at the floor in thought, and Eric peeked around the corner of the shelf at the entrance, his gaze unfaltering and focused, as if waiting for Caleb to appear like he had at the church.

Lance examined the knife inside the cane and stretched out his bad leg, just a little at a time, the pain coming in smaller waves.

"How long should we stay here?" Derek asked after a while.

"Until we get an update," Eric responded.

"And then what?"

Eric sighed. "One thing at a time, Derek." He raised an eyebrow. "Since when are you so antsy?"

Lance sheathed the knife and looked at Derek, who frowned at the floor. Eric was right, he hadn't been this antsy at the bunker… but Rob had been alive then.

"I'm not antsy."

"You once waited an entire hour, completely still, for a target to come out of a building so you could snipe them, and you can't handle a few minutes inside of a store?" Eric asked, the smile finally appearing on his face.

Derek glared at him. "You know I don't like it when you bring up those days… and besides, that was different. I was waiting to take a shot, but now I'm waiting to be shot." He scratched his chin. "We have no idea how long this cure will take. Are we seriously going to hide the whole time?"

"We're hiding *for now*," Eric insisted. "We're waiting to get updates on the cure. Unless you'd like to go to the Rose and be Malcolm's lab assistant, the best thing you can do is wait. Enjoy the silence while you have it. With our luck, it won't last long."

Derek grimaced. "You're right."

A tense silence overtook the room until Kaela broke it. "God, I hate beer." She slid the bottle away from herself. "But this beer is atrocious."

Eric chuckled. "If only you had wine. You could test your record."

Lance cocked his head to the side. "Record?"

Kaela smirked proudly as Eric spoke. "Kaela once drank a whole bottle of wine in under a minute."

Lance raised an eyebrow. "Did you really?"

"It was a dare… Hangover was so worth it."

The ghost of a smile appeared on Derek's face, but his eyes were dark.

Lance spoke up. "I have a TV in the back. Why don't you watch the news and see what's going on in the city?"

"Not a half bad idea. I think I'll do just that," Derek said, standing back up.

A few seconds passed, and the TV turned on, the sound barely audible from where the rest of the group sat.

It was a mystery that Kaela and Eric weren't connecting the dots with Derek's behavior, unless Lance was just getting better at reading people.

After a moment of silence, Lance said, "Under a minute, huh?"

"Oh yeah," Kaela said, her hands behind her head. "I need a nap."

Lance looked at Eric and shook his head. "Kaela, I also have a bed back there, you know."

Kaela stood up wordlessly and disappeared, leaving the beer bottle behind, nearly untouched.

Eric chuckled and slid next to the bottle, taking a large swig from it.

Lance thumbed the handle of the cane again while Eric gingerly sipped his beer and leaned against the cooler.

"I'm sorry about last night," Eric said.

"Don't talk to me."

Eric shook his head. "I'm trying my best here, Lance."

Lance tried to bite his tongue, but a string of anger lashed out, and he threw it at Eric. "How can you spy on me my whole life and *still* not know me at all?" He thought that would relieve his anger, but it didn't. He kept going. "The entire time I was in that orphanage, I *prayed* for a family. Nobody came. Nobody cared. So I started praying for my own parents to come back… Guess I should've been more careful with what I wished for, huh?"

"We went over this," Eric said. "I wasn't ready. You were way better off in that orphanage than with me. The life I was living was not meant for a child. That's why I was hoping you'd get adopted by a normal family and live a normal life." He looked toward the back room again, staring for a few seconds before continuing. “But then you didn’t get picked up by a family. And the last thing I was going to do was let you live on the streets like I did. Hence why I helped you get your store. And here I am now, offering you my business. It’s all I have.”

Lance scoffed. “Did you ever consider quitting the life that wasn’t meant for a child, you greedy, selfish bastard?” Already, tears started welling in his eyes again, and he dug his nails into his palms. “And for the last time, I don’t care about inheriting your damn business.”

Eric leaned his head back then said, “Just tell me what you want me to do, Lance. What can I do to make it up to you?”

Lance crossed his arms and tried to keep his breathing steady. “You can start by dropping the subject entirely. After that… I don’t know yet.”

“I–” Eric was silent for a long moment. “Okay.”

The sun was setting, and rich orange rays of sunlight shone into the store. Soon, they would be cast into darkness, and the thought of that sent a chill down Lance’s spine.

An eerie silence fogged the streets, more so than usual. No gunfire, no shouting, no late-night drinkers, no crickets chirping, and no bugs buzzing. It was as if they had been cast into some other dimension, all alone. Completely isolated.

Lance absentmindedly reached for a bag of pretzels behind him and opened it, popping a couple into his mouth.

The TV switched off, and Derek emerged from the room, grabbing a snack of his own. Kaela came out soon after, stretching and rubbing her eyes. She grabbed a bag of candy and snacked on the colorful treats inside.

“Anything interesting on the news?” Lance asked Derek.

“Talks about the ‘fugitives’, mostly.”

A knock sounded on the back door.

Everyone froze.

Lance tossed the cane to Eric, who caught it without looking. Kaela had her knife at the ready, and Derek aimed his pistol.

Lance closed his eyes and listened for the sound of whispers within himself. The beast stirred and awoke but didn't whisper to him. His stomach didn't twist, as if the beast was waiting for confirmation of danger on the other side of the door.

Derek eased to the door then cracked it open. "Amari?"

Kaela relaxed, and Derek let Amari in, locking the door behind her.

"What are you doing here?" Kaela asked, wrapping Amari in a tight hug.

"Malcolm sent me. I'm the only one quiet enough to sneak around the city," Amari said, releasing from the hug. "I think we're on to something with this cure. At the very least, we've figured out how we might be able to combat this drug." She stopped, as if gauging their reactions. "Malcolm said he's been thinking about it wrong, or something like that. He had me write this letter to give to you."

"You didn't bring any wine, did you?"

Amari pouted. "Sorry, girl. I should've, huh?"

Kaela waved a hand at her. "Don't worry about it. Just wishful thinking on my part."

Amari giggled. "I should get going."

"Already?"

"Malcolm needs me. Besides, I'm actually having a lot of fun working on this."

"Okay… Hey, be careful. And make sure to leave out the back door, not the front."

Amari nodded, and she slinked out, her steps silent. The back door clicked shut behind her, and Derek locked it again.

Kaela tore the envelope open and scanned the letter. "Oh…"

"What is it?" Eric asked.

Kaela offered the letter to Eric, who grabbed it and scanned the page. His jaw set, and his mouth formed a thin line.

He shook the envelope, and an empty vial fell out onto his hand. "Well, shit…"

Glass shattered.

A body flew through the air, past the aisle, and broke through the back door.

The beast's hiss in the back of Lance's head barely registered over Kaela's shout.

"AMARI!"

CHAPTER 19
AN EAR FOR AN EAR

Lance's heart dropped to his stomach. The only sound in the room was the tinkling of remnant glass hitting the floor. Eric removed the blade from his cane and tossed the body to Lance.

"Flip that switch toward the bottom," Eric whispered.

Lance did so, and a scythe flicked from the bottom of the cane. His throat constricted, Amari's body burning into the back of his mind. The ground swayed beneath him, and he leaned on the cane, his mouth dry.

A voice sounded from behind the shelf. "Hello."

Derek whirled and fired. Chips and snacks flew like shrapnel across the room and scattered on the floor as the bullets penetrated them and the metal shelf.

Silence lasted for only a moment before a laugh rang out. "Poor girl. She was so pretty. Seemed rather sweet too."

Kaela screamed and fired her pistol at the shelves. After the first handful of bullets sparked against the metal, her gun clicked. Empty. Lance's ears rang as the echo of the gunshots reverberated throughout the store. He readied the scythe in his hand. If Caleb rounded the shelf, he would be in for a nasty surprise. Eric stood at the ready at the other end of the aisle.

"Do you want to know the funny part?" Caleb was lighthearted in his tone, completely casual, as if the conversation was no less normal with a dead body just outside. "She wasn't even how I found you."

A crumpled bullet flew over the shelf and landed near Kaela's feet.

"Nice shot, by the way."

The bullet glowed. No, the blood *on* the bullet glowed.

Kaela's eyes widened. "Get down!"

The bullet exploded, and fragments of shrapnel flew across the room, shattering the glass doors of the freezers. Lance dove, pieces of the bullet grazing his back as his leg groaned in pain.

Lance gritted his teeth, using the scythe to pick himself up. Purple lines snaked around the shelf. The slithering lines grew slowly and steadily, wrapping the shelf in a tight hug.

"Run!" Lance yelled as the lines began to glow. He didn't wait for them to react and limped to the back door, broken off its hinges by Amari's body.

Lance covered his head as the shelf exploded into bits behind him, the shattering metal and glass deafening. The force of the blow shoved him farther out the door and into the alley. Eric, Kaela, and Derek landed near him.

Lance's leg screamed in pain as he tried to stand. "Everyone okay?"

"Yeah," Kaela said.

Derek groaned. "Same here."

Eric was panting as he glanced behind them. "Let's get the hell out of here."

Lance caught a glimpse of Amari's broken body, bent in unnatural ways and splayed over a trash can, her eyes wide in shock.

"Oh God," Kaela said, her face twisting with grief.

"Kaela, we have to go. Now," Derek said, his voice rushed.

"I'm so sorry."

"Kaela, now!" Derek grabbed her by the arm, and she broke out of her trance, running beside him.

There was no time for mourning, no time for a moment of silence, no time for anything. They ran down the alley, lit by one streetlamp.

They didn't get far before soldiers appeared at the end of the alleyway, guns pointed.

Lance froze, as did everyone behind him.

"Drop your weapons now!" one of the soldiers yelled.

Lance looked back at them, and after a few shared glances, they slowly dropped their weapons to the ground.

The alley filled with a tense silence, and Caleb calmly stepped out the back door. A businessman ready to strike a deal. He smiled at Amari's body, then adjusted his coat and cleared his throat. "I do hope you—"

Kaela swore at him, one foul word after another, a list she recited as if she'd been practicing for this very moment. Every horrible insult she could hurl at him, she did, until her ammo ran out, and she was left with nothing but her heavy breathing and fiery eyes. Her hands gripped the sides of her legs, her nails digging in fiercely. She appeared to either be fighting tears or the urge to claw his eyes out—maybe both.

"I do hope you all don't mind the new decorations," Caleb said with a smile pointed right at Kaela.

She took a step toward him, but Lance put a hand on the small of her back.

Steady, Lance thought, wishing she could hear him. *You kill him now, and we're all dead. Revenge is coming*, he wanted to say.

Her grip on her legs loosened—a response that seemed to say, *Fine.*

Caleb's brow furrowed. He didn't seem to notice the silent communication, and Kaela's now-blank face was all he had to gauge her emotions.

The soldiers rushed closer. They were trapped.

"As much as I wish I could kill all of you right here, right now, I need to know where Malcolm is… So you can tell me, and I'll let you go. Of course, I'll just hunt you down again, but there's nothing wrong with trying." He smiled, so amused by the position he had them in: mice caught in a trap of his making. "Or you could exercise your right to remain silent, and then I'll have my officers here kill you off. One by one. You'll have to forgive them if they opt for a slower approach than normal."

The killing calm didn't just stir within Lance. Finally, it seemed to realize the danger he was in, and it writhed within him, to the point that his stomach ached. His body urged him to move, to fight, to run.

No, he thought. *There's no way out.*

The calm froze, as if shocked to hear that. It whispered, urging him to do something.

But Lance refused again. He was stuck, and the calm inside of him would just have to accept that he had no way out. This was the end of the road.

This was where he died.

"You're lying," Derek said casually, as if mimicking Caleb.

Caleb noticed it, too, and he smiled. "This is a transaction of sorts. I truly will give you all one last chance to escape, and I'll be distracted with retrieving my brother, so there's no need to doubt me. Who knows? Maybe you'll escape me this time."

"That's cute." Lance hadn't expected those words to escape, but he embraced it and puffed his chest out. No point in showing fear to such a man.

Caleb frowned at him. "Soldiers," he said, raising his hand.

The soldiers shuffled and raised their guns.

"Take a warning shot at…" He assessed them, a strain on his face, as if he was truly having trouble deciding who he wanted to shoot first.

Lance's hand still rested on the small of Kaela's back. His hand grazed something. He almost looked but resisted the last second. The beast went wild inside his stomach. It was her knife. She must have stashed it before they were ordered to relinquish their weapons.

So that's what you meant.

A light growl rumbled in the back of his head.

The beast stirred within Lance again, only stronger, more forceful. He resisted a smile. He could see only one way out, and as terrible as the idea was, it was better than death.

The beast hadn't led him wrong yet.

The weight he put on his leg ached even as adrenaline surged through him. If he was going to do something, he would have to do it now.

Survive, the beast whispered to him, and Lance nodded.

Caleb smiled as his eyes drifted to Kaela for the third time. He made to lower his hand and signal for his soldiers to shoot, but Lance ripped the knife from under Kaela's shirt and sank it into Eric's hand.

Eric yelled, his screams and curses shattering the night. Caleb froze, his lip quirking up as he looked at Lance in confusion. The soldiers around them lowered their weapons, sharing glances with each other.

This was his chance.

Lance whirled around. Pain tore through his leg, but he pushed through it. The calm settled over him, the beast inside guiding his body's every move.

Yes, the beast purred. *Kill them.*

Lance's body moved. He kicked off the wall and tackled a soldier to the ground. The others fired, and Lance rolled, hiding beneath the soldier's body. The soldier convulsed as the bullets peppered his body, but then he went still. Violet blood splattered against Lance's face. The honeyed smell flooded the air.

He ripped the rifle from the soldier's dead hands and fired.

The bullets sprayed against the wall, and bricks shattered in a cloud of dust. Finally, they hit their mark, showering the soldiers with bullets. Purple blood painted the ground and walls. The remaining soldiers crumpled to the ground.

Breathless, Lance lay there for a moment, feeling along his body for any bullet wounds. He swallowed the lump in his throat, and a small laugh escaped him. *That was way too close.*

Lance shoved the officer's body off him. Before he could catch his breath, a foot slammed into his chest, shoving him back to the ground.

The beast hissed, and Lance made to roll, but a kick to the ribs stopped him. Lance coughed, and another soldier held him down. The soldier raised his arm, a knife in his hand.

Lance held his arm out, blocking the attack just in time. The knife hovered inches over his eye.

The soldier shifted his weight, crashing down on Lance's broken leg. Lance screamed in pain.

The beast growled and snarled, and with each passing second, Lance's strength waned. The pain was too much.

The soldier ripped his helmet off and leaned harder into the knife. It was closing in on Lance's eye, and as the beast desperately snarled, Lance freed his good leg and sent his knee into the soldier's groin.

The soldier merely grunted, but Lance threw his weight to the side just as the knife plunged into the ground, narrowly missing his cheek. Lance yelled and craned his neck, gripping the soldier's ear with his teeth and ripping it from his head.

The soldier screamed in pain and fell back. Lance gaped, the words leaving his mouth before he could stop them: "I'm so sorry."

The purple blood tasted just as coppery as regular blood, and for just a moment, the officer before him was a little boy, scared and cradling his ear.

Lance snapped out of his shock when Derek flew over his head, hitting the ground and sliding to the end of the alley.

Both of Caleb's arms grew in size and mass, and he swatted at Kaela and Eric like flies. Eric slashed at his neck, his arms, his stomach, but the attacks were met with only a stagger and another swing. Eric held his blade in one hand and the cane scythe in the other.

Kaela kept her distance, her eyes darting across Caleb's body. Her dagger was grasped firmly in her hand. Eric's blood soaked the blade.

She met Lance's gaze, rage seething in those cat eyes. Lance unholstered a pistol from a body and threw it to her. She caught it and shot at Caleb. The bullets hit his chest and stomach like bee stings.

One bullet grazed Caleb's eye. He roared, his voice deep and distorted, and fell backward into the trash can, knocking Amari's body from the lid. His hand smashed against his face as he rolled on the ground in pain.

Lance's stomach turned as Amari's empty eyes stared accusingly at him. Someone smashed into his side and shoved him against the wall, knocking the breath from him. The broken bricks were sharp against his side, and he cursed the assailant as his leg screamed in pain.

The officer held him in place, purple blood pouring from the side of his head.

A gunshot sounded, and the officer fell limply to the ground, revealing Derek standing behind him.

Derek shoved a pistol into Lance's hand. "Thank me later."

Lance nodded, and they emptied the guns into Caleb. The bullets barely pierced his skin. They aimed for his other eye, missing every shot. Derek cursed as his hands shook.

Caleb reared his head back and roared at the sky, his veins glowing in response. The beast stirred again, warning Lance of something, and when he looked around, the blood of the dead soldiers started glowing.

Lance started to yell for them to run to the street, but the beast stopped him, hissing for him to go the other direction. In the panic, he gave in. There was no time to argue. "Back inside the store!"

No one protested. They looked Lance's way, and their eyes all widened in shock.

As they dashed into the store, Eric jumped and sliced his blade across Caleb's hurt eye. He landed and threw his weight against Caleb's back, shoving him into the glowing bodies of his men.

The moment Eric dove into the store, a boom shook the walls, and blue flame ignited, billowing throughout the alleyway. A wave of the fire blew into the store, narrowly missing Eric as he dashed back into the aisle with everyone else.

Lance panted. The air smelled of sweat and blood. The crackling of flames sounded from the alleyway. They waited for footsteps or a voice.

Lance calmed his racing heart and stood, wincing as he put weight on his leg without thinking. It hurt worse than ever, and tears ran down his cheeks. He wiped them away. Snacks, glass, and pieces of metal were scattered all over the floor. The others moved, and he held a hand out to stop them. Eric handed the scythe back to Lance. Lance leaned on it, his steps crackling against the debris on the linoleum floor. Eric cursed then hissed. His hand, most likely.

I'll have a lot of trouble explaining that later.

Lance reached the doorway, and after taking a deep breath, he peeked around the corner.

Before he could react, a large hand wrapped around his throat and hoisted him into the air. The scythe slipped from Lance's grip. Caleb's smiling face glowed as he stepped into the store with Lance, holding him like he was a trophy. The beast inside panicked, dashing around inside him wildly. Lance kicked despite the pain, aiming for wherever he could reach.

Caleb didn't seem to care.

Gunshots popped, and small splashes of blood sprang from Caleb's backside. He was taller now; bigger. His entire chest, his head, his legs, all fueled by the nanobots.

Eric jumped and landed on Caleb's back, plunging his knife deep into his neck. Caleb yelled in pain and, with a heavy backhand, knocked Eric into the broken shelf.

Lance's chest tightened by the second. His body ached for air, the beast within clawing at him, screaming at him to do something, anything. His vision darkened. He reached blindly for the knife protruding from Caleb's neck.

He stretched his arm until his hand grasped the hilt of the blade. He ripped it from Caleb's neck and sliced his forehead. A waterfall of purple spilled from the wound, pouring into his eyes. Blinded, Caleb threw Lance with a roar.

Lance didn't know where he landed, but his back slammed into something. Glass shattered, and cold asphalt scraped his cheek.

He was outside, in front of his store. His body convulsed for air until finally his lungs permitted him to breathe. The air was cool and sweet. The metallic taste in his mouth didn't hinder the enjoyment.

Get up!

Caleb swung his body wildly, slamming into the walls of the store until he fell over the counter and crashed to the ground. Lance tried to stand. The beast urged him again to get up, but pain shot through his arm, covered in cuts and glass.

Eric, Kaela, and Derek bolted from the store as Caleb's cries rang from inside. They ran to Lance, and Eric helped him to his feet.

The beast hissed, and adrenaline muffled some of Lance's pain. He almost muttered a thank-you as Eric helped him limp away.

Eric kept close to Lance, and with every shot of pain that stabbed into his leg, Lance stumbled. Eric kept him steady.

"We're talking about my hand later," Eric said as they ran, his voice shaking with pain.

Lance refused to look back, refused to see Caleb's destruction. "Emphasis," he said, trying to get his breath together, "on *later*."

Eric laughed. *Laughed* in a situation like this.

Lance's leg yelled in pain, but the beast hissed again, silencing its cries.

Lance didn't know how long they ran, but they left the slums at some point. He stopped when the adrenaline ran dry, and he dashed into a nearby alleyway. His leg gave in, and he fell, but Eric caught him and lowered him to the cold ground.

The blood rushed to his ears, his heart struggling to catch up with his breathing. Eric panted between curses.

"Where," Lance tried to say, but the word came out in a gust of breath. "Where… where's Kaela and Derek?" He searched around the alley as panic rose in his chest.

Eric sat next to him, his back leaned against the wall. He was invisible in the patch of darkness, except for a peek of his leg jutting out. As if realizing that, he withdrew it into the shadows.

"Not sure." Eric smiled, his eyes wild. They shone through the darkness like a creature staring at him, stalking him. "That was intense, eh?"

"Amari's dead." Seeing that smile turned Lance's stomach. Every life-threatening scenario they got themselves into seemed like nothing more than a fun activity for Eric. "And now Kaela and Derek are missing."

"Wherever they are, I'm sure they'll be fine," Eric said, waving his hand. "I'm the one stuck with the cripple." He laughed then looked at his palm. "By the way, you owe me a hand."

Lance resisted the urge to punch him then forced himself to sit up. He tested his leg. Pain bit into his bone like a rabid hound. The adrenaline was already wearing off, and with it, the pain worsened. Lance bit his lip and waited for it to ease. It didn't.

"I don't get it," Lance whispered. He slid himself beside Eric in the darkness—no reason to make himself more of a target than he already was. "You threw him right into his own explosion… I don't think it even fazed him." He took a deep breath. *Just keep talking,* he thought. *Don't think about the pain.*

Eric nodded. "And the walls of the store didn't crumble like the church. It's almost like he weakened the explosion."

Lance shook his head. "How?"

"Well, Malcolm did say Caleb could control the nanobots. Maybe Caleb stopped the explosion from hurting him. Lucky we ran into the store and not into the street, huh? If Caleb wasn't sitting between us and that explosion, it probably would've killed us." Eric froze as a small sound came from the street. Like an animal, all his focus shifted to the mouth of the alley, his head peeking out from the patch of darkness. When nothing came of it, he relaxed.

Lance gulped, and the beast made no acknowledgement of what Eric had said. But it had told him to run into the store, not the street, as if it had known.

"We need to look for Kaela and Derek," Lance said, struggling to stand.

Eric groaned and hissed at his hand. "Yeah… before we do that, Lancelot, there's something I have to tell you."

Lance leaned against the brick wall, his leg throbbing with pain. "Spit it out."

Eric hesitated. "Daniel Landreau is alive."

CHAPTER 20
A CURE, A COST

Derek dashed across streets and through alleys, Kaela at his side. Caleb hadn't given chase, but that didn't stop Derek's feet from pounding against the concrete. Each breath he took was proof they'd been spared—this time.

They ran until they couldn't anymore, and they stopped in an alley. Derek, even with all the roof hopping he'd done over the past few years, hunched over and gulped down air. Kaela stood beside him, bent over, hair pulled back as if she was about to throw up.

Then she did. She ran to a nearby trash can and vomited into it. Derek suppressed his own nausea in response, leaning against the cold brick wall. His head spun.

Amari... Dead because of Caleb, yet he'd claimed she wasn't how he'd found them. Derek racked his brain for an answer, but none came. Maybe Kaela would have an idea.

Kaela wiped her mouth and sat across from him, her eyes filled with hatred. When she finally caught her breath, she swore.

"I don't get how he found us," Derek said.

Kaela didn't respond. Her face twisted, and she shoved her head into her hands. She brought her knees to her chest and sobbed.

Derek spoke slowly. "Where's Eric and Lance?"

Kaela shook her head. "I don't know." Tears fell down her cheeks. She looked at the ground. "Son of a bitch killed Amari. I'll *ruin* him."

Kaela tensed then went still. Something sparked in her eyes—realization.

"Oh my God," she said. "You don't think Malcolm…"

Derek swallowed the lump forming in his throat. "No… no, Caleb wouldn't have asked where Malcolm was, otherwise. But maybe we need to get to the Rose, and—"

"No!" Kaela shouted then looked around. "No, we can't. If Caleb doesn't know where Malcolm is, he doesn't know about the Rose. And anyway, Malcolm couldn't have ratted with George watching him. No, we can't risk it. If we go there, Caleb may just follow us and…" She clenched her fists. "I don't know."

"There you are," a voice spoke. Derek whirled, aiming his pistol.

Eric appeared from around the corner, stepping into the alleyway. "Probably shouldn't yell in the middle of a manhunt, Kaela."

Derek sighed and lowered the weapon.

Lance trailed behind Eric, cane in hand. He stepped over a dirty puddle, his limp more pronounced.

Kaela frowned when she turned toward Eric, and her eyes flashed. For a moment, she seemed ready to lunge at him and claw the smile from his face.

Eric shot a quick look at Lance, something resembling concern on his face, before turning to Kaela. "I don't mean to add to the bad news, but… well, I'm going to do it anyway. We need to go after Daniel if we're going to get that sample."

Derek froze. "What?"

"Eric… we barely survived Caleb. We're not strong enough to go take on another psychopath." Kaela's voice showed almost no emotion.

Eric's eyes lingered on her frown, and he widened his smile. "Why, Kaela—"

"Don't." She held a finger up in warning. There was a tense silence for a heartbeat. All she uttered was the one word, but somehow, it sounded like a threat. "I'm not playing games anymore."

Eric made no comment, but his smile weakened. "Like the letter said—"

"I don't give a jack shit about the letter anymore."

"Can I see?" Derek's heart skipped a beat. *They don't mean Daniel Landreau, do they?*

Eric handed him the letter, and Derek scanned it.

Attempts at cure unsuccessful thus far. Theory was to use my nanobots and rewire them to attack foreign nanobots. Like white blood cells fighting a virus. My nanobots are not good enough. Not designed for attack patterns. Caleb's are.

As are Daniel's.

Confession... Daniel is alive. Caleb told me Daniel was alive. Caleb said he was hiding in sewers, weak. Asked me to strengthen his nanobots. My research at the church, before you arrived... truthfully, was for Daniel.

Another confession. He is near. Arrived at the Rose and felt his presence. Near, but not close, the faintest whisper. I am sorry... Please do not be angry.

Daniel will not give sample willingly, especially after what Eric did. He is weak but not fragile. Caution is advised.

Eric spoke, but Derek didn't hear. He met Kaela's eyes. "The sewers."

Kaela shrugged. "Yeah, I heard you."

"We can get to the Rose from the sewers."

Kaela paused, then her eyes lit up. "I think there's a sewer grate in the alley next to the Rose." She nodded, and a smile played at her mouth. "I think that just might work." But then her face twisted into a frown again. "But we'll need to find a grate that's out of sight to crawl into in the first place."

"Well, there's one right there." Derek chuckled and pointed at a grate in the street just outside the alleyway, illuminated by an orange streetlight. "And even if anyone's watching, it would be way too difficult to track us." He ran over the idea in his head a few times.

Daniel was alive. *After that explosion? And how dangerous is he?* Caleb had told Malcolm he was weak, but if he regained his strength, he could join forces with Caleb. One rampaging Landreau was bad enough.

Derek shook his head. He couldn't let himself be distracted.

Eric smiled. "Then I suppose we should go then, yes?"

Kaela wrapped her arms around Derek. "Thank you, Derek."

Derek couldn't stop his smile, patting her back. "You're welcome."

Eric's teeth shone yellow. "Is the old Kaela back?"

"Shut your damn mouth, Eric." Kaela's eyes turned to stone, and she released Derek. Anger didn't lace her tone, just indifference.

Tension hung like a thick fog in the air.

Lance remained still, a smug grin pointed at Eric.

Eric frowned at her, but she stared into those black eyes with her own yellow ones. Eric's smile slowly grew, while Kaela's mouth formed a thin line.

Finally, Eric spoke. "Well then… I suppose we should head over to the Rose, shouldn't we?"

Kaela pointed at Derek and said, "You take the lead. You've maneuvered through this city enough, so your sense of direction should be good enough to lead us there."

Derek nodded, still searching for what could possibly have led Caleb to them if not Amari.

How many more would have to die before this was over?

"Sure," Derek said, clearing his throat. "Let's get going."

CHAPTER 21
THE SEWER AND THE CIA

Lance wished he could ignore the pain. Even with the cane, every step elicited a surge of it from his leg. With every passing minute, it seemed to worsen.

He wouldn't have minded a painkiller or two, if only he trusted himself with them.

But if he could be grateful for anything, it was that the pain kept him alert and rid him of the sleepiness tugging at his eyelids.

Derek stopped them before they stepped out of the alley, analyzing the street then the rooftops. "I don't think anybody's watching us," Derek said. "Let's go."

Kaela made a sound like she was about to speak but sighed instead.

She was furious, that much was obvious from how she gritted her teeth. Lance remembered being told his parents were dead, overdosed in an alley—how mad he'd been.

Though that story had been false.

Kaela wasn't the only one gritting her teeth anymore.

They stepped out into the street.

Lance racked his brain for any way Caleb could've found them. Had someone told Caleb about Lance's store? But who? Rotoya was dead, and if she'd told him earlier, Caleb would've been waiting for them.

Unless Rotoya is alive… Lance shivered.

The beast was quiet, slumbering and regaining its strength, sensing no danger. That didn't stop his heart from jumping at every shift in the darkness. Every sound from within the alleys.

With some trouble, Eric and Derek hoisted the sewer grate up, straining from the weight. Kaela slid down first, graceful even in the act of climbing down a ladder, while Lance bumbled his way down. He almost fell more than once.

Kaela looked at him with sympathy when he reached the bottom. Lance sat as the aching worsened. He leaned against the cement wall. Moss and slime pressed into his back, cold and wet. He didn't care.

Kaela visibly shivered as the light of the streetlamp peeked through the still-open manhole.

"You okay?" Lance asked, and his own voice trembled. The air froze him to the bone. The smell of sewage didn't help.

"I'll be fine once we get to the Rose," Kaela responded, rubbing her hands against herself for warmth. "But if you don't mind…" She didn't finish the sentence, instead sitting next to him and stealing warmth.

Lance said nothing as she did so, as she gave warmth of her own in return. A mutual exchange.

"Hey," she said. "In case we end up dying, I just want you to know I'm sorry about that night we got attacked on the hill."

"What are you apologizing for?"

"Just… freaking out on you afterward. What you did to that man scared me. It wasn't you." She paused. "But I guess you were just doing what you had to."

Lance sighed. "I'm sorry too. I said some pretty nasty things."

"Yeah… Let's forget it ever happened."

"Agreed."

Eric started his climb down the ladder, but he braced a hand on the cover, and Derek slid through the open space and joined him. They struggled sharing the same space on the ladder, but together, they slid the manhole cover into place.

The sound of heavy iron sliding against asphalt echoed all the way down the tunnels. The only light remaining was a ray of streetlamp peeking through the small hole in the middle of the cover.

Eric favored one leg over the other as he clambered down the ladder.

How is he able to hide his sprained ankle so well?

"Alright," Derek said as he hit the ground, followed closely by Eric. "Eric, if you will."

Eric adjusted his coat. "Gotcha."

The sound of shuffling followed. Then a lighter clicked, and a tiny flame erupted in the darkness.

Silence.

Eric's smile was terrifying, his face lit up by nothing but a small flame, the shadows dancing along his features and his dark eyes.

"Eric," Derek started, his voice a warning, "where's the light?"

Eric smiled wider. "It's right here, of course."

"You said you had a light," Kaela said.

"Yes," Eric insisted, holding out the lighter.

"Like a *flashlight*."

"Oh, of course not, who carries one of those around with them?"

Kaela groaned, then Derek. Lance shook his head.

"Well," Eric said, his playful tone grating Lance's ears, "I suppose if it's that much of an annoyance, I'll just put the flame out."

"No," Kaela said then sighed. "No, it'll do. Derek? I'm putting a lot of faith in your sense of direction here."

Derek said nothing. He took the lighter and held it in front of him. The flame served only to penetrate a few inches of darkness. "Shouldn't there be lights in this place, anyway?"

Lance shook his head again. "In the slums? You're lucky there aren't mutated crocodiles in here." He smiled at first then realized that, with all that'd happened, such a thing didn't seem so impossible.

Derek turned back toward them, his mouth set in a straight line.

"What is it?" Kaela asked.

"I just…" Derek sighed. "I really don't think this light is going to be enough. I need a little more."

Eric hummed then looked at Lance. "Lance, buddy, I'm going to need you to take one for the team."

Lance raised an eyebrow. "If you think I'm going to take the lead, you're crazy."

"Give me one of those wooden planks from your splint."

Lance raised an eyebrow then looked at Kaela. She offered nothing but a shrug.

"Come on, we don't have all night." Eric held his hand out. Lance hesitated, then unwrapped the splint and gave Eric one of the pieces of wood.

In a few swift motions, Eric grabbed the wood then wrapped the bandages around the tip. He removed the top from his lighter and poured its fuel on the bandages, closed the lighter back up, then lit the impromptu torch.

Eric smiled proudly as he handed the torch to Derek.

Derek shared a confused look with Kaela and Lance, then slowly turned and started walking.

"What… just happened?" Kaela asked.

Eric dusted off his hands and placed them on his hips. "Ingenuity, Kaela."

"Guys," Derek called. "We need to get going. There's no telling how long this torch will last."

Lance stood with Kaela's help, nothing left of his splint but a single piece of wood, which he held in his hand. The splint had helped with the pain more than he thought, and now his leg ached nearly twice as much as before. He breathed deeply, but the stench of sewage nauseated him. If he made even a single misstep, his leg would give out.

Even with Kaela on one side and the cane on the other, his feet and the cane slid on the slimy ground. One bad slip, and he would fall hard, maybe even into the dirty waters. Lance grimaced at the water and wondered what horrors lay within.

"At least I can kill a vampire if we run across one," Lance said. *Or a mutated crocodile.* He gulped. The poor attempt at humor didn't help his discomfort.

Eric shot him a smile. "There's that sarcasm."

They went quiet, save for the echo of their footsteps on the ground, the crackling of fire from the torch, and the tapping of Eric's cane on the slimy floor.

"I know you're skinny and all, but I really thought you'd be heavier," Kaela whispered after a few more strides. Derek seemed confident in where he was going, deathly silent the entire time, completely focused on getting them to the Rose. Eric checked his nails.

Lance glared at the back of his greasy head. At the very least, he could've been on Lance's other side, helping him walk.

Some father.

Lance allowed himself the quietest, breathiest laugh he could muster before responding. "Sorry to disappoint you."

Derek was getting farther ahead of them, then Eric. Slowly, they fell behind, then they regained their normal speed. It was as if Kaela had gained a second wind.

Something was off.

They were just out of earshot if they whispered, and now it seemed intentional.

"What are you doing?" Lance finally asked, keeping his voice a whisper.

She glanced at him then kept an eye on the two ahead. "Keep your eyes forward."

Lance did as he was told.

"Eric told me an interesting story about why he brought you into our group."

Lance stopped himself from gulping. *No way Eric told her...* No, it didn't make sense. "Oh?"

Kaela nodded slowly. "He did… and I just want to know your side of the story."

Maybe tripping and falling into the murky waters wouldn't be so bad, after all. "And why are you so curious about all of this?"

She shrugged. "Maybe I'm just trying to make conversation. Maybe some of Eric's information obsession is rubbing off on me. Either way… I'd like to know."

Lance's heart pounded in the silence that followed.

"Eric said you work for the CIA." She sounded unsure.

Now it made sense, Lance thought, mentally cursing the man ahead of them. He gripped the cane tighter; a reminder that he, even if only a little, relied on Eric. He almost scowled, but Kaela's eyes were on him, gauging his reaction. A drop of something fell from the ceiling and landed on Lance's shoulder, cold as ice. The smell was worse.

Do I go along with it? Lance thought. *Or do I just deny it here and now?* He didn't know everything Eric had told her. One misstep in the lie, and it would be over. She would know that not just Eric, but *he* also was hiding something from her. He could tell her Eric was lying to her, but she would just press for more information. He had no chance of winning, and Kaela was obviously aware of that.

More and more like a cat. He was the mouse caught in her trap, and she'd taken her chance to pounce.

"Anything you'd like to say?" Her tone was predatory. She was going to get an answer no matter what he did.

"And what if I did?" Lance finally said. "What difference would it make?"

Another shrug. She leaned into him, just a bit, hanging on the edge of every word he said. She had a good poker face but was too eager. *An advantage,* Lance thought with a steadying breath. *A foothold.*

Kaela continued. "I suppose it wouldn't make much of a difference at all, really." She gave him a wicked smile. "But if you tell me, I won't drop you into the nasty sewer water."

A joke. At least, it probably was. Lance's pulse spiked as Eric turned his head just slightly. He donned a smirk then faced forward again, an action so small that Lance barely noticed. Kaela was too focused on trying to get the info out of him.

Eric was *listening.* As quietly as they were whispering, he could still hear them.

But that smirk gave Lance nothing to go on, and he was still caught in the trap.

Eric, the spider he was, was watching from afar, relaxed in his little web.

Lance resisted rolling his eyes. *Great, now I'm using the spider analogies.* He shrugged. "You know, if I was a former CIA agent, I wouldn't be allowed to tell you. Classified information, and all that."

Kaela nodded. "I totally understand that. But can you look me in the eyes and tell me you're *not* an agent?"

She looked at him, but he didn't reciprocate. "I thought you said you wanted me to keep my eyes forward."

She lightly sent an elbow into his side, which hurt more than it should have. "Fine, if you're going to be literal about it."

Silence hung between them for a moment, then another. Lance thought Kaela was done until she finally spoke again.

"Okay, let's cut the games," Kaela said. "I know you're not some CIA agent, okay? Just be real with me, Lance. What's going on?"

"Look," Lance said. "I just… I just need you to trust me."

Kaela stopped in her tracks. "I *do* trust you."

Lance narrowed his eyes and saw no sign that she was lying. "Then why are you hounding me about this?"

Kaela kept walking. "Because I know Eric's story was bullshit. I knew it from the beginning. And after how you reacted, now I know that you're in on it too. I just… What's so secretive that you can't even tell Derek and me?"

"It's complicated," Lance said. "I just can't tell you. At least… not right now."

Kaela stared at him, her eyes brimming with disappointment. "Fine. I'll leave it alone. But once this is all over, will you at least consider telling me?"

Lance nodded. "We'll see."

What does it even matter? Lance thought. *Why should I care if anyone finds out I'm his son? There's no reason to hide it.* Yet even with that logic clicking firmly into place in his mind, the words couldn't escape his lips. Then again, it would hurt Eric. Maybe that made it worth it.

A storm of conflicting thoughts brewed in his mind. He stared at Eric's back. He'd eavesdropped on the entire conversation, or at least bits of it. Lance wondered what was going through his mind right now.

This time, the silence lingered. Kaela seemed satisfied enough, so Lance tended to the fire raging in his head.

Lance smiled. "You seriously trust me?"

Kaela rolled her eyes. "Yeah, I do. Maybe I hit my head harder than I thought."

Lance chuckled, and Kaela smiled back.

They walked until Derek stopped and looked around. The torch was dying out. They had little time left.

"Just in time," Derek said. He dipped the torch into the water, extinguishing the flame, then dropped the piece of wood on the ground. "Look. Light."

The light ahead was dim at first, but as they kept walking, it became more prevalent.

"Thank God," Lance breathed.

As they walked down a curve in the sewer, Lance saw them. Lights, jutting out from the walls. A new light every few feet. The group emerged from the darkness.

A railing was set at the edge of the concrete. Lance reached for it and leaned against it.

"You got it?" Kaela asked.

"Yeah," Lance said, limping and putting his weight on the railing. "Thanks."

Kaela stayed beside him as they continued walking through the now-lit sewer. Even the smell was more manageable, if still rotten. They had to be out of the slums.

They walked for what felt like an hour, stopping once for a break, before Derek paused. "I think this might be it."

Lance was out of breath as he crouched against the railing. God, he really hoped they'd reached the Rose. He tensed as Derek climbed the ladder and opened the manhole with a strain. Finally, it slid out of place, and Derek poked his head out. Lance held his breath. Caleb had followed them at every turn. Everywhere they went, he always found them, and someone died as a result.

Derek looked back down and smiled, and Lance relaxed.

Kaela sighed. "About time we made it." She turned to Lance. "You okay on your own for now?"

Lance nodded, and she walked to the ladder.

Derek climbed out, and Kaela followed soon after.

Lance caught his breath and limped to the ladder, where Eric was waiting. "Don't worry," he whispered. "I didn't spill your precious secret."

"That's not why I'm waiting," Eric said. "Let me help you up."

"I don't need your help." Lance started to climb the ladder. He barely made a few rungs before stopping. "Dammit… Fine, maybe I need a little help."

Eric helped Lance up, pushing his good leg up with every rung he climbed. When he crawled out into the alleyway, he breathed in the cool night air, and his eyes watered. He didn't know why, and he repressed it quickly, but the simple act of finally breathing that air and not seeing Caleb waiting for them removed a weight from his chest.

When Lance looked at the rest of them, they seemed to share the sentiment. Everyone sat on the cold ground and breathed.

"Well," Eric said after a few deep breaths. "I think I've done my part. Give my regards to the girls, will you?"

"What?" Kaela's head snapped toward him, her teeth showing in a silent snarl. "Where do you think you're going?"

Eric was already climbing down. Only his head poked out from the ground. "Isn't it obvious? I'm going to find Daniel."

Kaela groaned. "You can go after him later. We need to rest."

"Be my guest, but I'm going."

"He could be anywhere in those sewers."

"Mm-hmm. Anywhere close by, according to our rotting friend."

"Guys?" Kaela pleaded.

Derek looked from her to Eric, his mouth open like he wanted to say something. Lance wasn't sure what she expected him to do. Eric had made up his mind. If he wanted to go crawling through a sewer, more power to him. Whatever happened to Eric would be a result of his own stupid decisions.

"I suppose you have your answer." Eric smiled. "Adieu." His head disappeared, and the cover remained open.

Derek moved to close it behind him, and Lance turned to enter the Rose, but something pulled him away. It almost physically tugged at him, telling him to follow his father.

Don't. That was his only warning. The beast inside had awoken, and it begged him to stay away from the Rose. *Follow him.*

Why? Lance wanted to ask. Why should he follow Eric? His leg was already in enough pain, and he didn't want to be trapped in a sewer with his father. George could look at his leg, and he could get a fresh shower.

Go! The beast hissed, and Lance's body jerked in response. He fought his own body as it tried to follow Eric, and when he looked at Kaela, she sent him an odd look. Derek had the cover halfway closed. *Decide.*

"Are you constipated or something?" Kaela asked.

Lance looked down at his hands, wrapped around his stomach. He didn't remember doing that.

"No," Lance shot at her. Then he sighed. "No." Softer this time.

Derek nearly closed the cover. There was just enough room for Lance to slide through.

"Stop," Lance said. At first, he said it to the beast within. When Derek nearly kicked the cover closed, Lance repeated it.

Derek went still, his leg poised to kick, and Kaela cursed.

"So you're going down there too?" Her hands were on her hips now. "You're already injured. Eric is on a suicide mission down there, and the only thing you're going to achieve is digging your own grave when you get lost."

Lance walked to the cover, still open just enough for him to slide through. *You'd better not be getting us killed*, he thought, hoping the message was received. He got no response, but he knew it reached the beast.

Kaela put her hands on her head like she would pull her hair out. "You're as dumb as he is. Don't expect us to come after you if you don't come back, because we won't."

Lance stopped and turned toward her, and he couldn't help but smile. "Yes, you will."

Kaela opened her mouth, looked at the ground, then flipped him off.

Lance slid down into the sewer once again, and the smell of rotten eggs and feces crinkled his nose. Without Kaela's perfume to mask the smell, nausea punched him in the stomach. He descended anyway until he reached the bottom of the ladder. With a few more kicks, Derek closed the cover above them.

At least the place was well lit.

Lance's chest clenched in a tight twist, then someone spoke.

"I knew you'd come around," Eric said, leaning against the wall with his arms crossed.

"Yeah, well, call it a gut feeling."

"I brought you a gift," Eric said, holding up the partially burned piece of wood. "I took it after Derek dropped it."

Lance glared at the piece of wood. Even from where Eric stood, he could smell it, but it was better than nothing.

"Just get it over with."

"That's my boy."

"Don't call me that."

Eric laughed. "Okay, I'll just stick with Lancelot, then."

Lance opened his mouth to argue that as well, but the thought of what Eric might think to call him next shut him up.

Eric crouched in front of Lance, salvaging the splint. He wrapped it tightly with what little bandage remained, then stood. "How is it?"

Lance put a bit of weight on his leg. It still hurt, but it was better, at least. "Not bad."

"Then let's get going."

Lance gripped the cane tighter and followed Eric along the sewer, the pain in his leg better now that the brace was intact. He leaned against the railing for extra support.

I don't know why you brought me down here, Lance thought. *But you'd better have a good reason for it.*

The beast made a sound in response, almost like—a purr?

Lance scoffed and hobbled forward.

CHAPTER 22
A LOSS TOO GREAT

Kaela gawked at the manhole cover. All of that, just for those two idiots to get lost in a sewer.

"Is everything okay?" Derek asked, knocking her out of her trance.

Kaela didn't look at him, but the concern was evident in his voice. "Yeah… just wondering why Lance decided to go down there with him."

He'd probably decided to go down there at the last minute, a chance to be alone with Eric, to discuss her attempt at getting information. She shook her head. No—no, she trusted Lance. If he couldn't tell her now, he had a reason.

Still, she rolled the thoughts around in her head as she tapped her knuckle on the back door of the Rose. Whatever they were hiding, it had to be bad. Or embarrassing. She wrapped her arms around her shoulders, shivering as the cold air settled in her bones. Derek leaned against the wall next to her, looking out at the street.

Kaela knocked again, and this time, she listened.

Nothing.

Derek's eyes swam with worry as they shared glances.

Kaela rested her hand on the doorknob and pushed.

It swung open easily.

Time froze. The color drained out of the world, all melting together into nothing but gray.

She was on her knees. She was screaming, but it was muffled like she was underwater. Her screams were loud and piercing, but not enough to break through the cotton in her own ears. She only stopped to breathe, each gulp of air twirling her stomach in circles. Derek was at her side, his arms around her. She wailed louder than she knew she could, screamed for the bloody bodies scattered across the floor to get up and tell her they were pretending.

Blood had pooled everywhere, soaked into the carpet, and the bodies —some were riddled with bullets, others torn apart or crushed.

She cried and screamed. She couldn't stop. As hard as she tried, the sirens in her heart went off, over and over. Derek dragged her out of the Rose, but she kicked and screamed.

"You have to snap out of it," he said.

Kaela couldn't stop screaming. She could only hear the shrieks bouncing around in her own head, overpowering Derek's attempts to calm her down. They were in the alley again. Her back rested against the cold brick.

"If you keep screaming, they'll hear us."

Her screams turned into sobs.

Derek removed his hand from over her mouth, and her sobs regained their clarity.

"It's my fault," she cried over and over, trying to stay quiet. "It's my fault. It's my fault."

"No, it's not," Derek said.

Between every attempt to calm her down, Derek's eyes darted in every direction, as if scared that Caleb's men would burst through the walls. At any moment, they could come barreling in to kill them. She couldn't let that happen, so she closed her mouth and swallowed the screams that kept banging at her throat, demanding to be released.

Kaela tried to stand, only to fall to her knees. Her heart raced, and her stomach turned. The ground swayed beneath her. She had to get control of herself. She could mourn once Caleb was dead at her feet, she told herself. But the sobs still came, and Derek wrapped her in a tight embrace.

"I'm so sorry," he said.

She shook her head. "I can't… I can't do this."

"We should get out of here."

"No," Kaela pushed him away. "We have to see if Malcolm is still here. Or George. We have to know what happened."

"Let me go in there."

"No!" Kaela hissed. "I'm going too. I need to see if anyone's still alive."

Derek opened his mouth like he was going to protest, but the look she shot him changed his mind.

Kaela sat there for another few moments. "I just need a minute."

"Take your time."

Kaela breathed deeply, choking on some of the sobs that tried to escape her. After a few moments, she clenched her fists, gritted her teeth, and stopped her sobs. "Okay… let's go."

Derek helped Kaela to her feet. Her knees were weak, and her head ached.

This wasn't human. Whatever had done this was a feral animal. She stepped inside, and a puddle of blood splashed beneath her feet. She gagged.

They maneuvered around the bodies, avoiding the stares from the wide-open eyes of the corpses that were intact. The smell of the coppery tang of blood poisoned the air. They splashed the scarlet puddles with every step despite their attempts to step over it.

Blood painted the walls. Kaela called for someone, for any of the girls to come out and reveal themselves, to tell them what had happened. But every man and woman that Kaela recognized crossed a line through her mental list, rapidly shortening with each body she passed.

When she stood in the middle of the waiting room, she stifled another sob. "Caleb was definitely here." She looked around at the mangled bodies then at the bullet-riddled ones near the entrances. Caleb's swollen arms flashed in her memory.

"Caleb killed them. Tore them apart with his bare hands…" She pointed at the bodies near the doors. "He had his men waiting outside to shoot anyone that tried to escape."

"Jesus, Kaela," Derek said. "I'm so sorry."

"Not as sorry as Caleb's going to be." Kaela looked around at the bodies, some in worse shape than others. "I'll never let this happen again." She looked down at the closest body, twisted and broken into an unnatural shape. Kaela knelt down and closed the girl's eyes, wishing she had the time to do the same for the others. "Rest…"

Faint voices spoke beyond the walls. Kaela perked her ears then looked at Derek.

He heard them too.

One of them was rushed. Malcolm, for sure.

Kaela seethed as she recognized the other voice.

The voices came from just down the hall. Kaela took a step, then another, Derek close by. She inched farther down the hall until she pinpointed which door they were coming from. Just when she thought she could hear what the voices were saying, they halted.

Then someone said, "Come in."

Kaela's blood ran cold. Her heart skipped a beat, and when she looked at Derek, he offered only a shocked expression.

The person spoke again. "Don't bother trying to hide. I'm afraid my hospitality does not extend to asking twice. Now, come on in before I have to go out there and retrieve you."

Kaela balled her fists and composed herself. How could he murder innocent people just to get at her? Tears built up in her eyes, but she wiped them away as soon as they touched her cheeks.

Derek tensed. "We need to run."

"Go ahead," Kaela said.

She touched the dagger hidden at her leg. The smallest of comforts. *What did Malcolm say could kill them? Beheading?*

She could manage that.

Kaela took a deep breath, likely the last she would ever have, and said, "Get out of here, Derek."

Derek hesitated then stepped closer to her. "I'm not leaving you."

They shared a look for a lingering moment. Determination was set in Derek's eyes.

"Are you sure?" Kaela asked.

"I'm sure."

Kaela pushed the door open and stepped in. Bodies were scattered all over the room, blood covering the walls.

Caleb was sitting on the bed in the center of the room, the satisfied smirk on his face as sickening a sight as the bodies around him. Malcolm was sitting next to him. He twitched like he was being zapped every other second, his eyes blinking rapidly.

"I did some redecorating," Caleb said with that smug smile. Trying to rile her up, just as he had in the alley.

She would afford him no such pleasure, even with her heart screaming in agony. Derek stood behind her, his presence a comfort.

The knife strapped to her leg was also a comfort. Its cold steel dug into her. She would stab it right into that smiling mouth and cut every last tooth from it before she died so that nobody could ever see that disgusting smile again. If the drug could heal them like Malcolm claimed, they would grow back within the day, but it would be worth it as long as she got the opportunity.

"How rude," Caleb said, shifting in the seat. "I never knew you had my poor brother slaving away in that cold basement. And on a cure, no less?" He clicked his tongue, and Kaela nearly lunged to slice it out. "Funny that you would even consider it as such. This!" He gestured to himself. "This is a cure!" His eyes went wild, and his veins glowed brighter. His composure broke, and as he breathed slowly, he built it back up.

"You..." Her voice broke already. Kaela couldn't think straight. She kept avoiding the bodies everywhere. She couldn't allow herself to look at them, not if it meant showing weakness to Caleb. Not this time. She could mourn later, once she'd ripped his eyes from their sockets. "How did you find this place?"

Caleb shook his head. "I'm disappointed to hear you ask that question. I can find you wherever you go. It may take some time, granted, but I will do it eventually." He met her eyes, and it took everything inside of her not to attack him. "I suppose you do deserve an answer, however. I'll throw the puppy her bone since I did rid you of an entire business. After all, this is only the first of many I will destroy."

She nearly threw up again. That was all he could see of what he'd done—nothing but an end to her business, not the slaughter of the people she saw as her family.

"Thanks to the nanobots, I can sense when he is nearby, like a… a homing beacon, you could say. When I drove by this establishment, I sensed his presence." He chuckled lightly. "I thought I'd drop by for a visit."

"He lies," Malcolm said. "Found me bec—"

Caleb whirled his head toward Malcolm, his tone laced with fury. "Let's not ruin the surprise, dear brother, hmm?" He leaned back and crossed his legs, which brought his foot onto a puddle of blood. He didn't seem to care, entirely relaxed in this setting. "To my great surprise, none of the workers here seemed to know what I was talking about when I requested him." He laughed. "Well, I admit I got a little angry and went on something of a small rampage. Go figure, I find him in the basement, and he tells me he is working on this 'cure'."

He was no longer a man, Kaela thought, but a monster, influenced by the serum. It was her fault, then—her fault that everyone was dead, her fault for letting Malcolm stay here, cure or no cure.

Kaela dug her nails into her fist then leaned back slightly against Derek. God, she wasn't sure she could've done this without him here.

Kaela averted her eyes from Caleb's smug face and directed it at Malcolm. He hung his head and wrung his hands. Nervous and twitchy, with no sign of calming down.

"What did you do to him?" Kaela asked.

Caleb put a hearty hand on Malcolm's shoulder, making him flinch. "I did absolutely nothing. Though I suppose I shouldn't have allowed him to see that gruesome sight. All those people being slaughtered, it upset him." He stared at her for a long, lingering moment then leaned forward, demanding her full attention. "Aren't you wondering where my men are now? I'm sure you noticed the bullet wounds." He grinned. "I ordered the rest down into the sewer to go after Eric and the other boy with the long hair."

Kaela's heart fell to her stomach, and she went slack-jawed before she could stop herself. Her whole world was shattering into nothing. Caleb had lured them all to stand on his rug then pulled it out from beneath them to reveal a spiky chasm beneath.

Derek's breath caught. From behind her, she felt him tense so hard she thought he would tear a muscle. She shouldn't have let Lance and Eric go down there.

"How did you—" Derek started to say.

But Caleb held his hand up. "Wouldn't you like to know?"

"You don't care if they kill your own brother?"

Caleb hummed as he looked at his reflection in a puddle of blood. His face lit up. "No, not really." Caleb drew a knife and sliced Malcolm's head clean off.

Malcolm's head rolled forward to Kaela's feet, his shocked expression permanently etched on his face. His body was still for a moment then fell forward, landing in a puddle of blood. Purple blood poured out, mixing with the blood of her girls.

Kaela couldn't breathe. Her vision darkened, and her balance tilted. Derek put a hand on her back, and the cold of the knife on her leg called to her. The room filled with a sweet smell. Bile rose to her throat. As Malcolm's body lay lifeless on the floor, so did their chances of developing a cure.

"Poor brother," Caleb sighed, slicing the knife across his palm. "His only wish was to live forever. Shame he never accounted for decapitation." He laughed. "Poor bastard even admitted it to me. The nanobots can repair nearly anything, but growing a head back?" He sliced his other palm, pointing the knife at Kaela.

Kaela put a hand to her chest. She couldn't help it. Her chest ached and twisted, and her stomach writhed inside her. Derek paled.

"But as I was saying," Caleb continued, throwing the knife into the back of Malcolm's body, where it sank in with ease. "I don't necessarily care if my brothers die anymore. Malcolm was working against me, and Daniel shows no signs of becoming strong like he once was, and even if he did, I can't risk him trying to take his men from me. Besides"—Caleb's fingers danced, and the blood spilling from his hands danced along with them, shifting and moving in the air—"I've become much more powerful these past few days. I've learned a few more tricks, as you can see, so I don't need my brothers any longer."

Kaela stepped back. *This can't be real.*

"Now, you see, I find it very important that you all die. All of you... But Eric is my priority. He had the nerve to come to my building and threaten me in front of my coworkers. I don't appreciate being disrespected. Even worse, he escaped my grasp." He stood from the bed, and the smell of copper returned, mixing with the sweetness.

"What do you want from us?" Derek asked.

"Glad you asked, my boy." Caleb adjusted his tie. The blood floated above his head, steadily leaking from his palms and rising into the air. "You two are quite resourceful. I would like to offer you both the chance to join my side. All you have to do is take the drug."

"Like hell."

"The only alternative is death. So, what'll it be?"

As much as he claimed to hate Eric, Caleb acted just like him. A performer on stage.

Something shifted at Caleb's feet, and Kaela gasped as Malcolm's blood rose from the floor slowly, dancing and shifting until it also floated above Caleb's head.

Caleb raised an eyebrow, then a laugh escaped him. "Well, well, well... isn't that a fascinating discovery? I suppose my brother's untimely and permanent death allows me control over his bots." Another laugh left him as the large cloud of blood floated above him. "Thanks for the inheritance, brother."

Caleb took a step closer to Kaela and opened his mouth to say something else.

Kaela raked her nails across his cheek, right over his eye. He shouted in pain, turning and bending over, his hand over the wound. When he turned back to her, his one eye glowed, and the wound healed in seconds. It might not have done much, but it sure felt good.

"You stupid bit—"

She slapped him again, harder this time. When his head turned, she drew her knife and stabbed it into his neck. Derek charged, tackling Caleb. They fell to the ground, splashing red and purple blood all over themselves.

Kaela wrenched the knife, slicing it farther into his neck. Just a little more, and his head would come off. Caleb gurgled blood.

Kaela yelled as she wrenched the knife even farther. Derek fought and struggled to keep him down.

Caleb yelled up at the ceiling, and his veins flashed with blinding violet light.

The blood floating above him slammed into Kaela and Derek. The liquid reached her eyes, her nose, her mouth. She choked and coughed with every attempt to breathe. Derek choked somewhere beside her. Blood blinded her and stung her eyes. Another strike of the blood knocked her back, and she slammed against the wall.

Caleb coughed and sputtered for a few moments, but then his voice returned to normal. He was calm as he spoke but out of breath. "I was going to blow this building sky high anyway, so I suppose I'll have to leave you inside it."

A snakelike tendril slid around Kaela's arms and legs, and the blood pinned her against the wall. Panic seized her heart as she struggled in vain.

"But you fought like hell, so I'll give you that." Caleb laughed, and his heavy footsteps clunked out of the room.

The blood removed itself from her mouth then her nose, and she gulped air down, the smell of honey forcing itself down into her lungs, the taste of metal coating her tongue.

How could he have such control over the blood? Seconds passed, and the blood removed itself from her eyes. She blinked until her vision cleared, her eyes burning. Derek was pinned next to her, gulping down air and coughing.

Kaela struggled against her binds. Dark-purple ropes tightened against her arms and legs. He'd solidified the blood? But how?

"Kaela," Derek said, still getting his breath back. "Stay calm, okay? We can get out of here."

Kaela struggled harder against the blood rope, swearing and crying and scanning the mangled bodies of her girls. Every face that was still intact stared off into the distance. Their faces were painted in horror, and she could only writhe in her own anger and rage for having allowed them to feel that fear, to go through the horrors Caleb had made them endure.

Then she watched as the rest of Malcolm's purple blood pooled around his headless body. Their one chance at a cure was spilled across the floor, headless. She struggled more against the ropes, but the raw stench of copper and honey gagged her. After a few more vain attempts to escape, she stopped. A sob escaped her.

"I'm sorry, Derek," she whispered, tears trailing down her cheeks. "I'm sorry for getting you in this mess."

Derek struggled, fighting to escape his bonds. He knew it was useless as well. The hopeless glint in his eyes told Kaela that much.

He looked at her and shook his head. "Stop being sorry for everything. You did all you could."

Kaela let herself breathe. Foul as it was to smell, she breathed the air in, savoring the last few mouthfuls she would have before it was all over.

Malcolm's spreading blood reached another pool of blood. Red blood.

At first, it seemed like nothing more than a trick of the light, but Kaela blinked then blinked again. Malcolm's blood spread through the pool of red, almost contaminating it, as if the nanobots within sensed the red blood cells and hunted them down like prey.

Malcolm's blood moved on its own, consuming the red blood. Something awakened within her, a familiar comfort she'd thought she'd lost—hope. Its broken body presented itself before her, bruised and shredded but still intact. Just enough for one last push.

An idea clicked inside her head, and she reached for it. One last thing. She would try one last thing before they died.

Kaela craned her neck to her arm, raised above her head. Her neck popped and crackled, but she stretched farther. She clamped her teeth into her arm and bit down. Pain tore through skin and muscle. She screamed, but the sound was muffled. The pain only encouraged her to bite harder until the taste of copper filled her mouth.

Kaela sucked a mouthful of blood from her arm then spat it onto one of the ropes. It joined with the purple blood, slowly disappearing within the confine.

She dipped her tongue once again into the stream of blood sliding down her arm. She spat again, then again. She collected more and more blood and spat it desperately at the rope. Tears filled her eyes as pain sliced at her arm.

As she moved to gather more blood, the rope gave a little. It *softened.* She smiled at Derek, surely terrifying with her scarlet teeth.

"Kaela…"

"Don't ask questions. Just do it."

Derek shook his head. "Aw, hell."

He craned his neck and bit into his own arm, and together, they spat blood onto the ropes holding them. Finally, the rope of blood around her hand loosed just enough for her to wriggle it out. She laughed at the sight, joy flooding her body. Then anxiety as a sound caught her attention, a repetitive beeping somewhere beyond the room.

She squeezed her arm, coaxing even more blood out, and wiped. She spread the blood all over the rope. From her arm to the binds, she continued until the next rope loosened. She wriggled her hand free and fell forward, her ankles still pinned against the wall. Her breath quickened and rushed as she smeared the last two ropes with blood until they loosened. She fell to the ground, splashing into the purple blood. She wiped her face and held back a gag as she reached for her knife. She held the dagger in her hand, savoring the comfort it brought.

Kaela threw the knife to Derek, who already had one hand free, and he cut at the ropes until he was out of his bindings.

"You hear that beeping?" Kaela asked.

Derek paused then nodded.

"We've got to get out of here now before this whole place blows."

Kaela and Derek burst from the room and scrambled through the halls. The beeping was louder, sounding from behind the walls. How long did they have? Minutes? Seconds?

Of course Caleb had put the bombs on a timer, to add insult to injury and burn them in her own business, surrounded by the bodies of the people she'd worked with and grown to love. Hatred moved her forward until she finally twisted through the halls and reached the side door.

Kaela swore as she tripped over a body and landed in a pool of blood, splashing crimson onto her face. She paused, staring at her red hands. It took everything she had not to scream. Derek grabbed her and helped her to her feet as she stole one last glance at the bodies of her girls, her employees, her friends.

With a desperate push of her body, she flung the side door open, and the ground shook as a force threw them against the brick wall of the alley. Waves of flame shot from the side door, narrowly missing the duo. Heat scorched Kaela's side as the flames licked much too close to her, even as Derek shielded her with his body.

Kaela helped Derek to his feet, and they ran. Her body ached from the impact. It didn't matter if Caleb was waiting again, or if he had men sitting nearby. For all she knew, he expected them to escape. But as she sprinted into the street with Derek, no men rushed toward them. No mysterious figures watched them from the roof.

How did he get away so fast?

They crossed the street and slipped into a dark alley. Derek coughed and sputtered, leaning against the wall, and Kaela did her own share of coughing, trying to rid her lungs of the foul smell staining her insides. She sat on her feet, tears flooding her eyes as the building she'd worked in and managed for years erupted in flames, along with all her friends.

The sign at the front of the building flickered out and shattered. Smoke poured from within, and the fires spread greedily. Her heart sank into her stomach. Everybody in there was gone, and they wouldn't be identifiable once the flames finished their job. Sirens sounded in the distance, but by the time the fire department arrived, it would be too late. That was, if they weren't also under Caleb's influence.

Everybody in that building might as well have died by her hand. She was just as much at fault as Caleb was, and that was fine. Because she would find him. The more he took away from her, the less she had to lose, the less she had to live for. He would die by her own bare hands when she got the chance. He would find them again with some other diabolical plan to tear them apart, and she would be ready.

A warmth brushed her side, and Derek was there, a hand on her back. "How's your arm?"

Kaela brushed his hand away, gently. She couldn't accept his sympathy, not after how she'd let him go in there with her.

As the Rose collapsed with a loud rumble that pained her ears, all she needed was Caleb, dead before her—better yet, crumpled before her, broken, pleading with her, begging her to show him mercy.

She wouldn't.

CHAPTER 23
BONDING OVER BLOOD

Lance leaned more of his weight against the railing, despite how it froze his fingers.

Eric walked in front of him, never getting far ahead, even with how slowly Lance walked. The cane clacked softly against the ground, and the sound reverberated throughout the tunnels.

Neither of them spoke. Lance ignored Eric's every attempt at conversation.

Kaela and Derek were likely getting another shower and snacking while waiting for them to return, and here he and Eric were, scouring the rotten tunnels for someone that probably wasn't down here.

Why did you bring me here? Lance asked the beast. It didn't make a sound and instead continued swimming around in his gut.

The only living things they'd encountered were the occasional rats. Unless Daniel had gained the ability to turn into one, they were wasting their time.

"So Kaela was rather invested in that conversation you two were having," Eric said after the long silence—one last desperate attempt to get Lance to talk, surely.

Lance sighed and took the bait. "I had a feeling you were listening."

"I didn't exactly try to hide it from you." He turned with a wolfish grin.

"I can't believe you told her I was an operative for the CIA."

Eric stopped and turned toward Lance. "I can't believe she didn't buy it… I must be losing my touch."

"You realize that I could just tell her you're my father."

That wolf grin disappeared, and his eyes darkened. "No." His mouth formed a tight line. "No, that would be a terrible idea. If anyone found out, even Kaela and Derek, then—"

"It would ruin your reputation? Make you look bad?" Lance scoffed and made to push by Eric, even as it hurt his leg to do so.

Eric's arm went out, stopping him in his tracks. "Because if anyone found out that you're my son, you would be in danger."

Lance rolled his eyes. "As opposed to the danger you've already put me in? Making me drive recklessly through the city streets while Rotoya gave chase?" He gestured angrily at his leg. "You are the reason I have this injury, and *you* are the reason why I'm in this mess to begin with." He pointed a finger in Eric's face. "So don't give me that crap. Don't pretend like you're some loving father that cares so much for his son. If you truly cared for me, you would've stayed out of my life entirely."

"You're seriously not going to let the car-chase thing go, are you?"

"No."

"And I thought you were mad *because* I wasn't in your life?"

"Shut up."

Eric groaned and kept walking.

The beast whispered something, but Lance ignored it. His chest tightened as much as his fists. The continued whispering in his head didn't help the frustration—the beast's purrs and growls and words. With every day that passed, it seemed whatever was inside of him became more sentient. It wasn't just adrenaline or survival instincts, the sudden rush turning him into a combat expert. That had been confusing enough. Now, it spoke to him, urged him to take actions, and discouraged him otherwise.

Lance ignored the sounds of the beast and continued forward. With every step, he threw himself deeper into his anger at Eric, who was silent behind him.

Every ladder they passed slowed Lance down as he considered climbing to the street. If Eric protested, it wouldn't matter, not when he didn't have leverage over him. But every time he considered it, the beast hissed a violent no and told him to keep going.

So he did, muttering a curse as he walked past each ladder. They continued walking until the quiet pattern of Eric's footsteps stopped. Lance stilled and turned, a question already on his lips, but Eric held a hand up.

"Do you hear that?" he asked.

Lance tuned his ears for any sound other than the occasional drip of water. He nearly accused Eric of making another unfunny joke, but the look on his face was serious, focused, and… hopeful?

"Listen."

Lance did so again, this time closing his eyes. Something *was* there. Faint whispers. At first, Lance thought it to be the beast, but the beast was swimming silently within him.

This whisper was human, worldly.

His heart skipped a beat. Had Caleb found them? Down here, of all places?

He opened his eyes to make sure Eric wasn't making the noise, but he wasn't. Instead, his mouth was twisted into a smile.

"That's him," Eric said. "It's gotta be."

"Who?" Lance already knew the answer, but he wanted to hear it, to make sure it was real.

"Daniel."

As if in response, the beast stirred. A warning to get ready, to prepare for a coming battle. Panic seized Lance, curling around his chest and tightening in a viselike grip. If it truly was Daniel, could he even survive a fight with him? He should've just climbed that ladder.

"Let's go." Eric dashed ahead of Lance.

Lance remained still, tempted to turn back. If he just turned around, he could climb the ladder and find his own way to the Rose. But the beast growled, and his body was tugged forward by an invisible force. An order to follow Eric.

He did. He cursed himself for doing it, but Lance followed Eric.

Lance's leg ached as he pushed himself to reach Eric. He was putting too much weight on it. The beast kept encouraging him to move forward.

Lance followed the order and sped down the tunnel as quickly as he could, using the railing and the cane. When he caught up with Eric, he'd already stopped and angled his head to the ground with his eyes closed. Lance copied the action and listened. Hushed whispers of a man, too nonsensical to make out, came from their right. But no tunnel led to the source. Just pipes and wall.

Eric looked at him with a confused frown, and Lance stepped forward to convince him that there was no way to get through a wall. They could ignore the whispers, return to street level, and go to the Rose. A hot shower, a nice meal, and a long rest was all they needed.

But then Eric crouched, and he slid his hand along every inch of the tunnel wall. Around pipes and over concrete he searched until he gasped in excitement.

Lance's jaw fell as Eric dug his fingers around a piece of the wall and pulled. Just like the small hideout in that alley, a panel made of concrete slid out an inch.

Eric smiled up at him, wild and free like an animal, and braced himself against the wall. He pulled with all his might, grunting as he slid the panel out inch by inch. Finally, it slid out entirely, and the thick panel fell to the side. The sound was deafening and echoed throughout the tunnels.

When the echoes faded, so did the whispers.

Lance waited for an attack. He stepped back, waiting for Daniel to slide out from the crawlspace and slice Eric's neck open.

But nothing happened. Lance didn't move, his heart pounding in his chest, his breathing out of control.

The whispers still did not return.

"Come on," Eric said. He lowered himself to the floor and crawled through.

Lance grabbed his side before he could get halfway in, and Eric pulled himself back out.

"What?"

"You're seriously going to crawl right through there? You have no idea what's on the other side of that tunnel."

Eric rolled his eyes. "Which is why I'm going to go find out."

Stupid. Lance felt the word on his tongue, but he didn't say it. "Even if that is Daniel, you are at a huge disadvantage crawling through there. Why not lure him out?"

Eric smiled. "Aw, so you *don't* want me to get hurt?"

Lance almost slapped him. "I don't want to be left alone in this hell-hole with whatever is on the other side of that tunnel after me. How are you even going to fight it?"

Eric hummed. "You could always come with me."

The beast purred in agreement. Lance shook his head. "No, I refuse. Let's just get out of here. We know where he is, we can come back later."

"And risk him leaving this hiding place? Who's to say he doesn't know we've found him?"

Lance groaned and rubbed his face as Eric crawled into the tunnel again. *I hate you.* He focused on the beast. *But I think I hate* you *more.* The beast growled.

Go, the beast hissed at Lance, and his body urged him forward.

His mind struggled, but before he knew it, Lance was facing the bottom of Eric's shoes, crawling through the small, dingy tunnel.

"I hate you," Lance whispered. "I hate you so much."

"Yeah, yeah," Eric said. "I'll buy you a lollipop when we get out of this. How's that, champ?"

Lance sent him an obscene gesture, and though Eric didn't see it, it made Lance feel better.

They crawled until Eric slid out from the tunnel and into a small square room. Lance crawled out behind him.

The room was pitch black until Eric flicked open his lighter. The room was small enough for the flame to light up all four walls. It was a perfect square, as if it had been cut out by a laser. The air chilled Lance to the bone, and his breath formed a cloud in front of him when he sighed, standing up and staying close to Eric, the cane tightly gripped in his hand. The cold bit deep into his leg.

Lance's breath caught as he followed Eric's blank stare.

He was right.

Daniel was crouched in a corner of the room, shaking and staring at them with dark-purple eyes.

"Well, well, well," Eric said, and Lance almost hit him across the head for what he knew he was about to do. "Daniel Landreau, how have you been, my friend? It's been a while, you know." He laughed. "I thought you were dead, old friend… You know, I don't blow up my base of operations for just anybody."

Lance inched back toward the tunnel as Eric paced in front of Daniel, assessing him, gauging how much of a threat he was. As much as his body fought against it, Lance stayed close to that tunnel, prepared to dive through it at a moment's notice.

"I…" Daniel started. His voice and body shook. "I r-remember y-you." He looked up at Eric, no more than a lost child compared to what he'd been when Lance first met him. That confidence, that unwavering killer look in his eyes was gone.

Lance almost felt sorry for him.

Eric seemed to notice the innocent aura about him, and he stepped back, his guard lowering. "Why are you here?"

"B-brother came to m-me…" Daniel stuttered. "Told m-me I n-needed to h-hide."

"Caleb?"

He nodded.

"What is this place?"

"B-brother used b-blood to… slice c-concrete."

Eric stood straighter. "I see you have a bad case of the purple vein… but if you had burned up in that fire, you wouldn't be here. How'd you escape?"

"Men… p-protected me."

Eric was about to ask another question, but Daniel continued, "S-still burned m-my b-body."

Eric glanced at Lance then held the lighter closer to Daniel. His skin was charred and gray yet almost moving, as if the nanobots were working even now in an attempt to heal him.

"Why did Caleb tell you to hide?" Eric asked.

Daniel was silent at first, but when Eric repeated the question, he answered. "B-brother… said I was in d-danger. N-needed to hide. Said once h-he c-came to get me, m-my men and I would have c-control over s-sister cities."

Eric nodded then chuckled. He held his hand out, and Lance's body urged him to toss the cane. He did so without meaning to, cursing the beast again.

"I don't know how to tell you this, Daniel," Eric said, drawing his cane blade. The flame of the lighter flickered shadows on the blade. "But your brother has taken over your little private army. I have a feeling he just wanted you out of the way."

Daniel looked up at Eric again, his eyes sparkling with sadness. A pup betrayed by its master.

"Shame I have to kill you," Eric continued, raising the blade. "But don't worry… I'll get revenge on Caleb for you."

"P-please don't," Daniel begged, his hand held out.

"Eric," Lance warned.

All they needed was a sample of the man's blood. He didn't seem like a threat anymore. He didn't need to die.

"Sorry, pal," Eric said. "Can't take the risk of having you around to cause more trouble."

The sword went down.

And Daniel caught it between his hands. His veins glowed brighter, and when he met Eric's eyes, they too glowed, a bright purple.

"No," Daniel said, his voice no longer shaky. He pushed the blade forward and kicked Eric, sending him flying into the opposite wall.

Lance dove for the crawlspace, but Daniel shoved him aside. Like Eric, he slammed against the opposite wall. His breath left him as Daniel slipped through the crawlspace much faster than he should've been able to. Eric was on his feet, and he spared Lance a worried glance before diving in after Daniel.

Lance forced air into his lungs and stood, adrenaline rushing through him. He dove in after Eric, the beast poised and readied to strike. Adrenaline coursed through him, easing some of the pain in his leg. When he crawled out from the tunnel, he gasped.

Daniel shoved Eric's head below the murky water.

Lance didn't think, didn't know how he bounded over to them so quickly. He threw himself against Daniel, and the two of them slammed against the concrete wall. Eric's gasps of air were barely audible over the blood rushing to Lance's ears. Lance sent his foot into Daniel's head. Purple splashed from his face, and a few teeth scattered across the floor.

Eric, out of breath, joined Lance's side. His eyes were black as night but full of rage. He grabbed Daniel by the shirt and threw him into the water.

"Let's see how you like it," Eric said, a smile growing on his face.

But Daniel was already back on his feet, spitting blood into the water. His nose was broken, bent in a way that stirred Lance's stomach. *How are we going to take this guy down?*

Eric drew his cane blade once again and charged. Daniel's veins flashed, and the blade impaled the palm of his hand. The tip ended right at his eye, no more than a centimeter away from blinding him. Daniel shoved him away. Blade jutting from his palm, he swiped his hand at Eric. Eric dodged, but his movements were slow. He was tiring.

Water splashed, and the horrific smell of honey and sewage mixed. Lance held his breath and leapt forward. Daniel swiped again. Lance caught his wrist and struck Daniel's face with his elbow. It did little to faze him but gave Eric just enough time to rip his blade out of Daniel's hand.

Daniel hissed in pain, his veins flashing again. Before he knew it, Lance was thrown down the tunnel. He landed in the water and gagged as it entered his mouth, the taste sour and sickening. He spat out as much as he could and turned to join the fight again. But his leg protested, and he fell to his knees. The killing calm always helped, always worked; but his leg was too hurt to do anything, even with the beast giving him the advantage.

Eric was holding his own against Daniel, but worry covered his face.

Lance closed his eyes and breathed. The beast within coiled and hissed. He needed more. Needed to beat him. At this rate, they would be killed in this godforsaken sewer.

Let me breathe, the beast said, not in his head but his heart. From his very essence, it whispered, *Give me room.* Lance knew what it meant. He'd been allowing the beast to control him when his life was in danger, but he had never fully accepted it. Never allowed the beast any more room than the aid it provided. But just as it had said, with the little breathing room it had, they wouldn't beat Daniel.

Eric was slammed against the wall, his blade sliding across the floor. Daniel pinned him, whispering something in his ear. Eric's face melted in horror.

Fine, Lance thought. *Do what you need to do.*

It gave a pleased purr, and Lance stopped fighting. He didn't make any attempts to resist as the beast stretched and hummed. But he only allowed so much. A surge of energy ran through him, a surge of strength. Then he cut it off, stopping the beast before it could get greedy.

It hissed, but Lance ignored it. A snapping sound came from his leg, and a terrible wave of pain crashed into him. He crumpled to the ground, hands going to his leg before his mind could order it. But the pain only lasted for a few seconds. And as his hands traveled up and down the leg, feeling the bone beneath, it stopped hurting. The bone didn't feel broken anymore. *But how?*

No time, whispered the beast. Lance looked up again, newfound resolve filling his chest. Eric's eyes rolled into the back of his head, and his struggling weakened. Daniel's hands remained wrapped tightly around his father's throat.

Lance dashed through the darkness, and with one swift grab, Eric's blade was in his hand. He was fast, much faster than he'd ever been. Daniel only had time to look at Lance as he leapt.

Daniel's mouth opened in a gasp as the blade penetrated his neck. Lance grabbed the cane's body from the ground and flicked the scythe out. He whirled and sliced Daniel's neck. The shocked expression remained for a breath, two breaths. Then the grip on Eric loosened, and Daniel's body crumpled to the ground.

His head rolled into the water.

Before it could drift away, Lance grabbed it by the hair.

"About time," Eric said, coughing and sputtering. "Thanks."

Lance held the head in his hands, power swimming through his veins. The beast moved around in his gut, but it didn't feel nearly as uncomfortable. It had stretched out in its increased space.

God, this feels incredible!

"I know he's not breathing anymore," Eric said, rubbing his neck. "But I'm not done." After a few more seconds, Eric removed the vial from his coat and grabbed the head from Lance. He angled it over the vial, violet blood filling it and pouring all over his hand. He corked the vial and tossed the head carelessly next to the body.

Lance still held the blade, the adrenaline lessening little by little. With every bit of clarity that returned, guilt took its place. He'd lent the beast more power. Gave it more breathing room. He wondered what the consequences of that would be.

No, Lance thought and put a hand to his chest. Something in him, something greater than the beast, told him that it was the right choice—his instincts. The very thing that had kept him alive all those years on the streets.

The beast settled within him and returned to its slumber.

"What now?" Lance breathed.

Eric tossed him the cane, and Lance sheathed the blades.

"I don't trust leaving the body intact, beheading or no beheading," Eric responded.

Lance's breathing returned to normal, and as he took a step on the leg that was broken, he felt no pain. Not an ache, nothing. He hid his excitement, and for now, he gave a wince anyway, putting his weight on the cane. Eric couldn't find out his leg had healed that quickly, not without explaining… well, everything.

Whatever this beast inside of him was, it was scary—much scarier than he'd thought previously.

A demon?

"Right," Lance said after realizing Eric was staring at him, awaiting his input. "Burn it?"

He hummed. "When we first met him, he took a sip from a flask… I wonder." He bent down and rifled through the clothes on the headless body as purple blood pooled from the neck.

"Well," Eric said as he removed a flask. He wiggled it with a smirk. "Isn't that convenient?"

Eric opened the flask, sniffed, then swallowed a mouthful. He offered some to Lance. Just the idea of drinking after someone infected with those nanomachines… No, he wasn't about to take a sip of that drink.

Eric poured most of the alcohol out on the body, leaving a small amount. He picked the head up as if it was nothing more than a basketball and placed it on Daniel's chest.

Eric flicked his lighter and tossed it onto Daniel's body. It erupted in a golden flame. Then he poured the remaining alcohol on his wounded hand, wincing. "Let's hope that doesn't get infected."

Only when the sweet smell became overpowered by the foul stink of smoke did they walk away.

"What did he tell you?" Lance asked, faking a limp as he leaned on Eric's cane. "I've never seen you so scared before."

Eric said nothing for ten steps, then he cleared his throat, rubbing at his neck. "He said he was going to kill me and turn you into one of them."

"You were actually scared about that?"

"Of course I was." Eric looked at him, his eyes revealing something like offense. But then it was covered and hidden as quickly as it appeared. "You are my son, after all. Like it or not."

Lance's chest tightened at the words—in anger or sadness, he didn't know. Maybe both.

"Besides," Eric continued with a laugh, "after seeing what you did to Daniel back there? No thanks, I don't need you turning into a purple-blooded freak with those fighting skills."

Lance allowed himself a chuckle, and they walked in silence the rest of the way.

CHAPTER 24
HOW DID THIS HAPPEN?

It was gone. All the years of hard work, all the men and women she'd befriended then grown to see as a family.

Gone.

Destroyed in a breath of flame and a cloud of smoke.

Kaela shuffled along the sidewalk with Derek. She hung her head low, watching mindlessly as her steps dragged lazily across the concrete.

That was all she could bring herself to do.

Keep moving. One step at a time.

Derek walked beside her, scanning every rooftop and shadowy alley. At any sound or indication of an incoming car, they ducked into an alley until it was gone.

They didn't speak. There was no conversation to have after what they'd just been through; what they'd witnessed.

Her bicep pained her every few breaths, a constant reminder of what she'd had to do to survive. How desperate she'd been to get out of danger when, as she looked back on it, she regretted even trying. She should have burned in that building with her people. A captain going down with her ship.

Though, if she hadn't, Derek would have burned with her. Still, regret dug a hole in her chest, right through bone and muscle. A gaping hole where her heart had once been.

Caleb... He would die. At the first chance she got, she would take him down. It didn't matter who got in her way. It didn't matter if he took her down with him.

All her people had been slaughtered like animals within the confines of a place they'd thought was safe, all because of her stupid decision to bring Malcolm there.

Kaela looked up at Derek, the first time she'd lifted her head in minutes, and eyed his wound.

It had finally stopped bleeding.

"Something wrong?" he asked.

She was still staring at him. He looked at her, concern etched on his features. She had no right to have his sympathy, no right to have his concern.

None.

"Everything is wrong," she said back. *No point in lying.* "And everything will be wrong until Caleb is dead."

"We'll get him."

Kaela scoffed. "Oh, I know we will."

Derek's stare lingered on her. "Don't do anything drastic, Kaela. We can't afford to lose you too."

She balled her fists, which made him tense. "I shouldn't be *alive* at all. And that puts me at an advantage. I don't care if I have to strap a bomb to my chest, I *will* kill him."

She nearly stormed ahead, but her body was tired. Too tired to even keep her fists clenched. They loosened, and her legs turned to jelly. Suddenly, she was on her knees, and a hand was on her shoulder.

"Do you need me to carry you?"

She huffed a small laugh then broke it when he showed no signs that he was joking. She put one hand to her head and used the other to slap Derek's away. "Don't touch me."

But Derek put his hand on her shoulder again.

She looked back up to curse at him. But she met his eyes, those watery eyes, and the curse fell flat. The tears fell before she could stop them. She grabbed him and put her head to his chest, bawling her eyes out.

He shook. She wasn't the only one crying.

Derek led her into an alleyway and sat across from her. Kaela couldn't stop the sobs as they forced themselves out of her. Derek shoved his head into his hands, failing to hide his own tears.

"I can't do this anymore," Kaela said through sobs, trying to catch her breath. "I'm so tired of fighting."

Derek sniffled and wiped his face. "Yeah," he said, his voice cracking. "I know."

Kaela didn't know how long they cried together in that alley, but she kept sobbing until her head ached and no tears were left to trail down her face.

"What are we going to do about Eric and Lance?" Derek asked.

"I don't know," Kaela responded, wiping her eyes. "There's no telling where they are in that sewer right now. All we can do is hope they make it out alive."

It wasn't the grate next to the Rose, but it was good enough. Lance nearly forgot with each step that his leg had healed and that he needed to pretend. Eric didn't seem to notice, but he didn't seem to notice a lot of things until he brought them up later in conversation. Lance's chest tightened with every confident step he took by accident on his once-bad leg.

Having to pathetically hiss an occasional "Ow" grated on his nerves.

They walked along the empty streets, the sewer behind them mostly forgotten. The smell clasped onto both of them.

As if to confirm, Eric pinched his nose. "Phew. We smell like shit, huh?"

"That's because we're covered in shit, Eric."

Lance imagined a warm shower, a soft bed, and a hot meal, all awaiting him at the Rose. He could stand in the shower now, though he would still have the chair in there with him. But that didn't matter.

His only problem would be keeping George quiet about his leg. Lance wondered if HIPAA laws applied to him.

Regardless, he pressed on, putting as much weight on the cane as he cared to. Eric was smiling, despite his crinkled nose.

"Happy now?" Lance finally asked.

The anger of following Eric into a nasty sewer to kill a man almost melted away because he had his leg back—not to mention the cure. Maybe it was worth it after all.

"Oh, I'm very happy," Eric said, his eyes wide and bright like a child's. "We have one less Landreau brother to deal with, and we have what we need for the cure."

"It didn't seem that necessary to kill him."

Eric shrugged. "I still got revenge for my beautiful building." He fake sniffled and wiped his eye. "But I have a feeling if we'd killed Caleb first, Daniel would've gotten control of the soldiers." Eric furrowed his brows. "And once we kill Caleb, the soldiers and officers are sure to calm down with the man controlling them dead."

"And when they're calm, Malcolm can administer the cure."

Eric sent him a pair of finger guns, and Lance rolled his eyes.

"Please don't do that," Lance said.

"Aw, but what kind of dad would I be if I didn't embarrass you a little?"

Lance glared at Eric.

Eric's smile faltered. He cleared his throat and rubbed at his neck, where a dark bruise was forming.

That word still stung Lance's ears at its every utterance.

Dad.

He shuddered. The closest thing to a father-son activity they'd had was killing a man together and lopping his head off.

Eric opened his mouth, but the smile he was growing back disappeared as they rounded the corner. Lance lost his breath and had to brace himself on the cane.

The Red Rose had several fire trucks parked next to it. The firemen looked as if they'd just finished putting the fires out and were getting ready to leave.

When Lance stepped forward to ask them what had happened, Eric put a firm hand on his shoulder, pulling him back around the corner. “We can’t. We’re wanted criminals now, remember?”

He looked back at the firemen climbing into their trucks and allowed Eric to drag him into an alley.

George, Kaela, Derek… the employees. Were they okay? Where were they?

They disappeared into the shadows. *Malcolm,* Lance thought. It had to have been an experiment gone wrong. A fire started, and it spread. That made sense.

“What now?” Lance asked.

Eric paced in and out of the shadows. He lingered in the darkness for an extra second as a fire truck passed by, then continued his back and forth. “I don’t know. The only place they have left to go is Derek’s bar.”

“Which one?”

Eric shrugged. “The one closest to the Rose, I guess.” Something flashed in Eric’s eyes—for only a split second—then he looked away.

Lance didn’t need to read into it to know what he was thinking. *How many people died in this fire?* He shoved the thought away even though some deeper part of him knew that this had not been a victimless fire.

The beast within him shifted, and nausea swelled within Lance’s stomach. He’d nearly gone inside the Rose. Nearly allowed Eric to shuffle through the sewers alone. Yet the beast had demanded that he go along with his father. How could the beast have possibly known?

The only answer he received was a whine. The beast *whined.* Something told him this hadn’t been a simple fire, and he hoped with all his heart that the worst hadn’t happened.

Lance and Eric stepped into the dark bar, dimly lit by a small neon sign on the wall. The same as the one from Derek’s other bar, a beer being poured into a glass. The chairs were stacked on tables, and the quiet creaking of the floor below them broke the silence. The familiar smell greeted him. The greasy food, the cigarette smoke, the alcohol.

The door to the kitchens burst open, and Derek pointed his gun at them.

Eric raised his hands. "I'm starting to think you just like pointing your gun at me."

Derek relaxed. "You guys are okay," he said. "Thank God."

"What the hell happened?" Lance asked.

"Come on." Derek disappeared into the kitchen.

Lance followed, sighing in relief at the sight of Kaela fast asleep against the fridge. Derek sat on the counter and stared down at his hands. Desolation haunted his face, and his arm was wrapped in a bandage—Kaela's as well.

Though Lance didn't ask, Derek looked at him and shook his head. "Caleb."

Lance's heart fell to his stomach.

The beast had warned him to stay away, and it had been right in the end. *But why? I could've helped. Fought off Caleb, maybe. Right?* Lance asked. *Why didn't you let me help?*

Another whine. An apology. Surely Caleb wasn't so powerful that it scared the beast, making it back down and choose to fight someone else instead. Daniel had been bad enough.

Eric wordlessly walked to a separate corner and sat on the floor. His face was gaunt, his eyes empty. "George?" he asked.

Derek shook his head. Eric took a deep, shaky breath and leaned his head back on the wall, closing his eyes and going still.

Lance looked around at all of them. No words came to his mind, so he left the room. He needed to be alone, to collect his thoughts. He fake-limped to the bar and stepped into the bathroom, closing the door behind him with a light click.

The light in the bathroom was bright and cheery against the beige tiled walls. Something about this small space, with the exhaust blowing above him, calmed his nerves. It was the one place he could shut out the world for just a moment and collect his thoughts.

He leaned the cane against the wall and breathed. Slowly, he turned toward the mirror and looked at himself. Those piercing green eyes and that black hair—hair that wasn't his mother's after all. Yet those eyes were his mother's eyes. He could only imagine how beautiful they were on her. If only he could see them…

With a careful look behind him, Lance locked the door and propped his leg on the sink. He coaxed his pants leg up, revealing the bony limb underneath. It was perfectly intact. Not a lump or even a bruise left. No swelling, nothing.

He ran a hand over it, carefully touching and prodding it. No pain. He couldn't help smiling. His leg was healed. *Better* than healed.

Then he noticed something peeking from under his pants leg. A jolt shocked his heart. He lost his balance and fell backward, slamming into the wall.

Footsteps marched to the door, and Derek's voice rang out. "You okay?"

"Yeah," Lance called out, putting two fingers to his neck and breathing slowly.

He stood and propped his leg on the sink again. He reached with a shaky hand to pull the pants leg up just a little. He recoiled again from the sight, bracing his hand on the wall to keep his balance this time. He was out of breath, on the verge of tears as he lifted the fabric again.

Nothing stared back at him, and Lance realized with a relieved sigh that it had just been a trick of the light.

Then the beast purred.

And the veins in his leg glowed a dim purple in response.

CHAPTER 25
THE MIGRAINE RETURNS

Lance couldn't sleep. Everyone around him was breathing long and slow, curled up in the back corner of the bar. The room was nearly pitch black, and the door was closed and locked. The windows on each side of the door allowed him to look out at the street and the police cars patrolling. Lance had deemed it necessary for one of them to stay awake in case they were found. Anyone looking into the window wouldn't be able to spot them in the darkness, but if Caleb had found out about the Rose and about Lance's store, it was only a matter of time before Derek's bar was targeted.

Eric had told Kaela and Derek of their fight in the sewer while Derek disinfected and bandaged his hand. Derek recounted what happened in the Rose, but only after Kaela left the room in tears.

Hearing what they'd had to do to survive sent a chill down Lance's spine. He tried not to stare at their bandaged arms.

Lance was curled into a ball in the corner, watching the silhouettes of all the sleeping bodies.

Even the beast slumbered, certainly more comfortable than anyone else in this bar. Lance was wide awake. Fear was his blanket, and his heart could only settle for a handful of seconds before the memory of those purple veins flashed in his mind.

His head was spinning. Somehow, he'd been injected with nanobots. Yet the beast inside of him… What was it? A figment of his imagination? A side effect of the nanobots? The question he'd been replaying in his mind ever since was no less terrifying as it popped into his head again. *Can Caleb track me?*

However it worked didn't matter. It was the only logical explanation for how Caleb kept finding them. It also meant that Caleb already knew about Lance's nanobots. It meant that he couldn't control him. If he could, he would've tried already.

But that was how he kept finding them.

It was Lance.

Caleb could sense Lance's nanobots.

He had to put a stop to this, had to get away from the others. He couldn't afford to put them in danger. Had he been faced with that question days ago, he wouldn't have cared. But now Kaela, Derek, and even Eric were his family. The closest thing to one he'd had his entire life. He couldn't let them die because of him.

With a quiet groan, Lance sat up and surveyed the three sleeping bodies scattered across the room. Their chests rose and fell. They were all sound asleep. If he left now, he could get out before they knew what happened. He would go to Caleb. He needed answers—about how he'd been infected, for starters. Then he would fight him. Or he would try, at the very least. He could try to leave the city, but if Rob had been right days ago, plenty of soldiers were guarding the perimeter of the city. More than Lance could afford to fight or sneak through.

Lance stood and padded to the kitchen. He paused at the back door for a breath before stepping out. The night air was cold, and it dug its fingers around his body. A chill went up his spine as he walked, but it wasn't from the cold. This would likely be his last night breathing in such air.

He made it to the entrance of the alley, where he stopped and waited. He listened for any sign of movement, for any cars patrolling, before he took a step toward the street.

"What do you think you're doing?"

Lance nearly fell over, and when he looked back, Eric's head was peeking out from the back door. His eyebrow was raised, and a smirk played on his lips.

"I couldn't sleep," Lance said. It wasn't a lie. "I thought if I went out for a walk, it would help."

Eric closed his eyes and shook his head. "You're a terrible liar."

Lance gulped, helpless as Eric closed the distance between them, cane in hand.

Lance swore under his breath as he stood before Eric—no limp, no care about putting weight on his leg. No hiding it now.

When they were face to face, Eric spoke. "I think you forgot this." He held up the cane, offering it to Lance.

Lance made no move to grab it. Instead, he wiped his hands on his pants and refused to break eye contact with his father.

"What aren't you telling me?" Eric asked. "Because that pathetic limp you tried after we killed Daniel was not believable in the slightest. And now this?" He clicked his tongue. "You would be a terrible actor."

Lance crossed his arms. "Anything else you'd like to get off your chest?"

Eric raised that eyebrow again. "Getting a little confrontational, are we? If you'd like to keep that attitude, I can—"

"I'm leaving," Lance said. Also not a lie—not technically. "I'm sick of all this. I'm sick of being stuck with you three and almost getting killed at least once a day. I'm sick of being hunted down by a madman who only wants you to begin with." He took a step closer to Eric, inches from his face. "I'm especially sick of you. Of the mind games you play and the constant reminder that out of every bad thing that's happened in my life, the worst was finding out that *you* are my father."

Eric appeared unfazed by the harsh words, and Lance's anger grew. Before he could spout any more truths, someone spoke from inside.

"What?" It was Kaela. She was standing just outside the back door. Hurt glazed over her eyes as she looked at Lance. "Your father?"

Eric closed his eyes tightly, as if wishing this was a dream. Then he sighed and turned to Kaela. "Of course not. He's just…" He shook his head and cursed at the ground, clearly seeing no point in lying anymore. "Damn."

Anger slowly crossed Kaela's face. "Are you… Are you serious?!" She raised her voice, marching toward them. "Why the hell didn't you tell me from the beginning?"

Eric opened his mouth to answer, but Kaela just scoffed and turned away.

"Son… son?" She shook her head. "Why didn't you just say that all along?" She rubbed her face. "You strung me along like a puppet for *days*! I kept asking why you brought him into our group, and all he turned out to be was your son? Why didn't you just lead with that?"

"Kaela," Eric started, but Kaela turned away again.

Lance would've laughed if he wasn't scared she would aim her wrath at him next.

"Oh my God," she muttered. "You are such an asshole."

"Kaela," Eric said again, catching her attention this time. "I wanted to protect him." His voice was even softer than it had been when he'd told Lance. "I thought if nobody knew, he wouldn't become a target. He wouldn't be used to get to me."

Kaela glanced toward Lance then looked back at Eric with a frown. "If you really wanted to protect him, you wouldn't have brought him into this business to begin with."

Lance uncrossed his arms and shoved his hands into his pockets. "He wants me to take over when he's gone."

Kaela shook her head. "I can't believe this." She went silent for a moment. "Why are you two even out here?"

Eric turned his head back to Lance, a question behind his eyes. Great, now he had two of them to deal with.

"I told Eric I was leaving," he said.

Kaela's eyes filled with anger, and Lance's heart rate spiked. "Why?" Lance made to respond, but she opened her mouth again. "Are you stupid? Caleb knows who you are and what you look like. If we separate now, we're as good as dead. We need to stay together."

Lance shook his head. It wasn't supposed to happen like this. "I can take care of myself. Just let me go. I don't want to be a part of this anymore. I'm done."

Kaela crossed her arms. "I don't believe you."

Lance gritted his teeth. "I'm telling the truth."

"No, you're not." Kaela marched closer to him.

A voice rang out. "What's going on out here?"

Lance cursed at the starless night sky as Derek stepped out from the door, as quiet as ever. He eyed Lance carefully. "Lance?"

Lance shook his head at Derek. "I'm leaving, okay? It's over."

"Go to hell," Kaela said, her voice quivering. "After everything we went through, you seriously want to just leave us like this?"

There's no going back now, Lance thought. He was infected with the nanobots. Eventually, the beast would convince him to give in to it, like it did back at the sewer. It would seduce him into giving it more and more room until it took over entirely. Until he became a new Caleb. The thought sent a shudder up his spine.

The beast growled as if protesting the idea, defending itself.

How am I supposed to know you won't take me over?

The beast purred. *Show them,* said the whisper in the back of his head.

Lance physically shook his head. He was surrounded, and all he wanted to do was run off. Even with that, Derek would track him down. A wave of nausea crashed into him, and the beast purred again.

Show them.

No.

Yes. It was a hiss now. A demand. Lance's throat constricted, and he didn't know if it was the beast or if he was panicking.

Show them! The beast snarled.

"No!" He didn't mean to say it out loud. The word came out, and his throat relaxed. "I won't."

Worry crossed Eric's face. After another wave of nausea the beast repeated the order.

"What?" Eric's voice was drowned out by Lance's own thoughts. A single star in a black sky.

Lance didn't respond. Couldn't.

Do it!

"No!" Lance yelled.

Eric backed away. Traces of fear ran along his face, but he covered it quickly. Kaela didn't bother covering the fear on her face. Derek put a hand on Lance's shoulder.

He didn't even think as he blindly threw a punch.

Derek dodged, and Lance fell to the ground. He'd put too much of his own weight behind the punch. He tried to stand.

The beast growled a defiant growl, and Lance's body became weak. The beast stripped him of his strength.

It could do that to him now?

"No," Lance said again. "You have no say over my body."

He whirled to face the trio. The beast went silent then growled. His chest tightened, his heart pounded, and his teeth gnashed. He balled his fists, anger tainting his heart.

Lance wondered why they held such fear at the sight of him, then he looked down at his hands. His veins were glowing bright purple.

Neither Eric, Kaela, nor Derek seemed focused on that. They were all staring at his eyes. He looked down at a puddle next to his feet and nearly burst into tears. They, too, glowed a bright purple. The beautiful green irises of his mother were gone, replaced with the sick violet hue.

For just a moment, he considered clawing them out. In his clouded state of mind, he didn't know if this was even real. Then he knelt down and placed a hand in the freezing-cold puddle water.

He closed his eyes and prayed none of them would take the chance to kill him—not yet, at least. The beast stopped growling as the cold water seized his hand. Slowly, his body relaxed. His chest loosened its grip on itself, his heart settled, and the beast made no attempts to growl again.

When Lance opened his eyes, the emeralds were back. Tears trailed down his cheeks in his reflection, but he couldn't feel them.

Someone called his name. He didn't know who, not even when he looked up. Fear painted their faces, and he couldn't blame them. He was now the living embodiment of all the suffering they'd experienced the past few days. A mirror staring back at them with all their haunted memories.

"I didn't know," Lance whispered. He couldn't stop the tears from falling as he sat on the cold ground. His body was exhausted. The beast had tricked him, weakened him enough to reveal the secret hiding under his skin. Even now, as he shivered on the ground, stripped of strength, he looked at his hands. His veins were back to their natural light-blue color. “I swear I didn’t know.”

He looked up one last time, the fear on their faces replaced with confusion. They looked at each other as if expecting someone else to speak.

Lance controlled his breathing and composed himself. He wiped the tears from his eyes. The secret was out. He should have known he couldn’t keep it long.

“When did you notice this?” Derek asked. He looked disgusted to be near Lance at all.

He didn’t blame them, didn’t blame the anger that crawled over Kaela’s face. Because of these nanobots, Rob and Amari were dead, and Kaela’s employees were burned to ash, as well as George. Eric stared at the ground with his brow furrowed as if trying to figure out why he hadn’t put the pieces together earlier.

“Just a while ago, when I went into the bathroom,” Lance said. He could only focus on what he said and his own breathing. He reminded himself to breathe in then out. He let the breaths come and go like waves on a beach, back and forth.

“Your leg,” Eric said. “That’s how it healed so fast.”

Derek’s eyes widened as he looked at Lance’s leg then Eric’s cane.

“And the strength you showed. The ability to fight so well… That explains all of it.”

Derek scratched his chin and turned away. “The first time you showed something like that was after Daniel found Eric’s building. Right before we went into that little hiding spot, you took down that soldier.”

Lance tried to recall any time he could have been injected but came up with nothing. The first time the beast spoke to him was when that burned soldier tried to kill him. Before that… nothing.

“So that’s why you want to leave,” Kaela said. “Because you know you’re infected. What are you going to do?” She narrowed her eyes. “Were you just going to disappear… or were you going to join Caleb?”

“Kaela!” Derek scolded.

"What, don't act like you weren't thinking it too. What if Caleb has control of him and is calling him back?"

"He's not," Lance said. "I promise."

"Then where were you going?"

It hurt to lie, but he couldn't tell them. He took a deep breath. "Literally anywhere else *besides* Caleb."

Kaela unclenched her fists. "What?"

Eric stepped forward. "Let us go with you."

Lance shook his head. "No, the point is to get away from all of you. How do you think Caleb keeps finding us?" He hesitated, tears welling in his eyes. "Everywhere Caleb has found us, I've been there too." The tears ran down his face. Everyone that had died, died because of him. Their blood stained his hands. *Monster.* "He… He found us because of *me*."

Kaela tensed, her eyes wide.

Eric's voice was weak as he stepped closer to Lance and muttered, "You don't know that's true."

"It is."

"Let me come with you."

Anger flickered in Lance's chest. "Don't act li—"

"And if you make another remark about me not being there for you… I'm here *now*. You can hate me for all I've done. God knows I'm not a fan of myself, either. But you're still my son. If Caleb finds you, you're dead." He cradled Lance's face. "I can't lose you too."

Lance stared into Eric's black eyes. He was being genuine. He really wasn't lying.

Lance sighed then pushed Eric's hands away. "You never had me." He backed away. "And if he finds me, at least he won't find the rest of you." He gave a last glance at Kaela and Derek, at the sadness on both of their faces. "Don't follow me."

Lance walked away, rounding the corner and escaping those staring faces.

He almost smiled when Derek's voice rang out. "Wait… Did you just say *son*?"

The streets were hollow. Eerie. No civilians walked the streets, and no cars drove by other than police cars and armored vehicles. Lance didn't bother hiding from them.

The sky was pitch black, an ebony blanket over the city, and the streetlights cast a haunting orange glow on the path Lance walked. He couldn't tell if anyone was watching him from the rooftops, not that it mattered anymore.

He just walked. He walked the streets, waiting until he was found. Every turn he took, he held his breath, anticipating a gun in his face. He eyed every small movement in the shadows.

He closed his eyes for a few seconds at a time and just breathed, trying to ignore what he was doing and focus on the silence around him.

Doubt crept into Lance's heart as time passed. The beast remained silent, and he felt no eyes upon him. Still no people, and now even the patrol cars had disappeared.

Lance wrapped himself in his own thoughts as he walked, making no attempt at keeping his steps silent. He wondered what Caleb would've done if they'd all simply left the city. Would he have lost control? Allowed the nanobots to take full control over him and gone on a tyrannical rampage? The officers were already harassing citizens on the street. They were beaten, arrested, and treated like criminals. A man like Caleb didn't give up. He would've just moved from city to city if he had to.

They would never have been able to escape.

The beast stirred, and Lance stopped, listening closely. At first, the silence remained unbroken, but then the distinct sound of a car came his way. The beast growled, and Lance tensed. The sound escalated until a car rounded a corner.

A normal car.

Lance averted his eyes and continued walking, shoving his hands into his pockets. They trembled, and the beast didn't stop growling. The car drove past then stopped.

He kept walking, but when the growling didn't stop, he walked faster and prepared himself for a fight.

A door opened, and someone cleared their throat behind him. Lance stopped, his heart hammering in his chest, and he turned.

"Well, if it isn't the man I killed in the church," Caleb said. His eye was healed. He spread his arms out with a laugh and a wide smile, as fake friendly as a church pastor. His veins glowed—his eyes too. Even his skin had gained a purple tint. "I was just on a friendly drive through this quiet little neighborhood and—"

"You knew where I was," Lance interrupted, shifting on his feet. He could barely stand to look the man in the eyes for more than a few seconds. "The nanobots, right? That's how you always knew where we were. You tracked me."

Just like that, Caleb's arms dropped, and his smile turned more carnivorous than friendly. "I put a lot of work into making this entrance fun for both of us." He sighed. "Well, it wasn't like I could track Malcolm. Somehow, he made his nanobots invisible to mine. That left you."

Lance balled his fists and waited for Caleb to finish laughing. "You don't think the civilians notice those purple veins you have jutting all over your body? Not to mention your eyes…" Lance looked at them for a second too long and shuddered.

Caleb smiled and locked his hands together. "Good question." He looked over at a bench about five feet away and sat on it with a groan. "As far as Arachna is concerned, I was captured and injected with some foul liquid. It burned all throughout my body, and if my loyal soldiers had not found and rescued me, I would likely be dead. I was taken to my private doctor and miraculously healed. Though whatever I was injected with left me scarred. It changed the color of my veins and eyes." He looked at his hand. "And anyway, I may be able to return them to their normal color once I've discarded this city like the garbage it is."

"You sure about that?"

Caleb leaned back with a sigh. "Of course. I've done it before, after all. Malcolm helped me return them to normal after a particularly annoying couple almost exposed my operations. If I did it with Malcolm, I can do it without him."

"Your soldiers won't be so happy to find out you've been controlling them."

Caleb's smile twisted Lance's stomach into a knot. "I'll relinquish direct control over the soldiers, but the nanobots will continue to whisper in their heads. I will always have them under my thumb."

Lance gritted his teeth. The smug man sat before him, and it was all he could do not to leap upon him and tear his face apart.

"So why are you so carelessly prowling the streets tonight, Lance? Here to give Eric up, finally? Maybe you want revenge for me trying to kill you in that church? Perhaps you've even decided that running is futile, and you're surrendering to me." He listed the possibilities off on his fingers as if they were nothing more than an account of what he'd had for breakfast that morning. Prideful. Arrogant. That gentlemanly stature he'd had at the church was gone.

"I never asked to be a part of this," Lance said. The beast was poised and ready to strike. "Eric started all of this. It's him you want, isn't it? Not the others?"

"Ah." Caleb hummed. "So you didn't want to sell your friends out back at the church because of those two I met at the… What was it called? Red Rose?" He chuckled. "It certainly was once I was through with it." He looked down at Lance's tightened fists, and Lance relaxed them in response.

The way Caleb talked about those people suffering so casually. It was almost intentionally horrific, just to spit in Lance's face. Yet as Caleb smoothed out a crease in his pants, it became obvious that the drug had simply corrupted him to the point where he barely resembled a human.

Lance wondered if that would happen to him the longer the nanobots swam in his blood. The beast didn't respond.

"I guess that means those two survived my attempts to kill them?" Caleb grinned. "I'm truly amazed by how your group manages to escape so many of my attempts at murdering them." He looked Lance in the eye. "I would be furious if it weren't so impressive."

"I'll take Eric's place," Lance said. "You can do to me whatever you wanted to do to him. In return, you can continue with your plan to take over the world or whatever the hell you want… but you have to leave

Arachna alone. That includes Kaela, Derek, and Eric." Lance couldn't resist twisting his face in disgust when Caleb motioned for him to sit down. "I think we can agree there has been enough death."

Caleb patted on the bench, right next to himself. Lance took a hesitant step, then another. It wasn't until he sat down that Caleb smiled and spoke. "I agree that there has been way too much death filling these past few days. Especially when the point of this drug to begin with was to avoid such a thing." He laughed.

Lance frowned. A question sparked in his mind, and it was out of his mouth before he could stop it. "Were you ever planning on making the drug public?"

"No," Caleb said without missing a beat. "Well, Malcolm was, but he was always so naïve. Easy to manipulate too." He chuckled again. "I suppose that was how you corrupted him so easily. You convinced him to make a cure for something as wonderful as this." He gestured to his neck, where the veins glowed brightest. "I had to kill him. To save him from himself and your group. Breaks my heart. God rest his soul."

He put a hand on Lance's shoulder. Lance gritted his teeth so hard they hurt. It took every ounce of self-control not to snap Caleb's wrist.

The beast went wild inside of him, growling and snarling and snapping. Lance felt a chain break inside of him, and when he opened his mouth, he couldn't stop the words coming out. "You're so full of shit." He stopped his hand from shooting to his mouth as Caleb's grip tightened on his shoulder. Lance waited for the punch, the stab, the choke. Caleb's hand became more of a burden with each passing second. He opened his mouth again before he could stop. "You didn't care about killing Malcolm."

Caleb squeezed even harder then let go, leaving Lance's shoulder burning from the touch. "There it is."

Lance glared at him.

Caleb continued. "That thing writhing around inside of you. I felt it in that church basement too."

"What are you talking about?"

Caleb scoffed with a smile.

"Look, about my friends?" Lance said. "I need to know you'll spare them if you take me instead." The beast growled at him, but he ignored it. It was the biggest risk he'd taken yet, but even with the nanobots corrupting him, Caleb was still a businessman, and surely he wouldn't go against a sealed deal.

More cars arrived, then sirens. Police cars flooded in from both sides of the street. From around corners, they appeared, one after the other. Caleb stood, and when Lance did the same, Caleb pushed him back down. The cars drove to him and stopped, at least ten police cars and five armored vehicles.

All just for him?

It was almost flattering.

The doors opened, and officers used them as cover. Pistols and rifles and shotguns were all pointed at him by the heavily armored men and women. Caleb beamed at all of them, his hands firmly held together behind his back.

The beast growled at them, but seconds later, it whined. *Too many,* it cried. *Too many.*

Lance's head spun. Even the beast knew they were outnumbered. If he tried to fight now, it would be over.

One last police car drove beyond all the others and parked right in front of the bench.

Rotoya wore a proud smile on her face as she stepped out. "Miss me?"

CHAPTER 26
CAN WE TRUST YOU?

The sight of the chief punched Lance in the stomach. Caleb mirrored Rotoya's smile, looking on from behind her police car. Her body was covered in burns, her face scorched, and her smile twisted.

"I thought you were—"

"Dead?" The chief laughed. "Well, I almost was. I'll admit, you pulled a fast one on me. I'm impressed." Her smile disappeared. "But I'm still not happy about this constant reminder." She gestured at her face. "I thought the drug would've healed it by now, but… go figure."

"Then maybe you should've left us alone," Lance challenged. The beast circled his stomach with a low growl.

Rotoya emitted a pleased hum. "You've gotten brave since I last saw you."

"Are you done?" Caleb interjected, rounding the police car. "Because I'm ready to get this over with."

The chief closed her eyes and sighed. Annoyance sparked in her tone. "You've taken nearly all my men from me. The least you can do is give me this."

"I *did* give you this," Caleb spat back. His voice faded as he guided her far enough away to hiss in her ear.

Lance couldn't make out the words, but Rotoya's glare said it all.

The soldiers surrounding Lance kept their guns trained on him. If he ran, he'd be dead before he could round the corner.

An idea popped into his head, and he suppressed a grin.

The beast cocked its head to the side, as if wondering why Lance would want to smile.

Caleb would have taken control of me by now if he could... and if Caleb can't control me... maybe my nanobots are the alpha ones. Which means...

The beast purred, and Lance closed his eyes, picturing the soldiers, all of them, guns pointed. The beast shifted within him, pacing back and forth.

Let me in.

Lance ignored it. He kept his eyes closed and chose a soldier standing next to Caleb. He focused on him—just him. He reached out and grabbed in the dark, clawing for a foothold. Then, in the darkness, Lance sensed them.

Dozens of energies, like fireworks, inhabiting the bodies of the soldiers and officers. He sensed them all, felt their breathing in his own chest. Their hearts pumped purple blood. They were all tense, all waiting for the kill order. Lance focused again on that single soldier next to Caleb.

The beast growled at the soldier, but Lance calmed it. It whined back.

Let me in.

With all the guns pointed at him, Lance resisted the urge to shake his head. At least two of the officers were itching to pull their triggers. Their anticipation was tangible. He homed in on that one soldier for the last time. He gritted his teeth and dug deep within him.

There it was. Not just the breathing of the soldier, calm and even, but the blood flow. The nanobots swam through his blood stream, reproducing by the hundreds.

Lance reached out into the dark again, and he could feel the soldier's heart and the blood traveling through it. With that came his emotions.

Fear—the soldier felt fear. Had he seen what Lance could do? It didn't matter. He held that heart within himself and focused on what he wanted to say.

Check the rounds in your gun.

Lance eased his head up, keeping his focus as he painted disinterest on his face.

The soldier looked down at his gun, and his hand reached for the magazine. Then he stopped, shook his head, and pointed the gun at Lance again.

Lance cursed himself, and the beast joined in.

He made to reach for the soldier again, but the chief stopped in the middle of her argument with Caleb. Her eyes shot to the soldier, then to Lance. A smile played on her lips, then Caleb looked at him.

"What?" he asked.

"We can't kill him," the chief responded, the smile still on her lips.

Caleb sent Lance a nasty glare. "Why?"

"Because he's Eric's son."

Lance's heart fell to his stomach, and in his shock, he dropped what little control he held over the soldier. The soldier shook his head for a moment, as if confused, then returned to normal.

Caleb stormed to Lance, and the veins in his arm flashed a bright purple. In seconds, his arm grew large and muscled, and with abnormal strength, he lifted Lance into the air, his cold hand around his neck.

"Does she speak the truth?"

Lance tried to speak, but Caleb's grip was closing his airway. Caleb seemed to realize only when Lance's vision darkened, then he slammed him down. The bench cracked under the force, and Lance gulped down air.

Lance took a few precious seconds to reclaim his breath. Caleb demanded he confirm what Rotoya said.

"Yes," Lance said, coughing and rubbing his sore throat. "Yes, it's true."

Caleb whirled toward the chief. "Why didn't you tell me this earlier?"

"To be honest? I've never really known for a fact. More suspected. And it seems my suspicions were correct."

"You said it to me as if it were fact."

"Thirty years on the force, I'm pretty sure I've picked up a thing or two about reading people."

Caleb's veins flashed again, and his arm returned to normal size.

Lance cleared his throat, dots spotting his vision. "What about our deal?" The world seemed to still around him. "You're a businessman. Surely you know an opportunity when you see one."

"I offered you a deal the last time we met," Caleb hissed at him. "Negotiations are over." He looked at the chief, a glare that said, *You'd better be right about this*, and leaned into Lance's face. "I was going to kill you, but it appears you're useful to me. Temporarily. Play along, and I may just spare you."

Lance almost gagged from the sweet smell of his breath. His teeth were rotten. His eyes sent a chill up Lance's spine, and as Caleb turned away, Lance realized just how unhinged the nanobots had rendered him. *Will I become this way as well?*

The beast was silent, which was all the response he needed.

"Fine," Caleb said. "Take him back to Landreau Corp. I'm sick of seeing his face."

"I actually have a good hiding spot toward the edge of town," the chief countered. "We could use it, and you wouldn't have to see his face at all."

Caleb stopped halfway to getting in his car. "Not to be too honest here, Chief, but I don't have faith in any of your hiding spots. Eric and his goons are too clever. They'll find a way to get to him. Take him to Landreau Corp." He muttered profanities as he shut the door and drove away. Most of the soldiers put their guns down and entered their vehicles. They drove behind Caleb, disappearing down the street within the minute.

When they were gone, only the chief, four soldiers, and one armored vehicle were left.

So that was what she meant by Caleb taking her men… He'd taken *control* of them. One of the soldiers remaining was the same one Lance had nearly manipulated. Fear and excitement swelled in his heart. If he could force the soldier to make a distraction, he could get away. The plan hadn't worked as well as he'd hoped, but now he had a chance at fighting back.

Still, that he could even somewhat control one of these soldiers raised the hairs on the back of his neck.

Rotoya waved a hand, and her men crawled inside the armored vehicle. She sauntered over to Lance, and he waited with bated breath for her to punch him, kick him, even shoot him. She knew he could control her men now. The way she looked at him was the same way Caleb had looked at the sarcophagus he'd hidden in back at the church.

But the blows didn't come. Instead, she leaned close and whispered in his ear.

"I can help you." Her confident smile remained. She placed a hand on her hip, waiting for him to respond.

"What?"

"Get in the car. I'll explain on the way."

The beast purred and urged Lance toward the car. Was she telling the truth?

He followed her to the armored vehicle and slid into the passenger seat without a word, praying that the beast knew what it was doing.

It hadn't led him wrong yet.

A mental count revealed six men in the back of the vehicle, completely still, as if they were statues without the chief's orders. Yet somewhere deep down, their emotions remained. Even without control, Lance felt them—anger and fear and confusion. His head ached. Even just reaching for their emotions wore him out.

Rotoya waved her hand, and the officers' heads fell. Asleep just like that.

"I wonder," the chief began as she started the engine and eased down the street, "how it is you gained the ability to control my men."

Lance remained silent even as the beast urged him to respond.

"Though, with Eric," the chief continued, "I suppose I shouldn't be surprised you managed to get your hands on the drug."

"How did you know?" Lance asked.

Rotoya smiled, but her eyes remained on the road. "I could feel it the moment you tried to control Officer Cortez." Now she looked at him, a friendly gleam in her eyes.

Lance shifted in his seat. "Not that."

Rotoya glanced at him with a proud smile. "I didn't know, necessarily, but I strongly suspected. I thought you looked familiar when I saw you in my station. I'd recognize those piercing green eyes anywhere."

"You've... You've never even seen me before." Lance remembered what Eric had said back at the Rose. That Rotoya had been the one who told him about the fight back at the orphanage. "You investigated the case of my disappearance. You looked through the file they had of me. That's how you knew what I looked like. Did Eric know about this?"

"I was an up-and-coming officer, of course I took the case. Eric didn't have to know." She winked at him, and nausea crashed into his stomach. "Of course, I never found you. You were too well hidden in those slums. When I first saw you at my precinct then found out Eric hired you, I could only imagine how important you were to him. The most logical explanation was that you were his son."

"So you didn't know for sure?"

Rotoya shook her head. "But I do now."

"Why are you helping me?"

She was silent for a moment. "Like I said before, Caleb has taken control of most of my officers. Good men and women that shouldn't have a psychopath like him controlling them. When I was caught in that explosion, I... think I died... but only for a few minutes. The nanobots took their sweet time bringing me back, but they managed. When I returned, I discovered that Caleb had taken the opportunity to gain control of them. Now, he holds them over my head. So far, he's only given six of them back... He's already killed a few. Like little stickers for doing good and punishments for doing bad."

A spike of anger burrowed into Lance's chest.

Rotoya sighed, and she stared forward with an ice-cold glare. "Oh, and I'm not taking you back to Landreau Corp. I'm taking you to Derek's bar. That is where Eric and the rest are, right?"

Lance hid the frown that tugged on his lips, and as the beast growled lightly, he considered performing a repeat of their last encounter.

As if sensing his anger, Rotoya smirked. "I can't imagine any other place you'd be hiding after losing your store and one of Kaela's Roses. Notice how I kept that bit of information from Caleb?"

"But you don't know which bar."

"The one on Main Street, correct?" She laughed when Lance failed to hide the surprise on his face. "It's the one closest to the Rose that burned down. I didn't become the chief of police for nothing."

The beast settled, and Lance did the same. At the smallest hint of betrayal, Rotoya would find herself headless before she could crack another smirk. The beast purred in agreement. "So you want us to kill Caleb so you can get your men back?"

The chief nodded. "And once this is all over, I plan on bringing things back to the way they were before. When I woke up after the explosion, it was like I could see for the first time. I lost all interest in helping Caleb in his endeavors. Until the blast, it felt like everything he said made sense, like he wasn't wrong about anything. Then, after… it was the complete opposite." She frowned. "I think he suspects me, too. If I keep working for him, I'll likely find myself dead in a ditch. So if you have any reservations about trusting me, remember I'm doing this for myself and my officers."

The headache she'd suffered from so suddenly at the station… had that been Caleb taking over her thoughts?

The chief sighed. "Or maybe… maybe I'm just in denial of what I did. Either way, I plan on getting my people back, so that conversation can be held another day."

The remainder of the drive to the bar passed in silence.

Lance's heart thumped harder and harder in his chest as the armored car approached the bar. Lance exited the car first in case Eric or any of the others were watching. No movement came from inside of the bar. No voices.

The chief slipped out of the vehicle next, and when she rounded the back to let her officers out, Lance held his hand up and shook his head.

"If you let them out, they'll think we're after them."

"News flash, pal," the chief fired back, "they probably already do."

Lance rolled his eyes and stepped into the bar, the chief far behind. It was deathly silent, and when he peeked into the kitchen, nobody was there. *I wonder why the door wasn't locked?*

"Eric," Lance called. "Kaela, Derek."

No response. If they'd gone somewhere else, Lance would never find them. At least Caleb wouldn't either.

The chief entered the store, and when she opened her mouth to speak, a dagger plunged into the side of her knee. She yelled in pain. Eric flew over the counter and plunged his knife into her neck. The blade pierced through her and into the wall, pinning her. Derek dashed from around the corner of the counter and grabbed the pistol from her holster, pointing his own at her. Kaela appeared right behind him, ripping her knife from the chief's leg and angling it at her.

Lance yelled for their attention as they kept their distance from the chief. But then Derek pointed the pistol at him, and Kaela did the same with her knife. Eric returned to the counter and watched.

"Why are you with her?" Derek asked. "And how is she alive?"

The beast snarled at all of them, and the killing calm settled within Lance. The urge to attack them nipped at his heels, encouraged by the beast. He swallowed it and forced the beast to wait.

Calm down.

No!

"Lance," Kaela warned, "we kind of need an answer here."

Derek kept the gun trained on Lance's chest, his grip steady and stable. A professional, even when the fear behind his eyes revealed more than that.

"Please tell me you're not with her," Kaela said. "How is she even alive? Did you spare her, huh? Was this your plan from the beginning?"

"Listen," Lance started as the chief choked on her own blood and writhed, "if she wanted to kill you, she could have easily summoned the six men in that armored vehicle to come out and shoot us all. But she hasn't, even with that in her throat."

Derek made no move to lower the gun, and Kaela kept her purple-soaked dagger pointed right at him.

"Please," Lance said. "Just put the weapons down and give us a chance to explain... She saved me from Caleb." As Eric stared into

Lance's eyes, he stared back, not flinching in the slightest under his dark gaze. *You know I'm telling the truth.*

Lance waited for a bullet to hit his chest. Behind the fear in Derek's eyes lay anger and rage. That same look was on his face when Rob died. Lance recalled the sick smile Rotoya had worn when she shot Rob over and over. She continued to writhe with the knife in her throat, and suddenly, Lance didn't feel so bad for her.

After a long moment, Eric pointed his eyes to the ground. "Lower your weapons… but Derek? Keep your distance. She tries anything, you shoot her." He crossed his arms. "Alright, Lance… you have the floor."

To their credit, they listened. Even with a gun pointed at him, his stuttered words came out over the haunting sounds the chief made as the nanobots scrambled to keep her body alive. Explaining took longer than Lance thought it would, but by the time he finished, the gun was no longer aimed at his chest, and Kaela had sheathed her blade.

"So now what?" Derek asked. "We're just going to work *with her*?"

By now, the chief had gotten used to the knife in her throat, and despite the choking noises she still made, her head was down, and she picked calmly at her nails. At any moment, she could have removed it herself.

"That's the plan," Lance countered. "It's not exactly ideal, I know, but it's the best we've got."

The room was silent for a long, long time. Derek stared at the chief with seething hatred, and Kaela mirrored it. Eric stared at her too, but differently—with disappointment rather than anger. How long had he worked with the chief? How long had she looked away from his illegal activities, to now be covered with purple veins and murderous tendencies?

Kaela moved first. She ripped the dagger from the chief's throat and tossed it to Eric, who wiped the blood off and sheathed it within his cane.

Derek's grip on the pistol tightened as the chief stood, rubbing her neck as her veins flashed. The wound closed rapidly.

"So," the chief started, her voice scratchy and broken, "let's discuss the plan."

"What plan?" Derek muttered. His cold voice boomed, strong and unbreaking, though his eyes revealed the opposite.

The chief looked at Lance with a knowing smile.

Lance cleared his throat. "I managed to take control of one of her men." He inclined his head toward the chief. "Well… kind of."

Kaela closed her eyes and shook her head. "So… you didn't just get injected with the drug…"

"You got injected with the alpha drug," Eric finished.

Lance gulped. "I did… somehow."

When Eric looked at the chief, she held up her hands. "Don't look at me. Frankly, even with the alpha drug, he shouldn't have been able to make any of my officers do anything, especially while I was in control of them. Even Caleb couldn't take control of my officers until I almost died… He even had to convince Daniel to give him his soldiers. Never once did Caleb manage to rip them from that bond otherwise." She nodded at Lance. "But this one's different."

Something stirred in Lance's chest. Not the beast… something darker. A sadness and anger and fear slithered inside his body. The drug within him, however he'd gotten it, gave him a power that even Caleb didn't have.

They had an advantage. So why did knowing that open a hole in his stomach?

"So Lance can take over Caleb's men?" Derek asked.

The chief looked at Lance, and something like regret appeared on her face, an odd contrast to the smile she'd given when she shot Rob. "Not very well, but I suppose it's possible."

"I almost made a guard check his gun… That's about it," Lance said. "I'm not even fully sure how I did it."

Rotoya hummed. "And I wouldn't know how to teach you. I was able to control my officers from the beginning."

"Lance doesn't need to learn anything," Eric interjected. "We can beat Caleb without it."

The chief smirked at him, and Lance thought Eric would slide over the counter and pin her against the wall again.

"When we were fighting Daniel," Lance said, the words weighing heavy on his tongue, "I let the bea—the nanobots… I gave them… I don't know how to explain it. I gave them more access. When I did, that's when my leg healed. Not long after that is when my veins glowed." He swallowed the lump in his throat. The beast had urged him to give it even more room when he tried taking over the officer. "If I do that, I may be able to take some of Caleb's soldiers away from him."

Eric shook his head. "Doesn't matter. We can still fight Caleb without you giving this drug… more access, whatever that means. If all else fails, we'll use it as a backup plan."

Rotoya scoffed. "If that's what you call a backup plan, then surely you can come up with something better."

Eric looked down in thought then turned his eyes toward Lance. "No…"

Lance met Eric's eyes. "It's not ideal… but you need to trust me."

Eric's face flickered with doubt, and he looked away. "Fine… So what do you need us to do?"

They talked and argued until a plan began to form. Lance had to admit, they couldn't have done it without Rotoya's inside knowledge of Landreau Corp.

"We need to go. If we spend any longer here, Caleb will track you again and know something's up." Rotoya stood. "If there's anything else we need to discuss, do it now."

She was met with silence at first, but then Derek spoke up.

"What did you do to Rob?"

The room filled with silence, and Kaela's eyes filled with fire.

"When you shot him and dragged his body away," he continued, "what did you do?"

Guilt crossed the chief's face. "I gave it to my officers to incinerate."

"When this is over, and all that's left is us and you… I'm hunting you down and murdering you for what you did to him."

The chief acted as if she was going to smile but stopped herself. "That's fair. But I hope you realize it will not be an easy hunt."

Derek balled his fists, his mouth set in a thin line. "Makes it all the more satisfying when I take you down."

"*If*," Rotoya corrected.

Eric raised his eyebrows and clapped his hands together. "As fun as that sounds, we should really focus on the plan."

"Absolutely," the chief purred.

Derek glared at Rotoya and stormed to the bathroom. Lance held his breath until he disappeared. Kaela rubbed the back of her neck and grabbed a bottle of wine from the cabinet behind the counter. She disappeared into the kitchen. Eric remained where he was, watching the chief with that same disappointed glare.

"I thought you said you wanted things to go back to normal after this?" Lance asked.

"Wishful thinking, I guess," she said. "I'll need to face the consequences for what I've done." Sadness laced the words, but she smiled at Lance. "Let's get going."

Lance stole one last look at the backroom. He wanted to say goodbye to them, but when he turned to do so, the beast urged him away. *Fine, whatever*, he thought then followed Rotoya.

Eric grabbed his arm before he could exit, pausing long enough for the door to close behind Rotoya. She didn't look back until she reached the armored vehicle. "Listen to me," he said. "You need to be extra careful here."

"Yeah, yeah, I get it. I need to live so I can kill your not-so-secret admirer, now let go of my arm."

"What are you mad about now?"

Lance ripped his arm free. "I'm not mad. I just don't like you. And I definitely don't like you grabbing me." He sighed, his skin burning.

Eric lowered his voice when Kaela walked back into the room, wiping a hand on her cheek. The bottle was already half empty. "I'm trying, okay? Parenting is hard."

Lance sighed. "I get it. I get that you're trying, but I wish you'd just... I don't know..."

"Maybe we could—"

"Maybe we could talk about it later, huh?" Lance didn't wait for a response before he walked out the door, refusing to look at the smiling chief.

"Something wrong?" she asked.

"Yeah, we're not headed to Landreau Corp yet."

The chief nodded. "Eric used to get on my nerves all the time too. I can only imagine how infuriating it is when he's your dad."

Lance grunted in response as they climbed into the armored vehicle. Having to work with the chief was bad enough, but relating to her was a step too far. She didn't stop there.

"What is it like, having him as a father?"

Lance bit his tongue, his nails digging into his fists. "Not much different from having him as a boss." He opened his mouth to add something but shut it quickly. She wasn't about to suck any more information out of him than necessary.

"Are you ready for this?"

"I'm ready to be done with this, if that's what you mean."

"What are you going to do when this is over?"

That was the question that silenced Lance. He hadn't thought of it much. What he wanted and what would happen were likely going to be two different things.

Finally, he said, "If we get out of this alive, I don't really care what I end up doing afterward, as long as Caleb's dead and I can walk the streets without..."

Killing Caleb would stop the manhunt, but they were still wanted.

"I see that look," the chief said. "Between Eric and I, we'll make sure you're not considered criminals anymore. Though you may have to keep your friend off me long enough to do that."

Regardless of what they'd done, Lance was still considered a terrorist. Whether he cleared his name or not, that accusation would make anyone suspicious of him. The slums were hard enough, but if the residents found out a terrorist was in their territory, they would take it as a challenge.

He swallowed the anxiety that rose in his throat and chose not to think about it. Not now, of all times.

"Who's going to take over the police station if not you?"

The chief smiled. "I have a candidate in mind. Once she's not being mind controlled anymore, I'll have her take over."

Lance kept his mouth shut, wanting the rest of the drive to be in silence as he collected his thoughts and readied himself for the suicide mission ahead.

Still, a few more questions swirled around in his head like buzzing insects.

The beast purred in amusement at Lance's exasperation, and he found himself opening his mouth to speak. "So what exactly has Eric done to annoy you in the past, anyway?"

"—and the rest is history," the chief said.

Lance smiled. "Was he really covered in blood?"

"*Covered* in it. Looking back on it now, it's actually pretty funny."

Lance chuckled, not just at the story, but at the situation he found himself in: riding in an armored vehicle with someone who would have killed him mere days ago, laughing at her stories about his father, on the way to enact a plan that would likely result in one or both of their deaths.

Despite the coming dangers, he savored the calm before the storm. Streetlights hung over them, a flash of orange light before returning to darkness. The laughter eased the tension in his chest. If this plan did kill him, at least he was glad for these last few moments.

Even if they were with the woman who had tried to kill him only days ago.

Rotoya turned down a street, and the only thing between Landreau Corp and them was the road itself. The Landreau Corp building was a tower among them, a beacon to their doom.

Lance's chest tightened again the closer they drove. *Breathe in.*

Breathe out. Lance repeated it in his head, reminding himself that they had a plan. He ran through it over and over in his head, even the few details they'd managed to iron out before leaving.

The more Lance dreaded what lay ahead, the faster the car seemed to move. The chief lost her genuine smile and replaced it with one much more wicked. The entrance came into view, as did the soldiers waiting at the steps. They stood patiently, rifles in hand.

The chief stopped and handcuffed Lance in one quick motion. She awoke her officers, and they left the vehicle as if they hadn't been unconscious for the past hour.

The six officers surrounded the vehicle, and the chief left her seat, rounding the car to Lance's side. She opened the door and pulled him out.

Lance landed hard on the ground, groaning in pain at the impact of the cuffs on his wrists.

"Get up," the chief said, pulling him to his feet. Her face was stoic and angry. The officers around them wore dark helmets.

Their eyes were invisible behind their visors, but Lance could still feel the stares on him, the urges they had to pull the trigger now and be done with it.

The beast growled at every one of them. Somehow, it was a comfort.

Rotoya shoved him inside the lobby and kicked his legs out from under him.

The same six soldiers from earlier now surrounded him. The chief's stare burned into his back. A shudder traveled up his spine. He embraced it, allowing it to become as real as he could make it.

Elevator doors opened from down the hall around the corner, and Caleb stepped out, any hint of his smile gone. The beast hissed. Caleb approached Lance and raised his foot. Lance raised his arm in defense, but the kick met his chest anyway, and Lance fell back onto the tile. The beast snarled and snapped at its chains.

Lance didn't think. The killing calm settled over him. Even with the pain gripping his wrists, he rolled back from the landing and was on his feet again. He pushed off the ground and lunged for Caleb. Rotoya's hand scraped against his back in a vain attempt to grab him as he threw his body weight into Caleb.

But Caleb was too quick. He punched Lance down.

Lance slammed into the ground, his jaw screaming in pain. The beast didn't quit snarling. *Get up!*

"Don't shoot," Caleb said, his voice calm.

Lance suppressed a yelp as Caleb grabbed him and hoisted him onto his feet. The beast urged him to attack again, but he resisted the angry growls inside of him and focused on the plan.

"Attack me again," Caleb said, "I'll kill you on the spot. You're lucky I'm giving you this chance."

"You attacked me first, asshole!" Lance retorted, breathless.

"I didn't like the way you were looking at me."

Lance's veins hadn't shown. Or if they had, Caleb hadn't reacted. The beast gave an affirming purr.

Do it, Lance told the beast. *Show him.* He wasn't sure if the beast could laugh, but the sound it made resembled a dark and wicked chuckle.

Lance stepped away. One second passed, then two, and he swallowed the lump in his throat as nothing happened.

Give me more room.

No, Lance hissed at it. *No, you can do it without the extra room. This is* not *the time for this.*

After a whine, the beast purred. Gently, lightly, his veins answered. Slowly, the color turned purple, traveling across his legs and body.

Caleb looked at Lance's arms first, then his neck. His face twisted in anger.

"I'll gladly attack you again," Lance said. He made to lunge, but something hit him hard in the back of his head. He landed on the cold ground, and the beast went silent. His veins returned to normal.

Footsteps, then Caleb's voice rose above the ringing in his ears. "How did you…" He paused then swore. "So you're learning to control it. Hmm, that's unexpected… but I think I have a way of fixing that."

Lance rubbed the back of his head. The darkness surrounded him, and the voices became muffled. Hands grabbed him and dragged him across the floor. He was losing his grip, falling into the darkness. He fought against the heaviness in his head. He refused to go under, tried to follow which directions they took him. An elevator dinged, barely audible. His stomach surged as it dropped. He nearly vomited. More voices sounded.

The doors opened, then he was dragged across a cold concrete floor —left, then right, then forward, as if traveling down a long hall. Finally, after another right, he was dropped.

He almost gave in to the darkness, but a kick to the ribs woke him. He yelped in pain.

"I was just going to keep you down here, but now I have questions for you. I'll give you a few minutes to collect your thoughts. When I come back, you and I are going to talk."

Caleb's words were cold and angry, and Lance, unable to fight it anymore, submitted to the darkness and went under.

CHAPTER 27
I'M NOT LYING

Something had stirred in Rotoya's mind as she struck Lance with her pistol. It was a familiar feeling, one she knew but couldn't fully remember. A phantom pain—déjà vu. Caleb kicked Lance, and Rotoya felt it again. So familiar yet so foreign.

The biting cold of the underground level snapped at her skin, but her armor and the nanobots warmed her. Fixed lights brightened the hall yet somehow rendered it ominous. The concrete walls closed in on her, and she took a deep breath.

The chill relieved her burns, and when she closed her eyes and focused on the bots within her, they traveled to those burns. Even now, heat raged on within the wounds, as if the fire had seeped into her body and remained forever alive.

She missed this—being free of Caleb's influence. It was as if a fog had been removed from her mind and she could see again. She was herself, and she would never let Caleb take that from her again.

Caleb stepped out of the cold cell where Lance lay, slamming the thick steel door behind him. Only through the small, barred window in the door was Lance visible, unconscious on the floor. Rotoya had removed his cuffs before they threw him in.

Caleb glared at her, discontent written on his face. "What took you so long to bring him to me?"

"Little bastard tried to escape," Rotoya said.

Caleb raised an eyebrow.

"He's a crafty one. Like father, like son."

"So you almost let him get away?" Caleb asked, his tone condescending.

"But I didn't."

Caleb looked at the door as if deciding just how he wanted to respond. "If you and your officers can't bring in one man—"

"Look, I got him, didn't I? What matters is that he didn't get away and he's here. What more do you want?" When Caleb didn't respond, Rotoya drew a steadying breath. "I'll be in the lobby."

Rotoya walked away, her boots scraping against the concrete floor. The cell-lined hallway felt longer than ever as she traveled it, Caleb's stare burning a hole in the back of her head.

Caleb cleared his throat, and Rotoya stopped.

"One of your officers will be waiting at the front desk." A small flash of his veins, and she knew he was ordering the officer there at this very moment. She forced a smile and thanked him, the words bitter in her mouth, then walked to the elevator. She hoped Lance could withstand whatever Caleb had in store, at least long enough to initiate the next phase of the plan.

As the elevator rose, and her heart along with it, she wondered which officer awaited her at the front. This new pattern of working for Caleb was wearing her nerves down to thin strings. Getting her officers back at a trickle was an insult, as if she needed to *earn* her own officers back.

The only small comfort was that Caleb would be dead soon, one way or another.

She should never have accepted that drug.

Lance awoke on the cold concrete floor. He moved to sit up, his ribs aching in response, and he climbed onto a slab of metal attached to the wall by two chains, presumably a bed. The room was nothing but concrete otherwise, and the cold… why was it so cold?

At first, Lance was alone, but then the beast growled as it too awoke. Growling right at the door.

"I'm awake, in case you're wondering," Lance said to whoever was on the other side.

A voice muttered something, then keys jingled. As soon as the door opened, Lance made a note of which officer was holding the keys.

Caleb stepped in, his face pleasant.

He leaned against the wall opposite Lance, and one of the guards stepped in behind him, closing the door. The one with the keys watched from a small window in the door.

The officer in the room had a pistol at his side and was easily within arm's reach. It almost looked intentional. Lance ignored it for now.

"I have some questions for you," Caleb said. He seemed perfectly content in the cold, while Lance tried his best not to shiver.

"Shame," Lance responded, his voice shaky. "I thought you were just c-coming in here for a little visit."

Caleb smiled at him, as if enjoying the sight. "Are you cold?"

Lance focused on the guard next to Caleb. First on his breathing, on his chest rising and falling in an even pattern. He matched the breathing, trying to make a connection with it. If the chief hadn't been lying, then Caleb shouldn't notice the attempt, not with all the soldiers he had to control at once.

"I like the cold," Lance said.

Caleb chuckled. The sound spiked through Lance's head. Lance gritted his teeth and focused even harder. He reached out and felt something there. A small warmth. The blood of the soldier, coursing through his veins.

"So tell me," Caleb said, "how did you get a hold of the drug?"

Lance suppressed a curse. *Just shut up, already.* Every word Caleb spoke knocked him out of his concentration. This was his only chance. He had to take it.

"You wouldn't believe me if I told you."

"Try me."

Lance found it. He latched on to the warmth of the soldier and held on for dear life. He had something. It took everything he had not to smile. "I honestly don't know how I got this." He gestured at himself and nearly lost his hold on the soldier's blood for a moment, but he caught himself just in time.

Something about gripping the soldier made the cold more bearable, as if he was stealing the soldier's warmth for himself. A voice rang in the distance.

"Are you lying to me?" Caleb's words turned cold again, but then he stopped and calmed himself. The drug had gotten to his sense of business. He couldn't even speak calmly anymore, not without severe self-control.

Don't let him see, Lance told the beast. He readied himself to reach further into the soldier. If his veins showed, even for a second, even in the darkness of the cell, Caleb would suspect.

Lance shook his head as he dove deeper within the soldier, embracing the warmth that came with it. He felt what the man felt: boredom, tension, even a bit of sadness. Somewhere deeper down, his thoughts resided. Like voices in his head but dropped down a deep chasm. They echoed up to him.

I can't believe this is a terrorist. He's just a kid.

"I'm not," Lance said. "I'm not lying, I swear."

Caleb wordlessly scanned him up and down. Lance reached out one last time and latched onto the officer.

Cross your arms.

Lance's heart thundered in his chest as the officer crossed his arms. He waited for Caleb to look at the soldier, to furrow his brows, anything. But he didn't. He just stood there and frowned. Rotoya's theory was right. He held too many people under his thumb to notice a few out of reach.

Either that, or Lance had already improved.

"Well," Caleb finally said. "You're lucky." He slapped down a small, dirty journal beside Lance and smiled. "I believe you."

He left the room, and the officer left behind him. The door closed with a loud creak and slam, and Lance finally allowed himself to shiver, his teeth clacking together. A few minutes passed, and Lance eyed the journal then picked it up.

His hand rested on the front, where initials were carved into the leather.

M. L.

Lance considered ignoring it. If Caleb wanted him to read it, then surely it wasn't something he wanted to see. Yet whatever lay within these pages could have something to do with a cure, maybe something Caleb had missed.

The beast offered no growls, no hisses, no purrs.

So Lance took the decision into his own hands.

He opened the journal.

CHAPTER 28
THE CALM BEFORE THE STORM

He read it. Then he reread it. The first half was eloquent, but as he progressed, it worsened.

Malcolm had written it out plainly, as if he intended for Lance himself to read it one day.

The meeting with the man with a cane was miserable. It quickly descended into threats, and negotiating, I believe, was never on the table. His obsession with animals is also quite disconcerting... There was something in his eyes. An empty blackness that I have seen in no other person. Frightening, and yet so fascinating all the same.

There was someone with him. A young man, long dark hair. Beautiful eyes. There was something about him, as well. He seemed so out of place. As if he didn't even want to be there. After dealing with that man with the cane, I wouldn't be surprised. What was his name? Eric?

I refuse to tell anyone but you about this, journal, but I gave him a dose of the drug. In the moment, when the crazy man's black eyes were looking directly into mine, and he was threatening me like that, something shifted in the room. I had a vial of the medicine with me. The nanobots, contained in a small syringe. It was the beta strain.

Originally, should the plan have gone correctly, I would have considered giving the beta drug to the crazy man and having him under Caleb's thumb. Harnessing such a valuable source of information would have been crucial. Caleb would have been so proud, perhaps proud enough to increase my budget for experiments.

But the other one, the one with the emerald eyes, I stuck him with it.

The poor sap didn't even notice it.

I thought that if I stuck the emerald-eyed man with the beta drug, he would be more useful than the crazy man, even if the crazy man is the leader. The drug can change a man, make them erratic and somewhat unstable. An unfortunate side effect, even if rare. Still, as unstable as he clearly already was, I could not risk giving the drug to him. The other one, however, was clearly new and unfamiliar. A shift in personality would not affect his cover, and he could obtain most if not all of the information the leader retrieved. A very dangerous risk, one that only Caleb likely would have made. I am no businessman, however, and being one of the few risky investments I've made, I pray that it resolves in my favor.

I can almost feel judgement, even from an inanimate object such as you, journal. My thought process at the time was unflawed. I thought with my emotions rather than with my mind. A mistake that I have made more than once. I do not regret what I did, however. At least, I didn't until I realized I had given the alpha drug to the emerald-eyed man.

I find myself filled with a deep guilt at what I did. In my carelessness, I grabbed the wrong vial. Still... I cannot help but be intrigued by this new set of events that will take place. What will this man do with such power? A man given strength and endurance such as that. I wonder how it will affect him. Fascinating. Truly fascinating.

Perhaps it was meant to be.

Lance set the book beside him once he read those last few sentences. His heart raced as he stared at the wall. His throat was dry. Malcolm had injected him that day.

And he hadn't noticed.

He was going to be used as a pawn to gain information from Eric. The thought of it turned his stomach. A puppet—he'd been a puppet from the very beginning. When would he finally escape from people in power trying to control him? He clenched his teeth.

Time slowed to a crawl, and Lance could only guess an hour had passed before he picked the journal back up and kept reading. At this point, the writing was a scrawl.

Could not fix it! Was taken in the middle of night by mysterious men. Could not fight like brothers. My strain of the drug was strictly to keep me alive, to heal all injuries. Wanted all my nanobots to focus on that one thing, physical enhancements aside. Hypothesis unfortunately correct. Can die... can be killed. Nanobots do not prevent decomposition. Very unfortunate surprise. Grateful to not have my journal removed from my corpse. Death not implausible as I wished, but nanobots brought me back, all the same. Body weakened from decomposition. Still mobile. Intelligence uncompromised.

Calligraphy, however, is appalling.

So little strength when I first awoke. Could smell my own rotting flesh. Worms wriggled inside of casket. Gnawed on my insides. Killed them easily. Nanobots attacked them. Did not help the foul smell.

Time taken to crawl out of ground, unknown. Bloody hands. Couldn't see. Couldn't breathe. Could do nothing but claw hands upward until met with cold night air.

Hiding, now, in small crypt below the old church. Nanobots kept me alive. Did not preserve me... Failure, but also success. I am immortal. Not invincible. Can be killed but only resuscitated long after.

Must be careful. Should I be killed again... rendered unable... body will simply rot beyond resuscitation. Terrible fate, but must accept it to continue research. It is deserved, dear journal. Thought with emotions and not my head. Beginning to see pattern. Was not patient. Injected myself with experimental version of the drug... Grateful, for even if flawed, the nanobots saved my life. Perhaps... create a new version? Perfect them until they can not only resuscitate me, but heal horrible, rotted body parts? Can imagine it now. Nanobots working tirelessly to not only stitch skin and bone back together but create new skin and bone. Render me immortal and *invincible. What a fantastic bout of research this shall be. Next project shall be reversing the decomposition process. I cannot wait!*

Now, if I could only find some equipment... perhaps contact brother, Caleb.

What a shock it will be for him to hear my voice.

Must reach my office. Caleb shall take me. And what of the lab? I must gather the essentials.

The pages afterward were torn out, likely the notes for the cure. Lance needed those notes if he was going to get the nanobots out. There was no one left to do the research, but that didn't matter. Not one bit. If there was even the slightest chance he could silence the beast inside him, he would take it. Even if he had to teach himself, he would find a way.

The beast did not respond to the thought.

Lance set the journal beside him for the last time, refusing to look at it again, even as the temptation to reread those same lines gnawed at him. Nanobots were swimming in his bloodstream. He couldn't feel them, but he knew they were there. He grimaced.

Lance wrapped his hands around himself, not just from the cold, but from the sudden feeling that shadowed him, like he was infected. He closed his eyes and reached beyond the thick metal door.

The same officer he held in his grip was standing outside the door. His blood flowed freely through his veins, and his heart beat a steady, calm rhythm. It was a comfort, a distant hug. It felt warm, a wonderful contrast to the cold of this cell.

He ordered him to do small things every few minutes—cough, scratch his chin, sigh, even drop his gun and pick it up. The guard next to him felt the need to ask him if he was alright, as if he was being tested.

He urged the guard to speak, to say the words Lance wanted him to. A second of silence passed, and the guard still said nothing. His friend repeated the question, a hint of suspicion in his voice. Lance couldn't allow himself to let go of his grip on the guard, so he focused harder and mouthed the words along with him.

Sorry. Never had saying one word exerted so much energy from Lance. The air drained from his lungs. *Nervous.*

Lance forced the word out and fell from the bed onto the icy floor. The soldier didn't seem to hear it or just didn't care.

"I know what you mean," the other man said. "The guy in there's supposed to be some crazy killer… Weird to think of him that way, though. He looks so harmless." Movement, then a huff of breath. "Look at him. Lying on the floor like some broken little animal."

Not for long, Lance thought. The beast purred in agreement, and while the sound was oddly comforting, Lance wondered if the beast had something entirely different in mind.

"Rachel." The word escaped the moment the chief saw her. She hadn't seen her since Caleb activated the drug at the police station. She'd positioned her somewhere within Landreau Corp to keep her safe. Now, here she stood, Caleb's new choice pick for her. If he only knew what he'd done.

Rachel turned, her blond hair cut short to make room for the helmet she cradled at her hip. Her smile was a diamond light, and her eyes—disappointingly purple, courtesy of the nanobots. The shining cinnamon brown had been swallowed by the drug. Rotoya frowned but couldn't hold it as she made eye contact.

"Chief," Rachel said. A simple acknowledgement. Excitement shone in her smile, but she remained formal.

Despite being the chief, Rotoya felt lower in rank than the woman before her.

"What are your orders?"

Rotoya crossed her arms. "We're heading to a bar I suspect Eric or one of his accomplices to be hiding out in. With the boy in custody, Caleb can't track them himself anymore."

Rachel nodded. "Yes, ma'am."

The chief suppressed her smile as she led Rachel out the back, marching toward one of the police cars. *I hope you know what you're doing, Eric.*

"Would you like to take anyone else besides us, Chief?" Rachel asked.

"No," Rotoya said. "If they are at that bar, trying to hide a whole squad would be too risky. It's just you and me on this mission, Sands."

"Fine with me." Rachel grinned and fell into place beside Rotoya.

Sands. Rotoya was the only person allowed to say it. If any other officer dared to utter her last name, they were met with a venomous glare or even more venomous words.

Occasionally a venomous punch.

Rotoya had never asked why she was so sensitive about it. Never wanted to.

She sent a silent order to the six officers she had control over, telling them to get into the nearest armored vehicle and drive somewhere secluded. They would be needed later. Her nanobots transmitted the order in a flash, and the officers were on the move.

They slid into the car, and Rotoya drove out onto the streets, glancing in the rearview mirror. Her officers entered the armored vehicle and drove. Under her silent order, they chose a different street to travel down.

"I'm glad to be back on your team, Chief," Rachel said, looking out the window at the bare-bone streets. She sighed. "The city's so empty now."

Caleb had done that; he'd reduced this city to an empty maze. And with his grip over Agni tightening as well, nobody would be called. No military, save for Daniel's private army, which Caleb also controlled, especially with his brother's untimely death.

If Eric only knew he'd done Caleb's work for him.

A man with that much power and money was unstoppable. Rotoya ignored Rachel's questioning look. She always held contempt for anyone with such power, yet she'd taken the drug and allowed her brain to be muddled by his words.

She only ever found herself doubting Caleb after that explosion. She owed Lance for that. He'd made her realize where her true loyalties lay.

Granted, he'd done so by blowing her up, so the gratitude only extended so far.

Caleb would pay for his actions, the greedy fool.

Rotoya would pay as well if Derek was to be believed. She remembered killing Rob… shooting him over and over with a smile on her face. She didn't blame him for wanting her dead.

Rachel kept staring expectantly at her, and Rotoya realized she hadn't said a word in response to her comment. "I'm glad to have you back, too, Sands. How was it being ordered around by the big man?"

"Never as good as with you, Chief."

Rotoya glanced at her, a pang settling in her chest. How could she have let Rachel take that drug? Now, she followed the orders of anyone above her, anyone who had control over her, and she did so without hesitation. Mixing that with her already-loyal personality made her quite the threat. Practically a robot.

The chief reached out to her and felt her blood full of nanobots, thriving and breathing. A woman of power and discipline, infected with those things. *I did this to you.*

When the officers questioned taking the drug, Rachel had been the first to step up. She'd allowed herself to be injected in front of all the others, just to show them that they could trust Rotoya.

To be such a nice memory, it was tainted by what she knew now.

Lord, forgive me, what have I done?

Rachel's nanobots swam around in her bloodstream, attaching to every red blood cell they could. All Rotoya could do was will them to self-destruct, something Caleb had taught her. She wished she could shut them down completely and give her autonomy back to her.

Within minutes, they reached the bar, where a streetlight shone through the windows, casting the entrance in a haunting orange. Rotoya parked the police car in an alley enveloped in utter darkness. None of Caleb's scouts stood on the rooftops.

Good.

When Rotoya opened the door to step out, Rachel called out to her, keeping her voice to a whisper. "What are we doing, anyway?"

"We're taking Caleb Landreau down," Rotoya said.

"What?" Rachel said. "I mean, I'm with you, but… what's the plan?"

"I'll explain once we're inside. Come on."

Rachel did as she was told, and the chief felt nothing pull Rachel out of that car. None of the nanobots needed to force her movements. She simply did so of her own free will. Still, that didn't stop the nagging feeling that her willingness was being 'encouraged' by the drug, the way Caleb had her thinking she was doing the right thing in working with him. Knowing for sure was difficult.

She gestured for Rachel to follow her. "I want you to meet some new friends of mine."

She couldn't let this stand. She would cure her officers of these damn nanobots if it was the last thing she did. A promise to them all.

But mostly a promise to Rachel.

Lance sat on the metal bed, his eyes closed as invisible fingers reached out to the second officer keeping watch on him. Time moved at a snail's pace.

How long have I been in this cell?

Lance reached farther, grabbing at the second guard. The first one nearly slipped from his fingers with every attempt. He stomped his foot with a frustrated huff when the first guard nearly slipped again, breathing a sigh of relief when neither guard seemed to notice.

With a quiet, annoyed sigh, Lance reached out again. He felt cold emotion underneath the second guard—calculating thoughts, borderline paranoid, swam in his head. He focused on the nanobots within him and reached out. Then he latched on like a leech.

Next, he reached further, clambering selfishly for more.

Lance's energy drained, and he lay on the bed. His head throbbed in pain, and his stomach twisted, but he didn't stop. He climbed until the soldier's steady heartbeat thumped in his ears. Resentment and bitterness took refuge within the guard, washing over Lance with a chill.

Lance stretched past those emotions and grabbed.

On the other side of the door, the guard shuddered.

Lance felt it. He forced himself to breathe. He'd done it. Sweat poured down his forehead, and the beast purred quietly. Even it seemed tired.

He had a hold of two guards. He'd done it, and now he would wait and see if Caleb noticed.

If he did, Lance could only imagine what would be done to him.

How did Caleb do it? Just this one man had nearly thrown Lance to the floor again. And just keeping them both in his firm grip was weighing on him.

Give in, the beast growled at him. *Give me more room.*

It could work, Lance thought. If he gave the beast more room, he could control every one of Caleb's men, as far as he knew. The whispers tempted him. The soft growls of the beast became more convincing the longer it took Lance to catch his breath.

Still, Lance forced out a refusal, telling the beast no even though he wanted to say, *Yes. Yes.*

Lance's stomach twisted as the two men stood patiently, none the wiser, and his energy drained slowly but steadily. He closed his eyes and accepted the sleep that pulled him under.

Rotoya exhaled, shoving the growing anxiety out of her chest. She straightened her shoulders and stepped inside. Rachel said nothing as she followed her.

"Kind of a shame," Rachel finally said, her helmet secure on her head. "This place might end up burned down like the Rose was. I've never been interested in those places, but the guys always talked about how beautiful it was."

"I have a feeling it will be again one day," Rotoya responded.

It wasn't a lie. Eric was well off even though he rarely showed it. Once they finally killed Caleb, she had no doubt he would make off with a good chunk of his money—if given the opportunity, of course.

Rotoya passed the barren barroom and entered the kitchen.

Nothing.

"I'm not seeing anyone here, Chief. You think they left?"

"No… no, I'm sure they didn't." She paused. "And stop calling me Chief. It's Rotoya, remember?"

Rachel rubbed the back of her neck with an apology. "Sorry. Bad habit."

Rotoya padded across the floor, her eyes scanning the empty room. She racked her brain for where it could be. They'd said it was in the kitchen but never specified.

Rachel clicked her tongue. "You said they were friends… I'm sure Caleb wouldn't be very fond of that." Her tone was playful, but Rotoya's heart skipped a beat.

"And are you going to tell him?" She sent a wry smile at Rachel.

Rachel removed her helmet, mirroring the smile. "Not planning on it."

She was speaking the truth. The nanobots did not shift, didn't rush or slow down. Her heartbeat remained steady. That was the Rachel she knew. Even her eyes sparkled with mischief. It stung Rotoya as much as it warmed her chest.

Rotoya changed when she was under the drug's influence. She enjoyed the chaos, the violence, savoring it like a warm meal. Yet Rachel was herself. Did that mean she wasn't under anyone's influence anymore? Rotoya wanted to say something, anything—an apology, maybe. A confession.

Then she saw it. A door, painted the same white as the wall, barely noticeable in the corner of the room.

"There you are." She strode to the door and opened it.

A small set of stairs led down to another door. A smirk formed on her face as she shook her head. She called Rachel over, and Rachel wordlessly came to her side.

"Do you think…" Rachel trailed off, but Rotoya just walked to the door and knocked. She sent an affirming smile to Rachel.

The door groaned as it was pulled open, and Kaela's tired face met hers. Despite the exhaustion, she wore a wicked smirk. "Plan going well so far?"

"Without a hitch, as far as I know. Invite me in?"

Kaela stepped aside and allowed the two girls in, but her eyes settled fiercely on Rachel, and her hand rested at her side, where she'd sheathed her knife against her leg earlier.

Rachel paused, her hand hovering over her gun.

"It's okay," Rotoya said, holding her hand up. "You can trust them."

Rachel removed her hand from her gun and relaxed—almost too quickly.

Rotoya hesitated as she stepped inside. Bright chandeliers hung from the ceiling, and dozens of barrels lined the room on wooden shelves. The smell of wood and salt permeated the air. Kaela led them down the hall of barrels and took a sharp right, her steps clicking on the polished floor. Stone pillars marked the end of every row of barrels. The air was cool, but Rotoya's nanobots warmed her.

"This is fancier than the bar itself," Rotoya said.

Kaela smirked back, but her eyes held an inkling of hatred behind them. "Derek sells the barrels." She sounded bored, despite her smile showing a wicked interest. "Mostly to clientele with more refined taste."

Rachel's eyes widened as she surveyed the room. "Damn, I can only imagine how good the wine is."

Rotoya smiled at her. "Maybe I'll buy you a barrel once all of this is over."

Rachel smiled back, and Rotoya resisted frowning. The mischief was gone from behind her bright-purple eyes. Now, they seemed so… empty. *But she's still Rachel,* Rotoya thought. *She's herself. She's just being manipulated.*

They traveled down another row of barrels, and after a few more sharp turns, Kaela knocked on a dark wooden door. The door opened, and they stepped in.

Gun racks hung on each side of the room, with rifles, pistols, and shotguns.

Eric was sitting on a wooden table and leaning against the wall, his cane resting comfortably in his lap. The room smelled of incense and freshly oiled metal.

Derek stood near the center of the room, eyeing Rotoya. His hand hovered inches away from a pistol at the bottom of the rack. His eyes moved to Rachel. Despite being part of the plan, two nanobot-infused people were currently stuck in a tiny room with him.

"Don't worry about her," Rotoya said. "She won't betray us."

"Better hope Caleb doesn't take her back," Kaela remarked.

Rotoya sneered. "Then don't blow me up again."

"So what now?" Derek asked.

"We wait," Rotoya said. "Caleb will wonder why we haven't come back yet and *hopefully* send some of my officers here to check… which, knowing him, he will, just to remind me that they're not mine anymore." She looked at Rachel. "You ready to take down Caleb Landreau and bring everything back to normal?"

Rachel stared deep into her eyes, and after a moment, a smile grew on her lips. "Hell yeah."

Rotoya nodded then looked at the trio. "We're going to have to update her on the plan."

Lance awoke, the cold of the cell clamping its jaws harder on his skin. He shivered on the metal bed and rose, his hands wrapped tightly around himself. His breath turned to smoke in the air. Had Caleb made it even colder down here?

Beside the door was half a loaf of bread and a cup of water. He ignored them at first, refusing to look at them, but his stomach rumbled every time they crossed his mind.

He slid from the bed and crouched next to the food. He sniffed it, tasted it, then waited. The beast gave no sign that it was poisoned… and even if it was, with the nanobots inside of him, he likely wouldn't suffer any effects from it.

The bread was gone within seconds, and he washed it down with the nasty water.

Lance sat back on the bed, shivering and checking his grip on the two guards outside. At any moment, he could tell the one with the keys to unlock the door and let him out. Having that option floating around in his head was dangerous. He could get out, but the plan would be ruined if he did.

Still, he rehearsed what he would do if he *needed* to use the key.

Lance didn't have to wait long until that dreaded elevator sounded, and footsteps echoed down the hallway. How much longer would he make these trips before leaving Lance down here alone in the cold forever?

He latched on just a little tighter to the men, feeling the warmth they held within their uniforms. It helped more than it should have.

The door groaned open, and Caleb stepped in. He held a smile and eyed the journal next to Lance. A new officer stood next to him, and Lance worried for just a moment that Caleb knew. He swallowed the lump in his throat.

"Did you read the journal?" Caleb asked as he stood before Lance.

Lance reached out to the guard next to him, trying to find the warmth of his heartbeat in this cold atmosphere.

"Not going to answer?" Caleb prodded. "Well, I suppose that's fine. I know you read the journal."

The beast growled at Caleb, but Lance suppressed it. He reached out again and found the soldier's heartbeat, calm and confident, in perfect harmony with the other two Lance held. He reached for it, made to latch on to it as he had the others.

"I'm sure you noticed that some pages have been removed," Caleb continued, straightening his coat. "Filled with notes and diagrams to rewrite the nanobots." He pursed his lips. "I'm no scientist, but it is an interesting idea. Fight fire with fire. Fight nanobots with nanobots."

Caleb held an air of confidence in what he said. So sure of himself. Anger stirred within Lance's chest, and the beast snarled at him. He used that anger to propel himself further toward the heart of the guard next to him. He stretched and reached with every bit of his being, his body aching in response, his chest squeezing harder and harder. He couldn't breathe. Lance shut his eyes and held his head in his hands, pretending that he was about to cry.

He could feel Caleb's smile on him. He reached more and more. His grip on the other two loosened, weakened. He stretched just a bit further. Just a little more, and he would have three officers to himself. He could do it. But just as he reached the heart, something crackled, like a tree bending to the point of breaking. His other two connections bent, on the verge of snapping.

The beast purred. *Give me more room.*

Lance didn't shake his head, not in front of Caleb. He sobbed in his hands, as convincingly as he could manage.

Again, the beast purred. *More room. Give me more room.*

Lance refused.

More!

"No." Lance forced himself to look at Caleb as he said it. The threat, the quiet calm in his own voice nearly scared him.

Caleb narrowed his eyes, and the guard tensed. Lance could feel it but couldn't reach him, couldn't control him, not without losing one or both of the others.

"No?" Caleb replied. "I find myself very intrigued by you, Lance. The fighting abilities the nanobots have given you greatly exceed many of my trained soldiers. It wouldn't be surprising, since Malcolm gave you the alpha strain, but you seem to be fighting that. The nanobots are offering you a gift, and you're rejecting them. Yet even so, you can fight like the devil himself." He cocked his head to the side. "Just imagine how powerful you'd be if you *stopped* fighting."

Lance looked down again.

"You've left me with a difficult decision, Lance. You have too much potential for me to kill you. It would be a complete waste of your abilities. But I can't let you work for me either, not willingly. You're too loyal to your father for that." He crouched and met Lance's eyes. "So here's what I'm going to do." He cleared his throat. "I've thought about your deal. Here's my counteroffer… You tell me where Eric is, and I'll cure you of these nanobots. You won't have to fight them anymore. Or… I can inject you with the beta strain like I did the chief of police and make you kill Eric yourself."

"You're lying," Lance said. "There is no cure."

Caleb chuckled. "Not yet, but I'll have one made just for you. I may have jumped the gun on killing Malcolm. Oh well."

A moment of silence passed between them, in which Lance pathetically reached for the soldier's heart again. He didn't even get close. Exhaustion weighed him down, and despite the cold, the metal bed called to him.

"But don't you worry, Lance. I have someone special using Malcolm's notes to research it. In fact, he's in one of these very cells."

He had to be lying. Lance stared into Caleb's devilish eyes. No playful wickedness like Eric's—nothing but sheer corruption.

Caleb continued, "I haven't gotten my R&D team on it yet. They aren't exactly 'in the know' about this whole nanobots business."

Lance let out a bitter laugh. "Surprised you haven't drugged *them* too."

"*Say*… that's not a half-bad idea, Lance." His smile was too wide to be real. "Problem is, Malcolm only made a handful of extra doses besides the ones needed for Daniel's men and the police force." He sighed. "But that's okay. I have other plans for those anyway."

He really likes to ramble.

The beast purred in agreement.

Caleb extended his hand. "Do we have a deal?"

Lance glared at him. "How do I know you'll keep your end of the deal?"

"You don't." Caleb smiled. "But it's either that or die. I'll throw in a bonus. Kaela and Derek? Did I get their names right? I'll spare them too. But you leave this city and never return."

Lance hesitated then inched his hand toward Caleb's. He gripped it in a firm shake, and Caleb's smile settled into a more relaxed state.

"They're at a bar," Lance said. "Derek's Bar. It's the closest one to the Rose you burned down." He swallowed, the fear catching his throat. He was in too deep to doubt now.

"You have my word that Derek and Kaela will be spared." Caleb stood and made to leave. "I'll bring them here. You'll all be imprisoned for a time, but I'll see about getting you nicer cells. Warmer, too. Once you have your cure and the city has settled down, you'll be set free."

"Caleb," Lance said. The beast stirred in him, and Caleb's eyes flashed with excitement. "If you double cross me… I'll stop fighting it."

He let a pause rest between them. "You'll get to find out firsthand just how much potential I really have."

Caleb snorted. "Dramatic, just like your father. Don't worry. I don't back down from a good deal." He took a step away from the door. "But if I find out this is some elaborate trap, I have a nice, healthy dose of the beta strain with your name on it."

Caleb walked out, the door slamming behind him. Lance didn't let himself smile until the elevator doors opened and closed again. Then he huffed out a quiet laugh.

Lance reached out to the two guards at his door, checking his grip on them—loosened but not gone. Though he was already exhausted, he took the time to repair and strengthen his grip. By the time he finished, he lay across the metal slab, out of breath.

All he could think of as he closed his eyes was how things were going down at the bar.

I hope you know what you're doing, Eric.

Just before he fell asleep, the beast purred again.

More.

CHAPTER 29
SHATTERED LIKE GLASS

Rotoya sat in silence. Rachel sat next to her, arms crossed, leaning against the wall in the barroom. Both sat within arm's reach of the kitchen door. Rotoya combed through the plan in her head over and over. If more soldiers came than anticipated, Eric's group would jump out, and they would ambush them together.

For now, silence was their only company. They sat for what felt like forever, and Rotoya stole glances at Rachel. She hadn't bothered putting her helmet back on, raking a hand through her short hair.

"You know," Rotoya started, "I think I overestimated the drug when we first took it."

Rachel looked at her but didn't respond.

"I thought once we had the drug, we wouldn't get nervous anymore. Though this is the first time since I took it that I've felt this way, so who knows?"

Rachel looked down then asked, "You're nervous too?"

Rotoya nodded, and Rachel gave her a reassuring smile. *Nervous* was an understatement, but she swallowed every ripple of anxiety that washed over her. Nerves had never done anything good for her before, and they wouldn't now. Still, she wrung her hands and swallowed the lump forming in her throat.

What happened to her in this fight against Caleb didn't matter. It was her officers that sent her nerves into a frenzy. At any moment, he could order them to the slums and make them self-destruct.

Rotoya let out a shaky breath. Rachel was acting like herself—the way she sat, ran her hand through her hair, and bounced her leg over and over. The slight twang in her voice was as prominent as ever. She was Rachel.

But Rotoya had to know. "Rachel."

Rachel looked at her, meeting her eyes with those bright-purple ones.

"Point your gun at yourself."

Without so much as a blink of hesitation, Rachel pointed her own pistol at her head.

"Point it at me."

Again, without any pause, she pointed her gun, this time at Rotoya's face.

Rotoya cupped her hand over her mouth, hot tears welling in her eyes. She dug her nails into her cheek. She'd done this. *Shoot me*, she almost said. It was what she deserved.

"Put it down," Rotoya said, her voice cracking. She wiped her eyes as Rachel obeyed. She hadn't even taken direct control—just asked her, and she did it. "I'm so sorry."

"For what, Ro?"

Rotoya almost burst into tears. Her nickname, of all things.

The rumble of a vehicle vibrated under Rotoya's palms resting on the floor. She shoved her tears and nerves far under the waters and stood. The vehicle parked in front of the bar.

"Let's do this," Rotoya said. She marched out of the bar with Rachel following behind, gulping as the car doors opened.

Four soldiers stepped out of the car. A single squad. And no Caleb.

Perfect.

"Chief Rotoya? What are you doing here?" asked one of the soldiers. Two were armed with rifles, and the last two had pistols at their hips.

Rotoya ordered Rachel to flank them. A silent order from her nanobots. Doing so hurt, but it would be worth it when this was all over.

Rachel rounded the vehicle, silent as a wraith and casual, as if simply inspecting it.

"Caleb sent you too?" Rotoya sighed. "We've searched the place up and down, but we haven't found any sign of the fugitives."

Rachel balled her hands into one fist and slammed it into the back of a soldier's neck. He collapsed. The remaining soldiers spun at the sound. Rotoya sent her fist through the nearest soldier's visor, dropping him like a brick.

When Rotoya looked up, another officer was on the ground at Rachel's feet. She sent her fist into the stomach of the final guard then slammed her head into the car door. The impact left a dent in the metal.

"Nice work," Rotoya said.

Rachel smiled. "Thanks."

"Four down."

"How many more left?"

"I don't know… More than this."

They dragged the bodies off the street and drove the armored vehicle into a dark alley. Other than the unfortunate purple splatter on the road, it was as if nobody had come to check on them at all.

Rotoya tried to manipulate the blood, but even the small amount wouldn't budge. If only Caleb had taught her how to control the blood like he did, crashing waves of it into people. It would certainly make the coming fight easier.

Once the bodies were hidden in the cellar and their weapons stashed in the armory, Rotoya and Rachel sat back down in the barroom and continued waiting. A frown etched onto Rotoya's face after a while. Two of those four people were her own officers. She'd seen their faces when she removed their helmets. Having to beat down her own officers pained her, but if this plan went half as well as they needed it to, then it would all be worth it.

With any luck, Caleb was talking Lance's head off and revealing more information than he intended.

His pride would be his downfall.

And his mouth.

A pounding headache ripped Lance out of his sleep. Maintaining his grip on the soldiers, falling asleep, then waking up—that was the routine. He didn't know how Caleb possessed the energy necessary to control so many soldiers.

Lance lost track of how long he slept, of how much time had passed in this cell. Surely, it was no longer than a few minutes at a time. *Hopefully.* The room had no windows to check for sunlight.

What if he'd slept for hours? What if Caleb had gone to the bar personally? Lance shook his head, prompting a spike of pain in his temples. He stood and looked out the small window in the door.

Another person occupied one of these cells, according to Caleb. Curiosity gripped his heart the way he gripped the hearts of the two soldiers walking up and down the hall. One soldier looked in on a cell as he passed, two cells down, facing the opposite direction. Whoever they were, Lance could only imagine what they'd done to make Landreau Corp mad.

And what information they might have.

Lance took a steadying breath and ordered a guard to open his door. The beast—or the nanobots—sent the message, worsening his headache. The guard walked to Lance's cell and opened it, the door groaning loud enough to alert the whole city. Lance paused, waiting for any shifts or shouts to arise in response.

With another order, the second guard ignored what he saw.

Lance slipped out of the cell, and his heart leaped. Freedom nipped at his heels, and the temptation to run overwhelmed him. He ignored it and padded down the hall, two cells down. He stopped at the one to his right and peeked in. He blinked a few times then narrowed his eyes.

It... can't be...

George was lying across a cold metal bed. *Alive.*

So that was what Caleb meant? George was researching the cure for him?

Lance ordered the guard to unlock George's door. The risk was great, maybe too great, but plan aside, George might know something vital.

Lance readied himself to run if the elevator sounded, ordering the guards to do the same. With every order, his energy drained, and his eyelids weighed heavier. He paused and leaned against the wall, catching his breath. He had to hurry.

Lance wiped his hands on his pants and stepped into the cell.

"George?" Lance whispered.

George shivered. If Eric saw him like this, he would go on a rampage.

Lance shook George lightly. His skin was cold, but his round stomach rose and fell. Lance sighed in relief and shook him again.

Finally, George stirred. His shivering body turned to look at Lance, and his eyes lit up.

"Lance?" George said, sitting up in the bed. He trembled. "H-how did you get here?"

"It was intentional," Lance whispered, shushing him.

George nodded.

"We had a plan to infiltrate Landreau Corp. It's a long story. What are *you* doing here? We thought you burned in the fire."

"Yes," George said. "Y-yes, I b-believe that was Caleb's intention. He s-slaughtered everyone in the R-rose, took Malcolm to a room, and had his soldiers bring m-me to the vehicle."

"Why?"

"Wanted m-me to work on n-nanobots. Create m-more because I w-worked with Malcolm."

"Did you do it?"

George shut his eyes tight. "N-no… D-don't know how. He threw me down here when I refused. Now he w-wants me to research a cure."

My God, he was telling the truth...

"Are you okay?"

George nodded.

"Are you hurt?"

George's breath formed a cloud as he sighed and shook his head.

Lance bit his lip as exhaustion clouded his own thinking. "Try to move around. It'll warm you up. Can you do that?" The beast had to be warming Lance as his skin wasn't nearly as cold as George's.

George nodded.

"Look, I have to get going. Keep moving, okay? I'll get you out of here."

"Eric," George said as Lance made to leave. "Is he okay?"

"He's fine... You'll see him again soon." Lance slipped out of the cell.

George stepped from one side of the room to the other in one stride, his arms wrapped around himself.

Lance closed the door, and the guard locked it behind him. He stumbled down the hall to his cell. The door groaned again as it shut behind him, and Lance collapsed, his legs too weak to keep him standing any longer. The simplest acts exhausted him. He swore at the cold concrete.

He reached out to the heartbeats of his two soldiers. They were steady, calm. The beast purred again, but he shut it up before it could ask to be 'given more room' again. He extended his reach, stretching beyond the floors above to the main level. His body tensed.

He kept reminding himself to breathe as he felt the heartbeats of the soldiers walking around the main level. There weren't many. Not in the lobby, anyway.

He opened his eyes and leaned over, his strength draining. Again, the beast started to purr at him, but he shut it up. A growl in response, but then the beast went silent.

This isn't going to be easy.

He shut his eyes again and reached. A single guard ascended to the third floor, but his energy faded from Lance's reach. A stairway. If Lance remembered correctly, it came to the main floor right next to the elevator.

He swore. *How the hell am I going to do this*? With a sigh, he opened his eyes and looked at the two guards walking up and down the hall. He thought for a moment then ordered the soldier with the keys to let George out.

The cell door swung open, and George's footsteps clicked toward Lance's door.

"It's me," Lance said as George stared at the guard that had let him out. "I'm controlling these two guards. Don't ask questions. I think I can get you out of here, but you have to follow the guard that let you out. Can you do that?"

"What about you?" George asked.

Lance shook his head. "I have to stay here for now. It's part of the plan. Head to Derek's bar. That's where Eric and Kaela are. Did Eric tell you about the bar at all?"

George stuttered. "Back at The Red Rose, I think, yes. Which one?"

Lance cursed. "Um… Recluse Avenue. It's not far from the Rose that burned down."

Lance ordered the guard to guide George to the elevator door. The guard summoned the elevator, and the doors slid open. They stepped in, and the guard held his hand out to the doors, keeping them from closing.

"George, get ready to move," Lance said, hissing as the guard's distance made holding on more difficult.

He reached for one last time, his body aching, his headache returning. The cold bit into his skin like a rabid dog. He sensed each of the heart-beats of the soldiers in the lobby.

He closed his eyes, recalling the layout of the lobby and forming a mental map as the soldiers walked around. With one order, he had the second soldier in the hall pull his gun. George gasped, but he urged the guard to the stairwell. Lance ordered the soldier to fire.

Two rounds went into the ground then three into the wall. The sound echoed all the way down to Lance's cell. Every heartbeat in the lobby quickened, pulsing in Lance's ears. He sensed them as they scrambled.

They were descending the stairs. Lance ordered the soldier to run back down to the basement then fire two more rounds. More soldiers from the main floor rushed down the stairs.

Lance ordered the guard in the elevator to let the doors close. *Keep him safe, no matter what. Be quiet, and bring him to the back door. If there are guards in the parking lot, take them out.*

The elevator doors shut as dozens of heavy footsteps flew down the stairs.

The door to the basement swung open. Lance's vision darkened.

"What the hell's going on here?" asked a guard.

There was a tense silence. Lance forced the words out, just as he had before. Each word punched him in the chest. *Rat... startled me...*

"A rat?" the guard repeated, frustration lacing his tone. "I don't get paid enough for this shit."

The guards trudged back up the steps, their heartbeats settling to a normal pace.

Lance reached out and sensed the second soldier. He had to be in the hall. His heart was racing. Two more heartbeats were nearby. That had to be guards outside the back door.

Darkness edged around him, pulling him under. He resisted, drowning in the fog in his head.

The guard moved toward the back door. The two other heartbeats turned rapid, beating faster and faster until they descended to a slow rhythm. Unconscious? Had he done it?

Once George gets away, come back.

Moments passed, then Lance sensed the guard move back into the building, his pulse getting stronger the closer he got to the basement. When he returned, Lance allowed them to resume their usual walk up and down the hall as if nothing had happened.

Lance prayed that what he just did was worth it.

And that Caleb wouldn't find out.

The darkness pulled Lance under.

He awoke to the sound of an elevator door opening and wondered how long he'd been out. He groaned as he sat up, his energy slowly returning.

Footsteps approached then stopped at his cell door, but Lance didn't bother looking. He kept still.

"Two," was all Caleb said. Lance still didn't look at him, but the fury in his voice said it all. Rage danced off him, wild like a flame. Caleb's guard opened the door, and he stomped in.

"Is that supposed to be the time?" Lance asked.

Caleb sent a kick into Lance's side. He grunted, pain shooting through his ribs. He sputtered and coughed into the ground, grateful that no blood splattered onto the stone.

Wrath laced Caleb's words. "I know you helped him escape."

"And would you mind telling me who *him* is?"

Another kick to his ribs. Lance expected it this time and braced for the impact. The beast snarled at Caleb.

Caleb spat on the ground next to Lance's head. "You helped that doctor escape, and wouldn't you be equally surprised to hear that these two soldiers right here are acting strangely. One firing his gun down here at a rat and the other attacking the guards at the exit. Almost seems too convenient, now doesn't it?"

Lance shifted away from the spittle on the ground, fighting against nausea. So Caleb couldn't sense Lance's control. He could only suspect it. Lance stored that tidbit of information. "What does that even matter to me? Whoever it was didn't bother letting me out, so why should I care?"

A pause… Lance resisted the smile that tried to crawl up his face, and he refused to look at Caleb. That silence meant Caleb considered it. Considered that Lance wasn't the one who controlled the guards. It was his one chance to defuse the situation.

Caleb whirled and grabbed one of the two guards standing outside of Lance's cell. "Tell me, soldier, why did you fire those rounds again?"

Lance tensed. He shut his eyes and tried to force the word out, but pain seared through his head. Tears welled in his eyes. He tried again, but the word didn't leave the soldier's mouth. He'd used up too much energy. He couldn't let go of the soldier, either. If he relinquished control, the soldier might act confused. *Dammit.*

Caleb asked the question again then turned to the other guard. "Why did you punch those men?"

More silence. Lance sent the order to speak, but it didn't reach the guard.

Lance prepared for the thrashing Caleb would give him. But then the air shifted, and the beast growled again.

Caleb's tone revealed his smile. "I'll tell you why you should care, Lance, my friend. Without that damn doctor, there is no cure for you, meaning Eric will die, and you'll be stuck with those nanobots inside of you." He sighed. "Oh well. I have another solution."

Lance glared up at Caleb.

He slipped a syringe out of his pocket. “A fresh shot of the beta strain. Now you can kill Eric yourself.”

“No,” Lance said. A burst of adrenaline shot through him, and he was on his feet, pressed against the wall.

Caleb removed a knife and sliced his palm. “Don’t fight this, Lance.”

Lance scanned the three soldiers. *One last order. Just one.* Lance bit through the pain and ordered his two guards. *Fire.*

But Caleb’s guard was too quick. He drew his pistol and shot Lance’s soldiers before they could draw their own guns.

The beast hissed and snapped inside him as Caleb closed in. The killing calm settled over him, and the familiar dry voice whispered in the back of his head.

Survive.

Lance lunged forward and threw a punch at Caleb’s face. Caleb grunted, and blood splattered against the wall. He swiped at Lance with the syringe. The needle barely missed Lance’s shoulder.

Lance allowed his body to guide his movements. Faster than he could think, he dodged swipe after swipe, throwing quick blows of his own. Caleb hardly reacted to them.

Caleb yelled, his veins glowing brightly. His arm grew twice its size.

“Not this again,” Lance breathed. He narrowly dodged Caleb’s punch. The wall cracked on impact.

Caleb swiped his arm, slamming into Lance’s chest. Lance cried out and flew against the wall. He crashed to the ground, the breath leaving his lungs.

Getting real sick of him—

Caleb punched Lance’s face. Pain shattered into his jaw, and his head slammed against the concrete.

He groaned, too slow to stop Caleb from shoving the needle into his neck.

The beast roared, louder than ever before.

He tried to move, but his body ached.

Give me more room!

Lance refused.

More room!

"No."

NOW!

Lance was too tired. He let go of the chains around the beast. It roared again, and Lance screamed. Pain coursed through every part of his body. His veins glowed brighter than ever. Caleb smiled and backed away.

Lance's body burned with invisible flames. He screamed and screamed, too weak to even writhe. Zaps and jolts fired all over his body, like hundreds of needles poking and prodding his skin. The beast stretched and snarled and lashed out, taking up all the room Lance gave it.

The pain wouldn't stop. *Please make it stop.*

The beast roared and howled, and the zaps continued. Moments passed like hours until finally, the zaps popped fewer and farther between. Lance heaved a breath, sucking down as much air as his lungs would allow.

Caleb was still smiling as he said, "Get up."

Lance scoffed. "Go to hell."

Caleb's smile dropped, and his expression fell. Lance swore there was fear in his eyes for just a split second. "My God," Caleb muttered. "How?"

Lance couldn't speak.

Even the beast panted, exhausted. *None left,* it growled.

Lance almost smiled. *So that's what happened.* It had killed the nanobots, zapped them away like flies. *Thank you.*

The beast purred for a second before going silent—collapsing, probably.

"I don't understand," Caleb said. "What did Malcolm give you?"

Lance shut his eyes then forced them open again. His grip on the two soldiers released, and he was left cold and empty, pain searing all over his skin.

"Take him down to the *other* cell."

Lance couldn't fight back as the men healed from their wounds and picked Lance up, forcing him out of the cell. He smiled. Caleb showed fear in his eyes. He *feared* Lance. It was almost funny.

Lance weakly kicked at them, even with the beast faintly whining inside of him. A feeling vaguely like the calm settled over him, but it wasn't enough. His body was too tired to fight. The beast was too tired to fight.

Caleb sighed. "You could've been my best soldier, Lance. I don't know how you resisted the drug… Malcolm had to have given you a different strain, something unlike any other. But his journal didn't mention that." Caleb didn't seem to be talking to Lance anymore. "I don't understand."

"Affects everyone different," Lance muttered weakly. He chuckled, but it was breathy. "Maybe I'm just better than you."

Caleb said nothing.

Lance was too disoriented to mark in his head which direction the soldiers were taking him. All he knew was that they took several twists and turns, and that it was only getting colder the longer they walked. Then they were heading down a set of stairs, and with each inch downward, the cold air bit down harder and harder on his body.

"Maybe," Caleb said. "But it won't matter anymore. Until I figure out what Malcolm did to you, you're my lab rat. And you're never getting out of here."

Lance was dropped in another cell. He landed on a freezing black stone floor. The walls were the same. There was no bed—nothing but a dark stone-brick room and a dark metal door with no slit, no way to look out or in.

Lance looked up from his hands and knees at the guard holding the door open.

Caleb wore a wicked smile. "You know… I'm grateful to you, Lance."

Lance opened his mouth to curse him, but his breath caught. He was too shaky, too cold. He balled up with his back to the floor, his shirt doing little to block the cold stone from snapping its jaws around him. He didn't care how pleasing the sight was to Caleb. He just wanted some semblance of warmth. The cold only worsened his throbbing pain.

He reached out to the guards to feel the warmth of their heartbeats, of their armor. It always helped. But he couldn't. He couldn't regain his grip on them. The beast growled, but it was distant as well. Almost muffled.

Caleb continued, "No, really, I am. This cell will keep you tame for a while." He laughed, the cold sound bouncing off the stone. "It was originally intended for Daniel and Malcolm. Well, Malcolm died, and I wasn't going to leave Daniel in that sewer forever. I just didn't want him taking control of my men from underneath me. Regardless, once he died, I thought I would have no use for this little cell. And now, it seems the time and resources it took to make it won't go to waste after all." He laughed again, the sound haunting.

Lance couldn't stop fear from crawling up his spine. The beast whined distantly, unable to even raise its head. Tears built up behind Lance's eyes. A plea to spare him climbed up his throat, but he shoved it down, refusing to allow that weakness to show.

"What?" Caleb said. "Surely, you didn't think connecting to other nanobots worked like magic, did you? No, it's all electromagnetic. I'm not sure how my dearest brother did it, but the waves those nanobots emit to one another can pierce through just about any material." He slapped his hand against the stone wall. "This cell, however, is not just stone. Surrounding its infrastructure is a Faraday cage. Ever heard of it? I hadn't until Malcolm told me about it. It can block all electromagnetic fields within it. A beautiful invention, really. Malcolm made a few adjustments to it, specifically for the nanobots. Good luck trying to control my men in here. Hell, good luck using those damn nanobots at all in here."

Lance's breath quickened. His words caught in his throat as he tried to beg. He didn't care how pathetic he looked. He didn't want to be in here. It was too dark, too small.

Lance reached out to the guards, but he couldn't sense them.

"So thank you, Lance. For making this fancy little cell here useful again. I'll have food and water sent in here every day or so, and I'll be sure to check up on you. We're going to find out together what Malcolm injected you with."

He laughed as the cell door closed, and Lance tripped over himself trying to reach it first. But the door shut tight, and Lance was trapped in a black room darker than Eric's eyes.

Caleb released another laugh, muffled from the other side of the door, then said, "Can't believe I didn't think of it earlier."

Lance reached out to the guards again, but there was nothing to grab onto—no warmth, no heartbeat.

After a few long moments, he reached within himself and listened for any sign of the beast.

No growls, no whines.

Tears trailed down his cheeks, and he let them, for what little warmth they gave. He already felt weak, but the nanobots—they were gone. No killing calm or beast, nothing to reach out to for warmth. He was the same Lance he'd been before all of this. He forced himself to stand, to get his skin away from that bare stone. He stayed on his feet and walked around in the darkness. Kept himself moving.

The silence of the room weighed heavily on him. The only sounds were Lance's own feet padding across the stone floor and his tears tapping against it as they dripped down his chin.

He'd failed. The entire plan was in ruins, and he could see no way out. He had no strength left.

Eric, Kaela, Derek, George—all of them would likely die because he'd failed. But Rotoya—if she managed to do what Lance couldn't, they still had a chance.

There it was. A kernel of hope. A small piece of light to hold on to in the darkness. It wasn't much, but Lance held it close to his chest and kept walking, kept moving. Maybe, if they managed to win, someone would find him. One of them would come for him. He just had to have faith.

But with the cold chilling his bones, how long would it last?

Rotoya took another sip of wine, the bottle sitting nearly empty next to her. The more she drank, the more she realized the nanobots wouldn't allow her to get drunk anymore. A blessing and a curse, as far as she was concerned.

The bar door was left open, allowing a breeze to flutter in and caress Rotoya's cheek. That and the wine, with the dark of night shielding them —despite the danger they were in, there was a comfort in it.

"More of a brandy kind of woman, myself," Rotoya started, "but I can see why people buy barrels of this stuff from Derek."

Rachel nodded her head, taking a sip from her own glass. Rotoya wasn't sure if she did it out of boredom as well or if she was just following her chief's lead. Derek had set himself up on the roof of the building next to them, and Kaela and Eric were hidden in the alley with their knives and pistols ready to ambush whichever of Caleb's soldiers came along next. That left the basement empty, save for the soldiers and officers tied up. The honey smell had become more than they could bear.

Another car had come, holding four more soldiers. They went down easily with everyone's help. Just like last time, two of them were officers. With two patrols missing, Caleb would suspect something. One more patrol, and they would be ready to attack.

In a moment of quiet between the clacks of glass on wood, something stopped Rotoya. She held a single hand up, a signal for Rachel to get ready. In the distance, a tapping sounded. Almost like… footsteps?

Rotoya stood from the bar and walked out the door, fists clenched as she leaned against the frame, waiting for more soldiers to come. She looked up at Derek, who could see them before she could. His silhouette made no signal from the shadows, but his head kept turning from her to the street, and she signaled Rachel again, preparing herself for whatever fight was coming their way.

The footsteps closed in on them, and Rotoya crossed her arms, drawing up the words she would say when Caleb rounded the corner. She took a single deep breath and watched as a man rounded the corner, his face pale. When he saw her, he turned the other way and ran, but a voice rang out in the night.

"George?" Eric said. He emerged from the darkness, knife and gun dangling from his hands.

Rotoya had never seen a look like that on Eric's face—pale and scared but also relieved. Those black eyes watered, and Kaela emerged from behind him, mirroring his expression.

Derek climbed down from the building, and after he feasted his eyes upon them, he turned his gaze, full of rage, on her.

Eric approached George, hesitant, as if he thought it wasn't real. He smiled weakly, and Eric smiled back. They embraced, and tears ran down Eric's face.

"You're alive," was all Eric said.

George said nothing, too busy tightening his grip around Eric.

Derek approached her, a scowl like no other upon his face. "Did you know?"

The man did look familiar. He had the same round belly as the man in the cell near Lance. Caleb hadn't told her a thing about him, even when she asked.

Rotoya didn't meet Derek's eyes. "If I knew, I would have told you."

If this was the man in the cell, then how did he escape?

And what did that mean for Lance?

Some deeper part of Eric told him to fight against the tears trailing down his cheeks, but as he embraced the man that had practically raised him all these years, he didn't care. He told whatever was urging him to fight it to shut its mouth, and he held tight to the closest thing to a father he'd ever had.

George cried too. He tried repeatedly to talk to Eric, but he couldn't. Neither of them could.

He was alive. *Alive.* And Caleb would burn for making Eric think otherwise.

Moments passed, and when they finally parted, all they could do was smile at each other.

"How are you here?" Eric asked, finally able to speak, wiping the tears from his face. He glanced at Rotoya to see if she noticed, but she averted her gaze to Kaela, who was standing close by with crossed arms and a scowl aimed at the ground.

George looked behind him as if scared he'd been followed. "Caleb—he found me with Malcolm and had me brought to Landreau Corp."

A shadow grew over Eric's heart. "Did he hurt you?"

"No," George said. "I mean, he locked me in a freezing-cold cell, but he didn't hurt me."

Eric paused. "Lance… Did you see Lance at all? Is he okay?"

George nodded. "He's the whole reason I escaped. He…" He closed his mouth in a tight line, as if deciding whether what he wanted to say should be said at all. "Did you know that he…"

"He has the nanobots in him, yes. Is that how he helped you escape?"

George paused, and he shifted his eyes toward Rotoya and Rachel. "Uh, Eric… You want to explain your new friends?"

"I think we should all catch each other up to speed."

They retreated into the bar. By the time everyone was done talking, Kaela had finished Rotoya's bottle of wine and was working on a second, rubbing her temples. Nobody had managed to escape the Rose, as far as George knew. Caleb had been too fast, too wild in his rampage.

Kaela's eyes were watery. Eric didn't allow himself to show it, but he wished he could reach an arm out to her, tell her something to make her feel better. But no words would comfort that pain. She'd lost an entire family, and considering the heartache Eric had felt at just losing George, he could only imagine what she felt.

"So… Lance has already managed to control at least two of the guards," Derek said following a long silence.

George nodded. He glanced at Eric every few seconds as if he couldn't believe he was here.

How long did he think he would be stuck in that cell? Did he think he'd be forgotten? The thought itself put a dark hole in Eric's chest. He owed Lance. If Lance hadn't found him, Eric might never have known George survived the fire.

He shook the thought away when Kaela spoke.

"So he's making progress," Kaela said, her words starting to slur. She blinked like she realized it and slid the bottle away. "Do you think Caleb caught on?"

George shook his head. "That's what I'm concerned about. He made one of the guards attack the other two at the exit. And I think he made the other one fire gunshots in the basement to distract them."

"If Caleb suspects anything, Lance could be in trouble." Kaela didn't look at Eric, but the worry behind her eyes said it all. If Lance was in danger, Eric would burn down all of Landreau Corp to get to him.

"Wait." Rotoya stared at nothing for a moment. "I think something's coming."

After a moment, they moved. Eric ordered George to hide in the cellar. Derek climbed the stairwell of the neighboring building, and Eric and Kaela buried themselves in the alley, weapons at the ready. Rotoya stood in front of the bar.

A vehicle sped toward them—an armored vehicle, judging by the heavy rumble of its engine.

Eric's adrenaline pumped, and he balanced on his feet as he crouched. He was ready to spring. The darkness of the alley sheltered him.

Headlights flashed, and an armored vehicle parked in front of Rotoya and Rachel. One step on the gas pedal, and it would run them over.

No soldiers clambered out. Rotoya cocked her head to the side as she stepped toward the armored vehicle. Then the door opened.

Caleb stepped out.

Rotoya hesitated then sauntered to Caleb with her chin high. "Still haven't found anything. We've been waiting for backup forever. What took you so long? And where are the officers I asked for?" She looked back at where Rachel was leaned against the wall.

Caleb looked up at the night sky with a smile on his face. A cool night breeze whistled past as if he had summoned it himself.

Eric gripped his cane tighter. A charge hung in in the air. A fight was coming.

Caleb looked Rotoya in the eye. Something in the wind faltered. Caleb's veins flashed, and he backhanded her.

Rotoya flew back, shattering the glass window and landing on a table. The wood splintered beneath her weight. Rachel called her name and sprinted to her side. Rotoya coughed, and purple blood spilled from her mouth. She pressed a hand to her burns, and when she removed it, her palm was covered with violet blood.

Eric flinched when Caleb spoke.

"I know you're here, Eric!" Caleb yelled. "What a clever little plan you cooked up. Bring Lance to me, wrapped up in a little bow so he can control my men like puppets." He laughed. "I appreciate the effort, I really do. And as a gesture of good faith, I'll give you one hour to come to Landreau Corp, or I kill your son. I think we've all had our fun playing cat and mouse."

Derek's finger itched to pull the trigger. He had a direct shot at Caleb's head. If he fired a few rounds into each of his legs, then his head, maybe it would be enough of a distraction for Kaela and Eric to come in and separate his head from his neck. Anger burned his skin with every word Caleb spoke. He was alone, vulnerable. It was almost too easy.

He looked down the alley where Eric and Kaela were hiding, searching for some approval or disapproval from Eric, some other opinion besides his own. His mind was too clouded by revenge.

He spotted them crouched and waiting. Eric looked up at Derek and shook his head. *No.*

The sight sent a prickle of white-hot rage up Derek's spine. His instincts told him no, as well—told him that a lone man standing in the middle of the street, almost *asking* to be shot, was an obvious trap. Even so, the monster was in his sights.

Rob flashed in his eyes. His body appeared behind Caleb, lying in a pool of his own blood. He twitched then went still. It was the chief who had pulled the trigger, and his rage for her still held strong. But it was Caleb who'd controlled her, who'd made her see the world through his sick perspective. As far as he was concerned, they were both responsible.

He pulled the trigger.

CHAPTER 30
SUICIDE MISSION

Lance reminded himself that he was alive. He was breathing. He could make it out of this. The cold of the cell dug deeper into his bones, burrowing like ice picks. He shivered violently, and his teeth chattered. The cell closed in on him more with every passing minute, and the darkness was disorienting. The floor beneath him swayed, and every direction melded with each other.

His attempts to speak to the beast were met with silence, so he whispered aloud to it.

It made no sound, no movement within his stomach, but Lance felt deep down that it could hear him. That it was listening. That was all he needed. It didn't matter if the beast was just a part of him. He would take anything at this point, anything that would listen to him. Anything to feel less alone.

Lance sucked the frosty air down his throat and into his lungs. *There has to be a way out. There's always a way out, right?*

Sleep hung over him like a knife, but as it weighed down on him more and more, terror banged on the walls of his chest. If he fell asleep in this cold, he wasn't so sure he would wake up. For a split second, he closed his eyes, regardless of the consequences. He just wanted *out*—out of this cell.

But as he drifted, he gasped and opened his eyes. His heart hammered. *No,* he thought. *Not like this.*

Lance stood and bumbled around the cell. He felt along the walls, guiding himself. Keep moving. That was the goal now. *Keep moving.*

He didn't stop, and as the cold followed him in the darkness like a silent predator, he spoke to the beast again. Not a whisper this time. "If you can hear me, if there is any possible way you can help me, please do it." The plea bounced off the walls, and doubt crept in that the beast could even hear him at all.

Lance's hand grazed something on the wall. He stopped moving and felt again, then again.

A crack was in the wall.

Not a small one, either. A profound crack in one of the stone bricks. Lance ran his hand over it again, and a spark of hope flickered in his freezing chest.

Lance drew a deep, steadying breath, and he clawed at the stone. His nails dug deep. Pain seared through his fingers, but he kept going. He banged on the stone, reached his leg up high enough to kick it, then clawed at it more.

It went on for minutes, maybe hours. Time faded, and eventually, a warm trickle of blood ran down his hand, then his arm, dripping from his elbow onto the floor. He embraced the warmth it brought him, faint as it was, then swore as it fell cold within seconds.

Tears welled in his eyes the longer the brick didn't budge. He seethed at the pain in his fingertips. He shook his head and pulled one last time.

A crack echoed in the room.

At first, Lance smiled. He pulled even harder. More cracking.

Then an excruciating pain swept through his fingers.

His nails… The cracking came from his nails.

He pulled anyway. If this was the last time he could do it, he would make it count. He braced his leg against the wall and pulled with all his weight. The louder the pain screamed, the harder he pulled. A yell escaped his mouth, reverberating in the desolate room.

Finally, a loud snap echoed through the room, and Lance lost his grip on the stone. He stumbled and fell onto his back. Something clattered next to him, and he allowed the tears to come as he felt along his fingers. He found the pads that had been hidden underneath his now-missing fingernails and swallowed the urge to vomit.

Lance cursed in the darkness as if doing so would help.

He reached over to grab the nails that had landed beside him. But his fingers grazed painfully against something harder and colder than his nails.

He picked it up and rolled it in his hand. Sharp, like a fragment—a cold fragment of stone.

Lance ran to the wall and felt along the brick. An indentation marked the wall, where a small shard of stone had chipped off.

Lance allowed the tears to come.

He had hope.

He had a chance.

Sick satisfaction swept through Derek as he fired into Caleb's legs, a burst of rounds in each one, just as he'd planned. Amethyst blood spurted from the wounds.

Caleb fell to his knees, groaning in pain. Eric and Kaela leapt from their hiding spot. They fired their pistols as they closed in, Caleb's body flinching with every bullet.

Just as Caleb stood, Eric and Kaela leapt for him, plunging their blades into his neck. Time froze for an instant, then Caleb fell to his hands and knees. His veins flashed, and just as he had the chief, he swatted Eric and Kaela away with inhuman strength. They flew back, sliding across the asphalt. Derek fired again, this time at the blades, a desperate attempt to guide them deeper through his neck. Then he fired at his head. Surely, if enough bullets filled Caleb's head, it would come off.

"Get his head off!" Eric yelled to whoever would listen.

The chief hadn't returned from inside the bar, but Rachel dashed from the broken window. She sprinted at Caleb with a shout, her veins glowing. Derek's breath caught in his throat. She had to make it.

Caleb noticed Rachel sprinting at him and clawed at the daggers in his throat. Just as Rachel came within arm's reach, he ripped one from his neck and plunged it into Rachel's shoulder. He steered her with the blade and threw her against the armored vehicle.

Caleb ripped the second dagger out and rubbed his bleeding neck. He smiled down at Rachel as he raised the blade to finish her off.

Derek shot it out of his hand.

Caleb swore and cradled his now-bleeding fingers. He shook his head, and his veins glowed brighter than ever. He laughed and scratched his nails deep into his arms, bright-purple blood leaking from the wounds.

The blood moved, traveling down his fingers then winding down to the ground. It didn't drip like blood should but… *moved.*

Derek could only watch, paralyzed, as the blood formed into thin ropes at the tips of Caleb's fingers, glowing and humming.

Caleb smiled up at Derek and lashed his arm out. The whips stretched and sliced through the brick of the building. Derek threw himself back, narrowly dodging the strings of blood. Heat grazed his face as they barely missed him. He lay breathless as a chunk of the rooftop crumbled and clattered to the sidewalk below.

An engine roared to life, and Derek was back on his feet, pointing his rifle.

Caleb was driving away, the car swerving back and forth.

Derek shot at the tires, the bullets striking and sparking on the street. He was going too fast, driving too recklessly. Derek gritted his teeth and sprayed bullets at the car, wishing, hoping that somehow, at least one of them would reach their mark. He shot until no bullets were left in the magazine.

The vehicle left his sight, and the sound of the screeching tires faded. Derek dropped to his knees. So close—he'd been so close to avenging Rob. He threw the gun to the ground. "Dammit!" He punched the ground then punched it again. He panted, his heart thumping in his chest. Tears welled in his eyes, but he forced them back. Rob's face flashed in his vision. "I'm sorry…"

Voices echoed from the street. Eric muttered something to Kaela.

Rotoya groaned and asked Rachel if she was okay, stepping out from the bar. Her voice was distorted, as if her tongue was made of lead.

Derek sat there for a long minute, watching the empty streets as he collected himself and steadied his breathing. He climbed down the stairwell, preparing himself for a tongue lashing when the dark glare in Eric's eyes pointed at him.

"I told you not to take the shot," Eric said, not raising his voice. He didn't need to. His eyes did the yelling for him. "You'd better have a good reason for not listening to me."

Derek scoffed. "Did you not see what we just did?"

"I did more than just see it," Eric spat. He groaned and put a hand to his chest where Caleb had hit him. Kaela did the same. A twinge of guilt shot through Derek.

"We almost had him."

"No, we pissed him off. If he wasn't already on guard, he certainly is now. He'll be tougher next time."

"We'll deal with it."

Eric narrowed his eyes. "If he hurts Lance because of what we just did, I will personally make sure it reflects on you."

"Can we argue later?" Kaela asked with a grunt. She gently massaged her chest and coughed as if to test the pain. Her hand moved to her rib, and she hissed as she pressed into it. She swore.

The chief fiddled with her jaw. "Thr-o-ken," she said. "Gib it a minute."

"Suck it up," Derek spat. Just looking at her sent floods of hatred into him. Once this was over, he would kill her the same way she'd killed Rob—trapped under his boot, taking bullet after bullet until she finally went still. He kept his face neutral, but the frenzy settling in his chest burned his heart.

Concern painted Rachel's face. The chief stood, the nanobots flashing. By the time they all returned to the cellar, her jaw had healed, though she still rubbed at it as if it was sore.

"So, Lance got caught," the chief said, speaking to George. Guilt etched across his face.

"We're getting him back," Eric said. Not a suggestion or an order but a simple statement of fact.

Derek wished he could share that confidence.

Eric looked at Rotoya. "Can you control these soldiers?"

Rotoya surveyed the unconscious bodies, tied up and leaned against the wine barrels, then nodded. "Like I said, I can only control my own officers, but yeah, I should be able to… I think."

"How are you going to do that?" George asked.

Rotoya scanned her officers. "According to Caleb, Malcolm said the drug has something to do with connection. My officers have always been close to me, so my connection with them is stronger than Caleb's. Caleb took my officers from me when my heart stopped. The way I see it… if *their* hearts stop"—she gestured to her officers—"I may be able to get them back on my side. If not… we're screwed." She crossed her arms. "And I just let several of my own officers die."

A moment passed, then another.

Derek crossed his arms. "Try not to stab us in the back."

Rotoya shifted her weight. "Maybe you forgot, but it's in my best interests to kill Caleb too."

"And then what? You're going to shoot us next?"

"Watch it," Rachel said, her hand hovering over her pistol. Her shoulder had already healed.

Rotoya held her hand out, and Rachel relaxed. "Hate me all you want, but I want to stop Caleb as much as you do, so until that happens, we need to work together."

"Whatever," Derek muttered, leaning against the wall next to the armory door. If any of her officers made a move, he would grab a gun from inside and finish them off.

Rotoya stole a deep breath then looked at Eric. Her voice croaked as she said, "Do it."

Eric nodded and slipped his blade from his cane. Without any hesitation, he shoved the dagger into the chest of the closest officer. Rotoya shut her eyes and looked away. Rachel put a comforting hand on her shoulder.

Derek scowled.

When he was done, Rotoya let out a pained breath, and for a moment, she stared at the dead body of her officer. She took a step closer and kneeled next to him then placed her hand on his body and shut her eyes.

After several moments passed, Rotoya shook her head. "I don't think I can… Wait."

Rotoya opened her eyes, glowing bright and purple.

Derek rested his hand on the knob of the armory door. Kaela put a hand on his arm, shaking her head. He settled down, letting the knob go.

The officer's veins glowed a chilling purple. The wounds in his chest glowed the brightest, closing rapidly. When the wound closed, a long silence spread through the room.

Rotoya furrowed her brows and balled her fists.

Suddenly, the officer gasped for air.

Rotoya let out a long sigh. "Thank God."

Derek wasn't sure what he'd expected to see, but the officer roused and stood as simply as if he'd been given a light kick to the ribs. His wound was gone.

Rotoya straightened her posture. "Raise your arms."

The officer did so without question.

"Now lower them."

Again, he did so without question.

George's jaw dropped. "Incredible."

Rotoya gulped then nodded at Eric. One by one, Eric shoved his blade into the chests of the officers, and one by one, Rotoya commanded them back to life. They all gasped for air and rose like zombies from the dead.

Derek expected Rotoya to look proud or accomplished. Instead, her face was ridden with guilt. "Well, shit, would you look at that. I did it." She crossed her arms. "You all know what this means, don't you?" Some of the guilt scrubbed away, replaced with a wicked smile. "When we attack Landreau Corp, any of my officers we kill… I can bring to my side."

"In other words," Kaela said, a smirk on her face, "the more you kill, the bigger your army grows."

"Wouldn't call it an army, but yeah, effectively." Rotoya regarded her officers, guilt once again shadowing her face. "And I have no doubts Caleb will send my officers after me now that he knows I'm on your side. The man's pride has always been a weakness."

"Likes the sound of his own voice too," Eric said.

"Reminds me a little of someone I know," Kaela said with a sly grin.

Rotoya shifted her weight, blinking rapidly.

Derek raised an eyebrow. *Is she nervous?*

"Are you all ready to bring down Caleb Landreau once and for all?" Rotoya asked.

Her officers nodded in unison.

She straightened her shoulders. "Grab the guns from the armory and let's go."

"What do we do with them?" Derek asked, gesturing toward the remaining soldiers, unconscious and tied up against the barrels. "I don't want them waking up under my bar."

"Already handled," Rotoya said. Her veins flashed, and once her officers armed themselves, they hoisted the soldiers' bodies up and carried them out. "We'll lay them all in an alley. By the time they wake up, it'll be too late."

Derek didn't respond. He took a long deep breath and walked out with them. Whether they were going to their deaths or their victory didn't matter. Caleb was going to die by the end of tonight, one way or another.

Walking at his side, Kaela leaned in close to whisper, "Are you okay?"

Derek stopped glaring at the back of Rotoya's head and turned to Kaela. Worry swam in her eyes. "No… I'm sorry I jumped the gun."

"I get it," Kaela said. "I've been there. But we're close to finishing this, okay? You need to focus."

Derek nodded.

"We'll get your revenge after this."

Rotoya loosed a steadying breath ahead of him then leaned over to Eric and muttered, "I can say it now, but I genuinely had my doubts that this would even work."

Eric's heart raced faster the closer they drove to Landreau Corp. The armored vehicle they'd hidden in the alley was carrying them to the fight of their lives. Eric smiled in anticipation.

The smile lasted until Lance crossed his mind for the third time since they started the drive. If they'd hurt him in the slightest, the things he would do…

But a spark of hope flickered inside him. Caleb had said nothing about killing Lance. He knew Lance was infected with the nanobots now, which had to make him somewhat useful. That was the bit of hope Eric cradled as they rode through the empty streets. They wouldn't be empty much longer, he hoped.

Of all the insane plans Eric had come up with and been involved in, this was certainly the craziest. But once they killed Caleb, once his head rolled across those nice company carpets, it would be over. The city of Arachna could go back to normal. Hopefully Agni as well.

Eric swallowed the bile that rose in his throat. Never had his nerves attacked him so, not since the night Carrie gave birth. He wondered what she would think about all this. Would she consider him a good father? He wasn't—but he would be better. He would rescue Lance, take down Caleb, and be the father Lance deserved.

"Almost there," Rotoya said.

The vehicle stopped, and Eric stepped out. Derek and Kaela followed.

Rotoya smiled as another armored vehicle drove from around a corner and pulled up beside her. "You'd better hurry and do what you need to do." She tapped her wrist. "Tick tock."

Eric slinked into the shadows of the alley, Derek and Kaela behind him. His legs were heavy as he wound through the shadows, one leg still aching from his injury. The hum of the armored vehicle faded the farther they traveled.

They padded down the next four blocks in utter silence. As much as Caleb deserved it, killing him wasn't a priority until Lance was safe.

They stopped once they reached the end of the final alley. Landreau Corp stood grand and tall in front of them—a tower of sheer greed, full of men and women that would kill them in a heartbeat.

"Looks like there are more guards at the back entrance than last time," Derek said. "George said there were only two. I'm counting four."

They turned toward him, but he wasn't there. Then they looked up.

Derek was hanging from the stairwell. He continued, "I don't see any other extra security besides that." He dropped down and landed with a quiet grace. "Not too surprising. After all, he invited us here."

"The real security will be inside," Eric said.

"Still, we need to be careful."

Rotoya's vehicles revved in the distance. The three of them shared a knowing smile, and seconds later, tires screeched.

The soldiers out front yelled and pointed their guns.

The soldiers fired a hail of bullets then dove out of the way just in time as the two armored vehicles sped past and crashed into the entrance of the building. A thunderous boom shook the night, and Eric covered his ears. The entrance collapsed, glass shattered, and the soldiers not quick enough to dive out of the way were laid out on the ground. Still.

The soldiers that had dived out of the way clambered to their feet and took aim. Rotoya's officers were too fast, leaning out the windows and shooting the soldiers dead.

The guards in the parking lot sprinted inside Landreau Corp.

"That's one hell of a distraction," Eric said. "Let's go."

Gunshots rattled their ears as they sprinted across the street and through the parking lot.

Eric paused at the back door, his hand resting on the handle. "We ready?"

Kaela and Derek nodded, and they dashed inside. The moment they rushed in, two guards took cover in the hall, shooting at the two vehicles crashed halfway into the building.

The vehicle doors were open, and the officers, Rachel, and Rotoya all opened fire from their makeshift cover.

Eric and Kaela made short work of the two guards hiding in the hall.

"Which way?" Derek asked, standing by the door to the stairwell. His voice was nearly drowned out by the gunshots booming through the hall.

"You and Kaela go upstairs. I'll head downstairs. If you find Lance, bring him back here. If he's injured, take him out the back entrance and protect him."

Kaela snorted. "He's got the nanobots in him. I doubt *he'll* be the one that needs the protecting."

Derek huffed a laugh in agreement, and they parted ways.

Eric flew down the stairs, encountering two guards along the way. The first one only took a kick to the stomach to fall back and snap his neck on the stairs. The second's head and body fell separately with one swipe of Eric's blade.

The farther Eric descended the stairs, the more his mind shouted for one thing.

Lance!

Lance held onto the fragment of stone harder than he should have. Blood leaked from his hands, but he couldn't let go, as if it would fall into the darkness and never return should he drop it. In the bitter silence, the sound of blood rushing to his ears reminded him that he was alive. The air reeked of mold and copper. His head spun.

Footsteps resonated from the other side of the door, lightly tapping against the stone. A surge of adrenaline shocked Lance's heart, and he fumbled with the piece of stone in his hands, readying himself. His fingers shook with the cold clamping down on them.

The footsteps reached the door, and the lock clicked. Lance crouched, preparing to spring. But the door didn't open. Toward the bottom of the door, a small window slid open. Lance leapt.

Two hands tossed a tray of bread down onto the dark floor. Just as the hands retracted from the window, Lance caught one and stabbed the stone piece into its palm.

The officer screamed and reached his other hand into the cell to pull it out of Lance's grip. He stabbed twice more into the man's hand and arm, and when the other hand grabbed at Lance, he deflected it. Lance braced his legs and pulled, dragging the soldier farther into the cell and smashing his head into the door. The soldier grunted, and before he could pull back, Lance reached out and blindly grabbed at him until the cold grip of a pistol grazed his sore fingers.

The soldier's helmet clattered to the floor, and teeth bore down on Lance's arm. Lance screamed in pain as teeth punctured his skin. He pulled the firearm out of its holster and ripped his arm from the soldier's toothy grip.

Lance kept his hold on the soldier's arm as he aimed.

"No!" the guard shouted, but Lance fired.

He fired and fired until the gun clicked. His ears rang. He tossed the pistol aside and reached through the slot again, grabbing the keys at the guard's waist.

Lance sat still, holding the keys to his chest, the smallest bit of light entering the room. Even as dim as it was, Lance's eyes stung at the sudden brightness. He blinked it away and reached out of the slot once more, keys in hand. He cursed as he fumbled with them. He contorted his arm, his joints popping as he found the lock and inserted one of the keys.

His shoulder aching against the cold stone, he twisted.

The door clicked, a brassy click that echoed through the cell. Lance's heart swelled as he pushed the door open. He fell out into the dim hallway, right next to the soldier's body. Purple blood splashed on his arms and face, but he didn't care. He was free.

He stood, leaning against the wall, his eyes stinging at the dim orange lights hanging above him. Blood leaked from the deep bite marks embedded in his arm. He grabbed the empty gun and drunkenly stepped down the hall. He shouldn't have shot the gun that many times; he'd gotten carried away. Regardless, a metal object was a metal object, and it would do fine to smash through helmets.

When Lance reached the end of the hall, two guards rushed down the stairs. Likely the same two that had guarded his first cell. He was too drained to take on two at once, so he slid into a small patch of darkness and let them run past. They noticed the body and rushed to it, examining his injuries and looking inside the cell. Seconds later, they ran back down the hall and disappeared up the stairs.

Lance's head was pounding, but he carried on. He ascended one set of stairs then another until the dark stone turned to concrete. Tears welled in his eyes the closer he got to familiar ground.

He stopped when the stairway door flew open. He looked, but whoever ran through had already dashed down the cell-lined hall where he and George had been kept. Maybe it was Caleb. Or another guard. Either way, Lance didn't want to find out.

Hiding in the darkness, he scurried down the narrow hallway and crept into the stairway, rushing up the set of stairs to the lobby. His weakness began to dwindle slightly, enough to let him walk with more speed. The beast was still quiet.

How long had he been in that cell?

Lance passed the bodies of the two guards that had just run past him. Before he could even consider what had happened, he stopped and listened to the rumbling above him. *Gunfire?*

"What in the..." Lance shook off his confusion. He had no time to waste. He continued his ascent.

Something stirred inside him. His hopes rose, and when a small, weak whine whimpered from within him, he sighed in relief.

"I can't believe I'm saying this," Lance whispered, "but I am so glad to have you back."

The beast didn't purr, but he could feel it, worn out and tired. It wasn't ready to fight.

It curled up in Lance's stomach and slumbered. It would need as much rest as it could fit in before Lance would ultimately have to fight.

He reached the hall on the main floor, and the ringing in his ears worsened as gunshots and shouts bellowed from the lobby. Two more bodies were sprawled across the floor.

What the hell is happening up here?

Lance turned to dash out the back entrance, but something shifted inside him. The beast growled, already sounding stronger than moments before.

Lance hesitated. "Are you sure? You're still weak."

The beast purred in response, and Lance's veins glowed. He knew the next question the beast was about to ask, but Lance stopped it before it had the chance.

"I'm not giving you any more room than you have." He sighed. "Selfish."

It growled again, but Lance ignored it and turned around, his and the beast's curiosity taking hold. He reached the end of the hall and peeked around the corner. Two armored vehicles protruded in through the entrance, and two groups of black-clad soldiers were firing at each other.

Lance's jaw fell as Rotoya fired from behind the open door of a vehicle, spraying bullets at the opposing side.

The beast chirped curiously, and Lance just shook his head. "I don't know either, but…" A laugh played at his lips as a sudden rush traveled along his body, as if adrenaline was replacing his blood. He looked down at his veins, flashing purple for a second before returning to normal. "Damn, it *is* pretty cool." He clenched his fist. "Fine… maybe just a bit more room."

Eric reached the bottom of the stairwell. He swung the door open and entered a small concrete hallway. Metal doors lined the hall. Eric ignored the biting cold and glanced into each of them.

Empty.

Every single one of them was empty.

Surely these were the cells George had mentioned. Eric whirled and dashed back down the hallway, rounding the corner to his right. Another hallway faced him, dark and narrow; this one wasn't lined with any cells. Eric traveled down the hall and took another right then walked down a set of stairs. He shivered as an even colder air weighed down upon him. Much colder than it should have been. By the time he reached the end of the stairs, his breath formed clouds of smoke in front of him.

He hurried forward, deeper into the hallway. Concrete turned to dark stone bricks, and with them came an even harsher cold. The colder the air became, the hotter Eric's rage grew. *Are they keeping Lance* here*?* Dim orange lights hung on the wall, barely bright enough to guide his way.

That ghastly honeyed smell tainted Eric's nose, and he gripped his cane tighter. "Please tell me you're okay, Lance."

Eric descended another set of stairs, where the body of an officer down the hall lay next to a cell door, barely ajar.

He's free, Eric thought. His heart rose, but questions swirled around in his head. *Is he even still in the building, or is he running for the bar?*

Surely he would've heard the gunfire or the car crashing into the building.

Eric shook those thoughts from his head. Lance was free, and he had to find him before Caleb did.

Eric sprinted back to the stairwell. The thought of Lance being killed by Caleb made his blood run cold. His legs pounded against the ground. He forgot about being quiet—forgot about the nagging pain in his ankle. Anyone who bothered to get in his way would find themselves without a head.

Derek raced up the stairwell, Kaela at his side. Soldiers that met them died within seconds. A stray bullet had scraped Derek's arm, and Kaela had nearly taken one to the chest, but they didn't stop. They each had a pistol, stolen from the first two guards that'd had the displeasure of running into them.

The building had so many floors that they couldn't afford to give the rooms more than a passing glance. Soldiers waited in some, and they got bullets in their heads before they could fire first. Derek and Kaela had traveled up countless floors, and they slowed their pace, out of breath and exhausted. If not for Rotoya's distraction, they'd have been overwhelmed minutes ago.

"You don't think…" Kaela said between light pants. She cursed and muttered, "I hate stairs." Then she continued her original thought. "You don't think Caleb has Lance with him, do you? And that he's being guarded by, like, a ton of men?"

Derek regained control of his breathing, but he couldn't fight and climb stairs for much longer. "I don't know. But we knew this was a trap before we went in, so it would be no surprise if he did."

Kaela rolled her eyes, not at him, but at the soldier standing at the top of the current flight of stairs they were climbing. He made no effort to reach for his sidearm—just stood there as if frozen in time.

"Look, buddy, I'm sick of getting that nasty purple blood all over my clothes. Let's just go our separate ways, huh?" Kaela offered. Her voice held a twinge of sarcasm, and her hand casually rested on her hip. Her gun and knife were held at the ready.

The soldier remained frozen. Silently, he watched them. Then, as if time resumed at his spot on the stairs, he kicked off the railing and into the air. Kaela and Derek aimed their guns, but a sweeping kick sent both weapons clattering to the floor.

The soldier looked at them again, assessing them through that dark visor. His gait was casual. He had all the time in the world.

A distraction, Derek thought. And if he was trying to stall them, then Lance had to be close. Derek snarled and lunged. The soldier sidestepped and swept Derek's feet from under him.

Derek landed hard on his back, the air leaving him. Kaela swiped her knife at the soldier, but he sent a punch to her face, and blood spilled from her nose. He ripped the knife from her grip and kicked her into the wall.

Derek returned to his feet, winded, and jumped onto the soldier's back.

The soldier grunted and threw himself backward, slamming Derek into the wall.

Derek's back made a crackling sound, and he fell flat. The soldier raised Kaela's knife, but Derek craned his neck as the blade plunged into the ground, slicing his ear.

Derek swore and sent a blind kick to the soldier's groin. The soldier stumbled back but recovered quickly.

Kaela joined Derek's side, wiping the blood from her nose and helping him to his feet. Derek put a hand to the cut in his ear.

The soldier lunged, and Derek dodged and kicked him into the wall. He hit the handrail with a grunt. Another kick, and the soldier's visor cracked. The soldier recovered and lunged again, but Derek dodged. The soldier was getting sloppy.

Derek punched his helmet, and the impact sent the soldier to the floor, the visor cracking even more. His knuckles bled and stung, and he hissed as pieces of the fiberglass splintered in his skin. The soldier made to stand, but Derek kicked him back down.

"Go on ahead," Derek said to Kaela, hissing at his bleeding knuckles. "This may take a while."

Kaela hesitated then grabbed her knife and gun from the floor and disappeared up the stairs.

Derek stretched his bleeding hand and readied for another attack.

The soldier leapt and wrapped his legs around Derek's neck. They spun, and Derek was thrown to the floor. He rolled with the landing, but the soldier threw a kick to his stomach, sending him into the wall and knocking the air out of him. Nausea ripped at his stomach.

The soldier kept his distance, allowing Derek the time to stand.

They stared each other down, Derek panting while the soldier calmly paced. His eyes were visible through the broken visor, glowing bright and purple.

The soldier charged once more, and Derek stood his ground. They collided, and Derek nearly lost his footing. Gritting his teeth, he grabbed the soldier by the helmet and sidestepped, slamming his head into the railing. The visor shattered, and the soldier yelled. His voice was clear.

Almost familiar.

The soldier ripped his helmet off, small shards of fiberglass stuck in his face. His veins glowed a bright purple.

Derek raised his fist to throw a punch, but he stopped, his legs turning to jelly. The soldier clawed at his face, removing most of the shards, violet blood spilling all over the floor.

Derek choked as he tried to speak.

"Rob?"

CHAPTER 31
NOT AGAIN

Kaela dashed up the stairs. Her legs and lungs burned.

She reached the next floor, and as she peeked into one room, she paused. A different layout faced her. Boardrooms dotted the floor. Kaela only had to glance through the large glass windows to see that nobody was in them.

One boardroom, its blinds closed, sat against the wall at the very end of the room.

Kaela's gut told her to run. Her legs turned to concrete as she took the first step toward it. She almost sheathed her dagger at her leg, but something stopped her. Instead, she tucked it into her waistband, covered it with her shirt, and kept her gun at the ready.

The silence in the room was more deafening than the gunshots downstairs, and the ringing in her ears didn't help.

Kaela crept to the door and placed her hand on the cold knob. She rested it there for what felt like forever, every muscle in her body urging her to turn back, to let go of the knob. But she ignored that urge, and with a deep breath, she shoved the door open, painting a careless look on her face.

Even with the careless look, she flinched at the sight of Caleb.

She'd expected soldiers, maybe even a tied-up Lance, but he was alone.

Caleb was sitting on a chair, leaned back and looking at a large TV that nearly covered the entire wall. Dozens of camera feeds, showing areas where Kaela hadn't even seen any cameras: the back entrance, the stairwell, Derek fighting the soldier. Fighting… Rob? Her heart dropped to her stomach, not only at the sight of Rob infected with the nanobots, but Caleb whirling around in his chair to face her. She raised her chin at him, and his smile widened.

"What a pretty neck," Caleb said. "I can't wait to wrap my hands around it."

Kaela spat in his direction, for what little it did. "You sent Rob so Derek wouldn't come up here."

Caleb laughed. "I made sure not too many soldiers took the stairs. I wanted to tire you out, not kill you. But you two were still moving along rather nicely, so yes, I ruined the surprise a bit early and sent Rob down there. It worked, didn't it?"

Kaela's heart pounded, and her legs twitched. Her body screamed at her to run. "So you got what you want. Why do you want me dead, of all people? Why not find a way to lead Eric up here?" She scanned the TV for Eric or Lance, but Caleb shut it off, plunging the room into near darkness. Moonlight shone through the bulky windows.

"Because I see an opportunity," Caleb said. "And I don't like to pass up an opportunity."

A shadow disturbed the moonlight. Kaela whirled, but a dagger plunged into her side before she could avoid it. The gun slipped from her fingers. She gasped, and tears trailed down her cheeks as she sank to the ground, looking up at Amari's face.

She wore a sleek black dress, and her veins glowed a vibrant purple.

She met Kaela's eyes with a lopsided smile. "Hey, sweetheart. How do you like the new look?"

Eric reached the main floor. Gunshots rang out like rumbling thunder. Three soldiers took cover behind the corner of the hallway, one of them holding a riot shield.

Eric grinned. *Well, isn't that cute?*

They fired relentlessly toward the entrance, bullets whizzing past them. Eric stabbed the first one, covering his mouth so that he couldn't yell. The soldier with the riot shield died with a blade in his neck. With a swipe of his scythe, the final soldier's head rolled into the lobby. Eric ripped the shield from the dead soldier's iron grip.

Primal anger flooded through him. If he didn't find his son, he would kill every soldier in this building until he did. He wiped the purple blood from his face, the smell intoxicating.

Eric cleaned his blades and peeked around the corner. Dozens of soldiers fired at the chief and her officers. They were holding strong, but the soldiers had shields. The doors of the armored vehicle were riddled with bullets, and Rotoya likely didn't have much ammo left, even with Derek's extra stock. Eric wouldn't be able to help against all those soldiers.

Something caught his eye. Purple blood splattered against the small window of a door across the lobby. Kaela's words rang in his head. She'd mentioned a break room somewhere in the lobby. That had to be it.

Eric sneaked behind the soldiers, holding the riot shield up for protection and camouflage. They were all too focused on the chief to even notice him.

A few bullets whizzed past. Fewer still dinged against the shield, sending a new flood of pure adrenaline through him.

Eric reached the break room, but before he could slip inside, a soldier flew through the door, breaking it from its hinges. Eric fell back, the body landing on top of him. He struggled and pushed the corpse off, leaving the riot shield behind as he rushed inside, both of his blades at the ready.

Eric froze. Purple blood coated the walls and floor, and bodies were scattered throughout the room. Some were intact, some not so much.

Three soldiers were left standing, and Lance faced them all. His veins were glowing a blindingly bright violet. He was covered in purple blood.

Eric watched in silent shock as Lance made short work of the three soldiers left. Faster than he'd ever seen a human move, Lance tore through them. The first two went down in a flurry of feral strikes and blood. The last soldier dropped his gun and could only step back in fear as Lance faced him and leapt on him. Punch after punch, Lance pounded the helmet he wore until the visor cracked then shattered. Still, Lance kept punching until purple blood sprayed with every slam of his fist into the soldier's face.

The soldier's body had long gone still, but Lance didn't stop. Finally, Eric stepped over the bodies, nearly slipping twice in the blood. He reached out to his son's shoulder. The moment he made contact, Lance whirled. Before he even had a chance to speak, Eric was lifted off the ground and slammed on the metal table.

Lance stared down at him, fist raised, eyes glowing. But he stopped himself. His purple eyes flashed with recognition, and slowly, his veins returned to normal. The piercing green returned.

Eric wanted to say his name, but a different word came out. "Son?"

Lance stared down at him for a long moment, then a drop of blood—red blood—dripped onto Eric's cheek. Lance looked down at his hand then back up at Eric and said, "I… I can explain."

"Later," Eric said. He looked out the door as the gunfire raged on.

Lance stared at the ground as if listening to something. He nodded. But as he made to leave the room, Eric grabbed his arm.

"What are you doing?"

Lance looked out at the lobby then back at Eric. His veins glowed again. "Making a distraction."

And with that, Lance grabbed a pistol from a fallen soldier, tossed another to Eric, and sprinted out of the room. Eric followed him.

Caleb's soldiers were distracted by the chief and her officers firing at them.

Lance's veins glowed once more, brighter than ever, and he dashed toward the group with little more than a pistol.

Eric gaped.

Lance tore through their lines like a walking sword. Their shields did little against him as he shattered a soldier's arm and stole a shield for himself. Shield in one hand and pistol in the other, Lance bashed their heads and fired at their legs. Some of their heads rolled from the impact of the shield hitting them.

The soldiers caught on to Lance's attack and fired at him. He threw his shield and rolled, picking a new one from the sea of bodies, blocking the gunshots and firing his own.

Rotoya and her officers mowed down the ones Lance didn't kill.

Eric shook his head to regain his focus. He sprinted, carving his own path through the soldiers. His blade served well to decapitate some of them. The shield did well as a weapon, but the only guards that cared to fire at him were shot down by Rotoya before they could take their aim. The rest were focused on the real threat mowing through their defenses.

Eric sliced and bashed the soldiers. Three nearly fired at him, but a spray of bullets from Rotoya's officers shredded them.

Lance showed no sign of stopping, no sign of tiring himself out. The soldiers were nothing but obstacles. He looked different. Like a beast that had been trapped for too long and was finally free, snapping at anything it could.

Eric sliced at the leg of a nearby soldier. Before he fell, Eric kicked him into another soldier. He whirled and threw his shield into their heads. They dropped like bricks.

Eric flipped the scythe from his cane, holding it in one hand and his blade in the other.

With Rotoya and Lance covering him, Eric whirled and danced on his own stage, slicing and stabbing.

Purple blood painted the floors.

Lance turned, and a soldier raised his gun to fire into his back. Eric threw his blade, and it found the officer's neck. He fired anyway, and a bullet penetrated Lance's back.

Time froze, and Eric shook his head. But Lance turned and rolled his shoulder in pain then continued fighting, his veins glowing brighter. The bullet fell from his back as if something had pushed it from him.

With a roar of anger, Lance threw his weight into a bash with his shield, knocking a soldier down. He raised the shield and planted it in the soldier's chest. Blood splattered across the floor, but somehow, the shield held. Lance swept up two more pistols and took cover behind the planted shield, firing shots from each side of it.

Eric dropped to the ground, out of breath, and watched as the men fell like flies. The chief ordered her men to fire until they were out of ammo, and they did. The chief firing from one side while Lance fired from the other rendered their shields useless, and in a matter of seconds, every single soldier was on the ground, either dead or dying.

Eric ducked as bullets whizzed over his head and bodies fell around him. Their empty gazes stared at him.

Groans of pain traveled across the lobby. Before Lance's veins returned to normal, he shot each of the groaning soldiers until Eric could hear nothing besides the ringing in his ears.

He coughed and sputtered as the smell overwhelmed him. A gag climbed to his throat, but he hid it with another cough.

Lance was breathless, painted with purple blood. He fell to his hands and knees.

Eric was at his side in an instant. "That was one hell of a distraction. Are you okay?"

Lance gulped down air. "Yeah… yeah, I just used up a lot of energy." He rolled his eyes at apparently nothing. "Okay, *he* used up a lot of energy."

Eric raised an eyebrow. "What the hell are you talking about?"

"Forget it."

"Rotoya," Eric said. "Get whatever ammo you can from these soldiers. Revive and take control of the ones that belong to you."

Rotoya stood, and her officers moved forward, guns still pointed. "If you decapitated any of my people—"

"Then it was an accident," Eric snapped back.

Rotoya scowled. She and Rachel began removing helmets from bodies, reviving any that were officers.

Eric turned his attention to Lance. "What did Caleb do to you?"

Lance shook his head. "It's not as bad as you think… He put me in this cell that… It blocked the nanobots from doing anything. They just shut down." He took another few seconds to catch his breath. "When I got out… the beast, it woke back up, and… it was like it had been building the whole time I was in there… I saw the fighting, and I just… snapped."

The beast? What was that supposed to mean? "Well, try not to snap on us next."

"No promises," Lance said, but he flashed a sarcastic smirk. "I just… lost control a little bit."

Eric scanned the sea of bodies around them. Several of Rotoya's men and women rose, their wounds healing. Even the chief seemed surprised by the bloodbath.

Eric sighed. "I'm glad you're okay."

Lance nodded. "Did George make it to the Rose?"

"Yes, he's—"

"Eric," Rotoya said. Her tone held a warning. Her gaze was pointed out the few remaining windows of the entrance.

Armored cars, multiple of them, were driving up to the building.

Rotoya's eyes glazed over. "We have a problem."

Eric opened his mouth to ask Lance if he could still fight, but Lance shook his head, as if he already knew the question before it came out.

"I don't think I can do that shit again."

Eric helped Lance to his feet and guided him back to the break room, away from the awaiting battle. He turned to ask the chief how many of her officers she could bring back, but twenty men were already standing from where they'd been taken down, their wounds glowing through their armor as they healed.

Rotoya yelled, her voice deep and commanding. "I need five of you to go to the back entrance. Each of you grab a shield, a gun, and as much ammo as you can carry."

"We're dead," Lance said. "We're dead, we failed. *I* failed."

"Shut up," Eric hissed. "You just took out a couple dozen men. I think you've earned your rest."

"Maybe I can… Maybe I can control some of my own."

Eric shut him up once more. This time, Lance listened. Eric grabbed a gun and helped Lance to the bathroom inside the break room, locking them both inside.

"This is stupid," Lance said, sitting on the floor.

Eric chuckled. "Stupid but effective."

"My whole body is sore."

"Will be for a few days, too."

Lance groaned as he sat up straighter, leaning against the wall. "How did you know I needed help?"

Eric chuckled again. "Would you believe Caleb told us? He set a trap, and you were the bait."

"Doesn't seem to be working as well as he hoped, from what I've seen… Where are Kaela and Derek?"

"Looking for you."

Lance's eyes flashed with worry. "Shouldn't we go get them?"

Eric waved a hand. "They're fine. I'm not about to leave you alone here."

Lance opened his mouth, probably to protest, but he shut it when he tried and failed to stand.

They both sat silently as gunfire filled the lobby once more.

Kaela's plea didn't leave her tongue as she looked up at Amari, her eyes devoid of any sympathy, any warmth. With uncharacteristic strength, Amari tossed her onto a long wooden table in the center of the room. Kaela's ribs and back screamed in pain. Her side burned and stung. Bile rose in her throat as she tried to crawl away. The table shook. Blood pooled around her. Her blood. *Oh God.*

Kaela was flipped back over. Amari stood over her with a wicked smile. She leaned down to Kaela's face, caressing her cheek with the blood-soaked blade. "This gift… It feels amazing. Shame you'll never get to feel it." Amari raised her dagger, the tip of the blade aimed at Kaela's heart.

Caleb's voice rang out. "Stop."

A simple order—not a shout, just a single calm word. Amari paused then lowered the knife, stepping off the table.

"I control her," Caleb continued. "Consider her a souvenir from your admittedly impressive establishment. She gets to live for much longer than any normal person, thanks to a healthy dose of the beta strain. I can offer you similar treatment. You and that Derek fellow are quite the survivors. You're like cockroaches, constantly finding ways to escape imminent death. He'll be given his own special dose soon enough."

Kaela tried to curse him, but the words didn't rise to her mouth. The pain darkened her vision and fogged her thoughts. More blood pooled beneath her. Her vision blurred for a moment, but she blinked it away.

Caleb leaned forward in his chair. "I wonder how you managed to escape the Rose… It baffles me… but I'd rather you not tell me. The mystery keeps it interesting." He smoothed out a crease in his pants. "You know, if you accept my generous offer, you can spend the rest of your life with your friend, Amari. Derek can spend the rest of his life with, um… Rob. You'll all be a family… and you can all kill Eric together. Poetic irony, Eric being killed by his own people."

Kaela forced the word out. "No."

Caleb sighed. "Your crusade is over. I called in all my reinforcements from Agni. The chief doesn't stand a chance." When Kaela didn't respond, he continued, "Just take the drug, and not only will you survive… you'll be healed. Surely someone as desperate as you were to escape that burning building would choose life over death. After all you've fought for, why throw your life away?"

She glared at him. Hellish wrath stewed in her bloody gut at the man sitting so calmly in the corner of the room, watching her die on the table like some slaughtered pig. Her dagger was still hidden in her clothes. If she could get a good aim on him, maybe, just maybe, she could take him down.

She looked Caleb in the eye, tears dripping into the puddle of blood. The word tasted like poison as it left her lips. "Okay."

Caleb grinned and removed a syringe from his coat pocket. The liquid inside was blue. He slipped the plastic cover from the needle.

"This is the alpha strain of the drug, mixed with just enough of the beta strain for you to follow my orders. Other than the one your friend Derek is about to get… this is the last dose. I hope I'm not wasting this on you."

Kaela nearly spat at his words and the sick, twisted way he viewed the world. But she would let him get close to her, just close enough to make her move.

Her plan shattered when Caleb didn't get up from his seat. "Amari, would you be so kind as to inject our new friend?"

Amari hummed. "Of course, Mr. Landreau."

Mr. Landreau. It took everything in Kaela not to groan in disgust. Amari's light steps closed in on her. Kaela found her and followed her with her eyes.

Kaela tried to suck in a deep breath, but she couldn't. Tears streamed down her face as Amari clambered onto the table.

Kaela kicked Amari's legs out from under her. She fell back with a shout, and the syringe flew from her hands. Kaela rolled off the table, unsheathing her knife. It was coated in purple blood.

Caleb's arm grew to twice its size. Kaela barely dodged in time as he slammed his fist into the table. It splintered in half.

Kaela spotted an opening and stole it. In a blind lunge for Caleb's neck, she sliced. The blade carved halfway into his throat and stopped. Caleb choked and sputtered, clawing at his neck. He ripped the dagger out and stood, throwing a punch at Kaela. It slammed into her chest and knocked her to the ground, her ribs cracking. She ignored the pain and rolled back to her feet just as Caleb slammed his fist into the floor.

Pride. The man had let his pride lure him into a false sense of security. Kaela felt Amari's warmth behind her and dodged the knife aimed at her back. Kaela ripped the dagger from Amari's hand and sank her elbow into her nose. A small crunch, and purple blood gushed out.

Caleb's neck slowly began to heal, the wound and his veins glowing a brilliant amethyst.

Kaela lunged a second time, swiping at his neck again. The dagger sliced deeper into his throat. Kaela gasped, looking down as the blade in Caleb's hand pierced her stomach. He twisted it, and Kaela dropped to her knees.

Caleb dropped with her, grasping at his lacerated neck as the nanobots began to heal the wound again. He tried to speak, but the cut was too deep.

Kaela couldn't speak either as blood filled her mouth. The words she wanted to say, the hate she sought to spew, she couldn't.

She spat her blood in his face, and he gurgled out a yell of disgust. He released his grip on the dagger. Kaela screamed and pulled the dagger out of her stomach. Stars speckled her vision as searing pain consumed her body. She plunged the bloody blade into the remnants of his neck, then thrust the other one in next.

Caleb's eyes flooded with panic, and in a desperate attempt, he shoved Kaela away.

Kaela's grip on the knives held strong, and she felt the tearing of blade through flesh as she flew back.

The pain and excitement melded together in a cocktail in her heart as time slowed down.

Kaela landed on the ground, raw pain drowning her senses. She tried to gasp, but her lungs wouldn't listen. Her vision blurred then cleared again just in time to see Caleb's head roll across the floor and his body land next to it.

She scoffed out a laugh, but blood splattered out instead.

She'd done it.

Tears stained her eyes as she thought about her girls at the Rose.

At least she'd avenged them. Or most of them.

Amari leaned down and picked the blades out of Kaela's hands.

Kaela tried to swallow down air, but blood took its place. A sick copper taste saturated her mouth. Her body begged for air, but her lungs refused. Her skin crawled, and a sweet smell flooded the room as Caleb's blood pooled on the floor.

"How dare you?" Amari yelled. She raised the knives above her head.

Kaela's vision blurred again, and she closed her eyes. *So tired...* She waited for the knives to come. For the sweet release from the pain.

Amari gurgled as if she was choking, then after a long pause, she spoke. "Kaela… Kaela, oh my God!" she sobbed.

Though her vision was blurry, Kaela opened her eyes again.

Amari's eyes were riddled with panic and guilt. Her face twisted into a sob. "Kaela. Kaela, I didn't mean it. He… he made me, I—"

Kaela put her hand over Amari's, and Amari opened her mouth as if trying to force more words out, but her own broken sobs interrupted her.

Kaela tried to speak, to tell her that she was okay, that she understood. But she couldn't say the words. Couldn't even breathe. The world became fuzzy, the pain a distant memory.

She was content… She'd done what she needed to do and had sacrificed the only thing she could give in return for the deaths of her people.

Amari spoke, but it was distant. Forgotten.

She didn't have long. But it was okay. It would all be okay.

Something broke through the ceiling—a pinprick of light that slowly started to grow. It spread until it covered the whole ceiling.

It was so bright. So blinding. She tried to blink it away, but she couldn't. Despite the brightness, the beauty of it surpassed anything she'd ever witnessed. It was crystal clear. Peaceful and quiet. A flood of wind rushed past her cheek, warm like a summer breeze.

She sent a final request to her lungs, and they obeyed. She filled them with air one last time. Her final breath.

Something distant disturbed her peace, but it was no more than a ripple in water.

Shouting.

She ignored it.

Peaceful, content, Kaela released that final breath, and suddenly she was floating toward the light. Something pricked her arm, but she disregarded it. It didn't matter anymore. The light grew closer and brighter. Its warmth tickled her face, and strands of her hair quivered in its breeze. A smile crept across her lips, and she reached out to touch the light, to cross over and meet whatever awaited her on the other side. She gasped as a cold wave dug into her back, and she fell.

Ungracefully, she plummeted to the ground but felt no pain. The light shrank until it disappeared. The cold bite of the room returned, yet the pain in her stomach dwindled. Amari was crying next to her, then she wrapped her arms around Kaela's neck.

Kaela lay there, her head spinning. *Where did the light go?*

"I'm sorry," Amari said. "It was the only way."

Kaela didn't understand. But then she looked down at her hands. At the veins glowing purple beneath her skin. Her chest constricted, and she looked back up at the ceiling.

Come back! Take me back!

She looked at Amari and opened her mouth to speak. Whether it was a thank-you or a curse, it didn't leave her mouth. She froze.

Pain surged through her, through every inch of her veins. Her body burned, and she screamed, screamed at nothing. The pain burned and singed everything inside her. She laid a hand on her stomach, her side. Nothing—no wounds where there should have been.

Then something snapped inside of her, an audible snap from somewhere within her body, then the pain stopped. A growl rumbled within her.

A voice whispered to her, promising to stop the pain if she allowed it to move, to breathe.

Screaming at the top of her lungs, her body scorching and aching, she accepted the offer. The pain eased, but a presence moved and shifted inside of her as if it was alive.

She reached out and felt it. Felt that power.

Another snap, and a wave of calm washed over her.

The world clicked into place, and she breathed for what felt like the first time.

Amari was gone. Caleb knelt in her place, a worried look crossing his features.

Kaela flinched back in fear. She swatted at him with her hand, and he flew back into the wall. She looked down at her palms, her glowing hands, then back at Caleb. He stood with a groan. *But… I didn't even touch him.*

A voice whispered to her, bone dry.

Destroy him.

Kaela's mind was shrouded in fog. Her brain felt lost and empty. She looked to her left, and Caleb's body was still there, headless and limp.

"What the hell?" Kaela said, her voice drowsy and slurred. She looked back at the other Caleb, fear and sadness in his eyes as he stared at her.

Where's Amari?

Destroy him. Kaela didn't think. She followed the orders of the voice.

Caleb shook his head. "Kaela, what are you doing?" he asked, his voice higher pitched than before. "It's me."

Ignoring him, she held her hand out and felt the blood, the nanobots coursing through his veins. So this was what it felt like to control every bot in the bloodstream—an overwhelming power. Caleb's heartbeat turned rapid.

He was afraid.

Good.

A flick of her wrist threw him against the wall. Kaela ordered the blood to solidify, just as Caleb had at the Rose.

Caleb tried to make another plea, but he choked on his own solid blood. Guilt twinged her stomach, but she shoved it aside. He would pay for what he'd done to Amari.

She bent her fingers into the shape of a claw, and his body broke. The crackling of his bones turned her stomach. Kaela held Caleb in the air from across the room, those grisly sounds filling her head as every bone broke and every muscle tore.

The moonlight shone on Caleb's warped face. His crooked body floated in front of the windows. A smile crawled across Kaela's face though she didn't mean for it to. She could speak now. She could say anything she wanted, any curse, any snide remark she could think of. But she sealed her lips. No words would express the hatred she had for him. No words could ever do that.

She threw her arm out, and his body flew through the glass.

For a moment, as the glass shattered and the body flew into the outside air, her mind cleared. The fog lifted, and Caleb changed.

Kaela gasped.

She hadn't thrown Caleb.

Caleb's body remained lifeless to her left.

Amari's broken body stared back at her. Sadness and despair painted her face, her lifeless face, as her body plummeted to the ground.

Cold air rushed in, raising goosebumps on Kaela's skin. The floor tilted.

Kaela couldn't breathe, couldn't move as she stood there, looking at the broken window. There was nothing she could do. Even if she grabbed onto Amari's body again, it was too broken. Every inch of her had been shattered to dust. The ground would be a mercy.

Her stomach twisted and turned, and she dropped to her knees, sobbing into the floor.

"No." She looked at Caleb's body. She screamed and swiped her hand. His headless corpse shot through the glass of the office and flew across the entire level, shattering every glass pane in his way before dropping like a brick to the ground.

Kaela fell to the floor and curled into a ball, crying into the carpet.

That bone-dry voice spoke to her again. *She died at your hands.*

Every part of her being screamed, *No!*

"Shut up," Kaela said.

The voice growled somewhere within her then made to speak again.

"I said *SHUT UP!*"

Rage boiling in her blood, Kaela shut her eyes and reached down inside herself. She clawed for the source of the voice until she latched onto it. The moment she gripped it, the growls turned to snarls. She ripped and tore at it until, finally, she wrapped invisible hands around its neck.

As she smothered the voice, it cursed her, her family, her friends. She tightened her grip.

She squeezed harder until the growls became desperate whines, pleading for its life. Kaela waited until the voice fell silent then smothered it more. A sigh left her as the voice disappeared into nothingness and faded away like ash in the wind.

Kaela caught her breath and put a hand to her chest. The drug flowed through her body, humming with an energy that radiated power. She searched inside herself until she found them. The beta strain, swimming uselessly in her blood until some other bastard with the alpha strain could try to control her. Her fingers danced, controlling the beta strain and ordering them out of her bloodstream. Nausea punched her stomach, and her mouth stretched open. She retched, vomiting purple liquid all over the carpet. She coughed and gagged and sucked in breaths between new bouts of vomiting.

Finally, it stopped. She wiped her mouth.

It was gone. She couldn't feel any beta strain left in her body. She glared at the puddle on the floor, and the purple blood glowed brightly then crackled like a firework. Then it was gone.

Kaela crawled underneath the long wooden table, the cool night air blowing in from the broken window, and she lay there. Her mind cleared. The voice was gone. The beta strain was gone. Amari was gone… Her tears fell, and Kaela sobbed into the carpet.

Amari's name slipped off her lips repeatedly, asking—begging—her for forgiveness. Forgiveness that she didn't deserve, never *would* deserve. The wind blew in mercilessly, and her body shivered from the cold. The nanobots inside her moved. They were alive, just like the voice she'd smothered. Just like the betas she'd removed.

Amari's face burned into her vision, her heartbroken stare etched into her mind forever.

CHAPTER 32

SADNESS, SACRIFICE, AND SO MUCH DEATH

Derek defended against blow after blow, but he couldn't bring himself to fight back. Rob's attacks were unflinching.

A kick sent Derek to the stairwell. He gripped the metal railing, nearly flying over the stairs. His legs weak, his heart pounding, Derek rolled away from the stairwell, narrowly dodging another kick. Before he could recover, Rob swept Derek's legs out from under him, sending him crashing to the ground.

Derek held his hand out as Rob made to throw another punch. "Wait… wait." He just needed a moment, a single moment to catch his breath.

As Derek sucked down air, sweat dripping down his face, Rob cocked his head to the side.

"This… isn't you." Nausea roiled in Derek's stomach, and his chest ached as he rolled onto his hands and knees, his lungs begging for more air.

Rob reached into his back pocket and removed a syringe. Its plastic cover rolled across the floor. He lunged, tackling Derek to the ground, and plunged the syringe downward.

Derek blocked his arm, the needle an inch away from piercing his skin. He held strong at first, but Rob was overpowering him. Exhaustion weakened his arms, his body forcing air down his throat. The needle closed in on his neck.

"No," Derek pleaded. "No, I can't turn into one of these things." He sent his knee into Rob's stomach and threw all his weight into a punch to his face.

Rob staggered back, cradling his bleeding nose. The syringe fell from his hand.

Derek clambered for it. Rob dove for him, and Derek kicked him away, grabbing the plastic cover.

He covered the syringe and pocketed it, watching Rob carefully as he stood back up.

Derek spat blood onto the floor. Rob didn't give it a second glance. Derek couldn't bring himself to hurt him. Caleb knew Derek wouldn't be able to fight his own friend. *Bastard.*

Derek pointed at the blood on the floor. "You see that?"

Rob still didn't look.

"That was once yours. It's not too late. I know you didn't want this."

Rob made to attack again then stopped. He dropped to one knee and groaned, his hand on his head. It lasted for a second before he shook it off and looked at Derek. His eyes watered.

"I… Derek?"

Derek gulped. *If this is a trick...* "Rob… you okay?"

Rob shook his head—not a no but a motion to get something out. Like a bad thought he was trying to avoid. "What am I doing?"

Derek gawked as Rob stared at the ground, his face twisted in confusion. He stared for the longest time, and Derek waited for the trap, waited for Rob to charge again. But when he met Derek's stare, his eyes lit up.

Derek charged him, not to attack, but to wrap him in an embrace.

Rob choked on his words as he said, "I'm sorry… I'm sorry, I didn't mean to—"

"It's okay," Derek said. "I'm sorry I let them take you." He let the tears flow down his cheeks. It felt good to cry, not in mourning this time, but in happiness.

Rob was alive—alive and, for whatever reason, back to his old self.

When they separated, Derek laughed, wiping his cheeks. "I can't believe that worked."

A voice rang out from the stairs above. "It didn't."

Derek's smile shattered when he found the source of the voice. Kaela descended the stairs, her glowing purple veins and eyes flashing for a moment before she extended her arm and Rob flew back into the wall.

Derek reached out to Rob, but he escaped his grip. An invisible force held him aloft, flattened against the wall.

Derek looked at Kaela, a plea in his voice. "NO!"

Kaela didn't look at him, only closed her fist and lifted her chin. Her veins flashed again, and Rob's flashed in response. "I'm helping him." Her voice was eerily calm, and Derek made to charge her. Her eyes flashed at him too. "Don't. Just watch."

Derek's legs turned to stone, panic blurring his thoughts. Caleb had gotten to her. *Now what?*

Rob's body cringed. Slowly, his veins dimmed, and purple blood floated from his mouth.

Derek balled his fists and readied himself again to charge Kaela, but Rob's eyes met his. His stare was composed, as if telling his friend to stay put. Derek found it hard to breathe, hard to stand here and do nothing.

Kaela seemed to notice his impatience. "I said I'm helping him, you idiot."

Well, she was at least *acting* like Kaela.

Kaela manipulated the blood in the air into a ball, and it solidified. The ball glowed, then with a flash of her eyes, it flew up the stairwell. Seconds later, a boom echoed from above.

Rob gasped for air as he crumpled to the floor. Derek ran to him, kneeling at his side, a hundred questions already on his lips.

Rob's hand went to his chest. "What did you just do to me?"

"I took the nanobots out," Kaela said, walking down the stairs. "Well, most of them."

Rob laughed, though Derek didn't know why.

"There's still some in there, but at least you can't be controlled anymore."

Rob sat up straighter, his skin pale from losing blood. His breathing was unsteady.

Derek spoke. "We can't have so many people running around with purple veins. We still need a cure."

"And we'll get it." Kaela stared downward, as if sensing something. Wordlessly, she descended the stairs, quiet as a ghost.

"Where's Caleb?" Derek asked.

"Dead." Kaela kept walking.

When she disappeared, Derek sat down next to Rob, groaning at his aching back.

"You've gotten better at fighting," Derek said.

Rob smiled. "Well, I did have a bunch of little robots making me stronger."

Derek chuckled then went silent. "I'm sorry… again. I should have done more to help you. Instead of just watching them take your body away like that."

Rob shrugged. "It's not that bad. In the end, it's my fault I got caught." He sighed. "Besides, it all turned out for the better. Being dead was weird, though. But that's a story for another day." He rested his head against the wall.

Derek opened his mouth to protest, but Rob glared at him, so he closed it. They sat in the quiet of the staircase.

Rob laughed at his hands. "Guess I'll be stuck with these veins for a little while, huh?"

Derek nodded. He'd missed that laugh.

He had his friend back.

Rob's eyes didn't glow purple anymore, but they remained that color.

Derek sighed and laid his head back against the wall alongside him.

No matter what it took, he would make sure never to lose his friend again.

"So…" Rob started, still out of breath, "this is probably a bad time, but… I'm pretty hungry, and—"

Derek shook with laughter, and Rob joined in, hesitantly.

"Heh heh, yeah," Rob said. "No, but seriously…"

Eric stared at the fake wooden walls of the cramped bathroom. Lance was sitting across from him, his legs braced against the wall. His head fell forward every few seconds.

Eric chuckled. "All this gunfire, and you're still nodding off? You *must* be exhausted."

Lance didn't look at him. "I'm trying to get as much energy back up as I can so we can get this over with. I hate just sitting here." Now he looked. "And that gunfire isn't showing any signs of stopping. One of them is going to run out of ammo soon enough, and my bet's on the chief."

"It'll be fine."

"We also don't know where Caleb is. We don't know where Derek and Kaela are, either. Hell, we don't even know if they're alive. So why don't we get up and go check on them instead of staying in here?"

Eric glared at his son, but he couldn't meet those green eyes for long. Not when they looked right through his—just like she always had.

Kaela and Derek would be fine. That's what he told himself. He wasn't about to leave Lance, and he *certainly* wasn't about to let Lance leave.

But Lance seemed to take Eric's silence as an answer because he emitted an irritated groan and struggled to stand. Eric shoved him back down, ignoring the swears of protest.

Lance hissed, "I am *not* some child you need to protect. I'm a grown man, now let me out!"

"I *can't!*"

Lance stopped midstruggle.

Eric frowned. "I can't let you go."

"Why?!"

"Because the last time I let you go, you spent years in that damned orphanage, then more years in the streets…" Tears welled in Eric's eyes, surprising him before he could shove them down. "I've done a lot of shitty things, Lance! And I'm probably going to keep doing shitty things, but if there's one good thing I ever did, it was jumping in that taxi with

Carrie… That was the last night I had to spend with her, and I made the same mistake with you. I will *not* lose the one thing I have left!"

Lance just stared at him. Anger shadowed his face for a moment then disappeared. "I… What do you expect me to say to that? 'Thanks, Dad, I love you too'?" Lance made to stand again.

A heavy thud resounded outside the door, and Eric shoved his son back down. Before Lance could protest, Eric shushed him and put a hand to his ear, a silent order to Lance. *Listen.*

Footsteps sounded outside the bathroom. Eric racked his brain for a guess as to who was on the other side of the door.

The gunfire outside ceased, and Eric's cane blade whined as he drew it.

Eric burst through the door and found four guards standing before him. The moment their helmeted heads turned toward him, he knew they weren't the chief's. Fear clutched his heart at the silence in the lobby.

Eric almost lunged but stopped as the men looked around as if confused. Their guns were on the floor.

The officers stiffened suddenly, as if paralyzed.

Eric slowly weaved through the soldiers, their bodies as stiff as statues. The bodies on the floor—the ones still intact—were paralyzed as well.

Almost in unison, their helmets shattered, and purple blood floated out of them. Their faces were twisted in shock.

Eric sheathed his blade and tossed the cane to Lance. He caught it and leaned on it, exhaustion dimming his eyes.

Then Eric stepped out of the break room, surveying the dozens of bodies on the floor. All their helmets were broken, all their mouths open with purple blood floating out.

Rachel and the other officers did the same. Rotoya just looked around, her hand clutched to her chest as worry creased her face.

Even the soldiers outside froze.

"Chief?" Eric called.

Rotoya's eyes shifted to him, drenched in fear.

Then footsteps clicked on the floor from around the corner. Another prickle of fear hit his spine, and Eric readied himself. "Caleb."

But the footsteps, light and graceful, didn't resemble Caleb's at all.

And when Kaela rounded the corner of the hallway, Eric's legs buckled. The cane slipped from Lance's hand and clattered to the floor. His face twisted with emotions—fear and confusion, anger and sadness. He spoke, but no sound came out. He just mouthed, *He drugged her.*

Eric didn't know whether to run or to fight or to do what he was doing now: standing in fear, watching her carefully.

Kaela's sharp purple eyes shot to Lance as if she could hear what he'd mouthed. She shook her head at him, lightly, almost invisibly. Then she looked at Eric, and something calmed his fear. Not a threat. Not an enemy.

An ally.

Kaela scrutinized the men and women lying across the floor, blood leaking from their mouths. She focused on all of them, her fingers dancing at her sides. Eric gulped. She was ordering the blood. Manipulating it as Caleb did.

So where was Caleb? Where was Derek?

Her eyes met his again. "Trust me."

Her voice was still Kaela's yet monotone, laced with nothingness, as if all emotion had been ripped from her. Like her heart had been torn from her chest.

Purple blood continued to float from the mouths of the soldiers. Eric waited for blood to leave Lance's mouth, but none did.

Kaela's eyes repeated what her mouth had said: *Trust me.*

Kaela sighed as a flood of calm washed over her. The nanobots inside her… they granted her such power. Beyond her own, she could feel the nanobots in the rest of them. The alphas ignored her commands, save for the ones in her own body, but the betas listened. They obeyed her orders and left the bodies of the soldiers, inside and outside the building.

Most of the soldiers weren't truly dead. They were clinging to life by a thread. That thread was the nanobots. Their bodies were waiting for whoever was in charge to revive them. With a wave of her hand, every laid-out soldier was pulled by that thread, returned to the land of the living. Hearts beat to life, and lungs sucked down air—their last chance at living a life. Their last revival.

A second wave of her hand directed the bots she hadn't removed to heal their wounds. It would be slower, and it would only last until the remainder were gone, but at least they wouldn't die all over again. She kept them still and paralyzed for now as she continued the extraction.

She felt Rotoya's blood, but only a handful of betas were swimming around inside her. Not enough to rip out without hurting her, just as the rest of the soldiers risked injury if she stole every single beta from within them. The cure would finish off whatever she didn't remove, should one ever exist.

Lance, however, held none of the beta strain within his body. But *something* was inside him, just like the thing she'd held inside of herself. It moved around, snarling at her presence. She knew Lance felt it too. It would be easy to smother it, just as she had her own. But that would have to be Lance's choice.

Finally, most of the beta strain left the bodies of the soldiers.

With the bots gone, Kaela lost her control over the soldiers. The paralysis disappeared. Groans of pain and relief flooded the room, and slowly, Kaela closed her eyes and formed the gallons of blood she held before her into one large ball. She waited patiently for the blood in the stairwell, in the floors above, and outside to travel to her.

It took minutes, but time was a luxury she could afford to waste. Every ounce of violet blood, filled with billions of nanobots, formed into one large orb before her.

Kaela stole a deep breath. When she opened her eyes, her arms were stretched out. The bundle of nanobots and amethyst blood blocked the lights, plunging the room into a purple haze. She moved it out the front door. The ball shifted and flowed, pushing the armored vehicles out of the way. The blood floated high in the air, and the farther it rose, the weaker the nanobots held in Kaela's grip. They became a distant whisper.

She stopped, holding them miles in the air, barely feeling them anymore. Any farther, and she would lose her connection to them. This would have to be good enough.

Kaela took a steadying breath, and while she didn't see it, she knew the ball glowed brighter than any streetlamp in the city. Then a boom broke the night sky. The building quivered, and a tremor shook the ground. Silence fell until the soldiers groaned and moaned as they stood. A few from the break room screamed in pain. Several bodies still peppered the tile floor, all without heads. They wouldn't be coming back.

A weight lifted from her chest, and her mind cleared, rid of the whispers of their nanobots.

Eric stepped toward her, then Lance. She shook her head at them and scanned the men and women across the room, then outside. Some remained on the floor in pain, but the rest of the soldiers wasted no time in helping the injured.

Rachel hunched over like she was going to throw up, while Rotoya rubbed her back. The rest of the soldiers walked around as if they'd forgotten what the world was like without the foggy lens of Caleb's control over them. The officers did the same. Rotoya nodded at Kaela, a silent thank-you. Her eyes darkened as she scanned the headless bodies strewn across the floor.

How many had been her officers?

"How dare you?" Rachel spat, anger flashing in her eyes. "I *trusted* you! I took that damned drug because I thought you would never do anything to hurt us."

"I tried to release control, but I couldn't," Rotoya said as Rachel stepped back. "Sands, please understand, if I could have turned them off, I would have. I didn't know all of this would happen!"

Rachel's mouth formed a deep frown. "Do *not*... call me Sands." She stormed off and disappeared into the crowd.

Kaela took one step forward then another. Her steps felt light, like she was walking on air.

Some of the soldiers approached to thank her, their eyes and veins no longer glowing but retaining their purple hue. Some of them had seen past the lens, had known they were doing wrong, but had been unable to fight against their orders. It would take years for them to get over the things they'd done, but that would be their job. Their responsibility.

As far as Kaela was concerned, she only had one job. One job for one friend, and then she was finished, done with anything else for a long, long time.

Eyes followed her as she left the building, and a frown etched on her face. She couldn't turn their heads away. There weren't enough beta bots within them to control them anymore. So she wielded her frown as a shield and walked down the stairs. She looked out at the street, searching.

They hadn't been on the highest floor, yet… Amari was so broken.

Kaela ignored the stares as she picked up her friend's broken body. A pool of purple blood surrounded her, which meant there had been much more before Kaela destroyed the beta bots.

That purple blood trailed down her arms and clothes. Footsteps approached, and Kaela sensed Lance's presence before he made it known. Just like the others, she ignored him and kept walking, Amari in her arms.

She looked down the street for a long moment, considering walking the entire way. It was what she deserved, having to walk a body all the way to her destination, but that would take too long.

Kaela breathed a silent apology to Amari as she carried her damaged body to a police car and laid her gently across the back seat. She folded her arms over her chest, and the crackling sound that ensued chilled her to the bone. She put a hand to her mouth, muffling her sobs as she rounded to the driver's seat and started the engine.

She drove until the buildings turned to trees. The streetlights disappeared. Only the headlights and a sliver of moonlight guided her. The window was rolled down, the cool wind tugging at her hair and stinging her cheeks. Crickets chirped.

The entire way, she called to her own nanobots, begging and pleading with them to heal Amari's injuries. But despite how strongly she reached out, no answer came from the few nanobots left within Amari. Perhaps that was why she hadn't healed when the soldiers had. She'd lost too much blood and therefore too many bots to heal properly. That, and…

maybe her body had just been too broken. Kaela slowed the car, barely able to see through the tears in her eyes.

She ascended a hill and parked at the destination. She stepped out, surveying her surroundings before sliding Amari back into her arms.

The moon was little more than a crescent tonight, but it provided enough light for Kaela to watch where she stepped across the clearing in the trees.

Kaela set Amari's body on the cold ground with another apology.

She knelt and clawed at the ground with her bare fingers. It didn't hurt at first, but after she had dug a foot of dirt, her fingers bled, her nails ached and cracked, and her back groaned. She didn't care. Whatever pain she endured in doing this was nothing compared to the pain she'd put Amari through.

She didn't stop for an instant, even as her body griped. The nanobots provided strength and endurance, and even so, she ached. The nanobots healed her bleeding fingers, her broken nails, seconds after she broke them, over and over.

When she finally dug deep enough, the sun peeked over the horizon, and a morning breeze flowed like silk along her skin. They sat in the growing shade of the tree.

Kaela inspected Amari. Her face was so peaceful. How could she possibly look so peaceful when her last moments had been filled with shock, fear, and sadness?

Amari had likely blamed herself, Kaela thought as she lifted her body again. That thought weighed the guilt heavier on her chest. Gently, she laid Amari to rest in her homemade grave. Tears rolled down her cheeks, and she couldn't wipe them away in time before a few dripped onto Amari's face.

Kaela wiped her eyes, sighing at the cool morning air as it caressed her healed but still-sore fingers. The auburn light of the rising sun shone on the clearing. So quiet. So removed from everything else. A slice of the world where nothing existed but the hill, the bench, the tree, and the view. Kaela smiled, but only for a second. She reached down and wiped the tears from Amari's cheek. She looked over at the bench, where she and her parents had always sat. She remembered the laughs, the tears, the arguments. This had been their favorite spot. But now her parents were gone. She was the last one to enjoy its view, its peace—its last guardian.

"I should have brought you here when I had the chance. You would have liked it," Kaela said, looking down at Amari's sleeping face. "You would have covered yourself in hand sanitizer, but you would have liked the view, at least." She attempted a laugh, but it broke halfway through, almost into a sob. She glanced out at the city of Arachna, spread out below the hill. "I'm so sorry…" Kaela choked on the words as more tears leaked from her eyes. "I'm sorry for what I did. I should never have put you through all this." She cried until her head throbbed and the weight on her chest lifted, if only for a moment. It gave her a reprieve before it stomped on her chest once again. She didn't have much time left. If she spent too long out here, somebody would come after her.

In fact... She perked her head up.

Lance was headed in her direction, moving fast. She shook her head and looked down at Amari one last time. "I can't stay here with you long, but I swear I'll make up for what I did. I'll come visit you as well." Her voice shook. "I don't even know if you can hear me, wherever you are. But make sure you get some rest. You've earned it."

Birds chirped in the distance, and Kaela allowed herself to enjoy the sound for a few seconds before returning to work. Lance would be here soon, and he would insist on helping. She didn't want that. This was her responsibility.

CHAPTER 33
TO FAMILY

She wouldn't be happy with him, Lance thought as he drove through the city in the police car he'd taken from Landreau Corp. Derek and Rob said they would return to the bar to check on George.

Lance had tried to think of a way to apologize for the officers he'd killed, but Rotoya only blamed herself, and Rachel had glared at her from across the room.

"They all hate me," Rotoya had said. "I don't blame them, either."

Lance let out a nervous breath. The beast made an unrecognizable sound, but it was comforting, all the same.

At least he didn't have to spend all night in that horrid building, with those bright lights bearing down on him and the dozens of confused men and women freshly released from Caleb's control. All that confusion, all those people… He shuddered at the thought.

He shuddered once more at what Eric had told him. He'd worn that wicked smile when he told Lance he was staying.

"I want to explore. There's no telling what information I can get from this place."

"In the basement," Lance said. "On the first level of cells, at the end of the hall, there's a journal. Caleb gave it to me. If it's still there, you'll want to read it."

Eric winked and sauntered off.

Lance didn't bother to follow him, especially with the call of those dark cells below the floor. And after Kaela walked off with Amari in her arms, something had told him to follow her. Not the beast but something else. Something more than a voice in the back of his head.

He'd waited for as long as he could stand it, sitting on a bench in the lobby as Rotoya gathered her officers to explain what had happened. She didn't have to explain much. They all knew what they'd done. They'd all felt Caleb was doing the right thing until the nanobots left them. Their faces were haunted with guilt—Rachel's too.

Once the sun began to rise, Lance deemed that he had given Kaela enough time and stole a police car to follow her.

He could think of only one place to find her. When she started down the street with Amari, he'd run down the stairs to call to her, to at least offer to drive her there. But Eric had been out there with him just as quickly, shaking his head.

Now here he was, driving down the empty, sun-painted streets of Arachna. They would be full again, Lance thought, once everything was back to normal, once it was announced that the threat was over and their innocence was explained. Lance groaned. How would they even be able to do that? He shook the thought from his head. Rotoya said she would handle it. He chose to trust her. After all the help she'd already offered, he allowed himself to leave it in her hands.

Right now, he focused on Kaela. On the nanobots flooding through her veins. She couldn't have had them for long, yet she'd fixed everyone under Caleb's control by… doing whatever the hell she'd done.

Derek had said something about her taking out the beta strain but not all of it?

Caleb, Malcolm, and Daniel had all lost their minds because of the drug; how would Kaela be any different? Would she become crazed by the nanobots and turn into another Caleb? *Will I follow behind her?*

The beast whimpered, as if offended at the thought.

Lance reached the hilltop, where the sun was casting a peaceful orange glow over the clearing.

Kaela sat patiently on the bench, under the shade of the tree. A wooden cross was stuck in the ground, near a freshly packed mound of dirt. A makeshift grave, right near the tree.

Kaela's hands were folded in front of her, and she watched as he parked the car next to hers. She'd been waiting for him, Lance thought, and the beast purred in agreement.

The beast had been so quiet these past few hours, still resting from the explosion of power both it and Lance had experienced when he escaped his cell. That surge of power had felt so good—too good. And when the beast ultimately urged him to give in, to give it more room, he'd done it. He'd given in to the temptation.

It frightened him. The feeling was all too similar to when he'd given in to other temptations, to pop another pill or down another shot. He swallowed the lump in his throat.

Somehow, he hid that feeling from the beast, or maybe it just didn't acknowledge it—chose to withhold the fact that it knew until the right time. That fear kept Lance on the defensive, but as he left the car and neared Kaela, he wondered if he would ever finally give in and allow the beast as much room as it desired.

What would happen then?

Kaela stared at him for a moment, then her eyes shifted to the two broken pieces of wood tied together in the shape of a cross. "It was the best I could do," she said. "It's not great, but at least it's something."

Lance looked down at the makeshift grave, and the words came out without him thinking. "I think it's beautiful."

She looked at him with those purple eyes, a sad smile on her face. "Thank you."

Lance sat next to her on the bench. He eyed the veins on her neck, her arms. She noticed, as if calculating his every action. Could she sense what he was doing because of the nanobots?

She opened her mouth to speak, but Lance beat her to it. "So… about Caleb…"

"Dead."

"I figured that, but…"

She didn't seem to hear him as she said, "Amari was there. She was injected with the nanobots. He ordered her to kill me… She almost did."

Lance gaped at her. She didn't look at him.

"Somehow, I managed to kill Caleb, and… I'm pretty sure I died." Her eyes watered. "I felt it. It was so… peaceful. And serene. But then Amari injected me with the drug to save me. Caleb's death released her from his control." She swallowed hard.

Lance reached a hand out to touch her shoulder, to offer some form of comfort. But he stopped himself.

"When she did, I… I snapped. I saw her as a threat, and… it's my fault she's dead."

Lance opened his mouth then closed it. The words swirled around in his head, in different orders, different tones. None of them seemed an appropriate response.

"And now, I'm a monster." Kaela looked at her hands. "Covered with these nasty-looking veins."

Monster... "Yeah… I know the feeling." The silence between them lingered. "Are you going to take them out like you did the others?"

After a long pause then a deep breath, she said, "I removed the beta strain, but… no. No, I don't think I even can. Caleb could control his own alpha strain, but… if I can, I don't know how yet." She looked at him. "I'd remove yours if I could, but I can only sense them." She smiled. "*You* might be able to remove them, but you don't seem to have that much control over them yet. I'd just wait for the cure if I was you."

The beast growled, and Lance swore Kaela could hear it too. The prospect of a cure tempted him. A life without the constant growls and purrs and hisses. Being able to think clearly, not having a beast inside to urge him in one direction or the other.

"Did you… hear anything when you got the drug? Or do you hear anything now?" Lance asked.

Kaela smiled at him. A gentle, light smile. "How'd you know?"

"You did?"

"Yeah… it was like a living thing inside of me. It whispered these horrible things. I got so angry I just… I killed it."

The beast whined, and Lance cocked his head to the side. "How?"

A rough growl rumbled from the beast.

"That's like asking me how I took the nanobots out of all those officers. I have absolutely no idea. It just came naturally. It was like Malcolm said… The drug affects everyone differently."

"I have one too," Lance said, his voice breathy.

"I know," Kaela responded. "I can feel it sometimes. When it growls or moves around a lot. It's there."

"Could you…" There was no right way to word the question, and the beast was already snarling at him as if to say, *How dare you even consider it?* "Could you kill my beast if I asked?"

Kaela hummed. "The *beast*, as you call it, I think is different than your nanobots. I don't know how to explain it—I just… feel it. It would be hard to kill it without accidentally snuffing you out instead." She looked out at the sunset for a moment then returned her stare to Lance. "But I could certainly give it a try." An invisible hand wrapped around Lance's insides, around the beast. It snarled and snapped and struggled against the force. She looked at him. "Just say the word, and I'll do it." Her eyes glowed a bright violet.

Lance almost said yes. The word even reached his lips, but he didn't let it escape. The beast whined and whined, and something else told Lance that it was a bad idea. Not the beast itself, but something deeper, more powerful. His instincts. They'd never led him wrong so far, and they urged him to say no. So he did, and Kaela let go.

As the beast caught its breath, so too did Lance find himself suddenly taking deeper breaths.

"So… since you killed your beast… does that mean you won't go crazy like Caleb and the rest?" He almost punched himself for asking.

She stared down at Amari's grave. "I… I don't think so. If I start showing any signs, slip a cure into my wine to get rid of my nanobots." She laughed, but it was hollow.

Lance went quiet at that word. *Cure.* Was it even possible? It was a nice idea, but with Malcolm gone… But after what he told Eric to look for in his old cell, maybe they had a chance. That was, if Caleb even bothered to keep it there. "Wait…" Lance said as the words processed in his head. "Aren't you going to get the cure as soon as you can?"

Kaela swallowed, not breaking her stare from Amari's grave. She spoke quietly. "No."

"Why the hell not?"

Kaela shook her head. "Amari gave me this drug to save me… and I *killed* her." Her voice cracked, and tears welled in her eyes. "God… what am I going to tell her parents?" She shut her eyes tightly, the tears falling down her cheeks. A sob escaped her, and she covered her mouth. She tried to speak but couldn't. She gasped then sobbed more.

Lance reached his hand out again, inches from her back. Part of him wanted to withdraw, but he pushed forward. She didn't pull away from his touch, and he rubbed small circles on her upper back.

They stayed like that until she settled down.

"You don't think she would want you to take the cure?" Lance asked.

Kaela wiped her face, sniffling and coughing. "If I get rid of this drug, it's like… getting rid of her… of the last thing she did. It's… all I have left of her… I know it doesn't make sense."

"No… no, it does." Lance scooted closer. "You know… I've always known I got my eyes from my mom… I don't know how I knew, but I did. My whole life, I've been so obsessed with them. I'd stare at them in the mirror, I'd draw pictures of them… They always made me feel closer to her in some way." He picked at his nails. "I know it sounds really freakin' weird, but… Yeah, now you know."

Kaela nodded slowly. "That is pretty weird."

They shared a look for a lingering moment before both broke out into laughter.

When they stopped, Kaela looked down at her purple-veined hands. "Although," she said, "I'm not very fond of this color. Maybe…" Her lips formed a thin line, and she closed her eyes. Within seconds, her purple veins slowly turned blue. When she opened her eyes again, her yellow eyes, Lance's breath caught in his throat. "How do I look?"

Lance gulped. A word came to his mind, but he swallowed it and chose something else. "Normal."

She sniffled and wiped away the remainder of the tears. "Never had a man tell me that before. I'm almost insulted."

Lance made to apologize, but when she laughed, he just laughed with her. If he didn't know any better, he could have sworn the beast rolled its eyes. Did it even have eyes? "So I guess you can control your nanobots, then?"

Kaela furrowed her brows. "I guess I can, yet… when I reach for them like I did the betas, they don't listen. I try to order them out of me, but nothing happens."

"What did you tell them to do just now?"

"I—" Kaela blinked then scoffed. "I just didn't want my veins to look like that anymore, so I ordered them to… stop doing that. And they did." She clenched then unclenched her fists as if testing them. "I can still feel them inside me, but quieter. I don't feel as strong, either. And I guess whenever I need them, I can call on them."

"Caleb seemed to have trouble doing that… making his nanobots return his veins to normal like that. He only did it once, and that was with Malcolm's help."

"It wasn't hard for me." Kaela shrugged.

"I don't understand how you have so much power with those nanobots. How you have so much control. Even Caleb couldn't do what you're doing."

Kaela frowned. "No… but he could do things I can't." She glanced at Lance. Her eyes narrowed. "Keep an eye on that beast of yours, Lance. Mine manipulated me into… ugh, what'd it say? Giving it more room?"

A shock went down Lance's spine, and the beast was quiet. "Oh?"

"It knew I was vulnerable and preyed on that. I let it in without a second thought. Next thing I knew, Amari looked like Caleb, and—" She choked.

"By all means," Lance said. "Kill my beast if it starts getting out of control. Or slip me a cure if you can."

Oddly enough, the beast didn't growl. Now that it knew it would be killed if given more room, maybe it would stop pestering him about it.

It was certainly a nice thought.

"Well," Lance said finally, his eyes getting heavy the higher the sun rose, "I think I'm going to head back. You want a ride?"

Kaela looked down at Amari's grave one last time, smiled at it, then nodded. "Yeah… I'm ready." She walked in step with Lance to the police car. "I need a drink."

When they returned to the bar, Derek, George, and Rob were inside, talking quietly. All eyes shot to Kaela when they walked in, her eyes and veins perfectly normal.

She smiled at them and waved away the questions about why her veins looked normal. Even Lance, watching her sit on the nearest barstool with feline grace, nearly forgot that those nanobots were still swimming around inside her.

"Since you've effectively removed everyone's nanobots, do we even need a cure?" George asked.

Kaela frowned. "Sorry to burst your bubble, but those soldiers still have beta bots in them, just very few. They'll still need that cure if they want those veins to go back to normal."

"I thought that was just scarring left by the drug, maybe a permanent stain of the veins themselves."

"Speaking of cures," Eric said, strutting in, his black eyes wild. He reached into his coat, and his expression fell. He frowned as he retracted his hand, purple liquid and bits of glass dripping from his palm. "No…"

The room fell into silence.

"Wait." Derek reached into his pocket and took out a syringe. "Rob tried to inject me with this when he was infected."

A look of guilt crossed Rob's face.

"Maybe you can make something of it instead?"

George took the syringe. His eyes sparkled. "Is this the drug? The nanobots?"

"Yeah."

George grinned. "This is better than a blood sample. Malcolm was going to try to figure out how to separate the blood cells from the nanobots, and he didn't have the equipment for that."

"It's a mix," Kaela said. "It was the one Caleb had given to me… It's an alpha strain with betas inside."

"Well, damn, I need to put the spotlight back on me somehow." Eric winked at Lance and reached into his other coat pocket, pulling out a small book bound in leather. "Malcolm's journal. Lance told me Caleb put it in his cell, and the old geezer completely forgot to take it back out." With a laugh, he tossed the journal to George, who fumbled to catch it and ended up watching the journal fall flat on the floor. "I also did some digging in Caleb's office and found a couple of ripped-out pages with a bunch of formula crap on it. They're folded in the back of the book."

"Thank you," George said, already opening it and scanning a page. "This should help… with this and the syringe." He smiled widely. "We might just have a cure on our hands." The smile waned. "Except… I'm no chemist like Malcolm. I only understand what he explained to me."

"You let me take care of that," Eric said. "With Landreau Corp not hunting us anymore, I can reach out and find some chemists. Maybe even from Landreau Corp itself."

There wasn't a celebration as Lance expected. More a collective sigh of relief.

Eric, however, appeared elated. "You downers need to turn those frowns upside down because there's more news."

As if on cue, Rotoya and Rachel grunted as they stepped in, carrying a massive safe. Derek sent a glare at Rotoya, and Rob held fear in his eyes.

"Why are you making *us* carry this?" Rotoya groaned as she held the safe on one side while Rachel helped with the other. Rotoya's veins glowed slightly as she strained. "Rachel doesn't have the strength she used to, with her nanobots gone."

Eric gave them a knowing look and pointed to the corner of the room. "Put it over there."

Rotoya groaned. "Yes, Your Highness, is there anything else you need?"

"Another safe would be great."

"And if you find one, you're welcome to carry the damned thing yourself."

The sight drew a smile from Lance. Eric noticed, and his own smile grew wide, still as wicked as ever.

"Kaela, Derek, Lance—aw hell, *everyone*," Eric started. "Oh, and you too, Bob."

"Rob."

"That's what I said." Eric's chest puffed with pride. "You are now looking at the owner of his own private army."

The room went quiet, and most of their jaws dropped, except for Rotoya's and Rachel's.

I knew he was up to something, Lance thought. The beast purred in agreement.

"What?" Derek asked.

Rob frowned.

"Not the *whole* army, of course," Eric added, his smile showing no signs of narrowing. "But a tiny portion of it. As it turns out, being brainwashed and forced to do terrible things against their will is a deal breaker. The ones that aren't retiring or spending the rest of their lives in therapy are thankful for our daring rescue; they've decided they want to work with us." Eric glanced at the safe. "And the best part? Our dear late friend Caleb Landreau will be paying for their salary for the rest of this year… and the next."

Lance raised his eyebrows. "How much is in there?"

Eric's expression lit up as he raised a finger to speak, but both dropped as he turned toward the safe. "I'm not sure, actually." He smiled at Rotoya. "If you would."

Rotoya crossed her arms. "The hell do you expect me to do?"

"Blow the door open with your blood."

"Eric, I can't do that. Only Caleb could."

Lance turned toward Kaela, and several others in the room did the same.

She squirmed under their stares then muttered a swear. "Is there not a better way to do this? I don't even know if I can make my blood explode."

Eric drew his cane blade. "You could make that big purple ball of blood explode. I don't see how you couldn't do the same with a smear of your own." He tossed the blade to Kaela.

She heaved a frustrated sigh and shut her eyes. Her veins turned purple again, and she let out a small, relaxed gasp. How much power flowed through her when she did that, Lance wondered. She cut her palm, squeezing until violet blood spilled from her hand. She marched to the safe and smeared her hand against its door then stepped away, closing her eyes again.

"Derek, do you have a first-aid kit?" George asked.

"Yeah, just over here."

Derek led George away as Kaela scrunched her face.

Lance found himself clenching his own fists, and the beast let out a low growl—not of anger or rage, but of intrigue.

"I don't think I can do this," Kaela said, opening her eyes.

George returned and rushed to Kaela. He made to wrap her hand in the bandage, but the wound was already healing.

"Just try harder," Eric said.

"I told you I can't—" She stopped. "Wait… you know I couldn't take all of the beta strain out of everyone. Just enough so they couldn't be controlled."

"Your point?"

She looked at Rotoya. "If you can spread some blood over the lock of that safe, there may be just enough beta strain to blow it up. It won't be more than a pop, but maybe it will be powerful enough to get that lock off." She glanced at Rachel. "I can't take any more out of Rachel without hurting her… or worse."

Lance furrowed his brows. "How do you know?"

Kaela shrugged. "I feel it."

"It's not going to hurt me, is it?" Rotoya asked.

Kaela shook her head. "You have the alpha strain mixed in there, just like me. I was fine. You'll probably be fine too."

"Probably?" Rotoya sighed. "Let's get this over with."

Kaela shut her eyes and extended her now-healed hand toward Rotoya. Just like the soldiers and officers back at Landreau Corp, she stiffened, paralyzed. Her eyes widened, and she made gagging sounds.

Moments later, several drops of blood left her mouth, and she gasped for air, dropping to her knees. Rachel made a move like she was going to help her up then walked away instead.

Kaela floated the blood to the lock of the safe, and her veins flashed brighter. The blood began to glow, then seconds later, a pop snapped through the room.

Lance flinched, grateful that nobody seemed to notice. Goosebumps ran along his skin. The beast… chuckled? Or was it a growl?

Eric waved away the small cloud of smoke and looked into the safe. He smiled back at them a few seconds later, reaching in and rifling through the contents, counting the money within. "This might take a few minutes. Derek, come help me count this."

Rotoya caught her breath and returned to her feet. "I need some air." She let out something like a cough and rushed out of the building.

Rachel glared out the window for a long time then followed her.

Rotoya's insides ached, as if she'd just had a bad flu. She rubbed at her sore neck as she breathed in the fresh night air. Footsteps tapped behind her.

She shut her eyes. "I know you're raring to kill me, but you'll need to wait until I've pard—"

It wasn't Derek. It was Rachel. "I'm certainly tempted."

"Sa—" She cleared her throat. "Rachel…"

Rachel stared at her for one moment then another, as if she didn't recognize the woman before her. Maybe she didn't. Rotoya wasn't sure she recognized herself anymore.

"I… I don't know what to say," Rachel said. "I look at you, and I just hate you."

"What I did was wrong."

"Thanks for making me aware."

"I thought what I was doing was right."

"And now look at what happened." She scoffed. "I used to think you'd do anything to protect us."

"That's *why* I had us take the drug. I didn't know Caleb would end up brainwashing all of us!" Now Rotoya scoffed. "Jesus, Rachel, how was I supposed to predict *nanobots* that would take over our bodies and minds?

How was I supposed to predict that Caleb Landreau was plotting world domination?!"

Rachel looked down as if considering what she'd said. "I want you to leave the police station after pardoning those people in there."

"I was already planning on doing exactly that. And I want you to be chief of police when I'm gone."

Rachel paused, caught off guard by the words. She crossed her arms, her voice turning gentler. "Are you going to stay in Arachna?"

"Facing my officers was hard enough the first time… Facing you was the hardest." Rotoya shook her head. "No, I'm not going to stay in Arachna. I'll find somewhere to go, lay low for a while, figure out what I'm going to do next."

"I don't think I can forgive you for what you did."

"I know…" Rotoya wished she could reach over and pull Rachel into one last hug, one last show of friendship before it shattered forever. "Neither can I… but I really am sorry. I don't know if that counts for anything."

Rachel uncrossed her arms and made to walk back into the bar. "Maybe it would if my friends weren't dead."

Lance leaned his head against the table as Eric and Derek silently counted the money. Exhaustion nipped at him. His store might've been ruined, but maybe he could still go back and sleep in his own bed.

Rachel walked in with a look of rage on her face. Rotoya meandered in moments later. They stayed on opposite sides of the room, avoiding eye contact with each other.

Eric chuckled, and Lance lifted his head up. "Don't get too excited, Lance. It's not a fortune… but a couple million dollars should allow us to hire our part of the private army for quite some time."

"How are you going to get the headquarters rebuilt?" Lance asked. He narrowed his eyes. "And my *store*."

"And the Rose," Kaela said quietly.

Eric chuckled and waved a hand at him. "Don't worry—I have the money to rebuild all three. But *this* money is for our protection." He then looked at Derek and Rob. "And Bob, I figure you wouldn't mind having control over this little military group. I have other much more important things to do, you see, and—"

"Of course," Rob said, his voice filled with excitement. Then he cleared his throat, and his tone shifted to a more formal one. "Sir."

Eric and Derek placed the money back in the safe while Kaela scanned the bar for spirits.

A heavy silence filled the room—not a silence of anger, sadness, or tension, but a silence of relief. They'd won. *Won.* The word was foreign in Lance's head. They'd come out of this alive, and everything was finally starting to click together for them, despite their losses. The silence turned into quiet chattering. They shared conversation, but Lance just listened, too tired to contribute anything.

Eric was silent, too, though when he made eye contact with Lance, he nodded toward the front door. Lance took the silent message and stood with a groan.

Lance stepped outside the bar, shutting the door behind him. Eric joined him seconds later, stepping over the still-shattered window.

They walked down the street until they were out of earshot.

They sat in silence on a set of stairs. The sun had risen above the horizon. Lance savored its warmth.

Lance wondered what was going through the heads of the citizens of Arachna, especially with the explosions and gunfire last night. Not a soul was roaming the streets and likely wouldn't until the curfew was called off and the citizens were promised that everything was back to normal.

"It was getting a bit hectic in there," Eric finally said. "Too many little conversations going on at once. I don't like that."

Lance shrugged. "I just like to listen to them."

Eric snorted. "So do I, but I try to listen to all of them at the same time. To get as—"

"As much information as possible," Lance finished for him. "Why am I not surprised?" He sighed, and a question burned in his mind. "Why do you want to hire a private army, anyway? You already have Derek's agents."

Eric looked at him, an eyebrow raised. "I assumed it was obvious. I don't want anyone to be able to storm in on us like Daniel did that day. We'll have soldiers guarding us. Notice that Derek ordered his agents to go into hiding when everything went down? They're scouts, information gatherers, not fighters." He shrugged. "I mean, they can take care of themselves, but… an armed force to help us fight if anything like this goes down again?" Eric smiled. "Gotta learn from my mistakes."

"How many soldiers are you planning on hiring?"

Eric pursed his lips then said, "As many as will come aboard, which, admittedly, is only a small portion. I'll have enough money to pay them for a while, and by then, I'll have built some money back up to keep them employed. It won't be much, but it will be something for them to live on."

He ran a thumb over the wolf's snarling mouth on his cane, and Lance couldn't help but think of the beast. It even snarled a little in response, as if mocking the wolf. Or saying that it was one. That was how Lance pictured it, anyway.

"We'll still keep records on the ones not joining so we can summon them back when the cure is ready. Wherever they go, I think it's safe to say none of them will be returning for work at Landreau Corp—that is, if there is anyone left to inherit the business."

Lance stared down at his hands. "What happened in that bathroom?"

Eric blinked, and suddenly, he couldn't seem to meet Lance's eyes. "I can't seem to do the right thing when it comes to my family… no matter what I do."

"I thought you were having a mental breakdown."

Eric laughed. "No, I just… I don't know. I just didn't want you to put yourself in any more danger. If you died, I mean, I don't know what I'd do."

"You let me go on a high-speed chase through the city with the chief of police tailing me."

Eric rolled his eyes. "Come on, Lance, are you seriously going to keep bringing that up?"

Lance crossed his arms. "Whatever."

Silence formed between them, and suddenly the sun didn't feel so warm as cold air brushed against Lance's face.

"You know," Eric said, his voice low, "I don't ever expect you to forgive me for what I did, the decisions I made… But I want to be a father to you, even if I wasn't at first."

Lance didn't respond.

"Look, I'm obviously not good at… family and relationships and making people not hate me, but I want to try. At least with you." He sighed. "I meant what I said. I wish I had spent those nine months with Carrie, but I didn't. I can't go back and change it, as much as I want to, but I will never regret getting in that car with her, even if those were the last moments we had together." He ran a hand through his hair and released a frustrated groan. "I did the same thing with you. I left you, but… I want to come back into your life and be a father while I still can."

Lance rubbed his chin and closed his eyes as they watered. They weren't tears, he told himself—the brutally cold wind was the culprit. "I…" His voice shook, and he cleared his throat. "I don't *hate* you… not entirely." He expected to see Eric's smile when he turned his head, but even his dark eyes were sincere. "Truth is, I've made some stupid decisions too… Maybe it's genetic."

Now Eric chuckled, and Lance found himself doing the same though it made no sense. The beast chirped as if confused about why they were laughing.

When their laughter died down, Lance continued, "I don't know if I'll ever be able to call you a father. And I don't think I'll ever not wish Mom was here instead of you…" They were sour words, but the truth was the truth. "But I'm… willing to give this a try. Whatever *this* is." Lance fumbled with his hands. "After all of this, maybe a new start is for the best."

Eric smiled, and something like relief shone in his eyes. "That's all I needed to hear."

"We have some building to do."

Eric nodded then smiled at his son. "*We*? Am I hearing that you've changed your mind about taking over the business?"

"No," Lance said flatly. "No, I have no intention of taking over." Eric opened his mouth to counter, but Lance was faster. The beast growled, knowing what he was about to say. Even Lance held second thoughts about the words coming out of his mouth, but he said them anyway. "However… I do think you are at least partially responsible for all of this. So maybe I should stay for a while… you know, just to keep you in line. Like someone you'll have to answer to before you make a decision."

Eric furrowed his brow and frowned.

"Like you said, you've botched multiple deals lately. And you rarely listen to Kaela and Derek. Don't you think if anyone should be listened to, it's your own son?" Lance added, waiting for the frown to go away.

It didn't.

"If anyone else had said that to me," Eric whispered, "I would have completely laughed them off. But having my own son to tell me when I'm doing something stupid… maybe not such a bad idea. And it could be a good way to learn how to lead for when I get a little *too* stupid… as far off as that is, I'm sure." He laughed. "Should you ever decide you want to take over, of course."

"So is that a yes?"

Eric smiled. "A resounding yes."

He held his hand out, and Lance stared down at it. With a sigh, he grabbed Eric's hand, his palm burning at the touch.

"You start today."

Lance chuckled. "Sure thing."

"So, my consultant, my first decision is to go back into the bar and see if Derek can cook us some food."

Lance hummed. "Decision approved."

Derek and Rob pushed the kitchen doors open, carrying platters of burgers and fries. The smell alone had Lance's stomach growling. He was mostly sure it wasn't the beast.

The burger was juicy and tender, the fries crispy and salty. Every bite was better than the last. The burger was gone within a minute, and Lance munched on his fries, trying to slow down but failing miserably. Kaela finished hers shortly after he did.

Derek carried out a barrel of wine, and everyone poured themselves a glass except for Eric and Lance.

Lance glanced back at the bar door, half expecting Caleb or one of his soldiers to burst through. But every time he looked, they weren't there.

"Damn," Kaela said, finishing off her glass. "I never thought I'd eat a meal like that again."

"Neither did I," Lance said. "I could get used to it."

"Mm-hmm. Well," Kaela finally said, swirling the last bit of wine in her glass, "everyone seems to have drinks, and I feel just tipsy enough to do this, so…" She drained the rest of her wine, her eyes glazed over. She refilled her glass and held it up high. "To Derek's badass cellar wine!"

Laughter stirred throughout the room.

George took a long swig of his own and said, "To hopefully making a cure."

"To friends," Derek said as he looked at Rob and raised his glass.

Rob took a longer sip than even Kaela and said, "Also to friends. And, um… having my own private army, I guess." He smirked at Derek and looked toward Eric. "Lord knows how that's going to go."

More laughter.

"To finally killing Caleb. And to Kaela, for doing the killing," Eric said.

Despite the small room with not many people, it erupted with clapping and shouting that sent a spike of adrenaline into Lance's chest. He shifted in his seat, swallowing the panic. She nodded with a tight-lipped smile and took a long swallow of her wine.

Rotoya was leaned against the wall. She stole a long look at Rachel then averted her gaze and said, "To the men and women who've served under me for all these years." She cleared her throat. "And to the ones we lost."

Silence settled over the room.

Rachel looked around then raised her glass. "To Rotoya… May she find a path to redemption."

Everyone looked at Lance, and Derek was behind the bar in an instant.

Derek poured something into a glass and slid it over. "It's lemonade."

Lance nodded a thank-you, and all eyes were on him, all smiles.

Lance cleared his throat, feeling small with all the attention on him. "To…" He looked at Kaela and Derek and Eric. The beast seemed to perk up its ears, if it had them. A smile crawled across Lance's face, the words finally coming to him. "To second chances." *No, that's not it.* "And…" Lance bit his lip, but as he looked at Eric one last time, at the genuine smile on his face and the watery glaze in his eyes, the words felt more comfortable as they rose to his mouth. "To family."

EPILOGUE

THE FOX AND THE WOLF

Lance tugged at his eyelid, scanning his eye in the mirror. The piercing green irises stared back at him, and the veins in the corner remained red. He checked them every day before he left. Made sure the beast hadn't taken advantage of his unconscious state and possessed him. Every day, he was met with the same reaction; a soft growl from the beast, as if to say, *How dare you?*

Lance laughed it off. Always laughed it off because every time he looked, something inside him told him that it would be fine. That he was the one in control. But it never hurt to be careful. He blew out a single breath, a reminder that he was alive. That even after everything he'd been through, he made it out mostly unscathed.

He stepped away from the clean mirror and out the back room into his store. With a stretch, he grabbed a breakfast bar from the end of an aisle and was out the door. The sun peeked over the horizon, and the streets were quiet. The silence paired well with the orange haze in the sky.

But at night the silence haunted him, when the darkness of his room settled, the outside was quiet, and the beast was sound asleep. Apparently, it did that—not just rested, but *slept*.

That was when the fear came. When he was all alone in the quiet darkness, images of the pitch-black cell haunted him. Despite the short amount of time he'd been in there, he couldn't stop that fear in his chest, that nausea in his stomach. Sometimes, he even awoke the beast like a child yearning for their mother. It would awake with a soft grumble, but it would be there. Never did it growl at him in those moments. Never did it snarl. Somehow, it understood, and it cared. And when Lance waited for it to ask for more room, it didn't. It hadn't even bothered trying these past few months.

But even when Lance slept at night, nightmares preyed on him: nightmares of being trapped in that cell, cold, tired, and hungry, awaiting Caleb's smiling face somewhere within the darkness; nightmares of a woman with red hair and green eyes screaming in a hospital room; nightmares of everyone he knew and loved—Derek, Kaela, Eric—dead.

Sometimes, the beast snarled at Caleb even in his dreams, and while the beast never seemed to acknowledge it when he awoke, Lance knew it shared the nightmares he did. Being stuck in some dark void, completely powerless within the Fara-something cage.

Lance ate his breakfast bar as he strolled down the street, a jacket wrapped tight around him. He ran a hand through his dark hair, now cut short.

If Eric was to be believed, he wouldn't have to walk to the hideout much longer.

"I'll teach you to drive like a father should," he'd said.

Lance dipped into an alleyway, threw his wrapper in a nearby trash can, and shoved his cold hands into his pockets. Arachna was facing the heart of winter now. Once, he would've adored the cold, but it just didn't feel the same after that cell. He savored warmth more than ever. Even the shadowy alley gave him an uneasy, sinking feeling in his chest. He gulped.

He weaved down the alleyway and slid through a narrow passage invisible to anyone not looking for it. Within seconds, he was on the other side, and two armed men faced him. They guarded the front of the headquarters, nearly a perfect reflection of the one that had gone up in smoke. But now, it was much better hidden. The back of the building facing the street was paved with concrete, blending seamlessly with the other buildings. Eric had added secret pathways for quick exits—more contingencies, more backups. At least he'd learned from his mistakes.

And he'd listened to his son's advice. As time passed, he listened more to Kaela and Derek, as well. He didn't make any decisions without Lance, and he made few without Kaela and Derek, either.

The two guards wore black trench coats, hiding bulletproof vests underneath.

Lance resisted the urge to shake his head at the sight, regardless of how many times he'd seen them. A black trench coat was Eric's little uniform for his soldiers. It was laughable, but at least he'd had the sense to give them some armor underneath. They both had pistols at their sides.

Lance nodded to them as he walked past, and they nodded back, one of them opening the dark wooden door for him. He stepped into the dim room and sighed the cold air out of his lungs as warmth embraced him.

At a dark wooden table stretching from one side of the room to the other sat Eric, Kaela, Derek, Rob, and Rachel, the new police chief of Arachna. Rotoya had stepped down months ago then disappeared. Eric wanted to track her down, but Rachel stopped him.

As Lance made to sit down next to Eric, Rachel stood and stretched. "Thank you for the information, Eric." She smiled at Lance as she passed him. "I should be going now."

"How are the new recruits?" Eric asked. His smile was still as wicked as the day Lance first met him—only less frightening. More… playful.

Rachel kept walking. "They're adjusting very well, thanks for asking."

Lance shared a nod with Derek and Kaela.

Eric cleared his throat. "Now that Lance is here, we have some good news. The soldiers that volunteered are reacting well to the first strain of the cure. The most common side effect seems to be nausea, but for the most part, they're good." The door closed, sealing all of them in the warmth of the room, the old fireplace having been replaced with an electric one. "If things keep going as well as they are, this thing should be mass produced within the year." Eric looked at Kaela. "How's the recruitment going?"

Grief shadowed her face. "I'm getting there. The building just needs a few more details, and I finally hired a new kitchen staff. The grand opening should take place in a few weeks." Speaking of a grand opening should have filled her voice with excitement, but Kaela just sighed and took a long sip from her coffee cup.

"And you," Eric said, wild eyes pointed at Lance. "I have something I would like to run by my consultant." He winked.

Lance leaned back in his chair and crossed his arms. "And what would that be? I hope you're not considering coercing another pharmaceutical company."

Eric laughed. *Only* Eric laughed. "No… Something else."

Before Lance could ask what he meant, Eric stood and disappeared into the back room. They were left with the fake fire crackling behind them. Lance brushed off his jacket and let the warmth embrace him. The beast purred.

Lance eyed Kaela then Derek then Rob. They all wore proud smiles, and Lance's heart skipped a beat. If Eric was about to try to make him leader, he would step out. No way was he about to take that position. Slowly, they'd built an inkling of trust, and breaking it now would devastate him.

Eric returned, holding something in his arms. Some object swathed in a dark cloth. He set it down gently in front of Lance and placed his hands behind his back, his smile turning proud.

Genuine.

A cold sweat formed on Lance's hands, and when he hesitated, Eric said, "It won't bite… Well, not you, anyways."

Lance reached for the fabric and caressed the black cloth. Soft to the touch. He racked his brain for possibilities of what could be hidden beneath it. He surveyed everyone in the room, and they watched with wide eyes. Lance took a steadying breath and slowly unwrapped the cloth.

As he unraveled it, the room went silent, and the beast chirped curiously. Lance knew it wasn't dangerous, yet his heart beat faster and faster as the cloth gave way to the object beneath. All eyes in the room were set on him, all with matching smiles. Was this what it was to finally have a family? *It's nice.*

Whatever it was, it was heavy. Made of metal, he thought as he brushed his hand across its cool and unyielding shape. Finally, he removed the last of the cloth, revealing the gift.

It was an ornamental dagger, sheathed in a silver-and-orange scabbard.

Lance's fingers traveled up the sheath to the handle of the weapon. "Whoa."

The handle was shaped like a fox. A orange chrome fox with a silver chin and two emeralds for eyes.

"The fox was her favorite animal," Eric said. "Her spirit animal, she said. Even has red fur like her hair." He chuckled.

Lance didn't cover his eyes, but he tried to blink away the tears behind them. The fox was carved with intricate detail. Whoever had done it had taken their time. He ran a shaky thumb across it then across each emerald. They both shone in the sunlight spilling in from the windows.

Lance drew the blade. It whined against the sheath, and the blade itself was lightly etched all the way down with the pattern of a spider's web. The pattern was painted black, a contrast to the gray steel.

Tears pushed harder and harder against Lance's eyes, filling the dam to the point of breaking.

"Welcome to the spider's web, Lance," Eric said.

And as cheesy as that line was, as stupid as it sounded, the tears fell down Lance's cheeks. Those emerald eyes looked back at him, the only reminder of his mother. He wiped the tears away.

Months ago, he would never have let them see his tears, but after all they'd been through, it didn't matter anymore.

The mistakes and the choices he'd made had led them here—damaged, broken, but together.

Lance looked into his father's black eyes, and they stared back into his. They'd grown warmer in the past few months, like a dead flame had been revived. And the blond dye in his hair was washing out, revealing the black beneath. *Doesn't feel right anymore*, he'd said.

Lance grabbed the dagger tightly in his hand and sheathed the blade—his own blade, a constant reminder of his mother. He looked at the others, and Kaela had her face pointed up as she dabbed at her eyes with a tissue.

When she noticed Lance's stare, she said, "Shut up, it's a sweet moment, okay?" She swirled the coffee in her cup and took another sip. Derek chuckled while he and Rob sent smiles at each other.

Lance laughed, and he and Eric returned to their seats.

"Does my consultant approve of the decision I made without his counsel?"

Lance cleared his throat. "Decision approved." He rubbed his thumb against the fox's eye again. "Thanks."

"Well, I can't take all the credit. Originally, I was going to pay for it, but Derek and Kaela wanted to chip in. So they did."

"Thanks, guys."

They just smiled at him.

"Okay, everyone," Eric said, leaning back in his chair and clasping his hands together. "What information have you all gotten for me today?"

The television chattered in the background, some comedy about a group of friends and their antics.

Lance watched it for a few minutes, then his focus faded, shifting to the dagger in his lap. He stared into its emerald eyes.

He opened his mouth a fifth time, the temptation to speak to it alluring. It wasn't her. It was just a gift from Eric. Still, as he brushed his thumb over the orange chrome, he opened his mouth a sixth time, searching for the words to say to her, even if she wouldn't hear them.

He sighed and leaned his head back against the wall of his room. The lights were turned out, despite his own anxiety and the protests from the beast. If it wasn't for the TV, he would be scrambling for the light switch. But for the moment, he allowed it.

He told himself he needed to adjust to the dark again. He needed to recognize that he wasn't in that cell even if a chill ran down his arms every few minutes and Caleb's face appeared behind his eyelids just as often.

The beast growled every time, as if it saw him too.

Lance closed his eyelids again, but Caleb's face didn't show. Sleep weighed them down, and Lance drifted off, the laugh track from the TV fading.

"Hey."

Lance leapt out of bed, his dagger whining as it left its sheath, pointed at the intruder.

Laughter erupted from the door, and Lance rolled his eyes, putting a hand to his racing heart. "Son of a bi—"

"Ah, ah," Eric interrupted, holding his hand up. "Language."

The beast cocked its head to the side, and Lance mimicked the action. "*Language*?"

"How ya doin', Lancelot?" Eric continued, looking at the TV. "Used to love that show, but I stopped having time for TV years ago."

"Yeah," Lance said absentmindedly. "What are you doing here?" He crinkled his nose as the realization popped into his head. "Wait, how did you even get in here without me knowing? I thought I was supposed to have the best security system there was."

Eric shrugged. "You do. I just happen to have the keys to it."

Lance rolled his eyes. "Seriously, what are you doing here so late? It's"—he peeked at the clock on the bedside table—"almost midnight."

Eric ripped his gaze away from the TV. "You really don't know?"

Lance spread his arms out. *Enlighten me.*

Eric turned back to the TV. "Hmm… I suppose I'll have to add that to the list of surprises."

Lance crossed his arms. "Please tell me you didn't piss off *another* corporate leader."

"I did not. Ryan and I are on good terms with each other, thanks to my humble advisor."

Lance sat on the bed, sheathing the blade. "Well, your humble advisor had his work cut out for him." He laughed, but it wasn't an exaggeration.

"That's what I pay you for," Eric said. "Among other things. Speaking of which, did you get any good info today?"

Lance thought back, recounting every customer that had come into his store. "A lot of chatter about Ryan being the new head of Landreau Corp. No rumors, no conspiracies. For now, the city's buzzing with the idea of cleaner drugs for cheaper prices."

Eric hummed. "It was ballsy of him to make such a promise on live television."

"Even more so to do it with almost no experience running a place like that."

"I bet dear ol' cousin Caleb is turning in his grave."

"Better not be."

Laughter filled the room.

"So, how does it feel to know everything that goes on in Landreau Corp now?" Lance asked. Between exchanging information with Ryan, planting multiple spies while the company was distracted, and hiring several researchers and scientists to keep an eye on things, Landreau Corp practically belonged to Eric's organization. And good for it, too. Without them, the cure would never have been made. "I mean, after everything we've been through, is it all you ever wanted?"

"I did all of that for your sake, you know."

"I was just asking," Lance defended.

Eric sighed. "Like the city of Arachna is finally ours."

"All that's really left for you to do is find a way to get more information from the inner slums."

"Which leads me to my first surprise." Eric leaned closer. "How would you feel about having your own agents to gain information on the slums?"

The beast purred, but Lance scratched the back of his neck. "Eric, I don't want to lead anyone."

"You won't have to. Just tell them where to go, and they'll collect information and relay it back to you, to relay to me."

Lance started to refuse, but Eric interrupted. "It's only a handful of agents, and they'll get information in the deeper parts of the slums that you can't get from owning a store here. And if you ever feel like you can't handle it, I'll take it over until you can."

"I thought agents didn't like going into the slums."

"*Derek's* agents didn't. Besides, they have their own parts of Arachna to spy on. Moving them to the slums was always stretching them too far. But with our increase in profits, I can afford agents dedicated to the slums."

Lance blinked. Was this a trick to get him to become the leader? Slowly introducing new people until he guided Lance into taking over entirely? But Derek and Kaela had people, and they hadn't taken over. Lance bit his lip, and the beast purred again, urging him to accept.

The slums had been such a nice part of the city once, a humble section full of life and vigor. If he could gain some control over the inner slums with his own people, maybe there would be a chance of one day restoring them—if not to their former glory, then to something newer and better.

"Okay," Lance said. "I'll give it a shot. Only a few people, right?"

Eric nodded. "It's primarily to keep an eye on the gang activity in the inner slums, and that will leave more of Derek's men to keep an eye on the city itself." He nudged Lance. "Does my consultant approve?"

Lance chuckled. "Yeah… Yeah, your consultant approves."

"Good. Now let's stop the business babble and get on to the real reason I came here."

"Oh no."

Eric laughed. "How do you like your gift?"

Lance raised an eyebrow. "*That's* why you sneaked through my security system in the middle of the night? To ask me if I liked the dagger that I already told you I loved?"

Eric shrugged. "Is that so hard to believe?"

"With you… I guess not." Lance scoffed, but he couldn't hide his smile. It fell as he looked down at the fox handle. "Why did she like foxes so much?"

Eric crossed his arms, his smile turning warm. "She thought they were cute and smart. She always dreamed of having one as a pet. And she was so much like one herself. You should have seen how clever that girl was when it came to scamming people." He chuckled as he stood, leaning against Lance's dresser. "One time, she got a part-time job at this store. The manager was a real piece of work, so she had me go in there and pretend to rob the place on her first night. She gave me all the money in the register, gave them a false description, and quit the next day because she was 'scared to work there any longer'." He laughed harder than Lance had ever seen, bracing himself against the wall for support as he wiped a tear from his eye. "I swear, that was the smartest and luckiest girl I knew."

"Hence the fox," Lance said.

Eric nodded. "Hence the fox."

A silence settled between them before a thought popped into Lance's head. "How's George?"

"He's doing well. Has a nice influx of patients coming in, more than he did in Agni."

"Did he take the offer?"

Eric frowned. "He agreed to be our personal doctor, but he didn't agree to taking information from his patients to give to us. At least, not unless it's something extremely serious, like another Caleb situation."

Lance smiled. That was just like George. "Well, I for one respect his decision."

Eric rolled his eyes. "Yeah, I guess I do too, that old codger."

A knock sounded on the front door, and a voice spoke. "Are we supposed to stand here all night, or are you going to let us in?"

Lance stood. "Is that Kaela?"

"Don't get mad," Eric said. "I have one more surprise for you. Prepare to be very embarrassed."

Lance called out to Eric, but he'd already left the room. His heart skipped a beat as the possibilities ran through his head.

What horrid thing could he possibly have planned?

Seconds later, an orange light flickered from the hallway, and Eric strolled in, holding a tray of sandwiches. He flipped the light on, a party hat slanted on his head.

Oh God, it's worse than I thought.

"Happy birthday to you," sang three voices in unison as Kaela walked in behind Eric, holding several bottles of soda. She wore a hat of her own and blew into a party horn. "Happy birthday to you!"

"Happy birthday, dear Lancelot!" Derek came in behind Kaela, a large cake held in his hands, dozens of candles perched atop it. He set the cake down on a small table he was carrying with him. Lance buried his face in his hands, peeking through his fingers and laughing at the image of a spider in its web, drawn in frosting on top of the cake. The blood rushed to his face, and he knew it was beet red. He swore the beast laughed at him.

"Happy birthday to you!"

Kaela blew the horn again, and Lance prayed the redness would leave his face.

"Wow, I haven't seen a man that red since the Rose first opened." Kaela laughed and set the bottles down.

Derek placed his hands on his hips and said, "Go ahead and make a wish, Lance."

Lance laughed as he ran a hand through his hair. "You people are insane." The beast seemed happy as well, and a warmth surged through Lance that he hadn't felt in a long time. "Is today my actual birthday?"

Eric picked off a piece of a sandwich and popped it into his mouth. "That it is, Lancelot." He licked his fingers. "When was the last time you celebrated your birthday?"

Lance scratched his head as he racked his brain. "I got a muffin with a candle in it at the orphanage once."

"Ouch," Kaela said. "That's cold. Well, if I were you, I'd blow out those candles, make that wish, and eat the hell out of some cake."

Lance laughed again, looking at the many candles on the cake, tempted to pinch himself in case he was dreaming. "Thanks, guys… You're the best." He meant it, and after the events of earlier today, he squeezed his fists and refused to let the tears roll from his eyes as he leaned forward and closed them.

I wish… that no matter what happens, even if we get on each other's nerves, that we'll always be friends. No… family. Family, yeah. I like that.

Lance opened his eyes and blew the candles out, a puff of smoke dancing from each one. The room erupted with shouts and clapping, and Lance's face went red again. The beast purred. Or, actually, that was his stomach rumbling. But the beast did chirp and move around excitedly.

"Alright, let's get this cake cut. Lance, which piece do you want?"

ACKNOWLEDGMENTS

I want to thank God for gifting me my love of writing. This thing, this intangible feeling I have when I write, could not possibly be anything but a gift from my creator. And for that, I am truly grateful.

I want to thank my mom, who without I would not be here—who without my *book* would not currently be in your hands, dear reader. I don't know how I got so lucky to have such a loving, supportive, and kind human being in my life. As a writer, it is my job to put emotions and feelings into words. However, I fear I cannot put into the words just how much my mother means to me. I love you, momma.

I want to thank my wonderful sister. She is a beacon of strength and power, and her resilience inspires me every day to power through any adversity. She stood up for me when I could not. She may not be my twin, but she is the other half of my heart.

I want to thank my friends: Manprit Singh, Shane Adams, Amber Phillips-Temple, Kaylynn Phillips-Temple, Crystal, Raisa Bateman, and Shelton Spears. I have many others which I have not mentioned here, but these seven lovely people have been my largest supporters. They have offered advice and criticisms when needed; they have expressed excitement and joy at every advancement in the laborious process of creating this book; they have cheered me on in my darkest moments, where I even considered locking this book away forever. These people cheered loud for me, and here, now, I get to cheer just as loud for them. "THANKS, GUYS! WHOOP! WHOOP! YOU GOT THIS! YOU'RE THE BEST! YEAH!"

I want to thank my beta readers. Their invaluable advice made this book what it is today. Thank you all for taking the time out of your busy lives to read this book of mine.

Finally, I want to thank my favorite authors:

Leigh Bardugo. Six of Crows was the first book of yours I ever read, and it was that book that made me realize how deeply I wanted to be a writer. That book was the catalyst that sparked a fire in me. I wanted to take writing seriously. I wanted to publish a novel. And it would never have happened if not for you. I hope you realize just how many young writers you have inspired, and I hope it fills you with pride. I can only hope that one day, my books inspire someone the way yours have inspired me. The day that happens, I will know that I have truly made it. Thank you, Leigh.

Jenna Moreci. I don't even know how to describe the sheer gratitude I owe you. Your advice on writing and publishing is not only hilarious, but insightful. I would never have been able to publish any of my books without your help. I'd have given up on publishing long ago without your guidance and wit. And while I have made many mistakes on this journey, and no doubt will continue to do so, you have saved me from making so, so many more. So thank you. Thank you so much for sharing your knowledge with me. Rock on you beautiful, badass cyborg you!

ABOUT THE AUTHOR

A.K. Rohner has loved writing since he was a kid. He is the author of The Family Crest Duology and Arachna. This is his third book. He also loves to write short stories on his website: www.akrohner.com.

When he's not writing, A.K. loves piano, video games, and rubbing the bellies of any dog that will let him.

www.ingramcontent.com/pod-product-compliance
Lightning Source LLC
Chambersburg PA
CBHW020532310726
48979CB00014B/2303/J

* 9 7 8 1 7 3 3 3 8 4 5 6 8 *